And I Will Bring You Home

And I Will Bring You Home

Susan Wetherall

Merrimack Media

Newburyport, Massachusetts

ISBN: print: 978-1-945756-24-5
Copyright © 2020 Susan Wetherall

And I Will Bring You Home is a work of fiction. The people and events described in this novel are completely imaginary. The setting is not.

Published by Merrimack Media, Newburyport, Massachusetts

For my daughters,
Kathy and Cristina

The wonder of stories is the world they take us to, a world other than our own, a world in which we can become new and fresh again. And too, it is a world we can escape at any moment of our choosing.

Contents

Prologue

The termites come in April in Nicaragua. Like moths drawn by the light, they come at night, clouds of them, drop their wings and lie wriggling on the tables and floor and couch. On our laps and in our hair if we sit still long enough. And even if we sweep them up right away, some always manage to get to wood and lay their eggs before they die. So, once a year we paint all exposed wood with gasoline to kill the eggs before they hatch. According to local custom, this should be done in late March, during the suffocating stillness before the rains begin in early April.

This we did in 1967, and again in '68. And even though we did it again this year, it is now May and neither the rains nor the termites have come. It's certainly not for want of promising. The entire month of April was gray and gluey. The heat sat in our lungs and behind our eyeballs. Day and night. Already crops are ruined and people are angry over bus fares, the price of milk, the price of bread and eggs. *Señoras* slap their maids and children arrive home from school with bloody noses. Only last week our landlord, the lawyer Dr. Medina, had a shootout with a client in his office and the two of them ended up being carted off to the hospital in the same ambulance.

The newspapers had a field day with that one. Not surprising in a country where demonstrations over food prices are called Communist revolutions in the Somoza press, and where crimes of passion, especially those committed by government supporters, get banner headlines in the opposition press, squeezing out the three-headed chickens and bovine immaculate conceptions.

It's like a tropical cow town they said, when we got the news we were leaving Lima for Managua; so small, you'll meet yourself coming around the corner. Hot, said the previous bank manager; unbearably damp, said his wife. You might as well be going to Vietnam without a shooting war, she said, as if she knew all about wars and dying in the absence of one. The word "survival" laced their conversation as heavily as the gin did their drinks. They'd paid their dues and now it was their turn for a better posting. Somewhere like Lima. Not, for God's sake, another place like this.

It is now three years we've lived in Nicaragua. A full year longer than we've been anywhere else together, and Marshall is beginning to make noises about leaving. That goes against our unspoken contract. The contract says we arrive in a new place pretending we'll live there forever – until the moment we get on the plane for the next place. Then we seldom look back. This is supposed to create the feel of balance, of permanence, of roots going down.

Of course there are risks. When the next transfer comes, there is a wrench, a period of awful dislocation and confusion. A time to reschedule the loan, Marshall says. He is very good at that. He does it every day at the bank. So why not carry it over to our lives? What he doesn't know, and what I'm only beginning to realize, is that my roots don't feel like an illusion any more; they have gone down into the dry earth here and have begun to spread, surreptitiously, subversively. Even as I wonder where we'll go next — Colombia, Argentina, London — I have taken root.

I wake up early these mornings. Sometime before the sun comes up, during that in-between hour when the crickets have wound down and the first bird notes have yet to drop into place. Out on the patio the air is fresh and the smell of the trumpet vine is sweet. I flatten my bare toes against the cool marble, then bury them in the grass beyond, wondering that even in drought there can be dew. Fernando, *don* Claudio's tailless rooster, peers at me silently through the cyclone fence. He prefers noon for his concerts.

After breakfast, with Marshall off to work and Becka, tidy and self-assured in her school uniform, off to her nuns' school, I drop Caley at Mrs. Ferris' Kinderschool, back out of the driveway and go to the Eastern Market to buy the baby corn called *chilotes*, the *yucca* and fresh coriander for the lunchtime soup.

At the market, Bonifacio, who this March achieved the exalted age of twelve, pulls two of the enormous baskets from the back of the tiny station wagon and hops with them over the foamy brown sludge a washwoman's toss-out has made of the refuse in the gutter. I miss, splash, then wiggle my feet to clear the thought as much as the feel of filth from between my bare toes.

I bargain for everything. Onions up five *centavos* from last week, no thank you. Rice, beans, hands waving in the air, mock frowns, a turned shoulder and then laughter. The same noisy scene repeated again and again all around me. Tortillas are fifteen for a *córdoba*, same price as the first day I came here. No bargaining there. The woman I buy them from keeps her newest baby — two born in these three years — in a hammock slung above the metal drums holding the charcoal fires. She pats the tortillas, turns them with fingers hardened to the heat, and tells me that her son, the two year old, is better, thank God. The *enteritis negra* is a terrible thing.

For Calixto, the gardener, I buy five fat hand-rolled cigars from the blind cigar lady. The old woman rolls them on the inside of her wrinkled thigh, wraps them in a scrap of newspaper, then reaches to take the bill and slip it into the leather pouch between her shriveled breasts. She never speaks and her milky eyes stare through me.

For a time I feel that nothing will change, that here in the noise and heat and filth of the market, I am at home.

The cutter ants, in single file, each bearing a bright green jagged-edged sail five, six times its size, cross the back garden. Becka, Caley and I follow the stream from the plundered *lulo* I planted with seed smuggled in from Bogotá, to the cyclone fence out behind my sad cherry-tomato plants. We lean against the fence and watch them scurry out of view, watch others returning unburdened, clamber-ing in and around and over the outbound trail, using it to guide them back to the *lulo*. Shiny, brown-black bodies, three beads slung together, antennae and legs scrabbling.

When I was single, I ate fried ants once in Lima –– big, shiny, salt-speckled colony ants brought over the Andes from the Amazon jungle. They tasted of rancid grease and the legs stuck in my teeth. Marshall laughed when I told him. "Some things are better in fantasy than in fact," he said, and I thought about that for days. I barely knew him then.

Caley wants to know where the ants live. I point to *don Claudio's* yard. *Don* Claudio sets a feeder up in his back yard during the dry season in the hope that the Canadian geese will make it down this far south. But there are only two guests at his feast: naked Fernando, who flopped down at the *gallera* and whose noontime cock-a-doo-dles grace our lunch, and Serafina, an ancient *paso fino* horse *don* Claudio rescued from the slaughterhouse. The cutter ants will be safe in his yard.

The women in the lounge chairs at the swimming pool say that *don* Claudio Portillo Clarín has no relatives, that he is so old and so crazy no one wants to own him, that he was once a man of standing but offended in some long-forgotten way the Big Man's father. What saved him was a woman, but who she was and what she did, those things are also forgotten. They say he was once a poet and a philosopher, but the birds have pecked his brain away – *que lastima!* – and even his wife died in disgust. Their fingers flutter on their iced *milcas*. "But what else can one expect," they sigh. Only the old crone who passes for a maid and rocks in his rocking chair stays with him now.

And me? So many times I have lain there in silence on my towel and listened to their casual brutality, may God forgive me, wondering how those fluttering fingers stayed so beautifully manicured when they were always poking in shit.

Now we squat, Becka on one side, Caley and I on the other side of the skittery ant river, our foreheads creased by the wire fence. There is smoke in the air, thin, sharp, the smell of slash and burn. Too dry. Too soon for slash and burn.

The stream of ants slows, disappears. We walk back to the *lulo*, now only a stalk and bare, fuzzy stems. It took the ants less than two hours to strip it.

"Why didn't you stop them, Mommy?" my four-year-old Caley asks, now that the ants are safe. "Why didn't you put that stuff on them?"

"I don't know. They certainly got better use out of the lulo than we did. Maybe I really planted it for them."

Caley nods wisely, but of course, Becka, who is six years old, frowns. That does not make sense.

Marshall has gone to bed early. Because he can't sleep with the light on, I take my book into the living room, then sit and do nothing. Cerro Negro is at it again. From where I sit, I can just make out the volcano's red glow in the night sky to the northwest, out over Somarriba's coconut palms. It has thrown out tons of ash this year. Last week up in Léon, the boy I was interviewing for a scholarship to the States said they must sweep the ash off their roof every few hours or it will cave in. This critical stage is reached when the ash gets over ten inches deep, which was how deep it was on their neighbor's roof when it collapsed. He gave me a mask and took me up a ladder to show me the ruler he'd attached to the roof. And as the ash had already reached the eight-inch mark, he grabbed up a broom and began to sweep, while I perched on the roof's edge in the soft, gray rain and finished up the interview.

A beetle lands with a plop under the reading lamp. Its inch-wide back is shiny black with rainbow lights, heavy on the turquoise and blue end. It pulls the tip of a tissue-paper wing into its armor and starts its wobbly way across the table. A car turns into Somarriba's driveway. Two doors slam, then there are voices.

Becka comes from her room. "I can't sleep," she says. Usually she complains that Caley snores and that's the reason she can't sleep. But tonight she simply lies down on the couch and asks for a foot rub. I feel her forehead.

"No," she says. "I'm not sick." My cool, six year old child.

"I see."

Becka closes her eyes, giving me the chance to stare at her face all I want. It is a long face with a determined chin and a wide forehead. They say she looks like me. I think she looks like Marshall. Perhaps because her eyes, which are large and very gray, have that same look of unsmiling gravity that caught me up and held me when I first knew him.

"Do you think the *lulo* plant will grow back?" she says sleepily.

"I don't know, honey."

She is silent a long time and, just when I think the foot rub has worked and she is asleep, she says, "Will we live here always, Mother?"

I shake my head. And then she is asleep. My fingers stop moving. There is a tiny clatter. I look up and see that the beetle has fallen off the edge of the table onto the floor where it lies on its back, its legs waving in the air. It is too far away for me to reach without waking Becka up and I wonder how long a beetle can live upside down like that. With its legs waving so frantically? My thighs tense at the thought and Becka stirs. She is all boney legs and arms when I pick her up, really too big for me to carry, so I stagger and lean against the wall a moment to balance myself. She unfolds her body, slips from my arms and together we walk her to bed. The beetle is still upside down when I return. Crouching down, I turn it over with the tip of my finger and watch it wobble away. An old beetle at the end of its life. I cheer it on until it disappears in the shadows of the dining room.

There is lightning to the northwest over Cerro Negro. A red glow and above it the lightning. I walk out under the *jacote* tree in the front yard to watch. Night heat is thick around my body. It makes my skin alive in a way it never is up north. The volcano throws up rocks the size of trailer trucks. Jerry, the embassy geologist, flew over it one night to take pictures and a rock nearly knocked his plane into the crater.

Behind me to the southeast, a hundred miles out over the jungle, another kind of lightning is playing. Rain lightning, cool, grave, a flicker at this distance. Yet I think I can hear the rain pouring into the jungle, the fierce, wet roar of water on green leaves, on unpeopled land.

I am on borrowed time here. They've given us an extra year, and now each day in my little cow town with its white, hot sun and careless volcanoes is a fraction on the marker.

Book One

Chapter 1

José María watched the sausages come up out of the vat, crisp and tender. More than anyone, he knew exactly what went into them, and still his mouth watered.

"You're not hearing me," said his aunt Berfalia, dropping the sausages onto a towel.

"I hear you, *tía*." He glanced up at the smoke from the charcoal fires trapped against the zinc roof and counted back; he hadn't eaten since last night. He turned away and stared at the tortilla vendor's toddler who had wandered over from the next stall. The child stared back. Last night? Black coffee and a tortilla, that was it. He squatted down on the concrete floor next to his aunt's food stall and held his hand out. After a moment the child tottered forward, feet planted wide. The din of the food hall died away.

"José María. Are you listening?"

He caught the boy's small, wet fingers, and gathered him up. In an instant, the skinny fingers slid into the hair above his ears and the boy settled in, cheek to cheek. Thus armed, he pivoted and glanced up at his aunt. "I hear you very well, *tía*."

From this perspective, Berfalia was huge. There was the great belly and thighs, the huge arms that had cradled both him and his sister Luz as well as her own two boys. And then there was the face with

3

its round knob of a nose, high forehead, black hair, dyed and swept up into a roll, then flowing loose down her back. Her eyes were like twinkling moons setting behind enormous cheeks. It all added up to one gigantic cherub. Until you looked into those weary eyes.

He rose to face her, met her gaze and grinned. "I do. I hear you."

"No, you don't," said Berfalia. "You may think you listen, but you don't hear me." She skimmed more sausages out of the vat, rolled five of them into a piece of newspaper, and handed them to an old man who promptly sat down at the nearest table and carefully unfolded the paper. She slipped his coin into the pocket in her apron and turned back, her voice lower still. "If you were that good a listener, you'd quit pissing around."

I love you too, he thought and tried to smile. "You know it's not pissing around. The work really matters."

"Oh, so now you call it work,"she whispered. "Painting stupid signs on walls? Sending vitamins to a bunch of fools up in the mountains? Writing shit that'll get you shot before you even get it out the door? Why not just write a book on how to get yourself killed a hundred different ways?"

He stared at her. He had never seen her like this. Angry, yes. But angry and afraid? He shook his head. "You don't understand."

"Well, here's what I do know," she said. "You go away for years and when you finally come back you think you know it all."

Stung, he straightened up. "Know it all? That's the problem. I wasn't just away all those years, I was on another planet. Up there it's like Nicaragua doesn't even exist. And I get back here..." He held the child close and bent over so that only she could hear him. "...and people are dying, they're hungry, they disappear, they show up dead at the bottom of a crater, they float up like rotting sponges on the lake." He paused to catch his breath. "You don't think that matters, *tía?*"

Just saying it made him dizzy and he stood up even straighter. The child went limp against his shoulder and his ragged diapers were suddenly hot and wet. For a moment all José María could hear was the boy's ragged, asthma-caked breathing next to his ear; then he heard the sausage vat hissing and popping, and the child's mother in the next stall hawking tortillas with a side of stewed chicken feet. He sighed. He'd come to the market for comfort and instead what he'd gotten was pissed on. He didn't know whether to laugh or to cry.

"You're wrong," he said.

"Am I?" Berfalia's eyes turned to slits. "They'll make sausage out of you and those friends of yours."

The aching fear that had brought him to her flared up again. Premonition was her genius. And how liberally she had blessed him with it, this hard gut-ache that had driven him out of Hilaria's house before dawn, carrying reams of paper to Mario's place, spray paint to Digna's, and finally the typewriter to Augustín's. All that was left were his clothes. But first, he had needed this spoonful of ferocity.

"For starters, you could try getting that cut." Berfalia waved a thick finger at her own hair. "You'd stick out less."

He grinned. "As if you're the plain brown mouse." He made as if to duck behind the child. "No, no. Sorry. I didn't mean that. 'You're the author of my conscience,'" he quoted. It was a line from one of Mario's poems.

She wasn't amused. "No. Your conscience is no one's business but your own, and if you haven't figured that out by now – "

He cut across her. "Without you I could have been a wastrel." He grimaced as he remembered the propensities of her eldest son.

"Instead, you're an idiot. You'll get no rewards from me if you disappear."

"It won't come to that. I'll be alright."

"*Ajá!* You come in here with a face like wet shoe leather and tell me you'll be alright. I'm old enough to have a beard, boy. That counts for something."

He carried the child over to its mother, who settled him on her hip. "How old is he, *mamita?*"

"Nearly twenty months." The woman wiped the sweat from her eyes with the back of her arm and gave him a tired smile. She was a child herself, with the pouch of her stomach filling out again. "He wanders, but he's good."

"I can see that."

He turned back to his aunt. Enough. He had gotten what he came for. What was it the old man had called it, vinegar and piss? Vinegar and piss to ease the ache.

"I'll see you soon." He reached for a sausage from the pile of cooked ones.

"An old story." She swiped at his hand, missed and grunted. Her face softened. "Take care," she said and handed him a bundle of sausages she had made when his back was turned.

"You can count on it."

"It runs in the family," she muttered.

He blew her a kiss, a trick she deplored, calling it part of his "yankee shit."

By the time he got back to the house, the sun was low, filling the street with a hot, pink dusk that softened the whitewash and crumbling adobe. Poor Hilaria. He licked the last of the sausage grease from his fingers and walked faster. He had told her not to come home until he cleared out all traces of his stay. If the *guardia* came and found nothing at all, they just might leave her alone.

The street was nearly empty. He stopped to gauge if that was good or bad. Probably good; it was suppertime. Though why the neighbor should be sweeping her curb was a mystery. As he drew near, he watched her thin shoulders move rhythmically around the broom. She was a talker, someone to be avoided.

"*Buenas,*" she said, and knocked the broom against the curb.

"*Buenas tardes.*" Yes, a good afternoon.

She squinted against the sun. "Beautiful day." She nodded toward Hilaria's house. "Have a good rest."

"*Gracias.*" From her half open door came odors of supper cooking. His shoulders eased as he passed.

Supper? And sweeping? He frowned, fumbled the key, dropped it, then froze as the door behind the woman swung wide and the metallic clap of a rifle bolt shooting home sounded from inside. A soldier in army fatigues stepped out into the pink sunset. Ten feet away.

"*If the son of a bitch has you at ten feet, don't bother to move, Joe,*" the old man had said. "*Two feet, nothing to lose; fifty feet, sure; ten feet, don't move a fucking eyelash.*"

It took four of them thirty minutes to reduce the inside of Hilaria's house to rubble in search of the revolution. Not that he could see it from the back of a weapons carrier they produced from around the far corner, but he was close enough to recognize each item as it splintered. There was the muffled thud of Hilaria's stone mortar hitting the dirt floor, then hitting the inside wall. Thank God he had warned her. Then came the crack of wood — one, two, three, all of the wooden spoons.

The guard with him was five feet away, cattycornered on the other

7

side of the carrier, the butt of his rifle under his armpit, the barrel across his knee, his finger on the trigger.

José María closed his eyes. So, old man, what do I do at five feet?

He kept his breathing shallow, just deep enough to feed his racing heart. The street was filling with shadows. The woman had gone back to her supper, her job done. He closed his eyes. The sausages had turned to a hard lump in his stomach and the back of his throat stung with acid.

"You want one?" said the guard, holding out a pack of Marlboros, one thrust up above the others.

"*Gracias.*" He took it and waited. No light was offered. A pain as old as he could remember washed over him and settled in his gut. He tried to shrug, to smile. He could always chew the cigarette if he got hungry enough, if he was given time to get hungry.

The mouth of the rifle was dark and mysterious; behind it, the clip, the trigger, the finger, the guard with no light, all connected like the song in the old record his father had given his mother. He felt the needle descend on its articulated arm, down into the dusty grooves, high above his eye level, the tinny voice singing the flea on the fly on the knee of the frog on the log, and the green grass grew all around, all around, the sound sliding down as the wind-up mechanism slowed because he was too small to wind up the crank. Berfalia came to pick it up and return it to its resting place and to show him the small, soft thing they had taken from his mother's body. His sister, Luz.

There was a shout from the house and the pain flared up into his lungs. Another shout and the carrier shook as the officer jumped in on the passenger side. "*Nada,*" he called back over his shoulder.

Thank God. They'd found nothing.

"*Vamonos!* A *Los Pinos.*"

Christ! *Los Pinos*! The Pines.

The driver jumped in. Another guard vaulted up into the back of the vehicle; for an instant he filled the opening, blocked out the light. A voice said, "Piece of shit," and there was no room to duck as the butt of a rifle slammed into his head.

The sweet stench of decay. He opened his eyes. A long row of metal trash barrels. And closer, a blob of something pink and shiny lay inches from his nose; it was melting, running toward him, leaving behind reddish lumps the size of the nail on his thumb.

Rough hands grabbed at his shoulders and pulled him upwards. The sickly sweet odor filled his nose and he saw that it was ice cream, the remains of someone's dessert. Fear choked off his laugh.

He was pushed down on his knees. A rough bag, dark and sour dropped down over his head. The gassy stench of filth against his lips made him gag and he clamped his mouth shut.

There was a sudden babble and something hit him from behind.

"*Basta*!" said a voice above him. "Enough! There's no need."

He was lowered to the ground. He lay on his side and opened his mouth in gratitude. A moan rose from deep inside him.

"There now," said the voice in soothing tones, "that's better." A cultured voice, a voice of reason. Here...?

There was a tiny pause, a scraping sound like a match striking on stone. His mind made sense of it too late — the scrape of a shoe. The blow took him between the legs, once, and then again... His scream came from a long time afterward.

Chapter 2

Julia awoke with a jolt. The early morning light filtered through the curtains. Marshall slept on his back, his head tilted toward her on the edge of his pillow, his breathing light and even. She eased away from him, held her breath and counted down the seconds before the clock-radio clicked on to the last beats of a *cumbia*.

"Buenos días," shouted the announcer. "From Radio Managua, the eighteenth of June, we bring you the news. This morning at 4:10, Managua was visited by another tremor, this one registering five-point-two on the Richter scale. The epicenter was approximately sixty miles west of Puerto Somoza. Volcanic activity at Cerro Negro remains unchanged."

She sighed. She hadn't felt a thing. In the corner, the air-conditioner hummed into a higher note. Damn! If Marshall would only sleep without the air-conditioner on, she might actually hear the quake's rumble, and then maybe she would feel it. Five-point-two was plenty high enough.

"A den of Communist antisocial subversives was rooted out in a residence of the *Barrio Frixione* yesterday," crowed the announcer. "They were surprised in the early hours of the morning by the heroic forces of our National Guard. One of the traitors was killed and three others were taken into custody."

"Oh, my." She turned toward Marshall, ran the tip of her finger over the ridge of his shoulder and down his arm. "You hear that? They left out 'terrorists.' They're slipping."

He grunted and opened one eye. "Which station's that?"

"The Big Man's very own of course."

He rolled over, sat up and swung his legs to the floor.

"He left out anarchists," she murmured to her abandoned finger, "and licentious, and lawless, and no-count, and shiftless…The pinko creep must be going soft on Communism."

He yawned, reached over his shoulder and scratched his back. "You started the ice yet?"

"The party's a week away. How many ice cubes do eight people need?" She walked her fingers across the sheet to his rumpled pajamas, but before she reached him he stood and stretched. She fell back on the pillow wondering if he'd sensed her approach.

He turned around, still scratching. "So what are you going to do today?"

"Mattie called a meeting on the art show, and then Gerry's giving another lecture."

"What's it this time? More Arachnoids of the Middle Americas?"

"No."

"Because you know he'll bring his tarantulas again anyhow and ask you guys to hold them, they're sooo gentle." He held his hand out palm up, and cocked his head to one side. "So, do you think this time you'll actually hold one?"

She refused to take the bait. "Probably not."

"Because they're big and they're ugly and fuzzy and they bite or sting or whatever they do."

"They're not deadly," she said. "At least not — "

11

"So he says. The man's an idiot trying to get a bunch of women to cuddle spiders."

"I thought you liked him."

"I do. But the guy's a maniac. He's supposed to be a geologist. He's paid, with our taxes by the way, to look for oil."

"So?"

"So he's sure not looking for oil when he's flying over volcanoes in the middle of the night. Or studying spiders, or Mayan texts. Or looking into unions and the work ethic in Nicaragua."

"He's going to show us a movie he's made of the volcano."

"Just what I said. And he's going to bring those spiders again. I bet Mattie Schimmer holds them."

"Of course she will. That's Mattie. Dauntless lady holds deadly spider."

He frowned. "I thought you liked her."

She cast about for another subject when the slam of a car door sounded over the chug of the air conditioner. Fat Dr. Carrillo gunned the engine of his car every morning for five minutes before he left for his office, where he cured his fat patients of eating.

"You'd think he was still living in Alaska," she said.

Marshall looked at his watch. "Six fifty-two. He's early."

"That's what I'm telling you. Something's up. Did you feel the earthquake last night?"

"Nope." He tugged the seat of his pajamas out from the crease of his rear-end. "How big?"

"Five-point-two, according to the voice of Tacho here." She caught at the last words, tried to reel them back, or change their tone. But he only raised an eyebrow. Her fingers itched to push up those heavy lids and check the color of his eyes, as if by that she could check the temperature of his thoughts.

12

As he headed for the bathroom, she sat up. "You know, for a so-called legitimate president…"

He stopped. "For God's sake, Julia, this early in the morning?"

Caught between relief and sorrow that she could always call him back through anger, she shook her head.

"Purity, cleanliness, good health," sang the radio. "Drink *Leche La Salud.*"

He came back to the bed. "I'd feel differently, Julia, if you actually knew what you were talking about."

Why did it always come down to her and her deficits? She fell back on her pillow. "Tacho's a shit!"

"So he's a shit. Who isn't? You think we're so pure?" He pursed his lips and jerked his chin toward the north and the city. "Somoza just happens to be the one that makes things work around here."

"You're right. He may kill innocent people, but he does make the one train run on time."

A flush spread across Marshall's cheeks.

He moved toward the window, turned off the air-conditioner, swung the drapes aside and cranked open the glass louvers. Warm, flower-scented air tinged with exhaust fumes flowed in.

He peered through the louvers. When he spoke, his voice was flat and calm. "If it weren't for him, Julia, you wouldn't be living in the lap of luxury… Oh for God's sake, Carillo's gone in for a second cup of coffee and left the bloody car on!" He closed the louvers and turned the air conditioner back on. "We're going to die in our beds some day while he dithers."

When he turned around, he was smiling. He held a tail of the gold silk drapes in one hand. "You know what? I like living in the lap of luxury." The drape billowed toward her, helped along by the air conditioner. "I like cathedral ceilings and wrought iron chandeliers."

He pointed up and then brought his hand swooping downward. "I like marble floors. Oh, and I like being a bank manager and running my own show."

To her astonishment he did a little march-slap-step with his bare feet, ending up at the foot of the bed. "And from all the evidence I see, so do you. Not one, but two maids, a gardener, your own car — pretty good for a girl from Toledo whose parents owned a diner." He held his hands up. "Nothing against diners. But I don't see you serving your guests meat loaf and lima beans. Nope, it's *boeuf en croute* for you. And by God, a *croute* with little pastry buttons, I bet." His fingers plunked three buttons down onto an imaginary pastry.

She wanted to laugh, wanted to hug him. "Nope," she said. "How about a zipper instead?" She grinned at him and he grinned back.

"You're right," she said softly. "When I let myself, I like it, too."

"Then, for God's sake, try to enjoy it. Speaking of which, I've got a French white for that shrimp, and a Spanish red -- "

"Mother!" shrieked Becka. The bedroom door flew open. "She's got my uniform again. Make her take it off!" Becka stood in the doorway — school blouse, underpants, bare, skinny legs, white socks, heavy school shoes.

Caley danced past her, dressed in nothing but a brown and white checked jumper. It dragged along the floor and her belly button showed above the loose waistband. Becka made a grab, caught one strap. Caley twisted away and a button flew off.

"See!" Caley announced. "She tore it!"

Becka pounded the door with her fist. "I want my uniform."

"Caley, give it to her!" said Julia.

"Who, me?"

"Caley..." Marshall's voice dipped ominously.

Caley dropped the other strap off her shoulder and let the uniform fall to her feet. "I don't want it, anyway." She stepped out of it, kicked it across to her sister, slapped her belly and struck a pose.

Becka snatched up the uniform. "Someday you're going to get it, Caley Bennett. You're going to get it and am I going to be glad. I'm going to be so glad, I'm going to scream." She jerked back her head and screamed, "Oh God, oh God, oh God, oh God."

"Knock it off!" shouted Marshall.

"Thank you," said Becka in a normal voice. "Thank you, God." She clomped off to her room. "Thank you, thank you, thank you."

Julia looked up at Marshall.

"Unbelievable," he said.

"The Most Estimable Ambassador of our good neighbor, President Nixon," proclaimed the radio announcer, "the highly respected Bigelow Hunnicutt, will honor his Extreme Excellency, Anastasio Somoza Debayle, our General in Chief, our Veritable Hurricane of Peace -- "

Marshall burst out laughing and Julia tuned the radio louder. " — with a gala reception on Friday next, in celebration of the aforementioned Supreme Commander's Glorious Leadership in the cause of Freedom and Democracy."

Julia raised her arms, hands fluttering. "Oh, Glorious Hurricane."

"Put some clothes on, Caley," said Marshall. "You'll be late for Kinder."

Julia watched the bathroom door close behind him.

"Don't use up all the hot water," she shouted.

He poked his head back out. "I never have any trouble."

"That's because you always get there first."

"Yup." He closed the door.

She raised her voice again. "Have you called the landlord?"

"Not yet," he yelled.

"There's a leak. I know there is."

The door cracked open. "Yeah, right! Under the living room floor. You can feel it with your bare feet." He closed the door again.

She took a deep breath and rolled out of bed. "I'm going to call the landlord myself," she whispered to Caley who was watching from the doorway. Caley's eyes went round. That was Daddy work; even she knew that.

Julia took a slow, gliding step forward. "And I'm going to tell him…" She stopped. "What'll I tell him?" She took another step.

Caley shook her head but stood her ground.

"I'm going to tell him…" She bounded forward, caught a giggling Caley up in her arms and buried her face in the soft flesh of Caley's neck. "I'm going to tell him there's a leak in the system!"

Chapter 3

Premonition. José María pressed his head against the rough stone until the pain equaled the pain in his side. All others faded by comparison.

He pressed harder. And then there was…comparison…by comparison, he was in comparative pain, as compared to…he pushed against the words, against the pain, against the stone wall with its roll call of comrades, against the weight of stone all around him. Above him, Tiscapa's mountain crowned by a presidential palace pushed back until finally he floated free and there were no words left. Nothing.

And the Angel of Death bent close and spoke into his ear, a low caressing voice, the Spanish clean and clear, the words a meaningless stream. As the wires hummed and the electricity tore through him, he blocked the words out so as not to respond. But the voice buried itself in his bones like a homing beacon. Each blow, each torn square of flesh sealed it there, and some day, in a place of sun and light and people going about their lives, he would hear that voice and know it, feel it resonating deep inside him. That day was worth waiting for.

Premonition. He woke to the word once again. And this time there were tears from some forgotten dream, tears sliding down across the bridge of his nose, down around his mouth and onto the stone floor. He tilted his head to the side and his tears slid back into the torn membranes of his throat where they burned. As they should. It seemed fitting that the one injury he had dealt himself, the pulpy, raw residue of his screams, he should quietly heal on his own without their knowing. Good tears, salt tears, and when he swallowed, pain soared up into his ears on hot wires. His convulsive recoil brought alive his side, his feet and all the rest.

When the pain subsided a bit, he lay spent, floating in an icy stillness. A moment of coherent thought, a time of mercy. And a marker — for when it came, they were never far behind, with their boots and keys and fists.

He patted the rag that passed for a shirt, behind which he kept the hood. A rough cloth bag, stiff with the blood, snot and tears of others who had gone before him, it was meant to keep him from seeing the faces of those who tortured him. With it on, he couldn't breathe and the crust of dried filth rubbed the skin of his face raw in patches. And yet, for all its horrors, it became an odd kind of comfort in the dark and the silence. He kept it next to his chest, and talked to it when the silence threatened to overwhelm him. It was company, and he gave it names, none of which stuck. In his cell it was a friend, while outside it was another torturer.

The worst moment of his day was when he was forced to put it on before his sessions with the Angel of Death. In that moment, friend became enemy.

He refused to wear the hood in his cell, an act of rebellion that had earned him several beatings when he hadn't been able to get it on fast enough. Still he kept it stuffed between his bare skin and the shirt with a box of matches in the pocket, where he could get at them easily. With his hands bound before him, he'd had to learn to use both hands together. The hardest task was putting the hood on quickly when he heard them coming.

The matches had appeared one day with his dinner, nestled inside the tortilla, atop the two spoonfuls of sour beans. Slowly, his hands shaking, he had lit the tiny waxen sticks, a few each day, and in the short bursts of light, he'd read the inscriptions on the walls. Juan M, Plácido G, El Clarín. Dozens of them, unknown companions in the struggle, each listed without a last name. Some were written in fine script representing days of labor, others were only rough block letters. And some were only a cross or initials. These were the saddest. Men and women buried here, never having read a book or learned how to write their names.

He wept, remembering how Miguel taught him to read, and how Katherine fed him book after scrounged book in the States, all so he could stand here and read these names by the light of a match. "Juan M, 13 July 1967," angled downward above "Fuck the Guard."

José María searched for the names of friends who had disappeared, but they weren't there and so he gave it up when he had only one unread corner and one match left. And each time they came to take him to the Angel of Death, he put the match in its box in Juan M's corner, dry, clean, safe for his return, should he return.

He eased his head away from the corner and pushed himself up into a sitting position, taking in the sour stench of his own body. Proof that he lived.

When he was small, Miguel had beaten him up once or twice a month. One year older and a good deal larger, his cousin would swoop down from the stone sink or from the *nancito* tree in the back of the house and bash him silly. "It's because I love you," Miguel would say.

And he had come to half-believe that it was so. But he also became adept at sensing out a room before he entered it. And he had learned to run, though Miguel was faster and sneakier and seldom left marks. Berfalia, working at the market six days a week, never knew. And no way was he going to squeal on Miguel.

It was between the beatings that Miguel had taught him to read. And he'd helped Miguel load the huge baskets Berfalia used to carry sausages and meat to the market.

It was Miguel who'd taught him the anatomy of a pig and the parallels between pigs and humans. As Berfalia slaughtered and gutted and cleaned the animal, Miguel, a poet even then, had lifted the organs and discoursed on the transformation of food to shit and man to dust. He'd swung the testicles and the flaccid case for the corkscrewed penis and told of the wonders of the curlicue fuck.

"Enough!" Berfalia would thunder, prodding her son with the handle of her knife, and Miguel would yell back, "It's for his own good!"

José María pressed his clenched fist against his chest. Yes, my friend, my cousin, my mentor and tormentor, good had come of it. He'd learned to take a beating. He slid his hands up and touched his mouth. Like Miguel, they'd spared his face. At times, he would touch the soft lids over his eyeballs, the tender flexing lips and wonder. Not that it stopped or even eased the pain. But somehow, by the simple exercise of wonder, he knew he was defeating the Angel.

Just as he had finally defeated Miguel. The idea had come to him one day as Berfalia was moving in on a trussed and shrieking pig hanging from the iron pig frame. As the buzzards circled overhead, his sister Luz had hidden under Berfalia's bed. He and Miguel had stood next to the creature, each one with bucket upright and ready, their feet surrounded by empty buckets, this one for the last of the blood, that one for the offal, the rest for the cuts of meat or the little trash that was left.

As the knife swept across the pig's neck, he looked at Miguel and saw horror, sorrow, and something else, something fierce and urgent.

The pig bucked. Berfalia shouted for them to hang on and set the buckets, and they moved automatically, catching the blood, hanging on, staring at each other. In that moment José María realized that the look had been his own and his cousin's only the reflection.

The next day, he'd moved through the empty house saying good-bye to the things that had held him, struck by how few and yet how mysterious they were: the bucket of lard his aunt kept in the kitchen and used to heal wounds; the old Victrola and the pile of scratched records he had played over and over again. He'd run his hand over the flared horn, and thought of playing one last record.

Instead, he'd set his small suitcase down in the kitchen, walked out under the *nancito* tree and around the yard, washed down and spotless now. Years of experience had tuned his body well and he felt his shoulders curve and his back arch before he even sensed his cousin hurtling down from the top of the outhouse. His knees bent and he took a fraction of Miguel's weight, then snapped his body up and back. Miguel flew off and landed on his shoulder with his head against the gray, sunbaked slats of the outhouse.

Without a word, he'd pounced on Miguel, swinging hard, saying goodbye to the heat and the dust and his screwed-up cousin and the pig's blood. When he realized Miguel had stopped moving, he sat back, ready for a counter-attack, but Miguel was staring up at him with eyes already beginning to swell and a huge grin on his face.

"Cousin." Miguel spat blood out the side of his mouth, then wiped his face against his shoulder. "*Jodido*, cousin, son of a bitch."

"Fuck you, too." He'd rolled away and lay in the dust beside his tormentor.

"Hey cousin," Miguel had said after a while, "how about I come with you?"

Of course, Miguel would've known he was leaving; he'd probably known before the pig was dead. "Go see your own world, cousin."

As José María carried out the peeling suitcase, Miguel called his name. Miguel hadn't moved from where he'd fallen, hadn't even turned his head. His eyes still closed, he held one hand up toward the sky, two fingers stretched up in a victorious V.

That image had been his companion for fourteen years: Miguel, comforter, afflicter, mentor, who'd taught him the companionship of enmity.

With a gutteral cry, he welcomed the sudden onslaught of tears. He pushed his head back against the stones, opened his mouth wide and gulped in air until it scalded his throat and he clamped his lips shut.

He began to shiver. He'd seen once, in the forbidding bottom of Momotombo's crater, the blackened ruin of a human spine attached to blue jeans, packed tight and near to bursting with the rotting flesh inside. Buzzards flopped and pecked in ungainly attempts to break through the cloth. He'd pictured then, felt it now, the sickening rush of air as the man was thrown into the crater, his scream tearing through his throat.

José María slid his hands up beneath his shirt and clasped the small box between his fingers. Slowly he crawled into the fourth corner. The last corner. He pushed the box open with his tongue and slid his finger in to fish out the small, waxed stick.

They would come for him soon and yet he waited until his hands were steady and the faint mocking voice within was quiet. Only if you failed could something be called stupid, he reminded himself. Katherine had taught him that.

22

"Hey Joey, you screw up, then you stink," she'd said. "Do it right and your ass smells like a rose."

At last he had it right, the box in one hand, his wrists as far apart as the cuffs would allow, and he struck the match against the box.

Light flared, blinding for an instant, then steady. He moved the match slowly from the corner outward. There it was: "Efraín, Dec 1968."

Efraín, short, wiry, fast, and very funny. Efraín, who had disappeared six months ago carrying a message to Léon.

José María held the match close to the squared, wobbly letters. Only six months and he couldn't remember Efraín's face, his smile, or even his voice. As he reached out to touch the letters, it came to him — he'd not carved his own name on the wall. He was not here! Had never been here. The match fizzled out in his fingers.

In the distance, he felt rather than heard the faint clink of keys, the muffled tread of boots. He pressed his fingers against the dark wall, then rose, carried upward by his rage, for himself, for Efraín, for all the others. He drew out the hood, brought it up to his head, then threw it against the far wall. It disappeared without a sound.

Chapter 4

Julia scraped the onion skins into the garbage. Sweat ran down her forehead and into her eyes. She squeezed them shut, opened them and yelped as onion juice flooded her contacts. She snatched up a pot holder and groped for the spigot, forgetting that it was buried in a pile of dirty dishes.

"Goddamn!" She bent over double and rocked her way down to the floor.

"*Señora?*" Juanita called from the laundry room.

"*Mis ojos*! My eyes! I got onion juice in my eyes." She heard the water running in the laundry tub as she hunkered down.

"*Aqui Señora.*"

Julia reached out blindly.

"*Por favor*, please lift up your head."

Obediently, Julia raised her head and took the dripping cloth from Juanita. "Yes, oh God yes," she crooned as cool water flooded her half-closed eyes."I just wanted to get the onions done before I took another shower."

"I'll finish them, *Señora*. You go take your shower."

"No." Julia stood up and removed the cloth. Her eyes stung as Juanita's blurry figure took shape. "I'll just finish up here," she replied.

"I don't want you to wash the dishes when you've been ironing, certainly not in cold water."

"*Señora Julia*," said Juanita wearily, "it was Ninfa who told you that. If I were going to get rheumatism from wet hands and ironing, I'd have it by now."

"Oh." Julia sighed. "The *Señor* told me I was wrong about the wet hands."

A smile lit Juanita's face and she nodded.

Marshall only thought of Juanita as a mournful crow of a woman, with few teeth and a back so crooked she seemed to walk a little sideways with each step she took forward. He'd even gone so far as to scuttle across the bedroom one night in frustrated imitation because she'd refused to fire Juanita after some mistake with his laundry. But Julia trusted Juanita. And that alone, she told Marshall, made her worth keeping.

Julia handed the cloth back. "No, thank you very much, Juanita. I'll just finish up here."

The morning had started at six, when someone came to tell Ninfa that her child was sick with dengue. "*Muy grave,*" they'd said, gravely ill. So Julia had sent her home with money for the week and some extra for medicine.

"Stay as long as you need to," she'd said. "And don't worry about the party. Juanita and I will take care of all that."

Ninfa, silent and moody at any time, managed to express a vast skepticism merely by lifting one end of the single eyebrow that stretched from one side of her forehead to the other. Caught halfway between indignation and laughter, Julia barely managed to school her features into a look of caring concern and she wished her well. Ninfa was sharp and a quick learner. Not having her here would certainly make for more work. And Marshall would not be happy.

When the last of the onions were chopped, Julia covered them with a damp dish towel and headed for the bathroom. Crossing the living room, she noticed that parts of the trumpet vine were almost touching the paving stones and it would have to be trimmed soon. It was a shame. The children loved the cool, dark cave the patio became when the vine grew all the way down to the ground.

In the bathroom, she filled the sink with cold water and plunged her head down into it, eyes open. Once, twice, three times. She dried her face and sighed with relief. What a perfect gift the trumpet vine had been. It kept the patio cool and at sunset it flooded the bathroom with green and gold.

They'd been in the house just three weeks when one morning a bulldozer had roared around to the back of the house and proceeded to destroy the three car garage the landlord had just built to house the fleet of luxury cars he was sure a big-time banker would need. By the time they'd all scrambled out of bed and run out to the patio, the landlord himself, Mr. Medina, short and round, had arrived with two small potted plants, one in each hand. He waved one toward the rapidly disappearing garage and shouted at Marshall, "Not anti-earth-quake-proof." He galloped up to them, quite a feat in itself seeing as how the man was almost as wide as he was tall. He lifted the two plants. "You put dees plant here," he jutted his chin to the left side of the patio, "an dees one…", another chin jut to the right, "an' een no time…" He brought the pots together with a crash that shattered the clay and sent earth flying everywhere.

"*Úpale!*" he shouted. "Wow!" He banged his chest with a fist that still gripped a substantial portion of the pot rim.

They all stared down at the broken pottery, the clumps of dark earth at their feet, the impossibly bright green leaves and gray, spidery roots.

"They leeve," he crowed, and it took a second to realize the plants weren't going to get up and walk away but that they had survived their crash, clearly a cause for celebration. Soon they were all laughing, even Juanita and Ninfa, from the door of the laundry.

In a sudden shift, Medina pointed a shard of the broken pot at the maids and, with a great deal of shouting and arm waving and chin jutting, he had them dig holes on either side of the patio. The whole thing was done in the time it took for him to explain how fast the vines would grow up to the roof and across it until they met in a "*berytaable hungle.*" Marshall had goggled at the exquisite turn of phrase and, since then, had dined out on landlord stories.

But he still hadn't called Medina about the leak and it had been more than a week now.

As Julia started to put her face in the water again, she caught a glimpse of herself in the mirror. Well, I'll be damned! she thought. To hell with a cold shower — Medina's my landlord, too.

Before she could change her mind, she went to the telephone in the front hall. The landlord's number was listed by his first name. On the second ring, Anibal Medina Medina himself answered. After that, nothing could have been easier. Of course, he could come, he would do so today, this very morning if possible.

When she hung up, she was elated. Maybe, just maybe, she could get the leak fixed before Marshall got home from work. And after the rough start, the day would not turn out so bad after all.

She nearly danced her way back to the kitchen. She couldn't stop smiling as she started sautéing the ingredients for the filling. The crust she'd do later. And the dishes could wait until the main dish was wrapped up and in the freezer.

Things were well in hand. She could do this, if not with aplomb, at least with some grace. She caught herself up. How easy it is to be generous when your own hands aren't in a tub of cold, greasy dishwater, groping for sharp objects down in the murky depths.

The onions were turning golden in the frying pan and, if Medina came soon, the dishes might yet be washed in hot water before the day was out. They still had almost a week before the party.

Nicaragua had been their fourth move together and they'd become good at it. They'd hit the town running and within a week they'd gotten their furniture out of customs, they had a house that was ready for parties, and the kids were in school. They'd bought a beat-up Buick, had gone to two welcome parties, had even taken the kids to a birthday party. They'd hired a maid and had a lead on another.

Marshall had joined the bank baseball team and she'd found kindred spirits in Madalein and Carol, whose husbands worked for the U.S. State Department. Both of them lived on this street. With their encouragement, she'd actually joined the American Women's Club, surprising both herself and Marshall. "You never join clubs," he'd said, and went away shaking his head.

Julia rinsed her hands in the smaller sink to the right of the stove and reset her ponytail.

"Tell me about dengue," she said as Juanita passed through the kitchen with shirts on hangers.

Juanita stopped and frowned.

"Oh Juanita, I'm sorry. I don't doubt Ninfa's daughter is sick." With two kids and living in Acahualinca, said to be the poorest *barrio* in Managua, kids were always sick. "I just mean, is it dangerous?"

"Him," said Juanita. "It's the boy. And yes, it is dangerous if the child is sickly." Her mouth twisted into a small, painful smile. Her own grandchildren were often sickly.

"I'm sorry, Juanita. I wasn't thinking."

Juanita nodded and passed on through the kitchen. On her way back, with her arms unburdened, she sniffed the air and said, "That smells very good."

Julia smiled. "Thank you. I'm making extra so we can try some for lunch. Oh, and by the way, I've called *Señor* Medina about the water leak and he's supposed to come this morning."

Juanita stopped abruptly. "El *patrón*? This morning?"

"Yes, *el doctor* Medina." Julia tried to keep her tone neutral. She knew exactly what the problem was. She'd overstepped established bounds. Calling the landlord was Marshall's prerogative.

"Juanita, we need hot water, and the *señor* doesn't realize it because he takes his shower first."

"I can wash the dishes."

"So can I, but that's not the point." A little annoyed, she added. "We need hot water, and the Señor's too busy to see to it."

Juanita nodded and went back to the laundry.

Julia was adding the meat to the pan when she heard loud thumps on the front door.

"*Diós mío!*" said Juanita from the door to the laundry. "*El Patrón!*"

"That's okay, I'll get it." Julia turned the burner off and headed to the door. Good God, the man must have flown!

And indeed, it was the *Patrón*, in all his glory, thought Julia as she opened the door. Anibal Medina Medina and company, decked out in a gleaming white shirt and tan trousers with a little silver pistol poking out between his belt and the overhanging belly. His tasseled shoes were tan and brown suede and he lifted them delicately, as if he were dancing, each step pooching his belly down over the belt to hide the shiny weapon.

In seconds, he was standing over the spot where the leak was.

"With your feet?" he said, his pudgy face round with delight. "You can feel this leak with your feet?" He gazed down at her wondrous bare feet.

The word "*salvaje*"– savage — floated across her mind; there was something both savage and innocent about him. She glanced up and realized he was probably thinking the same of her.

She jabbed her bare foot at the marble tiles. "As I was saying — right there."

He offered a dreamy smile. His eyes sparkled. "But the heater is all the way over there." He pointed to the closet outside Marshall's study, managing in the process to brush against her arm.

Oh dear God, she thought. What had she done?

"That's more than twenty feet away. That could take a very long time." He smiled and looked around the room. "Such a wonderful house, so strong." His gaze came to rest on her feet again.

"Yes, Dr. Medina, it is a wonderful house, but there's a leak in the hot water system." She was feeling sicker by the minute.

"How sensitive your feet must be." He clasped his hands against his chest and stepped closer.

She took a step back, not even sure what lay behind her. "Dr. Medina. Please. The floor is warm there." She knew better! No woman should ever be alone with a man, especially in her own house. To him, Juanita wouldn't count.

She groped behind her, came up against the metal bar of the sling chair and broke her nail. Fuck! And it was she who'd made the overture, had invited him here when her husband was at work.

"Look doctor," she tried to make her voice sound hard and businesslike, "we're having a dinner party in a few days and I need hot water."

"You have no hot water?"

"That's what I'm saying."

He edged closer. "How are you bathing?"

"Very quickly." She stepped sideways and backed around the chair. "My husband also has to bathe very quickly, because the water is cold."

Husband? What husband? If anything, that only increased the sappy look on his face. "But I'll have to dig right across the living room. I might have to replace the water heater." He pressed his hands against his chest and winked. "How can we be sure?"

Not 'we,' you asshole. She pointed behind him. "It's there. See for yourself, touch it."

"I admire sensitive women."

"Senor Medina." Out of the corner of her eye, she saw Jaunita lurking in the door of the kitchen with a pile of folded laundry. Thank God.

"So sensitive." He moved to his right as though to come at her from the other side. "My wife is an invalid, you know."

"No, I didn't know that." She gave Juanita a nod.

"Yes. Unable to lead a normal life."

She nearly gagged. "I'm sorry to hear that."

"*Con permiso.*" Juanita crossed behind Medina.

"And you?" he barked. "Can you feel it, girl?"

Juanita stopped and shook her head. "No *señor*. But then my feet don't feel much." She went into the master bedroom.

Thanks a bunch, thought Julia.

Medina looked up into her face. "So ill. It's very sad."

"For God's sake, Mr. Medina." She caught herself. "I'm really sorry about your wife. I hope you have a long and happy life together — but I called you to get the leak repaired."

"You're not interested in my wife's health?" He looked genuinely

31

puzzled. Not care about the ailing wife? Not care about the sorrow-ing, abstinent husband? What was the matter with her?

"Yes I do care about your wife's health, but I need to have the leak fixed before — before the floor collapses and ruins this beautiful house."

"That's it?" His voice rose a notch. "You're worried about the leak? You stand there with your bare feet in this magnificent house like some maid just in from the country, in my house that is so beautiful, that my wife should be living in if she wasn't so sick with all those doctor bills, and all you can say is that you are worried about a leak?" He laughed and broke into English. "No bat, she say no bat; bat cold, she dirty, husband dirty, everyteeng dirty… "

It's a shower! she wanted to scream. You're too cheap to put in a tub.

Almost as though he'd read her thoughts, his little bully eyes glared into hers and he switched back to Spanish. "This won't do. Not in my house."

Her stomach gave a lurch. Oh God, the man was crazy enough to throw them out. "*Señor* Medina -- " Her voice cracked and she cleared her throat. "Are you going to fix the leak?"

"Look at that!" He pointed toward the patio.

"What?"

He headed for the sliding doors, his rear end wobbling like two garbage bags tied together. He fumbled with the latch, then shoved the doors open. "Those vines are growing onto the roof."

"Of course they are. That's what you said would happen — "

"They are damaging the tiles."

She grit her teeth. "The leak, doctor?"

"Oh?" he looked her up and down. "When did you say your party was?"

"Next Tuesday."

He nodded, then grinned and drew himself up. "Yes! We will work as quickly as possible so that your party may be an enjoyable one." He laughed, his belly shook and the little gun winked at her. "And de focking bat weel be hhott!"

Still grinning, he walked toward the front door. "I shall, of course, convey your best wishes to my wife," he said over his shoulder.

"Thank you, doctor, I would be most pleased for you to do that." She closed the door softly behind him and locked it. She felt dirty. And there was still no hot water. Half sick, she started to laugh. "No bat," she said throwing her arms up. "No focking bat! Wife dirty, husband dirty!"

Her laughter died and she rested her forehead against the door, dreading the moment when Marshall would come home.

33

Chapter 5

There hadn't always been this silence. Marshall glanced up at the rearview mirror and then over at Julia sewing the hem of her dress.

"How long did it take to make that?" he asked.

She reached up and turned on the car's overhead light to look at her watch.

"Don't do that," he said, squinting at the road.

"Going on five and a half hours." She turned off the light.

Again the silence. What could you say to a woman who made a dress in five and a half hours?

"All today?"

"No. I cut the pattern out yesterday." She broke off the thread, held the needle up and looked around. He grimaced. She would probably stick it in the leatherette dashboard.

"Don't do that," he said again.

"What?"

"Nothing."

He was intelligent. She was bright. Why the hell couldn't they carry on a conversation without grinding to a halt?

"I don't want to stay too late," he said.

She said nothing. Which meant she'd probably want to dance all night.

"I mean it."

"Fine with me." She rammed the needle into the dashboard.

"Dammit, you did it."

"What?"

"The dashboard. Did you have to do that?"

"Oh. I'm sorry."

He turned onto the country club road a little surprised she hadn't told him she hated the car anyway, and what did it matter, a little hole in the dashboard.

"It's not a very big hole," she said.

"The sun will make it crack."

"No, I mean in the living room floor."

"I don't want to talk about it." He still couldn't believe it. It was the most important dinner they would have in a long time, and there was a hole right in the middle of the living room, with a broken pipe half-buried beneath rubble. And now with Medina out of town or not answering his phone, it wasn't likely to be fixed soon.

"It stinks," said Julia.

"What?"

"The car. Like mold, and the clock doesn't even work."

"Of course." He smiled, his good humor restored. It was as good as an apology. "We could always light a fire in the goddamned hole and toast marshmallows for dessert," he said.

Marshall liked to watch Julia dance. She moved easily, looser than the Nicaraguan women but with the same fluid motion, as though the bandleader had her on a string, hooked onto something inside her. Maybe that's why she liked to dance close to the band. And why she never looked at her feet. She looked up at his face instead, her eyes wide, her mouth a little open.

"How many farms does he own?" she said and sidled past him.

"Who?" He turned to follow her. They were into a two-step and he knew it bored her. Every once in a while she changed to the three-step and then they bobbed away at each other at cross purposes, and he had to keep his eyes on her feet to figure out where she was going. He'd thought about taking lessons, but even then she'd probably go her own way.

"Montealegre," she said.

"Hey, give the man a break. This is his retirement party." He turned around and faced away from the band for several steps. When he turned back, she was into a three-step and her eyes were closed. Her pale green dress clung to her body and there was a series of round openings, like a necklace, just above her breasts. She was moving her hands around her wrists as if they were in water.

"I was thinking about the drought. It must be hard," she said.

"Oh." Talking with her was like dancing with her; you never knew where you stood.

"It is hard." He put one hand on her hip, plucked her right hand up with the other and brought her back to the two-step.

She opened her eyes and smiled, brought her left hand close to her face, as if she were going to thumb her nose at him, and brushed a stray hair from her forehead. A little wrinkle appeared between her eyebrows and she shook her head.

"What?"

"Nothing." She smiled that slow smile of hers, like she'd just come from a million miles away. "Something about the art show. I have the feeling I was supposed to do something for it, and I didn't."

The band started a slow song and he followed her off the floor. The back of the dress had those same holes in it, only these were bigger, and more of her back showed. He left her at the table talking with

Catalina de Salazar, and moved toward the bar, where a group of men clustered around Montealegre.

"*Hola*, Marshall. *Qué tal?*" They pronounced his name "Mushuh," a mishmash of open-mouthed sounds.

"*Hola, gringo beisbolero*," how's Chicago Federal's greatest third baseman tonight?" Manolo Helgar feigned a throw and ended with a clap to Marshall's shoulder. "Hear your team is in first place."

Marshall grinned. "Certainly is, no thanks to me." He hadn't played baseball in the last two seasons, but they never forgot. There was something about an American executive playing on his company team that tickled them; the fact that he'd done it for even one season gave him an exaggerated standing and was always good for a comment or two.

Soon enough, they were talking about the weather, the heat and the severity of the drought.

"What difference does it make?" said Quiñones, eyeing the amber liquid in his glass. "Droughts, floods, wars, they just mean more interest for the banks."

"Disaster produces opportunities," said someone behind him.

"It drives borrowing to the limit and requires creative exiting," said a familiar voice.

Marshall turned. Jaime Salazar was offering his hand. "Just soup and nuts," Jaime said with a smile.

He shook Jaime's hand. "I've lost you." Jaime was probably the only man in the world who could get away with wearing his hair parted in the middle. Put a pair of glasses on him and he'd be Casper Milktoast.

"How does it go?" asked Jaime. "One man's soup is another man's nuts, isn't that it?"

Meat and poison, thought Marshall. He smiled.

Nobody else did, or corrected Jaime.

"Anyway," Jaime said, "it's just reality."

"I suppose so." Marshall didn't like the funding crunch any more than they did, particularly when there were people out there who weren't going to make it. Today he'd had to drop the bad news on Clementina Pineda. Next week, Beal Jackson. He grimaced. That's what he got for trying to help Julia's widows and orphans. But dammit, he couldn't have done it any other way once he'd approved their loans contrary to Head Office's negative hints.

Jaime took him by the elbow and led him a few steps away from the group. He lowered his voice. "How about coming up to the farm tomorrow? The new airfield is finished. We could make it for lunch and be back by dinner. It's a beautiful spot, the Pacific Ocean, volcanoes, the works."

"Sounds great." Marshall grinned. A casual hop on a plane, a dance at a country club – how about that for the kid whose first job was sweeping the floor of a menswear shop in Jefferson, Ohio? "How's the farm doing?" he asked.

"So much for cotton this year. But ..." Jaime shrugged. "We'll make do. Thanks God for diversification."

Marshall nodded. Diversification, hell. God could dry up the continent and Jaime Salazar would survive. These men were survivors, every one of them.

"Are you up to starting early?" said Jaime.

"Sure. How early?"

"Seven o'clock? Out at the airport?"

"Fine." With anyone else in this crowd, you might get started by noon, if you were lucky. But Jaime was punctuality itself.

Marshall turned to watch Mattie Schimmer walk by. So did the other men. With red hair and a figure like a siren, she was a knock-out. "Did you say you had a volcano on your place?" he asked Jaime.

"Not on my land." Jaime grinned. "Still, there may be something of interest for you there."

"Hey Marshall, what's up?" Garv Schimmer dropped into the chair beside him and spread his elbows on the table. "Hear you beat Palacios last weekend."

"It was almost as easy as walking on my nose."

"I bet." Garv leaned forward and spoke to Julia on Marshall's other side. "What kind of nut plays tennis in this climate? Baseball is sweaty enough, but tennis?"

"A cashew," Julia said. "Have you ever seen a cashew growing, Garv? The nut grows outside the fruit." She stuck her little finger out like a hook from her fist.

Garv grinned. "I think that describes you more than Marshall."

She laughed. "You may have a point there." She raised her finger as though she was going to give a speech.

"How're you doing, Garv?" said Marshall quickly.

"Not bad." Garv ran a finger and thumb over his Pancho Villa moustache. "Got some time tomorrow morning?"

Garv probably wanted to clear up the factory loan. "Sorry, I can't tomorrow. Jaime Salazar is flying me to one of his farms up north."

Garv gave a low whistle. "Nice."

"How about the day after?" asked Marshall. Word was that Unity Foods was in a buying mood and, with five years in the black, Garv's cookie factory was a good deal. Here was another way around a drought.

"Okay with me," said Garv. "How's the branch in Montoya going?"

"Should be opening next month."

"A lot of work, opening a new branch," said Garv.

"Not that much. Fidelia's taken care of most of it. She's amazing."

"You should make her the manager," said Garv.

"That's what Julia said."

"Smart woman." Garv tapped a finger on the table in front of Julia. "When're you going to run that phone patch to your mother?"

"Thanks," she said. "Not for a while."

Garv winked at Marshall. "So, if your first line doesn't work, try another… Julia, my love, how would you like to dance?"

Marshall watched them thread their way out to the dance floor. Cashew? What the hell was that about? Men told him he was lucky to have such an attractive wife, but sometimes it was more work trying to figure her out then he had the energy for.

She looked good in that dress though, even with her hair in a roll in back and strands of it flying about her face. It was somehow provocative, having her hair look uncombed like that, as if any minute she'd pull out that ridiculous pin that held it together and it would fall down her back in a tangle. Like she'd just gotten out of bed.

The Nica men always smiled up at her when she passed, as if they knew exactly what that would look like. Which was strange because she wasn't beautiful. She was pretty, but not a beauty like Mattie. Or a flirt like Mattie, either. The thought made him laugh. Julia flirt? She was too blunt, too direct.

When he first knew her in Lima, she was a mystery, someone who could carry on three different conversations in the marketplace and come away with a basket of bargains and a story from each of the vendors. She was curious about everything, this tall, gray-eyed woman who listened so intently, especially to him.

  • And you fell for it, he thought. You loved it. She was the first woman who even came close to Silla. Once, on the train going to Machu Pichu, passing through an area where wild flowers grew on the mountainside, she disappeared for a while and when she came back she handed him a bunch of flowers. He asked her how she got them, but she simply pointed out the window and smiled. After a brief moment picturing her dangling off the side of the train, plucking flowers in the wind, he finally decided she must have struck up a conversation with someone who already had them. She'd probably listened and listened, and the poor sap had simply handed them over in a rapture.

The hitch with all that listening was that she actually expected him to tell her everything: his thoughts, his feelings – it drove him nuts. If he wanted to tell her what was on his mind, he'd do it when he was ready.

He'd finally managed to get that across to her. But look at her on the dance floor. Garv talking away, waving his hands while she looked up into his face with the exact same fascinated expression she'd used on him. No, Julia really wasn't like Silla at all. You could depend on Silla. What you got one day, you'd get the next day and every day after that. Julia was too much herself. You couldn't count on her to meet you even halfway.

"You look a little sad." Mattie Schimmer's voice was soft and breathless. She slipped into a seat across the table.

"I wasn't aware of it." He smiled.

The band started a slow tune.

"They dance well together," said Mattie, with a nod toward the dance floor.

"Yes. How's the art show going?"

"S'funny. We've lived here ten years and I'm learning about places

41

I've never heard of before. Wiwili, Comoapa, Solentiname." She laughed. "Maybe I'll even learn how to pronounce them."

Mattie was famous for her awful Spanish. But, with a face like that, no one gave a damn.

"It's a big undertaking," he said. "The art show, I mean."

"Hey, I like doing this kind of thing." She leaned forward. "One-upping the Nicaraguan women. They aren't exactly friendly."

He frowned. He hadn't figured her for a whiner. "Has it been hard?"

"A little lonely at times. The American women come and go and the Nicaraguan women can't be bothered."

He couldn't picture Mattie lonely. He shifted his weight on his chair and looked away. Out on the dance floor, Julia was dancing at a small distance from Garv and talking a blue streak.

"I manage," Mattie said softly. "I do the best I can. Would you dance with me?"

His blinked. "Of course."

It only took a few steps on the dance floor to know Mattie would follow him. She was shorter than Julia and he was able to close his eyes and brush his chin lightly on her hair, knowing she wouldn't notice because of that beehive thing that lifted her hair way off her scalp.

She wore perfume, which made him think of all those bottles of perfume he'd bought in the duty free shops over the years that just sat unopened in Julia's closet.

Mattie's hand on his shoulder drew him closer. Well, even if he wasn't a good dancer, he was managing well enough. He looked down at the red hair beneath his nose, it looked great with those little curls over his ears. He took a breath and moved into a three step and she followed him perfectly. She bent her head back and looked up at him. He had never really noticed how blue her eyes were.

"Marshall?"

"Yes?"

She ran her finger over the hollow beneath his ear and smiled. "Nothing."

Her breath was warm on his chin and he nearly stopped moving. It was almost as though he could feel her bare breasts against his chest. "Nothing" was definitely not what she meant.

Her fingers pressed lightly against the back of his neck, pulling him to her, and his outrageous thought floated away in a jumble. No, he told himself calmly. Had he spoken it aloud? But he was leaning into a step and now her thighs were against his. There was no space between them. None at all.

Chapter 6

Hands gripped his ankles and dragged him out of the truck. As his raw back scraped along the metal grooves of the truck bed, José María screamed, but the croak that came out tore at his throat. The men laughed so hard they dropped him on the ground and again he cried out.

They picked him up by the armpits and the ankles. The guy at his head leaned over to look at him and José María tried to slug him with the back of his fists, but they were tied together and his swing went wild. He kicked out with his feet but only succeeded in making the bastards stumble and drag his butt along the ground. He forced the croak up into a scream and they howled with laughter and made a see-saw of him so his back scraped along its length against the ground until the pain shut him down.

When he came to, they were arguing in whispers.

"…shit's a faggot."

"…a fuckin' crybaby…all that snot on his face."

"You want to see him piss his pants?"

"He already stinks of piss."

"Look, he's comin' around."

"Someone sit on him…"

"Enough," said a voice louder than the others. "He's blown his voice. You won't get shit out of him now."

"At least get the blindfold off."

"Yeah, let him see what's coming."

"I said GET IT OVER WITH!"

As they lifted him, someone shoved his head to the side and fumbled at the blindfold.

"*Uno, dos…*" The blindfold fell away and he caught a glimpse of dark shapes against a star-filled sky, sensed the vast, steaming crater below, the vultures circling overhead.

"Out and over, motherfucker!" someone yelled, and he was airborne. Wind rushed past and he screamed and screamed until his lungs filled with the rushing air and something hard struck his leg, his back, his head…

A flame of light touched his eyes; he opened them to a low sun slicing between the trunks of trees. Morning, or evening? He struggled to keep his eyes open, but they closed of their own accord. When he woke again, the sun was gone and the sky was dark with stars poking through the heavy canopy here and there. It must have been sunset when he woke the last time and that meant he was facing west. On the west side of a steep hill that seemed covered with trees and foliage.

From above came the sound of a truck shifting down, the grunt and burr of an engine climbing and, overlaying that, the unmistakable, belly-to-the-ground backfire of an overloaded bus heading downhill in low gear. Highway traffic. He was in one of the ancient, overgrown craters off the South Highway.

He couldn't believe it. He was still alive, could still see and hear and recognize where he was. He rested in that thought, floating in a sea of relief and gratitude. Until he started to move.

He tried to block the hideous scream that came from his throat. He swung his arms up to smother it only to bash his nose because his wrists were still tied together. Groaning, he lay back.

His shirt had become glued to his back with dried blood, the cloth jammed into the gullies left by the bastard's belt buckle. He tried shifting from side to side to figure out the extent of the damage, but the pain was too much, so he rested his head against the earth and closed his eyes. About the pain he could do nothing. But fast or slow, he had to get out of here.

At least they'd cuffed his hands in front. That would make for an easier piss when he did get up, though he wasn't sure how easy that piss would actually be, given that his kidneys were probably melted cheese by now.

He closed his eyes and ran a slow inventory of his body: he was thirsty, but not desperate yet, light-headed, a bit nauseous. There were pangs he'd always associated with hunger in his stomach. But he wasn't sure he could get anything past his throat. His feet felt okay, his legs bruised but intact. All in all, he decided, it was just his back and his throat. The rest would be okay in a day or two.

He held his hands up against the darkening sky and sniffed. The tie around his wrists was a porous fiber of some kind. A plant fiber, like the ones the women used in the marketplace to tie the blue sea crabs together. He could probably chew them apart. The very thought brought hot bile up into his throat. So, it was either shout and rip his throat apart, turn over and lay his back open, or chew the fibers apart past his gag reflex. And it was probably going to take all three to get out of here.

With one sustained groan, he rolled over and hauled himself up onto his knees. He felt along the ground until he found a sharp rock

46

and wedged it between his knees. That would keep him up. Then he rested.

There was something to be said for breathing. With his mouth closed to keep from screaming, he took slow, deep breaths through his nose until his pain eased.

When his hips and legs started to cramp, he bent forward and started working the fiber against the rock. Each movement lifted up tiny sections of scab from his back, then closed them down again. He took another deep breath and established a rhythm between breathing and grunting. In a short time, his shirt was soaked with sweat, and probably with his blood.

Somewhere off to his left, a rooster crowed, then a dog barked from up the hill. He paused to wipe the snot from his nose with the back of his wrist. He'd thought he'd never hear something so simple as a rooster crowing again.

When the last fiber gave way, he toppled over, curled up on his side and let the pain wash over him. He was almost too grateful to care. He was not in some steaming crater being picked apart by vultures. He'd glimpsed his first sunlight in weeks. Heard a dog bark, and a rooster crow. This small piece of now, pain and all, felt as close to heaven as he had ever been. Now he could manage; he could live inside that still space and stretch it out forever.

The thought brought him up short. What was it Katherine had said about heaven back in San Francisco? "Heaven ain't forever, boy. And neither is Hell. They're both all around us, all the time. So think and keep your eyes open and watch out." That had been her mantra; it had seen her through years of homelessness. It was the *not forever* part that had kept her from giving up. "Because now is all we got to work with. You got that?"

So then, think. Why was he here? Why wasn't he dead of thirst in some stinking crater? Why had they tied his hands in front where he could work at them?

So he would live! Of course. And they could watch. Watch him go back to the *compas*, so they could grab them all and do with them what they'd done to him. Augustín, Mario, Pedro, Migdalia, all the men and women who were fighting and dying to get out from under that motherfucker Somoza and his fat cats who'd taken the land away from them. But not their spirit. Fuck! The sons-of-bitches were waiting for him to lead them to all the others, so they could pick them all off. Like they'd done with Efraín, and the one who could only carve an X on the wall because he couldn't write.

He needed to get out of here. He needed to make up for lost time, he needed work. But how could he work without endangering the others? He couldn't! The thought was like a knife run straight through his chest until he couldn't breathe, and when he finally could, he couldn't stop weeping.

He woke up thinking of them. Seeing their faces. Migdalia, the other half of his heart when he was a child; Augustín, who had had faith in him from the start; and Mario, who had cheered him on when so many of the others had no use for him. He knew what *they* were thinking. Who was he anyway? Gone for 14 years, and in the United States, Somoza's joyland? He'd become a foreigner, a lightweight. He could be, and probably was, a mole. He was sure there were some who still harbored those thoughts.

Eventually some of them did come around. Like Efraín, before he disappeared, and Claudio, whose body had been found in a ditch outside of Masaya. After that, he was back to square one with the hardliners. To them, he was at best a Jonah, or worse, a snitch.

Thank God Augustín had believed in him right from the start.

Augustín had been in the movement a very long time and his credentials were impeccable. His father and his grandfather had fought with Sandino himself, and they'd paid the price when the senior Somoza rolled in on the backs of U.S. dollars. For Augustín, his fourteen years in the States was a good recommendation. And besides, "I know your cousin and your Aunt Berfalia." Augustín had whispered her name with a mock shiver. "You're fine."

Even after Augustín spoke up for him, he'd been kept out of the loop or been given jobs that connected with very few people. He made flyers, looked for a printer, carried messages to places rather than to people.

And that was when he met Mario, who seemed to be everywhere, in the mountains up near Matagalpa, down somewhere on the San Juan River, then over on the east coast. Mario, who never heard a joke he didn't like, or told one he didn't botch. But that didn't matter; Mario's botched lines were often funnier than the right ones.

Far to the west, a jet with its running lights on moved slowly across the purple sky and disappeared. Something rustled nearby. He stiffened, turned his head and opened his eyes wide. There was movement to his left, darkness – no, a shadow floating toward him across the leaves with barely a sound. Something gleamed in the darkness and was gone.

He closed his eyes and held his breath. It was right above him now, its fuggy breath warm on his face. Something rough and wet dragged across his cheek. Dog.

"*Hola*," he whispered and was answered by a soft whine and the movement of a tail wagging at the other end.

José María let his breath go in a whoosh. From roosters to wagging tails – a day of miracles. Tears came again, running down across his temples and into his hair. "You nearly…" Even whispering hurt, so he gave it up.

The dog woofed and went down on its front paws, its head cocked to one side.

When José María didn't move, the dog gave another whine. It rose and scratched at the leaves and dirt a few times, then turned in a circle, eyeing the ground.

José María thanked whatever deity kept wild animals away from lonely, misbegotten travelers. This dog was civilized.

As though it understood, the dog thumped his tail, once, twice, then flopped full length along José María's side.

Make yourself at home, boy. He reached out to stroke him, and a cool nose followed by a warm tongue found his hand.

It was still dark when José María woke to the drone of crickets. He breathed in cool air, felt the ground beneath him, solid and comforting. He hadn't died, not yet. There was a soft grunt close to his ear.

"Still…there?" he croaked. He could talk. A little. Just that bit of rest had eased his throat some.

The tail was thumping.

"Time…to go?"

The dog rose and waited.

"Okaaay." Clenching his jaw, José Maria struggled to his feet. Before he could tumble head first down the hill, he caught himself on a bush and the trunk of a sapling. Christ, God in heaven but that hurt.

Just one look uphill and he was dizzy again. He waited for it to pass. The strange thing was, as far as he knew, they'd never touched his head. And yet the day they'd stopped coming for him, he had all the symptoms of a concussion, the dizziness, the headache, the difficulty thinking.

Back at the nursing home in Missouri, the patients fell a lot and he'd learned more than he ever wanted to about head injuries. Head injuries, hip fractures, broken wrists, ankles. At one time or another, Katherine had had them all. And still nothing stopped her. She'd been determined to make it to her sixty-fifth birthday and she almost did, though what portion actually got there he could never be sure. For a woman whose passion was books, early senility seemed a particularly grievous burden. He'd read to her, book after book, until she'd stopped him. Why, he didn't know and never would, because by then she was beyond explaining anything.

The dog had come around to stand before him. Its muzzle poked José María's thigh, then it backed off and stared upward, mouth hanging open, tongue dangling. It whined softly, butted José María's thigh again, then stepped back and barked.

José María sighed. "Okay then, if you say so."

As he started up toward the highway, the dog kept nudging his left side, forcing him to take the hill at an angle.

"Yes, okay, but where are you taking me?"

It was a hard climb and he had to stop frequently to catch his breath. But the dog's muzzle pushed up into the palm of his hand again and again and he never rested for long.

During one stop, José María heard music. As clear as if the people playing were only yards away. Not quite live — by the sound of it, there would be real speakers, big ones. Nothing tinny like the old record player with its trumpet speaker that his father had given his mother. What a piece of junk; it was always breaking down.

He shrugged before he could stop himself, then hissed until the pain went away. He'd become almost as good at repairing sound systems as he was at refrigerators and washing machines. At the nursing home, he'd learned to repair almost anything, especially after the janitor died, and he'd taken over until they found someone permanent, which they never did.

He stopped abruptly. They had come to a clearing. In the center, a huge house with a wooden veranda was surrounded by a vast patchwork of dead grass and dirt. Only two windows at one end of the veranda were lit, and the music came from there.

The dog had left his side and was crossing the clearing. It stopped once, turned around, gave a low woof, then continued on. At the foot of the steps, the dog sat down and waited.

Swallowing against the hard knot in his stomach, José María followed. To his right, out near the dark corner of the veranda, furniture gleamed white and ghostly. Cautiously, he veered and made his way toward that. Chairs, a table, a Masaya rocker. And there, perched on the edge of the table, was what looked like a pack of cigarettes.

He was up over the railing and crouching down in the shadow of the table before he even questioned whether his body could do such a thing. His thighs were trembling and the ache in his gut had mushroomed until it sat up under his ears. He reached for the pack of cigarettes and rose slightly to scan the table for matches.

With a click, a light went on overhead. The harsh, white glare blinded him for a moment.

"Hold it," said a man behind him.

José María dropped the cigarette pack, saw it bounce on the wood floor. His hands rose of their own accord.

There was a long, slow intake of breath. "*Carajo!*" said the man. "What the hell happened to you?" The Spanish was faintly accented, and there was something else, a *gringo* with a lisp?

Keeping his hands up, José María straightened and turned slowly as a figure stepped from the shadows at the far end of the veranda. A gun, yes, an old pistol. Then he saw the face above and he stumbled back against the table. "*Jesus!*" he said. "What the fuck happened to you?"

The man's eyes gleamed beneath half-hung white lids. Something like a laugh escaped the ruined mouth.

"Icarus," he said, coming to a halt under the overhead light. "Not everyone is so direct." He glanced down at the dog which had come to stand beside him, and another rumble of laughter shook him. "Most people prefer not to look."

You're not giving me much choice, thought José María. What with the gun, and the light there was little he could do but concentrate on the face before him. Only burns could have created that melted flesh. "Icarus?" he asked.

"Fell from the sky." The man gestured with the gun. "And you?"

"Fell from a train."

"With a back like that? More like you fell from Grace." A gravelly voice with a definite *gringo* accent. A *gringo* with a huge house. With a gun, and a strong, steady hand.

"Does it matter?" said José María.

"In Nicaragua? You're asking me?" The man reached into his shirt pocket and brought out a folder of matches. "You were looking for these?" He tossed the matches onto the table.

José María lowered his arms, took the matches and nodded toward the cigarettes on the floor.

"Go ahead."

"Thanks." His hands shook as he pulled a cigarette from the pack and lit it. At the first drag, he started to cough. He fumbled behind him for the chair and sat down.

"Water?"

José María nodded. The coughing wouldn't stop; his throat was tearing apart, his eyes were streaming, his breath came in sobs. He felt the dog's warm breath next to his ear and he looked around to see it inches away, head cocked to one side, watching. The man was gone.

He pulled himself out of the chair. He had to go before the man returned. Another wave of coughing shook him and he fell back, crying out as the arm of the chair hit his butt. The coughing filled his ears, and through it he heard the words he'd spat into the Angel's face come back at him, hoarse, jagged, like the hot, thick, shameful echo of an old love. They broke into syllables, then into nonsense. Now, spent and sick in a gringo's chair, he realized he had spoken in English, the language of his father. And the Angel had understood!

"Here. Drink this." Icarus held out a glass of water.

"Thanks." José María drank, spilled water down his shirtfront, handed the glass back and pulled himself up. The gun was still pointed at his head.

"You'd better come in," said Icarus, inclining his head toward the house. José María glanced at the room with the light on. Where the music came from.

"Is that an order?"

"No." The man snapped the safety catch on, crooked an elbow out as if to slip the heavy thing in his jacket pocket, then shrugged and lowered it to his side.

The music stopped. Only the crickets and his own heartbeat were left. Inside the window, a green-shaded lamp stood on a table. He looked again at the mangled, unreadable face before him. "Icarus," he said softly.

"It looks like you could use some coffee."

Coffee! Warm coffee, sweet coffee. José María felt his knees begin to give. He reached behind him for the arm of the chair and sat. "Yes, coffee." He glanced up. "Coffee would be wonderful."

He sat with his elbows on the table, his head in his hands, until the man brought out a tray holding a mug of coffee, a sugar bowl, a *rosaquilla* on a small plate, and a little jar of some kind of salve. José María picked up the pastry first. Cold, heavy, utterly plain, it nearly brought him to tears. All those years in the States, all those chilis, burgers and chiliburgers, and what he would find himself wanting was the bland simplicity, the comfort of a *rosaquilla* or, at Christmas and Easter a *nacatamal*. He hooked his thumb through the *rosaquilla*'s center hole, took up the cup of coffee, then dipped the pastry and bit into it. He chewed slowly, reluctant to let the soft paste down his throat. He added more sugar to the coffee, sipped and added more. And even as he sipped and chewed, a tiny shudder started up in his stomach, a soft queasiness.

Icarus had sat down and was looking out over the veranda railing. He had put the gun away and his hands, one of them badly scarred, lay folded loosely between his knees. The dog, not quite matching the man's delicacy, lay stretched out on his side across the top of the steps, his eyes trained on José María. Some time before the man returned to the porch, the music had begun again, piano music now, soft and mournful.

José María managed to swallow the last of the pastry. He licked his fingers, then laid his hands in his lap. For a moment he let the music and the quiet presence of the man fill him. There might be generosity in that silence. There probably was. He wished he could believe in it; he wished he could stay here and rest.

He rose. "Thank you."

"You can stay," said Icarus.

Fear, familiar and protective, blossomed. Beneath the fear, there could only be loss. "No thank you," he said quietly.

Icarus nodded. A faint twisting of the lower half of his face could have been a smile, yet his eyes, one half-shut, were the saddest José María had ever seen. The fingers, until now so still, began to move slowly to the music, hovering, not quite touching down on the arm of the chair, an almost imperceptible farewell.

José María started for the stairs.

"Here, take this with you. It's an antibiotic salve. It should keep that back from festering."

José María took the jar. "Thank you." Maybe he should stay after all. The thought of actually putting the salve on his own back seemed an impossible task. He smiled and shook his head. "Thanks."

He turned toward the stairs. The dog lurched to its feet, looked at its master and gave a whine so nearly human, of such sorrow and discouragement, that both men laughed.

Icarus rose and came to the top of the steps. "It's okay, boy," he said softly.

The dog laid a paw on his master's foot and groaned.

Icarus crouched down. "There, yes, it's okay."

José María descended the stairs and crossed the wide lawn to the protection of the trees, hearing their sad murmurings long after he was out of earshot.

Chapter 7

The plane dipped hard to the left as Jaime turned it out across the bay. "I'll give you a shot at the volcano." His voice was clear as a bell over the headphones, which were so cushioned around Marshall's ears that he could barely hear the sound of the engine.

"It blew the hell out of the place once," said Jaime. "All the way to Panama, they say."

In the passenger seat, Marshall grinned. Swashbuckler was not a word he'd have used to describe Jaime Salazar before today. But then again, "siren" was not a word he'd have used for Mattie before last night.

They turned back toward the beach and the water went from deep blue to green to a thin, white line of foam on the sand before they were once again over the harsh, brown land. The drought was worse than he'd imagined. From up here everything was the color of dirt.

Fifty miles back, on the other side of the mountain, they'd crossed over the area where Clementina Pineda had had her farm. For two years, he'd been promising himself he'd go out and see it, but he never had. Now it belonged to the bank. Like Beal Jackson's would next week.

"You don't like it?" Jaime said.

Marshall shook his head. "No. It's just the drought. Worse than I thought."

"Nature is creative. Take a look at that."

The volcano rose up before them, the top lopped off at an angle like a pig's snout, its brown sides were streaked with black and gray lava flows.

The engine's shriek spilled through the headphones. Marshall looked up. The mountain was rushing toward them. Christ! He opened his mouth to scream. Instead, he froze. Oh fuck, he was going to piss his pants! He closed his eyes and clenched his butt. Son-of-a-biiitch. He heard Jaime laugh.

At what felt like the very last minute, Jaime pulled up and they slipped over a shallow dip on the crater's rim. A wind buffeted the plane. When it settled, Marshall took a deep breath. The pressure in his bladder eased. His relief was so enormous that at first he didn't register what flowed past beneath the plane.

When he did, he gasped. Below him stretched a vast field of green velvet, with clusters of tiny yellow flowers dotted here and there. He hadn't seen this much green in almost two years.

The small plane rocked as it hit some turbulence. Then it banked into a steep turn and they flew out of the crater the same way they'd come in.

Marshall sighed; he felt lighter than air. Better even than he felt after sex. He rested his head against the headrest and glanced at Jaime.

The man was laughing! Marshall forced a grin. "Well," he drawled, "for a minute you had me."

Jaime nodded as though he'd proved a point. "So what did you think?"

Think, you little prick? What did you want me to think? "Why is it so green back there?" he asked finally.

"Not sure." Jaime shrugged. "Who knows? They say it turns green whenever there's a drought. And damned if it isn't so. Maybe there's water coming up through the old lava tubes."

He brought the plane around and headed north again. For a while, neither of them spoke. Soon they were flying over field after field of brown skeletal bushes, speckled here and there with white bits.

"Is that cotton?" asked Marshall.

Jaime nodded. He wasn't laughing now.

"Yours?"

"Yes."

"How many acres do you have?"

"It's *hectares* — more than twice the size of an acre — and I'm not completely sure how many. You'll see when you look at the books."

The plane shook. "It's the heat coming off the land," said Jaime. "You're not nervous, are you?"

"No. I was just thinking of how Julia hates to fly." He'd actually been wondering what it would be like to sleep with Mattie every night and have that same lighter than air feeling afterwards. That dance last night sure felt like a come on. He took a deep breath and stared out the window. Garv certainly looked happy enough. Was he unaware of Mattie's seductiveness?

"Julia?" said Jaime. "Afraid to fly? I was sure she had the heart of the lion."

"No, she hates flying, but she does love to travel. I mean in trains and buses. And boats. She's a good swimmer," he finished lamely. He looked out the window. They were coming down. "I don't know what that makes her."

"It's curious," said Jaime. "If there's no fear, there'd be no such thing as bravery. Right? And no fun, either."

Marshall faced forward. Fuck bravery. What he wanted was a wife, not a lion. As for fun, he was still waiting for that part.

A dirt airstrip ran alongside a series of low buildings. Jaime flew over it, waved at someone on the ground, then pulled up to make another circuit.

They came down so fast that Marshall gritted his teeth, but Jaime set the plane down as if he were laying a baby on a table. And then he smiled. "Welcome to my second home, Marshall."

"Thanks. How long did it take to get here before you had the airstrip?"

"A day by jeep. Back in the forties, it was weeks by mule."

"Ever do that?"

"We haven't had it that long. My father pulled it together in the fifties, when cotton got big. Before that, it was just a bunch of dirt farmers."

Like Clementina Pineda, thought Marshall. Who had almost twenty acres until a week ago. Was she a dirt farmer?

A Jeep was waiting for them. Marshall barely had enough time to feel the earth beneath his feet before he was hurtling through a tour of Jaime's vast holdings: all cotton, yellow and snow white puffs, but most of it dead before it had sprung. The roads were awash with sifting dust. There were sheds, pesticides, fertilizers, harvesters, tandem flatbeds with wire cages to keep the picked cotton from flying out — hundreds of thousands of dollars in equipment alone. Jaime ran him through it all at top speed. Twice Marshall asked him how big the farm was. And twice Jaime put him off.

The tour ended in an air-conditioned office where Jaime called for coffee and interviews with a procession of employees: the farm manager; a man who handled supplies; the *capataz* or Head Honcho as Jaime called him, who managed the two thousand seasonal workers and their families; and the bookkeeper, who came in carrying a huge ledger bound in worn red leather and eased it down onto the conference table in front of Jaime.

"This is Horse, my accountant," said Jaime.

Horse? Rising to shake the man's hand, Marshall saw that the right shirtsleeve was empty. The man swung his left arm up and they fumbled at each other's fingers.

"Faustino Horse," the man said. "*Mucho gusto.*" A slight man, with close-cropped hair, he wore very thick rimless glasses tied on with elastic.

"*Mucho gusto,*" Marshall replied.

Horse nodded at the ledger. "This runs from July 1966 to yesterday — a little under three years." His Spanish was accented.

"Please sit down, Horse," said Jaime, waving a hand toward the chairs. "Would you care for some coffee?"

Horse hesitated.

"Well then, what is it?"

"The lady is at the house, *señor.*"

Jaime looked at Marshall, then shrugged. "Perhaps not today, Horse."

"As you wish, *señor.*"

There was a small silence. Could that have been relief that crossed the man's face? Somewhere out of sight, a shortwave radio crackled. Jaime waved at the ledger. "Well, it's your show now."

Horse cleared his throat. Marshall held up his hand. "Before you start, it would help if I knew the extent of the acreage *Señor* Salazar owns."

"Approximately seventy-two thousand *hectares,*" the man said without looking up from his book.

Astonished, Marshall shot a look at Jaime whose face was vintage blank. A little more than 140 thousand acres. Christ, just how many dirt farmers gave up their land so that — Marshall brought himself up short. Dirt farmers, Jaime had called them. They were subsistence farmers. And Jaime and his father had saved them all from a hand to mouth existence by giving them a steady income for harvesting his crop. With 20 acres, Clementina Pineda had not been a dirt farmer. If she were, he wouldn't have invested in her in the first place.

Marshall sat back. In fact it was a brilliant idea all the way around. The land benefited, the farmers had steady jobs cultivating it and picking cotton, and Jaime could make a handsome profit, which would come to the bank. Absolutely brilliant. Julia would disagree, but that was exactly how the economy should work. Besides, what wouldn't Julia disagree with?

In a quiet monotone, the bookkeeper presented a picture of the farm as viable while at the same time giving a chilling picture of the drought depressing food resources and exports. Cotton exports had doubled since the early sixties. But now, after two years of drought, the industry had taken a dive.

"Well done, Horse," said Jaime when the man had finished. "You should be in Managua. You're wasted here."

"Gracias." Horse stood. His glasses reflected the light from the window and a ghostly line of buildings beyond. Marshall marveled at their thickness and how hard it was to see the eyes behind them.

"It is an old discussion," Jaime said to Marshall. "And one I have yet to win. *Lástima!* A pity." He glanced at Horse. "Still old man, there are some advantages to having you here, eh?" Jaime stood up. "Lunch must be ready by now. He turned to Horse, Perhaps it would be nice to have the lady with us, after all. It would be a nice touch."

It was a delicious lunch: cold *ceviche* made of a sweet, white fish, rice, dark, rich beans, fried plantains, a tomato salad with capers, and icy beer. The woman who served it was striking; her hair was dark, her skin light golden tan. She was barefoot and wore a shapeless white robe with irregular holes cut out at intervals. A bit like the dress Julia had worn last night. Only this dress had holes everywhere.

Jaime leaned forward, holding up a piece of fish on his fork. "Some people think of Nicaragua as a dusty, frontier town, with a cowboy mentality. The truth is, all frontiers are edges of opportunity, of possibility." He popped the fish into his mouth and spoke around it. "People think 'what a disaster, all that violence, flood, drought, let's stay the hell away from there.' What they don't realize is that everything that happens, all of it, brings opportunities. A war, an earthquake, and you have a whole new set of variables."

Marshall sat back and tried to collect himself. Opportunities? Variables? Was there a business proposition in here somewhere? Marshall smiled. "What are you proposing to do, Jaime — make an earthquake? Start a war?"

"God does that well enough. My job is to keep my eyes open." Jaime took a long drink. "Take this farm. Droughts are slow — wars, too. They give you a lot of time to think and require a lot of patience. People get hungry, they get frightened — most people stop thinking and just try to survive. Of course, it's all very sad. But it's also a good time to keep your eyes open. Like you, with your new bank branch in Montoya. You clearly believe that there are opportunities to be grasped here."

The woman reached to pour water into his glass and Marshall found himself staring through one of the holes in her dress at the dark place around her nipple and a hair, darker still, just this side of where it.

"Yes, it's a time to keep your eyes open," said Jaime.

Marshall felt his face flush. "What did you have in mind?"

Jaime's eyes followed the woman across the veranda. "Droughts are slow," he said again. "Plenty of time to think about it."

Marshall tried to keep his expression neutral. All this wooing was not necessary given Jaime's connections and his assets. Nor was it his usual demeanor. Perhaps it was a style he had when he was up here in a slower, more peaceful place. Tomorrow or the next day, he would come into the bank in his suit and tie and with an unbeatable scheme for importing basic foods, or buying up more land, something that would net him huge profits and earn a bundle for the bank as well. Marshall smiled.

They were just finishing the fish when a call came in over the shortwave and Jaime excused himself. He'd be back before dessert, he said. Marshall was to have another beer.

Don't mind if I do, thought Marshall. It won't be me flying the plane back to Managua; it'll be me with a shit-eating grin, clutching my seat. He drank the last of his beer, held the bottle out to the woman, and signaled for another. She disappeared and Marshall sat and tried not to think of that tan skin beneath the shapeless dress.

He could still feel Mattie's body against his, moving to the music. She'd said nothing more throughout the rest of the dance and they'd walked wordlessly back to the table when it was over. But there it was, the feel of her finger under his jaw, her thighs against his, and his aching response. Christ, there it was, stirring again just thinking about it. As if he could ever do anything about it. There was the bank, there was Julia, and Garv was a friend and a client. Besides, he'd always felt that men who cheated were self-indulgent fools. They should have gotten it right the first time.

He closed his eyes, remembering the drab university chapel where he had looked into Julia's eyes and spoken his marriage vows, willing himself to mean every word. He was so sure that he could come to care for her. How could he not? She had the language, the poise, the grace, the intelligence. She was warm and funny. From the very first meeting he knew she would make an excellent wife for an international banker.

So what had happened to the perfect banker and his ideal wife? He hadn't really been looking for perfection. And he wasn't looking for passion. That'd been Silla, and Silla was over, by her own wish. There would never be anyone like her again. But did that mean he should never marry? Never have children? Never have a congenial, comfortable marriage and family?

What the fuck! What was he doing sitting here whining? He stood up, knocking his dessert knife onto the concrete floor. He pushed back his chair, but the woman was already bending to pick up the knife and he was staring down at a tiny dusting of hair at the top of her butt crack.

He backed away and went to stand at the other end of the patio. He was a banker. A businessman. He made decisions that affected people. He looked at the bright green potted plants surrounding the table, the white tablecloth and silverware all set down in this desolate burnt-out corner of the earth. This was the reward, this strange mix of luxury and ruin on the frontier of opportunity that Jaime spoke of. Marshall smiled. Jaime was not crazy, he was creative. As Jaime's banker, he was lucky to be here at this time. He slowly turned around, drinking in every detail — the string of low, tin- roofed buildings, the flat land with the heat coming off it in waves, the blueness of the sky.

"Thinking to buy the place?" Jaime called from across the patio. He was seated at the table again, pouring two flutes with champagne.

Marshall walked back to the table and sat down. "Not a chance. I'm a city boy."

Jaime raised his glass to Marshall in a toast. Not champagne, it was one of those fruit drinks. Peach, or mango — Julia would know.

Jaime gestured out toward the improbably green patch of lawn and the brown fields beyond. "It's curious. When there's drought, the volcano's crater blooms just as you saw it this morning. It seems when the ground is dry, then the water finds its way up through the ancient boreholes. At least that's my theory. But when it rains, when there's a real rainy season with floods and wash outs, the crater dries up. Just like that." He snapped his fingers. "They can't seem to work together." He twirled his glass then held it out to the woman for more.

It all seemed a little forced. If this was a business deal, why was Jaime being so cagey?

"You want fruit?" The woman spoke for the first time. She had a harsh voice, as if she seldom used it, and her Spanish was slurred.

"Yes, thank you," he said. "Anything but papaya." The nipple's dark aureole flashed again. Smooth, he thought, it would be smooth to the touch. Except for that single hair. He couldn't figure out whether he was turned on by it, or turned off.

"You don't like papaya?" said Jaime.

Marshall looked up. "It has an odd aftertaste."

"Yes, of course. Like vomit." Jaime laughed. "Does that bother you? The papaya has papain in it, an enzyme you have in your own stomach. What you're tasting is something of yourself."

Oh great. Just what he'd always wanted to hear. "I guess that's why I don't like it," he said, and held his hand up to stop the woman from overloading his plate.

She moved to Jaime's side of the table and dished the papaya onto his plate.

"I've always believed the fruit Eve offered Adam was really

papaya," Jaime said. "And that it did not acquire that taste until Adam ate it… *Ya, basta.* Enough!" He took the woman's wrist and guided her hand back to the bowl, did something with his thumb and the spoon clattered down. "I happen to like that particular taste." His hand remained poised above the bowl, the woman's fingers dangling out below his. "Out here, life is simpler than in the city. A man can relax and let go."

Marshall couldn't take his eyes off those dangling fingers. Yes. It was true. He was relaxed. He hadn't felt this relaxed in a very long time.

Jaime brought the woman's hand across the table and held it open before Marshall. "You are sure, Marshall?"

Sure of what? That he didn't like papaya? The woman's eyes were nearly shut. She was bending forward, barely breathing. The holes in her dress were shadows, pulling him in. Marshall remembered the silence in the office with Horse. *Un detalle,* a fine detail — holy shit!

Her name was Yelva Inez and she wore nothing whatsoever under her dress. Not a shred. He stood at the shuttered window, his back to her, looking at the bars of light slice across his shirt front while somewhere behind him she stood there stark naked.

She had to be Horse's woman, and this was some weird game of high courtesy, *un detalle,* a detail, something special. He was being given some kind of papaya, by God, whether he liked it or not.

Except for the huge bed in the corner, its white sheets crossed with bars of sunlight, the room was empty.

What did Jaime expect to get from this? All that talk about tastes and passion fruit and then something strange about the balance of payments and Garv Schimmer…Was this something Garv had done?

He'd opened his mouth to say no, and there were the holes in the dress and the thought of Mattie, and he'd said yes. Or more exactly, nodded his head.

The dress had fallen into a crumpled heap beside the door. It had slid down her body as though the door closing behind her had pulled it off, and there he was, gaping, his mind revving at high speed, gears disengaged, before he fled to the window. He hadn't expected this. He could hear her behind him, moving closer. The soles of her feet had to be rough to make that stroking sound, each step lagging a little behind the other so that she seemed to hesitate as she came nearer. He could only guess what she was doing but whatever it was, he was getting hard. He couldn't believe it.

He forced himself to turn around and look. She *was* dancing! Her eyes were closed, her arms wove around her body, she swayed, haunch-smooth, head bent as if listening to the sound of her feet.

My God! She was a tiger stalking him, gold and brown in the bars of sunlight, her nipples large and erect. He wanted to touch them, to breathe on them. He wanted to take her into his mouth, all of her.

She stopped. A slight shudder swept across her belly. There was nobody to see whether he touched her or not—his cock had never felt so hard, so ready. She tilted her head to one side, like a cat, then sank down, cross-legged, completely open to his gaze. He felt a surge of aching, swelling heat in his legs, his groin, up his spine.

Somewhere far away, a combustion engine started up with a tiny, popping, machine-gun rattle. Goddamn them! Goddamn them all! He bent down and held both hands out to her.

Chapter 8

Her name was Maggie Peters and she reminded him of Katherine. A little dab of a woman, she was heading for Patagonia in her jeep and Silverstream trailer and she picked him up at kilometer 12 on the South Highway. A retired gym teacher from Pennsylvania, with two married daughters, she'd coached a high-school football team during World War II when all the men were off to war, and her team won the city championship two years in a row.

"How tall are you?" José María asked. She was his third piece of luck today.

"Pinch that." She flung out an arm. The movement startled him. "I'm five foot one," she said, "but there's not an ounce of pinchable flesh on that arm. All muscle." Her arm was firm, the skin smooth and warm to his touch. He thought he might like to rest his head on it.

He'd slept beside the highway in a small, leaf-filled gully and had awakened before dawn with a clear head and the knowledge that his choices were few and easily made. He could bolt or stay. As he had no intention of bolting, and Managua was too risky now, he would head for his sister Luz's house down near the coast.

The second bit of luck had been finding the shirt and some clean towels in a small garden shed beside a swimming pool. It had taken far too long to soak the old one off his back, but he'd taken the time anyway, easing himself down into the pool, keeping an eye out for lights in the house.

And now Maggie Peters with her mirror-bright trailer completed his day. She was the perfect cover — who could quarrel with a little old lady, a *gringa* at that? He took another sip of water. He could ride down the road like this forever, the miles piling up, distances covered. He felt so good he finally held out his hand and broke the rule. "My name is Joe."

Her handshake was firm. He sensed that once again he was in good hands — the man last night, his dog, now Maggie. Her broad face and dark eyes were easy, and her gray hair hung loose down her back, like Katherine's. Her resemblance to Katherine was remarkable. She even had the same faint moustache and curling hairs on her chin.

"So how far is this turn-off to Pochowhatever?" she asked. Her English was flat and brisk.

"Pochomil. About six more miles."

"That's a beach town, isn't it?"

"My sister lives off the main road a ways."

She gave him a quick glance, then shifted down so fast both trailer and jeep bucked. "Where'd you learn your English?"

"In the States."

"Figured. You must've been there a long time."

"Almost half my life." He watched the road sliding away in the side mirror.

"You don't look so good," she said. "When did you last eat?"

"Last night."

She pulled off to the side of the road, rummaged behind the front seat and handed him a box of soda crackers before getting her jeep and trailer moving again.

The salt tasted good, but after the second cracker he closed the box, set it between his feet and stared at a point twenty yards ahead of the jeep. "All the way to Patagonia alone?" he asked.

She pursed her lips.

"A lot of people say that?"

"Yep."

"Well, if you go around picking up strange men…"

She reached over and pinched his arm. "Feels like I could handle you." She double-clutched from fourth to second to take a steep hill.

He smiled. "I don't doubt it. So why Patagonia?"

"Because I always wanted to. My husband and I planned to drive the length of the two continents, from top to bottom." She slowed to let an overtaking bus slip in front of her. "But he died when the girls were still young. So we never went."

She tapped the brake as the bus made a feint toward the oncoming lane. "I don't mind telling you, Joseph, driving down here is a lot more challenging than fielding a winning football team. Anyway, this is something I always knew I was going to do. So here I am, the girls grown, grandchildren set, nobody back there but a couple of friends who are probably still in their bathrobes drinking their coffee and wondering if I'm still alive."

It was Katherine all over again, hugely delighted with herself. "Hey Joey," Katherine would say, "look what I got today; wait'll you see this!"

He shifted back in his seat, careful to take the weight on his shoulder and the side of his arm. He missed Katherine, especially as she'd been those first years: a celibate, a teetotaler, mean, ornery, an omnivore of stolen books, a scam artist, and a bag lady of infinite grace.

Katherine came from a family of drunks, lechers and anarchists, where piss and shit were, as she put it, lifted to the level of context rather than content. It was years before he even began to understand what she meant by that. It had been one of his first, conscious lessons in politics.

"You dope, what the heck are you doing?" said Maggie Peters. The bus ahead was weaving back and forth across the center line.

"He wants to make sure you don't pass him."

"I can see that."

He closed his eyes. Katherine was as much his family as Berfalia or Andres, or even Luz. By the time he hit San Francisco, Katherine had been on the streets for more than twenty years. She'd picked him out of a gutter one day when he was only fourteen, sobered him up, found him a sleaze-bag room, and paid for it with the proceeds of her scavenging until he got himself a job.

While Miguel had taught him how to find the strength to leave Nicaragua, Katherine had taught him everything he knew about surviving in an alien world. She repaired and sold the stuff she scavenged. She read every book she could get her hands on, from Mickey Spillane and Earle Stanley Gardner to Howard Fast and Charles Dickens, then argued about each one regardless of whether he'd read it or not.

"Finally!" Maggie Peters swung the jeep out to pass the bus as it stopped to pick up passengers.

"Uh-oh. Now he's going to get you for sure."

"No he won't."

In the side mirror, José María watched the bus fall behind. "I guess you're right."

It was Katherine who'd persuaded him to look for his father, the Marine called Wheeler from Missouri, who'd served in Nicaragua in 1936. The man who'd enticed an Embassy laundress from her suds long enough to impregnate her, and then, before going back to the States, had given her his Victrola and records. The idea of finding him was crazy, but nevertheless, they had set off one spring day, heading for Missouri, each with a bar of soap and a change of underwear.

The plan was simple if a little surprising for a woman who hated cops: go to the police station in each town and ask. And she was right. The story of a lost father, a former Marine, was a winner. The older cops in particular took the time to give them leads to veterans' hospitals and nursing homes, or they scratched their heads and tried to remember if the old guy out West Patchell way or over in Knob Lick was a Wheeler or a Wheeling. And all the while, they would look him over with appraising eyes as if wondering how they would feel if he had washed up on their doorstep and called them Daddy.

The jeep swerved violently. "Well, I'll be damned," said Maggie Peters. "That son of a gun! Would you look at him!" She waved her fist at the bus as it trundled by on a downgrade.

"I told you."

"So you did." She grinned as though she found that immensely funny. "Next time, I'll remember."

Next time. He closed his eyes and stretched his neck. All through that long, hot summer, sleeping rough, eating out of trash bins, bathing under garden hoses late at night, they'd crisscrossed the state from St. Louis to Kansas City, from Peculiar to West Eminence, arguing and laughing. When he'd become discouraged — after all, there were a million fathers out there, and he didn't know why he was even bothering with the enemy who'd invaded the land of his birth — Katherine had given him just enough hell to keep him going. If only he'd been able to give her the strength to keep her alive.

"We're here," said Maggie Peters.

José María woke with a start. The jeep had stopped.

He sat up stiffly and shook sleep from his head. "How long have we been here?"

"A couple of minutes."

"Oh." He felt woozy.

"This is where you're going?"

"Yes. Thanks a lot."

"It doesn't look like there's anything down that road."

"My sister's house is down there."

"I remember, off this road a ways. How far a ways?"

"A bit."

She turned the key in the ignition, shoved the jeep into first, and made a wide turn onto the descending highway. "Just say when."

"Hold it," he said. "You can't go down there."

"I can't?"

"It's over twenty miles. It's way out of your way."

"Over twenty miles? That's what a hoofer calls 'a bit'?"

He shrugged. "I'll hitch a ride."

"That's what you're doing, Joseph."

"You'll never make it to Patagonia this way."

"That's not the point, is it? I got plenty of time. More than it looks like you have energy."

As they started the winding descent toward the ocean, his stomach began to churn. This would not be good. He was going to arrive sick. His brother-in-law Antonio would be shit-faced and Luz would have to appease him. Another toxic homecoming.

When Katherine had collapsed in St. Joseph and the doctors said it was meningitis, he'd been terrified. The same disease that had addled his cousin Andrés's wits. And Katherine's luck had been no better. Worse when you considered how smart she'd been. Her body had recovered, but her mind never did.

74

He'd begged for a job as an orderly at the nursing home, mopping floors, emptying slops. Heavy snows, hopeless springs, iron-hot summers. Later, as assistant janitor, he'd learned to repair the nursing home's machinery. So something had come of it. Every day, he'd visited her, hoping she'd come back. But she never did. "Get me outta here!" she'd shriek. "Get me outta here, you shit-filled asshole. Get me outta here."

That was when he'd begun to understand what she had meant by 'context,' rather than 'content.' Pain and terror and sorrow were the context, her words, his actions, even Eddie Brown, were the content. Eddie, a fellow nursing home resident, had appointed himself her bodyguard. He'd wheel her to the front of the veranda when José María came, and then Eddie stood to attention and waited. Eighty-seven years old, Eddie claimed he'd fought in the war of 1812, the war between the states, the Spanish American war, the two great wars and this last mess in Korea. Now that it looked like this new mess in Vietnam was going to fall into the shithole, Eddie wasn't of a mind to participate. He'd been stationed here and had a job to do.

So while Katherine had yelled obscenities, Sergeant Eddie explained how a musket was loaded, what it was like in the field hospital at Chancellorsville, what to do when you found an unspent grenade, when to attack and when to cut your losses. "If the son of a bitch has you at ten feet," he would say, "don't bother to move, Joe. Two feet maybe, fifty feet sure, but ten feet, don't move a fuckin' eyelash."

Those were the real parents of his Missouri homecoming, Katherine and Sergeant Eddie Brown. They were both context and content, and by the time Katherine died two years later, there was a powerful tenderness between them. A new kind of context. After years more of wandering, it was what had finally brought him back to Nicaragua. Home was the context, the content was what you made of it.

"What's her name?" asked Maggie Peters.

"Who?"

"Your sister."

"Luz Alba María."

"Luz Alba María. It means light, doesn't it?"

"Light of the dawn and Mary. Our mother was optimistic." He closed his eyes again. The pain and weariness would pass. He was free now; they had let him go and he had work to do.

"And your father?"

"Who knows? Luz is my half-sister." The words sounded strange. "My father was a U.S. Marine, hers was a lottery vendor."

His foot jiggled on the floorboards; he pressed his hand on his knee. How fitting. Spill out his guts to a stranger, an old woman who would disappear down the road and carry the pieces of his life away with her.

They pulled up under the *ceiba.*

"That's some tree," she said. "How old is it?"

"Close to three hundred years, they say."

She whistled. "And your sister's house."

"Over there." He pointed to the faded pink and blue house.

"Looks like the best house in town," she said.

"My brother-in-law thanks you." He pushed down the door handle. "And I thank you."

A figure came to the door. He waved. Luz? She probably couldn't see him from there. He stepped down out of the jeep. Children were gathering around the trailer, stroking it, staring at their own faces in its polished surface. "You keep a hell of a shine on that trailer, Maggie Peters." he said, buying time against the figure in the doorway.

"Yup."

"Best trailer in town," he said.

Maggie Peters looked past him at the doorway, then at the line of dusty shacks. She opened the door and got out of the jeep. Her hand trailed along the hood and around the side, then she was staring up at him, and he wanted to stroke the wild gray hair, the chin fuzz, that wonderful face. He looked back into the jeep. He would give anything to get back in and go with her, all the way to Patagonia. Just go with her anywhere.

She shook her head slowly. "Not now, Joseph. Not yet." She touched his shoulder. "It's never easy, but it's alright."

"As in 'can be done'?"

"You got it." She put her hand under his elbow and turned him toward the house.

Chapter 9

Julia came out of the bathroom still drying her hair. As she started getting dressed, she ran through her countdown again. She had twenty minutes until the guests arrived. The table was set and the butter, garlic and sherry were in the pan, waiting for the shrimp to defrost. The *chayotes* were peeled and in cold water. The salad greens, disinfected, rinsed, and dried, were wrapped in wet paper towels cooling in the fridge. There were little bowls of roasted almonds and marinated olives in the living room and out on the patio. She wanted to remind Juanita to take the *croute* out of the freezer when she had served the shrimp. She knew she was forgetting something, but what?

Dancing on her bare feet, Julia pulled on her underpants, slipped her dress over her head and padded out to the living room. Something flickered near the patio doors. Her stomach took a turn. It was coming from the hole in the floor. Gas? Holy shit!

Julia raced over and skidded to a halt. "Caley! What in heaven's name are you doing down there!"

Crouched into a ball, her head against her knees, Caley didn't look up. Thank God she was not on the pipes, though there was little enough room between the pipes and the wall she was leaning against.

Julia crouched down and ran her hands through Caley's soft hair. "What is it?"

"Hmff, mmm." Another shake.

Julia stretched out on the floor, her face at the edge of the hole. "What's wrong?" she whispered as she slipped her finger under Caley's chin and gently lifted her head. Caley's eyes were red and her nose was streaming.

"Oh sweetheart, you've been crying."

Caley rocked from side to side, her toes just missing the pipes.

"Careful, Honey. Were you hiding?"

A nod. And then a shake and Caley's eyes flicked toward the front of the house where her father had shut himself in his office almost an hour ago.

A wave of frustration flooded through Julia. The hole was her fault and she had apologized. More than once and handsomely, she thought. But Marshall was still so furious he was hiding in his room less than half an hour before the guests arrived. What was he thinking?

Three days ago, Dr. Medina had finally sent his minions around to fix the hot water leak. Yesterday they'd gotten the hot water up and running. But today, nobody had come to fill in the hole and replace the marble tiles.

Julia could only guess how many times Marshall had called the landlord today but, by the time he'd gotten home from work, he was so angry he'd disappeared into his office without even looking at the hole. What glued the man together? Was it just anger?

With her thumb, Julia wiped the snot from Caley's upper lip. "I know he's angry, Honey, but I think he wants to cool down alone so he can feel better when the guests arrive."

"Why?"

"Sometimes we just need to be quiet and alone."

"Why?"

"And sometimes…" Julia rose up on her knees. "…sometimes we need a good hug to feel better." She reached down and Caley came scrambling up.

By the time she finished her last minute checks in the kitchen, Julia gave up on whatever it was she couldn't remember. The guests were due any minute. And it was hard to remember anything with Marshall still closed up in his study. Well, whatever it was, it was too late now to worry about it.

Becka had not quite finished placing her guest cards on the table when tiny Catalina Salazar and her husband Jaime arrived.

"*Qué bello*, how beautiful," said Catalina showing her card to Jaime.

"Yes," he said. "These are very, very good." He smiled down at Becka. "May I take mine home?"

"Oh yes." Becka's face flushed. Julia could sense her surprise. Men didn't usually sound like that.

"Did the nuns teach you calligraphy, Becka?" asked Catalina.

"Yes," Becka whispered, then cleared her throat and said it aloud.

"They taught me as well, a long time ago, back in Colombia. But I never did it as well as this."

"Thank you."

Caley, who had come up to lean against Julia's hip, was staring up at Catalina with her thumb in her mouth. Catalina was indeed a lovely woman, with enormous dark eyes and hair wound up in a thick braid that went perfectly with the cream silk pantsuit.

Julia gave Caley a small hug.

"And you are…?" said Catalina.

Caley whipped her thumb out and hid it behind her back. "Caley," she said.

"Caley. That's a wonderful name. Two syllables. The perfect number." She laughed at Caley's surprise. "I always wanted a name with two syllables. Mine is Catalina, and that's four. Way too many."

"Couldn't you be Cata?" asked Becka. She blushed at her own forwardness.

"You know, I tried that, but no one else liked it, particularly the nuns at school. In fact, I can think of only one person who calls me that now." She glanced at Jaime and the look that passed between them caused a sharp ache to bloom in Julia's chest. The man was both courtly and kind, a perfect match for Catalina.

The doorbell rang again. Juanita went to answer it and brought in Manolo and Vilma Helgar.

"Thank you so much for inviting us, Julia." Vilma embraced Julia and pecked at both cheeks.

Oh crumb, oh shit, thought Julia. That's who Vilma Helgar was! Marshall had given her the list of the guests, but it took seeing the big woman again to connect her to that day down in front of Richardson's Hardware Store. Was it a year ago? No, more like two.

"And what lovely young ladies." Vilma threw up her arms and swooped toward the girls.

As one, Becka and Caley closed ranks and stood firm, and Vilma stopped in her tracks. "I know, I know, I'm way too big to come charging at you like that. But how pretty you both are." She spread her arms wide again, nearly bashing Marshall, who had suddenly appeared from his study.

"Whoa," he said.

Vilma laughed at him. "You can say that again."

"Whoa," he said with a grin and they both laughed.

"It's just that I'm so…" she flipped her long blonde hair over her shoulder.

"Spontaneous?" said Marshall.

Bountiful thought Julia.

"Your daughters are so lovely."

"I think they are," he said. He shook her hand and reached out to shake Manolo's hand. A round, slightly disheveled man with a wonderful smile, Manolo was at least three inches shorter than his wife.

"Would anybody care to have something to drink?" Marshall offered as he walked to Catalina and Jaime to shake hands.

Julia tilted her head toward the girls' bedroom and they took their cue and disappeared.

The last of the guests, Clara and Rafael Valdés, were from Guatemala. Julia had never met them before. Somewhere in their middle forties, both were dressed with quiet elegance as though they did their shopping in Europe. Rafael wore his hair just a tad longer than men here wore theirs, and it was parted just off center. Clara's dark hair was teased into a beehive about the size and shape of a small, fat poodle.

"What a wonderful hairdo," said Vilma. "Where did you get it done?"

Julia caught a gleam in Catalina's eyes. It was there and gone in seconds.

"Thank you so much," said Clara. "In the salon at the Hotel Tequendama."

Vilma walked around Clara. "How long did it take?"

Clara laughed. "I'm not sure, I was reading a book. I always take a book with me."

"What were you reading?" asked Catalina.

"These lovely little curls are a wonderful touch," said Vilma, actually touching the one that was nestled in front of Clara's left ear.

Once the women had arranged themselves around the coffee table and the men had leapt over the trench and occupied the patio, Julia sat down. Only then did the ache in her back she hadn't realized she still had suddenly let up. She allowed herself to sink into the chair and relax. She'd been thrown again yesterday, trying to get Pepsie over a log about a foot high. Luckily, they hadn't been too far from the stables and she could walk back, unsaddle the horse and wipe him down. She'd hoped the walk would loosen up her back, but the pain was still there and had been all day.

Thankfully, the ladies were deep into conversation. It was something you could always count on here. What with children and servants to talk about, there were never any awkward pauses. How many children, how many boys and how many girls, their ages, each thought spawning another. There was laughter, little stories, no one held the floor entirely and it could roll on forever without Julia having to do more than listen and wonder at the infinite variety of maternal joys and concerns there were in this world. It was like sinking into a warm bath.

Until she realized all three women were looking at her.

"I'm sorry, I was thinking about the dinner. What did you say?"

It was Clara. "You have just the two daughters?"

"I have two girls. Becka and Caley."

"And when will you have a little boy?"

Julia opened her mouth.

"Oh, Julia doesn't like little boys," said Vilma. "Right?"

Julia flushed. She should have been ready for this. It had definitely not been one of her finest moments that morning in front of Richardson's Hardware Store. She'd only met Vilma once at a cocktail party when, a few days later, she'd run into her in front of the hardware store. With almost elegant formality, Vilma had introduced her four-year-old son, Manolo. The little boy had promptly hidden behind his mother. Julia couldn't remember what she and Vilma had been talking about when the boy had yanked on his mother's skirt. After one glance, Vilma had cut the conversation short and had dragged her little Manolito across the sidewalk to pee on the front of the store, explaining to Julia how it was bad for a little boy to hold himself back because it might affect his later sex life. Julia's jaw had dropped and she couldn't think of a thing to say. But clearly Vilma had read her thoughts.

"Oh, you must like little boys," said Clara. Her Guatemalan Spanish had a slightly rolled, guttural quality. "I'm sure you'll like little boys when you have them," she said, and then she hit her stride — boys were so much easier to manage than girls, easier to satisfy. Direct, uncomplicated, fiercely loyal...

And what did that make little girls? thought Julia, just managing to keep the smile and a deeply attentive look on her face. Little girls were devious, cowardly, and dirty? And irreverent. Definitely irreverent. She shook her head and reminded herself that these women belonged here and she was a visitor. She saw that Catalina was watching her. To her surprise, Catalina winked and followed up with a smile quickly hidden.

But Clara had the bit in her teeth. "With boys, there are none of the worries that come with girls." Her tone was light, innocent, even compassionate.

Vilma agreed — one mistake and girls were marked for life.

Julia looked down and saw that the knuckles of her clasped hands were white. That day down at Richardson's she'd asked Vilma if little girls could be allowed to pee on store fronts. And, if not, what about their sex life? Oh no, said Vilma cheerfully, girls could always benefit by learning to control themselves. Later they would learn whatever they needed to know from their husbands. It had been a depressing thought to Julia back then. Now it made her a little sick.

The sliding glass doors opened and the hum of the cicadas flowed in ahead of the men. Julia watched them jump over the trench.

"You're right," Julia said to Vilma and Clara. "Little girls may be more complex than little boys. But not always. The other day, in her kinder class, Caley knocked Jeremy down for bullying her. They called me to come and get her. And when I got there, I told her, right in front of the teacher and Jeremy, who was not being sent home, that it was good to learn to defend herself instead of whimpering and expecting others to do it for her. And then I told Jeremy that bullying was always bad and should always be called out. Preferably by a responsible adult."

Vilma and Clara looked shocked. Even Catalina seemed taken aback.

"The Principal was observing everything from the doorway to her office," said Julia. "She thanked me and said she had just called Jeremy's home and told them to come and get him."

"And Jeremy?" asked Catalina

"Jeremy had the grace to look a little scared."

Marshall's voice cut across Julia's. "Shall we sit down to eat?" He was looking at the wall behind Julia and the lower lid of his right eye trembled.

"Yes." Julia stood and gestured toward the dining room.

At the table, there was a buzz of pleasure as people searched out their place cards. Chairs scraped against the floor.

"What a lovely table you set," said Clara.

"I hear she is a wonderful cook," said Vilma.

"She is," said Catalina. "She made the most wonderful mushroom and shrimp strudel at the last American Women's luncheon I went to.

The sound of the cicadas outside of the window behind Julia seemed deafening. She suddenly wished the evening were over and she could hide her head under her pillow.

"Please sit down," she said to everyone, and followed suit herself, nodding her thanks to Jaime Salazar who had somehow managed to seat Catalina and was now holding out her chair.

As Marshall made his way up the side of the table with wine, he made a comment to Manolo Helgar about the vintage of Chilean wines, then moved on to Clara Valdés, who was smiling as though she were being served a goblet full of stars. Marshall nodded back gravely.

Handsome, at ease, and remote, these were the qualities that drew women to him, thought Julia. The perfect gothic hero.

When he got to her, she covered her glass and shook her head, hoping to catch his eye, but he only nodded and put the bottle back on the sideboard. She smiled blindly down the table. "I'm sorry about the cicadas," she said. "Would you like me to close the window?"

"No," said Catalina. "I love that sound. It reminds me of the mountains outside of Matagalpa, with the last of the sun on the far trees and the cicadas starting to warm up. It's like they take in all the warmth as the air begins to cool."

Jaime smiled and shook his head. "She's got the mind and spirit of a poet. And I am continually delighted by the many ways she sees things."

"Have you written anything?" asked Vilma. "I love poetry."

Catalina laughed. "Jaime would like me to, but there is so little time. Just living fills me up."

"I don't know how she does it," said Jaime.

"Oh I do," said Julia. "It's like this world, this place, this moment fills you, and becomes you."

"Yes, that's it!" Catalina exclaimed. "How did you know?"

"It sometimes happens to me like that. I'm out riding and suddenly everything is united, or all of one piece, and there's no need to be or do anything else." Julia twirled the stem of her empty wine glass. "It doesn't happen often, but when it does — " She looked up. " — it's wonderful."

Vilma and Clara looked puzzled. The men looked absent. Even Jaime had lost interest. Catalina gave a tiny nod and smiled wryly.

Juanita came in with the platter of sautéed shrimp and Julia caught yet another of Marshall's raised eyebrows, this one accompanied by the slight pursing of the lips as his eyes followed Juanita's party walk. Damn you, she thought. Lay off her.

"Excellent shrimp," said Jaime. "Must be from Bluefields. Did you get them at the supermarket?"

"No, I bought them at the Eastern market."

"They are good," said Clara and reached up to touch one of the spit curls next to her ear.

"I fly to the east coast regularly," said Jaime. "Bluefields, Puerto Cabezas, Corn Island. I'd be happy to take you all any time. Well, probably just two at a time."

Julia smiled and opened her mouth to thank him.

"Oh, that would be lovely," said Vilma. "Wouldn't it, Manolo?"

Manolo grunted agreeably.

"Julia hates to fly," said Marshall.

Julia turned her smile on him. "But I love to travel," she said. Even that mild pleasantry put him off.

"Yes, that's what Marshall told me yesterday," said Jaime.

87

Marshall seemed even less pleased with that.

There was a time, Julia thought, when this self-possessed man had seemed to hang on her every word. Well, maybe not hang, but he seemed to enjoy what she said. She centered the last shrimp on her plate, eased the tail around to form a comma, an ear, the back end of a parentheses, one hand clapping, then she speared it with her fork and turned to Jaime. "How was your trip, yesterday?"

"Didn't Marshall tell you about it?"

"No. He's been busy."

Jaime nodded toward the table and the food. "It seems you've been busy, too. As for yesterday," he shrugged, "it turned out to be a work-day like any other. But the farm is a beautiful place. You should see it." He patted his mouth with his napkin and glanced over at Marshall, "Maybe you should go to Bluefields first."

"We'd love to," said Julia.

"Oh my, yes," said Vilma, favoring Jaime with a shy and girlish look.

"Fine." Jaime turned to Marshall. "I'll give you a call at the bank when I'm flying out that way."

"Thanks," said Marshall.

"The turtle industry is still strong on the east coast here?" Rafael Valdés asked Jaime.

"Yes. Much as it is in Guatemala."

"Stronger," said Manolo Helgar, barely raising his head from his plate. He was already finishing up seconds of shrimp and was looking around to see if there might be thirds. The man was a pig, and Julia loved him for it.

The air was warm and still. A soft whinny came from *don* Claudio's place. The cicadas wound up a notch. Then Juanita brought in the main course.

Julia stared aghast. Marshall, standing to pour the red wine, was staring down at the long, lovely, golden pastry shell on its platter. Down the middle of it, where the fine, straight, neatly incised zipper should have been, was a gaping wound where the oven's heat had cracked the thin shell precisely along the sculptured zipper's length. And worse, the contents didn't just peep out, they swelled out, a grayish surge of cooked, ground beef. She looked up at Marshall who gave back a look of perfect blandness. She gestured for Juanita to cut it into servings at the sideboard.

The steady hum of the cicadas seemed louder than ever.

"Do you ride?" asked Catalina, gesturing toward the window.

"Oh, that's not my horse. It's the neighbor's. He rescued her from the slaughterhouse."

"Oh right, that would be *don* Claudio Portillo," said Vilma with a laugh.

Julia kept her eyes on Catalina. "He's really a very gentle man." She felt rather than saw Marshall staring at her. She could hear him thinking "and how would you know that?" He circled behind her. She smiled over her shoulder at him. "We've had many conversations…about nature… and the treatment of animals."

Marshall came up on her right and poured the red wine into her glass. The room was quiet. Nothing could be heard but Juanita's shuffling feet, the cluck and gurgle of the wine being poured, and the loud buzz of the cicadas.

The *croute* turned out to be delicious; everyone said so and Vilma asked for the recipe. "How refreshing to make it out of ground beef instead of a slab of beef. I would never have thought of that. Nicaraguan beef is too tough even when it's ground."

"Yes," said Julia. "But then you can add things like bread cubes soaked in milk, and butter and eggs." She opened her palm and gestured toward the Croute.

Slowly the conversation picked up again. Jaime brought up the Vietnam War and cotton prices and Manolo jumped in — did they know that Nicaragua was the only U.S. ally to send troops to Vietnam?

"What about Puerto Rico?" asked Rafael Valdés, and there followed a discussion about whether Puerto Rico could rightly be considered an ally of the United States or a dependent. In any case, the fact that Nicaragua, an independent country, was sending troops to someone else's war, was what mattered.

"I understand you run a scholarship program, Julia," said Jaime when the conversation lagged.

"I don't run it; I just do the interviews. It's an exchange program out of New York."

"Exchange program?" Rafael Valdés had to raise his voice in order to be heard over the cicadas, one of which was now quite clearly inside the window. Marshall signaled to Juanita to get rid of it.

"Yes," said Julia. "It's high school kids who want to study in the States, or families here who'll take U.S. kids for a semester."

Juanita brought a cup and disappeared behind the curtain.

"What kinds of families?" asked Jaime.

"All kinds. From everywhere. From the cities. Up in the mountains, down on the coast."

"And their financial resources?"

"From all levels, rich and poor. There is no distinction."

"Ah," said Rafael with a nod, and Julia could almost hear him thinking "that's where the problem lies."

The curtain billowed into the room with every move Juanita made.

Marshall's face glazed over, as if everything that could go wrong, had now done so.

Jaime was watching the curtain. He switched to English. "I should think very poor people would not be good candidates."

"That's what the program thinks too," said Julia in English. She hated it when they spoke in English just so the maids wouldn't understand. Yet persisting in Spanish was another kind of rudeness.

"You don't agree with them?" asked Catalina.

"They worry that kids from very poor families would be lost in a middle class U.S. family."

"Exactly," said Manolo Helgar in his heavily accented English. "And besides, some kids could be very dissatisfied when they came back home."

"While I'm not from Nicaragua," said Clara, "I think that would be dangerous because they would end up wanting — "

"What we have," said Vilma, and Clara nodded in agreement.

There was a small pause, then Rafael spoke slowly, his eyes on one of the candle flames. "It's natural for people to want to better themselves, but if everyone wanted to be rich, then there would be no one to do the work that makes the country progress. Of course, industry can make some people rich. But they have earned it with their intellectual capabilities, and the time and expenditure of educating themselves, not to mention the cultural advantages they have grown up with." He thought for a moment. "Differences are natural in any society, but people without education, or — " He hesitated. "– or without preparation or the right kind of values, those who are dissatisfied could start a revolution." He paused and looked up. "And nothing can be solved by violence."

Everybody looked impressed by Rafael's excellent summation. Or maybe they were just relieved he'd gotten through a sticky place with no casualties. Then one by one, they turned and looked at the curtain and the silent struggle behind it. Marshall stared down at his plate, clearly unhappy with the awful mess sitting on it.

"I've got an interview tomorrow morning," said Julia, "with a girl whose father owns a general store down on the coast."

Jaime rose and went to the curtain. "It would be particularly hard for young North Americans to live with such poor people." He pulled the curtain aside, revealing Juanita in a half crouch, one hand reaching up, the other holding the cup. Jaime cocked his head for a moment. With a movement almost too quick to see, he reached to a point on the curtain an inch or so above Juanita's head, closed his fist and the cicada was silent. "These people often live in very primitive conditions," he murmured.

He held the curtain aside for Juanita to stand, and indicated with a nod his closed fist. Juanita hurried away and brought a damp towel from the kitchen.

"Gracias." Jaime took the towel, wiped the cicada's remains away and handed the towel back.

With dessert, the conversation split and wandered on separate tracks. Manolo was talking about Communist agitators stirring up the farm laborers in the north somewhere and comparing notes with Valdés on agitators in Guatemala. The women, still in English, were talking about maids, petty theft and the lack of good, honest workers. Vilma lamented the difficulty of getting good help and, to make matters worse, seamstresses, manicurists and hairdressers never came to the house anymore. Julia recommended Juanita's daughter, who was a seamstress, but Vilma was politely not interested. Julia understood. *Gringas* were famous for spoiling their maids.

"These union organizers," said Jaime. "Useless, idle people who have no true work of their own, *sin oficios.*"

"Wonderful expression," said Julia abruptly. "Without office."

"Without shift," Jaime corrected. "Shiftless."

"Does that mean without work?" she countered.

Marshall raised the wine bottle to refill Jaime's glass and Jaime shook his head. He held up a finger and beamed at Julia. "It means idle and useless."

"Or idled and without..." Julia's voice trailed off as she saw Marshall's face.

"I didn't catch that," said Jaime.

Julia shook her head. Her stomach ached with the effort to keep from taking it all back, everything she'd said this whole awful evening. She felt like a bear lumbering into someone else's cave. Soon she'd be scrambling back out, terrified, and running for home.

At least now the dinner was over. Soon they would be going home. She sat up straight. And then what? Would Marshall speak, or would The Silence truly reign.

Rafael was the first to stand up. "Gentlemen, I have here four Cuban cigars and with your permission, Marshall, I would like to share them with you out on your delightful patio so that we don't offend the ladies' delicate sensibilities. I also have a bottle of excellent French brandy for all of us." He disappeared into the front room, whistled up his chauffeur and brought back a very fine bottle of brandy and four cigars, each contained within its own gold tube.

It was quite a performance, and it was followed by a fitting bustle as Marshall went searching for glasses, thank God they were clean, and Julia went to look for wooden matches, because the best Cuban Cigars should only be lit by matches that came from a real tree such as those that grew in the jungles of Guatemala and which Rafael used in the manufacture of golf clubs which he planned to sell throughout Latin America. Somewhere in the middle of all this hurly-burly,

Clara produced a box of Italian marzipan which delighted the ladies and turned Marshall green at the thought, no doubt, of combining good French brandy with Cuban cigars and that most despised sweet of all, marzipan. Julia managed not to laugh out loud.

"I rather like the smell of cigar smoke," said Vilma wistfully as they gathered around the coffee table. "At least the first few puffs." She sat down on the couch. "But truth be told, the conversation is so much more interesting when the men aren't here."

Clara laughed. It was very close to a giggle and quite a difference from her regal bearing at the beginning of the evening.

"Clara, you were saying something about getting your own back with the maids?" said Vilma.

"No, it was some beggars that came to the door. They had a sick child with them." Clara turned sideways and drew her knee up so that she could face Vilma at the other end of the couch. "My friend Lisa was there and she said the only reason they would take a sick child from its bed was for effect."

"That I can imagine." Vilma raised her eyebrows at Catalina. "If you're going to go begging, you want to look pathetic, isn't that right?" She waited for some response, but none came.

"Anyway," said Clara, "Lisa said, 'Let me take care of this,' — and she was amazing."

"Oh?"

"She told them she had some used clothes, and she took them to my back patio where I was airing out some of my cool weather clothes. And she offered to sell them my mink coat for fifteen thousand U.S. dollars."

Vilma spluttered and then cackled.

"Yes, really," Clara continued. "It was pure genius. She said it was a bargain, that she'd bought it at forty thousand dollars. First she let them look at all the clothes and then she went around and put prices on them." Both women were laughing now. Catalina's eyebrows were flat and her hand was covering her mouth.

"Weren't you afraid they were looking the place over?" asked Vilma. "So they could rob it later?"

"Yes, we both thought that afterward." Clara laughed. "But the truth is, they never bothered me again. Of course, who knows what they're up to now while we're away."

"Surely you have guards."

"Yes. And they're armed."

Julia rose. "Excuse me, there's something I forgot to do." She headed for the kitchen.

Goddamn them! But...and this scared her, was she much better? This whole shitty night, so much of it her own fault. And all she could do was sit there in silence? Julia stared down at the heavy, cast iron frying pan. A creamy brown residue from the sautéed shrimp clung to the bottom of the pan. She set her index finger down hard against it and watched her fingertip go white from the pressure. She pressed harder. She wanted to cry, but Juanita, clanking dishes in the sink, was too close. Julia turned on the flame under the frying pan and measured the heat as it came up under her finger. Idle hands, idle hands. Not to mention a big mouth and a foolish tongue. She jerked her finger back. Not just foolish, but thoughtless.

"Julia?" Catalina stood in the doorway of the kitchen, her small, brown hand up on the stucco wall.

Julia glanced at her reddened finger. "Idle hands are the devil's playground," she said in English.

"Oh, yes, *trabajo del diablo*. Idle hands make devil's work,"said Catalina.

95

"You know that one?"

"I most certainly do." Catalina's English was precise, with a tiny lilt to it. "My aunt was the Mother Superior of a Catholic order. She ran a nursing home in Barranquilla." Catalina smiled. "She was a tyrant. My hands were never busy enough. And when she feared for their salvation, our salvation, she persuaded my grandfather to send me to a nun's boarding school in Bogotá. And there…" Catalina came forward and held one perfectly manicured hand out toward Julia. "…I learned that God didn't keep his eyes on little birds. He kept them on my hands. Twenty-four hours a day."

Catalina moved to the stove. "I think you were right to tell Caley to stand up for herself. I wish someone had told me that when I was young."

"Thank you. I needed that."

"I've come to ask if I may speak with your maid. I need some sewing done for my daughter. She's having her fifteenth birthday this year."

"Of course." Julia turned to Juanita. "The *señora* would like to speak with you."

Julia poured water into the pan to loosen the drippings and watched Catalina speak with Juanita. The maid, almost a head taller than Catalina, held one elbow awkwardly with the other hand and kept her eyes on the floor.

"Did you like that school?" Julia asked when Catalina had finished.

"No. I hated every minute of it." Catalina laughed. "Do you know, one of their rules was that when you woke up in the morning you were allowed to pee, then you had to wait until the evening to pee again. And if you broke that rule, you were punished."

"Oh my. I wouldn't last there half of a day." She saw again Vilma's

96

little boy peeing on Richardson's wall and asked, "what was the punishment?"

"You couldn't eat or drink for the rest of that day."

"My God, you must have had bladders of steel."

"Oh my dear, you have no idea. We were supposed to have perfect control in every way." Catalina crossed her perfectly manicured hands across her breast.

"Like perfect little angels?"

"No. We were none of us angelic. Angels can fly. We were more like statues, unable to walk or talk without permission."

"Holy cow."

"That would be the Mother Superior." Catalina fluttered her fingers. "I have so many stories. You wouldn't believe half of them."

"I'd love to hear them."

"Then perhaps you will."

"Do you manicure your own nails?"

"Are you kidding?" Catalina pronounced it "keeding." "Entrust God's little birds to someone else's care?" She laughed. "Not every one of us is a lazy cow, Julia. But those two in there are worse than most." She frowned and shrugged. "Though I should never say it aloud, they are not too different from their husbands. Looking at them, I sometimes fear for this small world we so love."

Chapter 10

Marshall counted twelve bottles of perfume on Julia's closet shelf. They stood in a circle on the unpainted particleboard. One lay on its side and he set it upright, surprised that no perfume had leaked out. He knew she had opened them when he gave them to her. He had watched her sniff and declare them lovely.

He looked at the worn, discolored riding boots, the battered hard-hat, that awful cotton underwear folded neatly on the shelves, and the row of brilliant, long, party dresses. All of it had her smell, part animal, part vegetable, as if she'd moved her pantry here, including the onions and spices. He thought of Yelva Inez, and the scent of papaya if that's what it was, the bars of sun and shadow on their flesh, hers tawny, his pale. And Silla. Would it have been like that with Silla when they had gotten over that first awkward bit?

Quickly, he backed out, closed the bathroom door and climbed into bed. That was over, dammit. Silla's choice, not his.

Julia came in from the kitchen, already peeling off her clothes — the sandals shed near the door and scooped up by the straps, the dress flipped open down the front and shrugged off next to the dresser. All of it in one long dancing motion, talking all the while about something Juanita had said or one of the women at the party, or both. As if nothing had happened. As if everything she'd done this evening was fine.

When she started on her bra, he turned out his light.

There was an immense space between them on the bed. Julia could see his outline in the dim light, toes up, face up, his hands by his side under the sheet. Clenched, she was sure.

"The President's cousin, for God's sake." Marshall punctuated his sentence with a stab of his big toe against the sheet. "You don't just up and pronounce judgment on her."

"Vilma is not the President's cousin."

"She's married to an in-law of Jaime's, and Jaime is Tacho's cousin through his aunt's husband."

"And I'm descended from Noah."

"Christ," he growled.

Let's get out of here, she wanted to scream, or I'm sorry — anything to keep them from fighting again. "The woman was a bitch."

He punched his fist against the mattress. "I don't give a damn if you don't like them. They can be sons-of-bitches, but they're clients. Can't you get that through your head? They're clients. It can't be that hard to be civil when you're around them."

"What wasn't civil?"

"All of it. You don't talk to them. You make these judgmental pronouncements. You tried to one-up Jaime."

"I what?"

"That crap about Unions. You mouthing those cute little answers back was a pretty obvious crack at his politics. And then you disappear and they have to come out to the kitchen to talk with you." He jerked his head toward her and then away. "You are not a maid, Julia, no matter how hard you try. And they are not ordinary people."

"I suppose that makes us not ordinary people."

"That's right. Not any more, and not here. Jesus! I can't believe you served them meatloaf."

Look at me, see me, she thought, not the stupid meatloaf. "They liked the meatloaf."

"Of course they did. They were embarrassed for you."

"You were the one who was embarrassed."

"Damn right I was. Why do you do these things, Julia? All I ask is a good meal and pleasant conversation. Is that too much to ask? I told you these were the most important clients I have right now. And then that ridiculous maid comes tottering in with a meatloaf! It's a goddamned good thing I didn't say hotdogs the other day."

She burst out laughing. "*Wienies en croute,*" she said and sailed off into laughter again.

"Stop that!"

"With a zipper," she gasped.

"Christ!"

She turned her head into her pillow and the laughter drained away. Would she ever learn? They didn't do easy laughter. Or intimacy. Ever. At the merest hint of it, his face would shut down, his lips, those wonderfully mobile lips that seemed so often on the verge of revelation, would flatten and thin to a straight line. It was the lips that she hated, with their promise of untold secrets.

She rolled away from him and pulled her knees up. So many secrets. That was how it had felt in the beginning. To tap those secrets, to share her own, to whisper them to each other, their faces pillowed only inches apart, that had been her dream. Sadder still, her expectation.

"I don't understand." He seemed not to have noticed that her back was to him. "Whenever I begin to think it's okay, we're going to be normal like everybody else, then you make it perfectly clear you're not with me. You don't like my friends; my clients aren't worth your attention. Apparently I'm not worth it, either."

She rolled back over so fast she almost rolled into him. "You're not what?"

He turned toward her and in doing so managed to get farther away. "You aren't interested in what I do; you don't even care enough to learn what the GNP is."

"I'm sorry?" she said.

"They're decent people, Julia."

"Yeah, sure." She blinked back tears. "You want to buy my fur coat?"

"That's one isolated incident. I'll bet you Catalina had nothing to do with it."

"Yeah, sure."

"You don't like Catalina?"

"I do like her. But I like Juanita, too."

"For God's sake, what's that got to do with anything? You don't *have* to like Juanita. She's the maid, she works for you. For us. We have nothing in common with her. She can't even read. What are we to talk about? How to mop the floors? How to serve a meatloaf? How to walk, for crying out loud?"

"That's the way she walks when she's trying to be elegant."

"Well, she looks like a chicken and she – " He stopped abruptly. "You've done it again."

"What?"

"You changed the subject again."

"Did I? Is it really a different subject? I thought you said — "

"Stop it!" He jabbed his foot against the sheet, and she waited.

He began again, this time more gently. "Admit it, you dismiss people like Vilma and Clara because they happen to have money."

The accusation struck home. "You're right," she said. "Because they're rich and they despise people who are poor." Her voice petered out. Be quiet. You've said enough. But when the silence dragged on, she added, "It's just that I hate people who dismiss other people because they're poor."

"You might as well be dismissing me," he said very softly.

"I'm not." But she was, wasn't she? All of it. The blind, dull movements when they made love, no light, no words, only numbing white sound from the air conditioner. The nightgown rumpled at her waist, his pajamas to his knees. Cramp in her thigh. Don't interrupt. Don't tell him. Pretend. Oh God, will it always be like this?

His hands suddenly sliced the air above his chest and his voice was thick. "Vilma, Juanita, myself — people are people. They're decent. But do you care? I should be a Goddamned truckdriver, and then you might be satisfied."

"For God's sake!" She rose up on her elbow. "Would a truck- driver's wife drag two bone-poor women into her house and try to sell them her fur coats?"

"Fur coats!" He sat up and snapped on his bedside light. "That's what I like about you, Julia. You are a continual *non-sequitur*. You fuel yourself with resentments; you have a penchant for the imagined offense." He rolled to his feet in one motion. "You have the most amazing capacity for the inappropriate. Meatloaves. Hiding in the kitchen." His voice got louder. "Telling your daughter to beat up a little boy. For God's sake, what kind of conversational gambit is that?"

"Maybe it's penis envy."

"What?" His voice swooped upward and she caught her breath. "Penis envy? Christ!"

She sat up. "Maybe I'm just jealous because my daughters can't piss on a wall."

"You're crazy."

"What's wrong with penis envy?" She knelt and hissed up at him. "Penises are not such a bad thing to talk about. I think they're a fine subject for conversation. Let's talk about penises, Marshall. We can start with the one I'm never allowed to see."

His face went smooth and tight. He started to move around the bed.

"And oral sex," she yelled. "Ever heard of that? What is it? Going down? Blowing? Eating? Say what it is."

"You're disgusting." He was heading for the door. "I have nothing to say to you."

"Oh, now you have nothing to say. You pick and pick, you call me crazy or disgusting, you can barely stand to touch me, and now you have nothing to say?" She hopped off the bed and shrieked, "Come back here, you mother-fucking son-of-a-bitch."

And he did. In a swoop, arms flailing, he was on her, driving her back on the bed. As she fell, she rolled her knees up to her chest and rammed them into him, but he twisted around her and came at her from the side, upending her. His fists came from everywhere. Grunting, she fought back with her feet, her knees, her elbows. He was huge. She couldn't breathe.

Then it was over. He wasn't there anymore. She opened her eyes. He was near the bathroom door. She could hear his jagged breathing over her own. Even in the shadow, she could see the horror on his face.

103

"My God," he groaned, "I've never, I've never..." His fist hammered the door frame. He stopped and turned away from her.

The humming in her head slowed and became the chugging of the air-conditioner. Behind it, barely audible, came the cicadas, and the distant clink of silverware being put away.

His voice came at her, thick and low. "Why did you marry me if you don't like being with me? Why in God's name did you marry me?"

Her eyes were hot and now she could barely see him. "I guess both of us have the same question."

Book Two

Chapter 11

The car started rough, but it started. Then the road flowing past, mile after mile, brought its own sweet comfort. Julia savored the deep blue bowl of the sky, the day still fresh enough to smell good, the peace of being alone. Back in December, the poinsettia had bloomed along here like wild flowers, huge bushes of them, and clotted in among them, the white helix flower that made the Nicaraguan Christmas colors. White froth and scarlet swords. Now the bushes were grayish branches trying to survive the drought.

She passed the wrought iron gates of huge homes, *Gracias a Diós,* thank God and *Villa Hermosa,* Beautiful Villa in curlicue letters arching above the entrances. The back roads where no other *gringa* drove, this cranky little hatchback, the time alone, it was all healing. Like her silent slide through the pool this morning as the sun came up, with only the birds and the night's residue of bugs floating on the pool's surface for company. No one to see a black eye, a swollen cheek, or the remnants of sorrow and anger binding together into a new pattern.

Marshall had slept in the study and for that she was grateful. No one had said a word about her face and for that she was not so much grateful as worried. Each had reasons for silence. Caley gave her a wordless goodbye hug, and Becka gave her a pat on her back and they both fled.

Of course, Marshall had been silent. As he always was after any disagreement they had. And this was not just a disagreement. This would call for a week or more of silence.

Julia turned off the highway toward Pochomil. For a short distance, the road wound around a series of small hills. As she got closer to the ocean, it opened out into fields of sugar cane. Dust coated the tender green shoots the irrigation had coaxed out of last year's blackened stubble. These were the President's lands: sugar here and farther down, cattle.

She had been down here before, to the President's beach home. A huge place with miles of veranda. It had been a Sunday reception, with oceans of rum and tonic, several baby steers roasting on the beach, white-coated servants shuttling platters of meat to the house, a marimba band. The men shot skeet off the veranda while the women paced behind them, protecting their lacquered hairdos against the wind with shimmering, translucent scarves tied beneath their chins. Off to one side, Julia had watched a lizard stake out its territory on the veranda's railing and defend it against the marimba player who, between runs and without missing a beat, whacked the railing with his mallet, inches from the lizard's flicking tongue.

Nobody else had noticed. And afterwards it seemed so bizarre that she wondered if she had imagined it.

The roar of an engine startled her. She looked up through the windshield. A fumigator plane zoomed low overhead and banked. She stamped on the brake and the car stalled. On a downgrade, thank God. She pressed the accelerator and slowly let out the clutch. Damned cowboys! They pounced on you out of nowhere, then disappeared, pulling half your skin away with fright and leaving you to sniff the trailing pesticide. It was a wonder they weren't all killed in action. And then she thought of Beal Jackson.

When he'd crashed, his family was with him. Wife and daughter, up in his plane for a birthday ride. My God, what would it be like to see the earth slamming into you, then to wake up and smell their bodies burning, and not be able to get them out?

She shivered. Maybe she wouldn't fly to the east coast in Jaime Salazar's small plane after all. That is, if the offer was still open after last night.

San Rafael del Sur, the last town before the turn-off, had a general store, a guard post, a Texaco, and a ragged string of wood and adobe houses. But it was a metropolis compared to San Victorino, which was only a cluster of houses surrounding an ancient *ceiba* tree. The road actually split around the tree, staggered on a few yards and petered out just beyond the houses.

Julia parked the car under the tree and gathered up the interview forms. "The largest house in town," the girl's father had said. "Easy to pick out." Yes, it was far and away the largest. She gazed in admiration at its mottled pink sides and its faded blue pediment. There was a pig rooting near the front step. Julia glanced around. The pig was the only sign of life in the entire place.

As she stepped from the car, she kept an eye on the pig. The thing was a monster. Its flanks and mountainous rump were mottled gray on a background the same tone of pink as the house. Coarse hairs stuck out of the backbone and the tail looked jammed on, as if the big winner at a birthday party had done the deed and fled.

She settled her straw hat on her head, hitched her purse on her shoulder, took a firm hold on the forms, and started forward. The pig gave a snort and shifted its weight. An eye came into view, small and distinctly malevolent.

"Hello," she said softly. The thing was even bigger than it looked from the car. Its udders were hugely swollen. Which meant... She froze as it took a step toward her, and there they were, a clump of seething piglets below the bottom step of the porch.

"Oh shit!" she said, and then in Spanish, "Hey there, piggy — whoa!" The pig started toward her. Julia shifted her weight, ready to dash for the car. In her sweetest voice, she cooed in English, "Stop right there, you fucking big lard-ass bag of pork chops."

"You called?" A thin, bearded man stepped out onto the porch. He was grinning. "Hey, *Chuleta,* Pork Chop!" he called in a raspy voice. With a flip of the wrist, he chucked something at the pig.

The pig stopped in her tracks, stood swaying for a long moment, then she trotted back to her brood and stood over them, eyes darting back and forth.

Julia stifled an embarrassed laugh as she realized he had spoken in English. "Thank you," she said and carefully stepped around the beast and up onto the porch. The man watched her coming, a mild frown on his face.

"I'm from the scholarship program — to interview María Antonia?" She heard the hesitation in her voice and cleared her throat. "I have an appointment."

He raised his eyebrows. "An appointment?" His gaze fell to her cheek and the faint smile faded. He stepped back, swept out an arm toward the plastic covered furniture glowing in the dim interior of the house. "Please sit down."

She watched as he walked down the porch stairs and disappeared around the house. There was something odd about his gait. Not quite a limp but something close.

She took off her hat and sat down on the sofa. A plastic Christmas

110

tree, decorated with florescent pink balls, sat on a low coffee table. A statue of the virgin stared down at her from the top of a refrigerator.

A short, thin woman came from the back of the house in a burst of mumbles: please forgive, she hadn't known, she'd get her husband, and the child. She stopped, stared at Julia's cheek, then hurried away, returning a minute later to thrust the "child," a large, chubby teenager in a tight blue and white checked school uniform, into the room.

Julia rose. "María Antonia?"

"Papi," the girl called in a strangled voice, and kept on walking until she was out the front door. Julia sat down. The program in New York had said the girl was fifteen and she was certainly big enough for fifteen, but good heavens! Julia tried to imagine her in a high school in Cleveland or Boston. But the memory of the boy up in Leon measuring the volcanic ash on his roof with a stick came up instead. Damn. She should have brought him up last night when the men around the dinner table were ranking candidates by their fathers' bank accounts.

She leaned back and tried to clear her head of comparisons. As far as she was concerned, each candidate should be a clean slate, no matter what the New York program advised. She knew there was a hook in her reasoning, somewhere. But that too she cleared away.

It took twenty minutes before father, mother and daughter were assembled around the coffee table. The mysterious man at the door was not present.

Before Julia could do more than introduce herself, *don* Antonio, a short man with a bit of paper stuck to a fresh shaving cut on his chin, stood up and laid a finger alongside his nose in a gesture so slow, so fulsome, she half expected him to start rooting for goodies.

"It is a great honor," he said in a voice that carried the thunder of

111

a born orator, "to welcome so distinguished a representative of our great neighbor to the north."

A disembodied cough floated in from the next room.

"*Gracias*," said Julia.

"A neighbor who has brought democracy to our humble country. Also stability and economic order. Out of chaos."

The unmistakable sound of cot springs creaking came from the next room, two thuds, a pause, then the squeak again. *Don* Antonio sat down. He smiled and his eyes slid toward the wall behind Julia. "Not an easy thing to do, in this place of godless people."

María Antonia beamed and fidgeted. *Doña* Luz stared at the far wall. "Perhaps you would like some coffee?" she asked.

"Certainly," said *don* Antonio. "We are ready for your questions."

"Thank you." Julia watched the woman slip into the back of the house. Courtesy required that she accept the hospitality. She would wait until the woman came back before she started. She turned back to see *don* Antonio staring at her.

"You may begin," he said. "We are ready."

Oh hell. Julia took a breath and began. It took less than two minutes to realize *Papá* considered this to be his interview, another two to realize that neither María Antonia nor her mother had ever expected to open their mouths. And maybe a half an hour more, a long, uphill slog, to lose hope altogether. Health, hobbies, interests, school record – the irrepressible *Papá* plowed into each topic with gusto, interjecting little speeches on how the baser elements in Nicaragua contrasted with the finer instincts of the great people to the north.

Doña Luz carried coffee in from the back of the house and *Papá* produced a pitcher of milk from the refrigerator and praised the virtues of cold milk and its unheard of luxury in this place. He himself did not take it in his coffee but he knew *Americanos* did. She didn't, but she dutifully held her cup up.

While he poured, she said to the child, "Tell me about your reading, María Antonia."

Don Antonio closed the refrigerator. "She reads the classics, the very best."

"Have you read *Don Quixote?*"

"Of course she read that. So many questions! She has even read Charless Deeken's story about two cities."

Julia tried one last time, switching now into English. "Did you read it in English?"

The girl's mouth sagged. *Doña* Luz closed her eyes.

Don Antonio hitched his chair up onto the small carpet. "What did you say?"

In the next room, the cot creaked and feet hit the floor. "She read it in a comic book," said the bearded man from the doorway in perfect English.

María Antonia smiled at him and he grinned back and turned to Julia. "You know, comic books like the ones your embassy puts out about the Red Terror. Simple to understand."

Doña Luz cleared her throat and said in Spanish, "This is my — "

Don Antonio's voice overrode hers. "This is my brother-in-law." His face was red and he hit the word hard. The man in the doorway burst out laughing, and for the first time Julia recognized the similarity of the Spanish words for in-law and cunt.

"Yes, I am José María — " He paused and she wondered if he were actually going to repeat his brother-in-law's pronunciation. "-- the divine and godless one," he finished in English and bowed. His nose was crooked above the scruffy beard and moustache, and his skin was an odd grayish-brown, like a dusty nutmeg. "My niece," he nodded toward María Antonia, "knows no English. You will not be doing her any favor sticking her with a family in Kansas for a year. Besides, she hated 'Tale of Two Cities'." He laid his finger alongside his nose in exact imitation of his brother-in-law. "It was not a happy ending."

Don Antonio's chair tipped over as he stood up. *Doña* Luz made little choking sounds in her throat and ran to pick it up.

"*Ay, Luz, Lucita,* I'm going, little sister," said the man in Spanish.

Limping slightly, he walked back through the door he had come from. "It is a far, far better place that I go to than I have ever known." The words floated back with the clarity of someone who was born in Kansas City.

When the paperwork was done and the apologies and reassurances ended, *don* Antonio walked her out to the car and shook her hand. The speck of paper had fallen away from the razor cut on his chin, leaving behind a single drop of red already turning brown.

"An excellent car, the Volkswagen," he said, patting the roof, and then, so softly she almost didn't catch it, "She will be accepted?"

Julia reached out to touch his arm and thought better of it. "You should go instead."

"I?" He turned and stared at her. His eyes narrowed and he stepped away from her. "It has been a great honor, *señora,*" he said coldly. "May you go with God."

Too shocked at the sudden transformation to do more than mumble, she watched him turn on his heel and walk back to the house.

She had been dismissed!

Shaken, she got into her car and started the engine. It stalled and she gripped the steering wheel to keep from screaming. What had just happened? He'd spent nearly an hour prancing around and fawning all over her and now he was angry?

On her third attempt, the VW coughed and started. Without turning to look, she knew *don* Antonio had disappeared into the house.

She had only gone a few kilometers, was gliding into a little dip in the secondary road, when the fumigator plane tore down out of nowhere. She ducked, pressed the accelerator hard and the car died. She slammed into second, popped the clutch, but the car bucked to a stop on the upward climb. She stomped on the brake pedal to keep from sliding backward.

"Damn!"

She pulled on the emergency brake and cranked the engine, once, twice, and it flooded. She sat back, her head pounding. The road was empty in both directions. She could be here for hours. There was no breeze and the shallow bowl held on to the midday heat. The oily smell of pesticide and the gas fumes from the flooded engine permeated everything. Dead bugs, dead engine, the long, useless interview. Useless and sad. And then that ending. She turned the key again. The engine coughed and died.

"You stupid shit!" she screamed.

A hundred feet ahead, a piece of red flower detached itself from the dusty undergrowth at the side of the road. A red baseball cap, below it a face, a black moustache, a blue shirt. A machete dangled from the man's belt. With a deliberate gesture, he pushed his cap back on his head and stared at her. She twisted the key, put the clutch in and drifted backward, hoping to gain enough momentum to get part way up the other side and perhaps get a start from there, but the car settled at the bottom and she swallowed another screaming curse.

Her mouth felt like dust. Up ahead, the man crossed his arms over his chest and turned his head toward the undergrowth as if to spit. His hand went up in a beckoning gesture and her skin prickled as another man stepped out of the bushes. Thin, bearded, this one moved onto the road like an old man. Only he was young, and he, too, had a machete. His head was turned away as they conferred. After a minute, the first man sat down against a tree. The second man ambled down toward her and her breath came back with a gulp. It was *don* Antonio's brother-in-law, José María.

With a sigh of relief, she released the hood latch and stepped from the car. Her knees were rubbery and she leaned against the fender.

He stopped at the bumper and smiled, wrinkling his nose. His eyes were green with brown flecks at the edges. The skin beneath jumped in little spasms.

"I think you flooded it." He reached for the catch to lift the hood. "It's probably the carburetor."

"You speak perfect English," she said.

"Thanks. Your Spanish is pretty good, too."

He handed her the wing-nut screw, lifted the air filter out and balanced it on the fender.

"This is the air filter," he said.

"That much I know."

"Sorry."

"But not much more."

He went to the side of the road and cut a branch the thickness of his thumb from the bushes. In two or three quick strokes of the machete, he peeled the smaller branches from it, came back to the car and buried his hand inside the engine. All this time, the man in the baseball cap sat beneath his tree, watching.

"Want to crank her up?" José María leaned out and nodded toward the driver's seat.

She got in the car and cranked, the motor whined, but when he took his hand away it died again. He ducked around the hood and peered at her through the windshield. "You got a screwdriver?"

She checked the glove compartment. "This okay?" She held up her Swiss Army knife.

He examined it, opening each blade and tool. "Clever bastards." He looked up and grinned. "Did my brother-in-law give you any satisfaction?"

She lifted an eyebrow. "No. Nor, I'm afraid, did I give him any."

He bent over the engine again. "Though you tried very hard." He burst out laughing, glanced up at her and pushed the hair out of his eyes, smudging his forehead in the process. "Did you read it in English, María Antonia?" he mimicked, and laughed again. "It was wonderful."

"Cheap shot!" she snapped. "You sat in there and laughed the whole time?"

"Not the whole time." He bent over the engine again. "No, not the whole time. Crank her up, please?" His body dangled out from underneath the hood. His heels were worn down and one sole was loose on the side.

He could probably use a good tip, she thought. But speaking English like that, he might take offence. With a sudden shock, she realized that if he hadn't spoken English so well, she would probably have dismissed him out of hand. And she from the great democracy to the north! She glanced up at the man sitting under the tree. He hadn't moved.

"Don't pump it," José María called out. "Get your foot off the pedal."

"It's off!"

"There." He slid off the fender. "It'll work 'til you get home, I think." He closed the hood and rested his hands on the metal.

"Thank you." She waited, uncomfortably aware that he was hiding another grin.

"Aren't you going to offer me a tip?"

"Certainly not!" She felt her cheeks grow hot.

He looked past her, back toward San Victorino. "Then I must beg for one. Are you going to Managua?"

"Yes, of course."

"Can I hitch a ride?"

"Certainly." But she couldn't keep her eyes from sliding beyond him to his friend beside the road. Not him, she thought, not two of you.

"Don't worry," said Jose Maria softly, and then again in Spanish, "*No te preocupes,*" only the Spanish had gained something in the translation and she didn't understand what until he turned to wave away the man in the baseball cap. He was laughing at her, or smiling. Nevertheless she felt better when the other man stood, saluted, and disappeared into the trees.

José María wiped his hands on the grass beside the road before he came to the passenger door. She leaned over the hot plastic seat to release the lock.

For the first five minutes they didn't speak. She drove and, having deposited his machete on the floor behind her seat, he played with her Swiss Army knife. Once again he opened up each blade, each instrument, and whistled when he came to the scissors. "Clever bastards," he finally said. "This one knife could be a whole surgery."

"You're a doctor?" That would make sense. With his English, he must have studied in the States.

"I'm a refrigerator repairman." He smiled. "It is my brother-in-law's one consolation for my continued existence in his life. I can repair the Holy Ark, the sanctuary of the milk. He did offer you milk for your coffee, didn't he?"

She said nothing. He had, after all, been listening.

118

"You were greatly honored," he said.

"I know. He wanted that scholarship."

"Don't give it to her," he said and stopped. "Ah, the past tense."

She nodded, then said quietly, "I almost wanted to give it to him."

He laughed. "I hope you didn't."

She could feel him watching her.

"Oh. You did, didn't you?"

"I did. In a way."

"What did he say?"

"He said goodbye."

"I'll bet he did. And closed the door on you."

"Yes, he did. Just walked away." She shook her head, "I couldn't figure it out."

He, too, was shaking his head. "Yes, it's a cultural thing."

What the hell? She glanced over at him and then back to the road.

"Oh, I see," she said in as cold a tone as she could manage. "It's just a cultural thing. What you're really saying is I'm just a foreigner, so I can't understand?"

"I didn't say that. At least not the way you're taking it."

"Well, then enlighten me."

"It's just that in the States you like long pauses and unfinished hints. It's a kind of hubris."

"Hubris! Oh well, that makes me feel a whole lot better," she said. "Long pauses and unfinished hints? I'm afraid that's a bit over my head."

"See what I mean? You expect to be understood without understanding."

She gripped the steering wheel, unable to decide which was worse — what he was saying, or the quiet, thoughtful way he was speaking. A cloud of water rose abruptly out of the irrigation pipes in the field to their left and blew across the road ahead of them. Spray hit the windshield and flew toward her window as they drove through it. She dropped her arm out to reach for the water, but it was gone and her hand bucked in the dry wind.

He spoke softly. "What I mean is that you are generous in the United States, ready to rescue anybody in distress without considering who they are and what they want, or don't want — just what you think they need. You lead with your heart and expect to be understood at the same time."

"And you call that hubris?"

"Yes."

"Isn't hubris a universally negative trait?"

"Probably, but it's different in different places."

"So, since I'm a foreigner, I can't understand that or act on it?"

"Did you with my brother-in-law?"

She said nothing. She still wasn't sure what she'd actually done wrong.

As though he had read her mind, he said, "You were telling him the cold truth, that he was a buffoon who needed to go back to school in the greatest country in the world, where he could be remade into a grownup."

"Oh my God!" She sat up straight. "I didn't mean it that way."

"But he didn't know that. It's how he took it."

Was he saying that she could never understand what a Nicaraguan was feeling? That she and *don* Antonio had been talking past each other all through the interview, each in their own separate worlds?

Her hand rose to the bruise on her cheek. "I am not a tourist."

"Are you sure?" he asked.

"Wow! Talk about hubris."

"A tourist sees the people of another country as objects of curiosity

— interesting, odd, possibly even wonderful. And they all too often see themselves as very clever to be present to observe such oddities."

Bloody damn hell! thought Julia. This conversation is over!

After five minutes of silence, he cleared his throat, coughing in the process. "What is your name?"

"Julia," she said without looking at him.

"Julia?" He said it first in English, then in Spanish with its softer intonation. "Julia. *Doña Julia. Todo una dama.*" And in English again as if she needed a translation, "Every inch a lady."

She felt deflated. And annoyed she hadn't seen it coming. Next he'll ask me if I'm married. And after that, the titty-boos. Shit!

"Where do you come from with such perfect English?" she said primly.

"Where do you come from with your perfect Spanish?"

"I asked first."

"But I'm your guest."

She almost laughed and was late shifting. The car lost momentum going up a grade.

"I'm sorry…" He looked into the back seat and the silence went on a tad too long. "Perhaps I am your enemy."

"Oh no." She laughed out loud. "Let's just say you are no longer an object of curiosity. You are an interesting guest."

He leaned back against the passenger door and smiled as if to acknowledge her sarcasm. His beard was so sparse it was almost a non-beard, and his nose was crooked, the cheeks chuckled up against his greenish-brown eyes. She had never seen such sad eyes. And just like Caley and Becka, he'd not stared at the bruise on her cheek after that first glance on *don* Antonio's porch.

She felt the cheek begin to throb again as she swung the car wide

121

around a curve and headed into the switchbacks before the South Highway. The fields had turned to hilly, untenanted land.

He sighed, pulled his knees around toward the front and stared down at his knees.

"Where are you from, *doña* Julia?"

"Cleveland, Ohio."

"Ohio." He spoke dreamily. "Where's that?"

"With English like yours, you ask?"

"I am an ignorant man," he said. "A simple proletarian."

She laughed. "As my daughter would say, 'bee poo'!"

"Ah, you have a daughter."

"Two."

"They must be very beautiful," he said, almost inaudibly.

She frowned and he chuckled. "You are thinking, 'how predictable. He is now going to make a pass'."

She flushed but kept her eyes on the road and slowed as they came up to a tractor chugging along. She checked her rearview mirror and pulled out to pass it.

"Far from making a pass, *doña*, I think I'm going to vomit."

"What?" She looked over.

"Watch out, here comes a truck!"

"I see it."

But she hadn't. She goosed the accelerator and the car wheezed around the tractor just in time.

"Poor car," he said, his hand up on the dashboard. "Poor me. I am quite serious, please stop the car."

She pulled over to the side of the road and he opened the door. He got his feet on the ground, attempted to rise, and groaned. He dropped his head down between his knees and retched violently into the dirt. She could see his ribs heaving through his thin shirt.

She reached out, as she would to Caley or to Becka, and put her hand on his back. He flinched. Her stomach gave a lurch. Under the cloth there were huge welts, crisscrossing his back like a tangle of ropes. She made her hand lie still on them as he shuddered. She brought her left hand next to her right, gently lifted her right and slipped it into her purse on the floor in back. No Kleenex. Only an old head scarf. She took it out and waited.

His hands were clasped around the back of his neck and with each heave his knuckles knotted white. When he slowed, she slipped the scarf under his fingers.

"*Gracias.*"

His back was warm under her hand and, without moving, she tried to feel what they were, those dreadful ridges. The tractor had long since passed them. She didn't remember seeing it go by.

At last he stood up and went to sit on a grassy hummock ten feet from the car. He drew his knees up and rested his forehead on them.

At the far edge of the road where the earth had been cut away to the roadbed, exposed tree roots hung down. She winced and thought about those welts under her fingertips. Who could have done that to him? And why?

She turned off the motor, set the brake and went to sit beside him. A truck rumbled by, going up toward the South Highway, and she watched it round the bend. The shoelaces on his boots were knotted in three places. His breathing evened out and she began to hear birds, a breeze tacking down the roadbed, a cicada out before sunset. She closed her eyes and let her mind float.

The muscles across her shoulders eased and she was startled to feel sadness, that hard-ache belly cramp that comes before tears, and then fear, so abrupt it brought her head up. He was looking at her. She looked away.

"Thanks," he said.

"Who did that to you?"

He did not answer.

There seemed to be nothing more to say. She wanted to go, to stand up and drive away, but she didn't move. A car was coming up the hill, would round the bend in a moment. She gathered herself to stand, but his hand came down over hers. He was saying something, his expression so urgent she could not turn away from it. Out of the corner of her eye, she saw a jeep pull up in front of the Volkswagen. There were four soldiers in it. She lifted her head and they stared back at her.

"*Qué pasa?*" said the soldier in the front passenger seat.

She looked at José María. He brought her hand up slowly to his knee, then looked toward the jeep, a strange, tired grin on his face.

"Nothing," she called out, "*muy cansados.*" She hit the 'd' hard, as though she were a *gringa* tourist. "Him, me, *mucho* tired." She mimed it.

The soldiers looked at each other.

"Too much play," she said, "*demasiado jugar,*" almost tipping the word into *joder*, the word for fuck. She felt rather than heard his indrawn breath.

The soldiers burst out laughing. "*Vaya gringa*," they yelled. "Look at the steam coming off them. She's worn him down. When you're through man, give us a chance."

The man beside her stiffened, then relaxed as the jeep's gears crunched down into first. The smile and the tired expression on his face had never changed.

They were still shouting when the jeep disappeared up the hill, and their voices became the sounds of birds and one mad cicada, and then she could feel the shape of his knee under her hand and his hand above, still, light, the fingers settling slowly down between hers.

"That was stupid," he said softly.

She was shocked.

"Very stupid. They could have come after you." He was staring straight ahead without looking at her. "How could you know it would work?"

"I didn't."

He lifted his hand away. "I'm sorry."

"Sorry?" She let herself breathe again. "How about thank you?"

"You're right. Thank you." He shook his head, wiped his face, grimaced at the smell on the scarf, looked at her. "Jesus, they could have come after you."

"And you know what that's like, don't you?"

He turned away without a word.

At the crest of the hill above Managua, when the first faraway glimpse of Lake Managua showed between the trees, she said, "Cleveland is south of a lake, too."

He nodded. "Let's hope it's cleaner than this one."

"Where did you learn your English?"

"From California to Saint Joseph, Missouri."

The lake disappeared again. A blur of burnt-out bushes and curlicue gates flew by on the right side. A marker said twelve kilometers to Managua. Twelve K's to heat and dust and being on her own, six more out the Masaya Highway to the children, the maids, and Marshall.

"How long were you there?" she asked.

"Many years. But I'm still ninety-nine and forty-four one-hundred percent pure Nicaraguan." He smiled. "The rest is air. Like the soap."

"And so you float?"

"For now." He took a deep breath. "It was a hoax, you know."

"The soap?"

"They got air in it by accident and it floated, so they made a selling point out of the fact that it floated, even though with all that air, there was less soap in it."

"So you float by accident?"

"Or by hoax."

"Sort of defies the laws of physics."

"How's that? Oh yeah, I see, I'm still a man of some substance. Just liable to sink." He took a breath and held it, his cheeks puffed out. His eyes closed. "Quick and sudden sinkage."

"Are you alright?"

"It was very quick of you, what you did back there. Again, I thank you."

He seemed to doze off. When he spoke it startled her. "Have you ever been to Acahualinca?"

"No, I haven't." Ninfa's children lived in Acahualinca with their grandmother. "That's where the million-year-old footprints are, isn't it?"

"Ten thousand years old. Some say only six. But yes, they're there. You should go and see them."

She let him out on the by-pass between the South Highway and the Masaya Highway, near the turn-off to the *barrio* San Judas Tadeo. Juanita's daughter lived somewhere in San Judas, she thought.

He came around to her side of the car and handed the Swiss Army knife through the open window. For an instant she thought he was going to touch the bruise on her cheek. Instead, he rested his hand on the windowsill.

"It's quite possible for someone to observe," he said, as if he were giving a lecture on the uses of the wing-nut screw, "from a perfectly neutral perspective, that is, that your hair's the color of the trumpet flower, and your eyes are gray with laugh lines at the corners, and that your daughters might, probably do, have some of this same brightness. From a perfectly objective viewpoint, you understand." He cleared his throat, "Without wanting to make anything more out of it."

She was speechless.

"Thanks for the ride." He limped across the road, the machete flapping against his leg. "You should go see Acahualinca," he called, and turned south into San Judas Tadeo.

Chapter 12

Marshall pulled the phone away from his ear and stared at it in disbelief.

"Hello?" At this distance, the voice was tinny.

"Yes, uh yes, I'm here. I just didn't catch what you said."

"I said, Mr. Bennett, that the Supreme Commander would like you to come to lunch with him today." The man spoke in exactly the same clipped, impersonal Spanish as the first time around and Marshall still couldn't believe it.

He closed his eyes and grimaced. Bloody hell. The very first time he'd been invited to the presidential palace in three years and it had to be today of all days.

"Please tell his Excellency that I accept with pleasure." He was going to have to call Mattie. Cancel their lunch. Again.

"Good. Lunch will be served at one p.m. Please be at the main entrance of the palace at 12:45." Smooth, impersonal, without any hint of arrogance, and yet the voice carried the assurance that this was a momentous invitation.

"Yes, certainly. Thank you." Marshall glanced down at his dusty shoes.

"Thank you. Oh, one moment, sir," said the man. "Please hold for a moment." The phone clicked off and he was left holding the receiver, trying to decide whether a shine would be enough, or if he should drive home and get a better pair. He looked at his watch and shook his head. Just a shine. No need to go overboard.

The line crackled open. "His Excellency, General Somoza, would like to speak with you in person, sir."

In person! Marshall straightened in his seat.

"Bennett, good to talk with you." The President's voice came through in perfect, unaccented English. "Having a small lunch today with Rafael Valdés. Thought you might like to come."

"Of course, Mr. President." So Valdés was back in town.

"Excellent. I'll give you my secretary for the details. Heard you flew up to Jaime's farm. Nice country up there, isn't it?"

Marshall stiffened. Was there something more than friendliness there? "It's certainly an impressive layout," he said and then regretted his choice of words.

"Yes." There was a pause. "Jaime told me you play baseball for your bank."

"Not any more, sir."

"Too bad. What position?"

"Er, third base, Your Excellency."

"No shit. The hot corner. Well, good to talk with you. Here's Gualter." He clicked off and Gualter came back on to repeat his instructions.

Marshall hung up and sat back in the soft leather chair. He couldn't believe it. He'd finally been invited to have lunch with the President. After three years, an invitation for a small lunch at the presidential palace. He didn't know whether to be happy or worried.

He sat up. He'd have to be prepared both ways. Jaime and the President were pretty tight. Clearly they wanted something from him. Or from the bank. But he was no novice, he knew how to handle a deal whether it came disguised as a fabulous opportunity or not.

He stared out through the gold mesh curtains at the street he saw every workday — the line of traffic headed toward the lake, the large blue and orange AGFA film sign above the camera store across the street, the woman selling lottery tickets and plastic toys from a tiny wooden table at the curb, and the shoeshine boys. In here, the cool stillness, the soft carpet, the gleaming sweep of the conference table. Holy shit! Three years as manager of the bank and now lunch with President Anastasio Somoza, Tacho himself. Local boy makes good. That's what they'd think back in Jefferson — not that he'd ever let them say it. Or print it.

He glanced at his watch. Eleven-fifteen. Well, he'd planned to have his shoes done on his way to lunch anyway. Damn but he'd been looking forward to the cool darkness of the restaurant with Mattie sitting on the other side of the table. He'd had to wait for two weeks for their schedules to mesh, and every one of those days he'd had second thoughts. But he couldn't shake the image of Julia's face on the bed that night, her look of hatred, her lips peeled back like an animal. Each time he thought of it, he could hardly breathe. He wanted to get a million miles away from her. The thought of going to another country with her, going anywhere with her, made him sick.

No wonder he'd never even got close to calling Mattie to cancel. But now?

Anxious to get the call over with, he went out to his desk for the American Society Directory. Once again, Fidelia had moved the pictures of the children and Julia to where she could see them. One photo of the kids had them in party dresses. The other was a shot of Julia standing up against a wall in Cuzco with her head raised, her hair nearly gold against the blue-gray stone, her eyes half closed, laughing.

He grabbed the directory and headed back to the privacy of the conference room. He'd have gotten rid of the damned photograph if it weren't for Fidelia and the unspoken explanation that would hang between them like a dead dog. This changing of the photographs was the only sign of softness he'd ever detected in the woman. It was like she was made of steel. He'd always imagined her on a Marine survival course, catching a squirrel with her bare hands, finding shelter, working her way down off a mountain alone while the rest of her platoon holed up, ate dirt and thought of hamburgers.

He dialed Mattie's number, missed the third digit, dialed again.

The maid had to go get her, the *señora* was just leaving.

"Hello, Mattie? It's Marshall Bennett."

Mattie's voice was soft and happy. For about two seconds. Oh yes, she understood, Tacho was Tacho, you never refused the President. Smooth, cool, yet he heard the anger, felt it in his back.

"Tomorrow?" he asked.

She had a planning meeting tomorrow that would probably extend into the afternoon and Thursday was the general meeting of the American Women's Society.

For a wild moment, he thought of seeing her for breakfast.

"Well, some other time," he said.

"Yes." Her voice was already distant — she was off to something else, a meeting, a person. He laid the phone in its cradle. Damn you, Julia. Goddamn you.

Because there'd been a line at the shoeshine boys, he ended up passing his card to the guard at the gate with two minutes to go. Then, after three different checks of his clothing and briefcase, he arrived at the dining room where a man in a dark suit relieved him of the briefcase.

"If you should need something from it," said the man, "just signal the waiter and tell him you want it."

As he entered the paneled room, Marshall glanced at the table. Five settings, four men already in the room. He was the last to enter. Was that by design? It was exactly one o'clock.

Rafael Valdés was talking with the President. Another man was partially obscured by the long, morose figure of Carl Lindstrom from New York National. So, there were two *gringo* banks invited — not a singular honor after all.

Massive and beaming in his perfectly cut silk suit, Tacho drew Marshall into the circle and introduced him to a man from Honduras named Arévalo. They shook hands, then Marshall turned to Valdés and grinned. "I'm still thinking of that Cuban cigar. My first, and it was great. I can still taste it."

Valdés grinned back. "If you're still tasting it, it must have been terrible."

You got that right, thought Marshall. It had tasted like shit. And the worst of it was he knew he would forever connect that taste with what happened with Julia in the bedroom later.

"Not at all, Rafael. I just need to find a source in the States. You know, because of Castro, they've stopped importing cigars from Cuba." Jesus, he told himself, don't overdo it.

"What'll you have?" asked the President, martini in hand. The bar man, in a white jacket, stood at the ready.

"A bloody mary, please." He was counting on the tomato juice to keep him sober. The drink appeared almost instantly. He took a sip. It was even stronger than he'd feared.

"We were just talking about football," said Tacho. Your soccer; but

132

then, baseball's your sport, right?" The tinted sunglasses didn't hide the President's shrewd eyes.

"Not exactly, sir." Marshall relaxed. It was interesting that Tacho had them stand around until he got here. Also interesting that Valdés was here and Jaime Salazar wasn't. Maybe Jaime hadn't said anything to the President about the woman at the farm. Maybe they weren't as tight as he'd thought.

"Bennett here played third base," Tacho said to the others. He raised his glass and chuckled expansively. "The hot corner."

Marshall almost laughed out loud. The man probably hadn't held a baseball in his life, but he had the slang down pat. "I can take the heat, Mr. President."

"Good man." Tacho slapped him on the back. "So, what'd you think of Jaime Salazar's farm the other day?"

"It's beautiful country, sir." When there was no reaction, he added, "And it's certainly a productive operation."

"Yes." There was just the tiniest pause. "I hope you all like fish," he said, turning away. "I'm on another diet. I have yet to find one that combines everything I want." He waited for a chuckle and got it.

The photographer arrived. The President put his glass on the bar and invited them to sit down at the table.

For official photographs, Tacho liked to stand in the middle of a group of men, towering over them all; today, others were taller, Marshall just barely and Lindstrom by a good deal, so the pictures were shot up the length of the table, with the President standing at its head. Several more were taken from each side, with Tacho sitting and the photographer shooting past his broad shoulders.

Lindstrom sat to the President's left, Valdés to his right; Marshall was next to Valdés and opposite Arévalo. Valdés was talking about his custom-made golf clubs. He already owned one of the biggest timber operations in Guatemala and, with heavy backing from First Chicago, he'd recently acquired controlling interest in a steel mill.

A two-foot high silver gamecock sat at the foot of the table. It was unbelievably ugly, and Marshall surprised himself trying to find words to describe it to Julia. Well, that wouldn't happen any time soon. In these last two weeks, they'd barely spoken to each other. Still, he wished he could tell someone. Mattie? Tell Mattie about the damask covered walls, the brocade drapes, the Louis-something furniture? And at the head of the table, the Supreme Commander, his extreme Excellency, President Anastasio Somoza, Glorious Hurricane of Justice. Julia would scoff at the operatic extravagance of a third world ruler, but it was he, not Julia, who was actually sitting here with the President of a country.

He wished he could tell Mr. Peel, back at the Jefferson National Bank. Poor old Peel had never had lunch with the President of any country; he'd probably never flown over a volcano. And he certainly had never been offered a woman like some post-prandial cigar!

The man from Honduras was boring Lindstrom about bananas. It made up for Lindstrom sitting next to the President. Consommé came in silver bowls along with a land deal of some kind. Marshall's ears perked up. A million hectares north of the Río Coco to go to Honduras in exchange for electricity? Marshall sat forward and tried to make sense of it. Tacho was smiling at him as if waiting for him to say something.

Marshall removed the slice of lemon from his consommé and laid it on his saucer. "What did you say it was for, sir?"

Tacho's eyes widened. "Why cheap electricity, of course. For the people of Nicaragua. Every peasant will be able to hook up to the system for pennies."

Marshall was glad he wasn't looking at Lindstrom. Giving away a million hectares of land was hardly cheap. At that rate, you could electrify Nicaragua off the map. Valdés, sitting beside Marshall, seemed unusually quiet. What was really going on here?

Then it came to him. The President would take his free electricity, sell it cheap as the benefactor of a nation, the bearer of light, earning new titles, new divinities. Meanwhile those pennies would mount up, along with higher rates for industry, government offices, even the military. Yes, millions of *córdobas* would find their way into Tacho's pockets.

Giving up the land would bring the border down to the river, which made sense, too. A river frontier was more secure militarily and in the international courts. So what was this luncheon all about? It seemed a closed deal with nothing in it for the banks. Or Valdés, for that matter.

He glanced at Lindstrom. If anyone knew what was going on here, he did. The big Swede's face held its usual vacuous stare and pursed lips that made him such a skilled negotiator, but even he looked a little baffled. So who here did know?

"Tell me Marshall," said Tacho, smile in place, amusement in his voice, "you think Jaimito could use public electricity? Or does he generate enough snap and crackle up there on his own?"

Marshall's skin prickled. The bastard knew! Marshall picked the lemon slice up and bit into it, peel and all; the acid knifed through the glands beneath his jaw. "That's a question for Jaime, Mr. President."

"Well, I've asked him, of course. It seems our friend Jaime would need a substantial investment in infrastructure to make joining a grid worthwhile." Tacho's hand reached out toward Rafael Valdés, "and the same is true for you, Rafa." He pressed his napkin to his lips, "And that's where you gentlemen," he looked at Marshall and then at Lindstrom, "can be very helpful."

Marshall's hands were still shaking when he took the photos from the man at the front gate and climbed into the taxi.

"A lot of traffic," said the driver.

"Do the best you can." He leaned back against the seat. He wanted to whoop aloud, and he wanted to go somewhere quiet and hole up. His knee gave an electric jump and he squeezed it. He'd landed a deal, a fantastic deal. No, he and Lindstrom had been handed the deal and neither of them had done a thing to land it.

He sat forward, the plastic seat suddenly too hot against his back. What about the woman, Yelva Inez, that the President so obviously knew about? Snap, crackle and pop? Christ! He could feel his head start to pound. That was no coincidence. People didn't just hand out post-prandial fucks without wanting something big back. Not unless...

He caught his breath, then let it out explosively. He'd been set up! All that papaya philosophy Jaime had spouted at the farm. And today, Tacho's seemingly innocent questions in a setting where there was no choice but to nod and answer yes. Tacho's comment about Marshall playing the 'hot corner.' And he, fool that he was, saying, "I can take the heat."

No. That didn't sound right. He sat back.

If they were doing this to him what had they done to Lindstrom? The Swede didn't have a family to worry about. He didn't have a wife to fuck up his mind.

Marshall stared down at the envelope with the photos he hadn't yet looked at. 'I can take the heat?' It hit him like a blow to the gut and he felt the fish start to come up on him. He might as well have said, 'here, take me, I'm yours.' One stupid comment and they had him on their playing board. And only they knew the rules.

"No!"

"*Perdone?*" said the driver.

"*Nada!* It's nothing " He settled back. Cool. Stay cool. And think. Jaime was too much of a gentleman to play the heavy. He hadn't even been there today. Besides, men screwed around here all the time. Why was this any different? Because it was handed to you on a plate, you fool.

He twisted around to look back up at the hill behind the Campo Marcial. The Presidential Palace was invisible, tucked away behind the Intercontinental Hotel. But he'd been there, invited to the home of Nicaragua's Hurricane of Peace, Julia's "Man who Made the Trains Run on Time."

Goddamn her and her smug pronouncements. What the hell did she know about the real world? She never listened to him. When he tried to explain the facts, she always came back with her ignorant, negative, narrow-minded ideas.

Stop it, he told himself, or you really will bring up that lunch. He stared up at the taxi's broken dome light. Somebody running by the taxi passed a piece of paper through the open window. A mimeographed sheet, a confused mishmash of issues: jails, the rise in milk and gasoline prices, wages. Three typos. Written by agitators. Students probably.

He dropped the paper back out the window, picked up the envelope from the seat beside him and opened it. Glossy black and white photos. The silver gamecock glowed in the foreground of one, its wild plumage out of focus; Tacho in the background, with half moon teeth and dark glasses. The well-heeled guests all turned away, no doubt smiling at the President.

Nothing of the cross-currents or the confusion showed in the pictures. This was just a pleasant little get together. And then, from the head of his luncheon table, plowing into his third plate of Pompano snapper stuffed with shrimp, Tacho had unveiled the biggest deal Marshall had been dealt since he came to Nicaragua. Land, electric power transmission, cables and cement, plantations, engineering consultants, roads…

The U.S. banks were in on the ground floor to supply high-interest loans and credit lines, currency exchange and tax rebates. They could charge off losses to companies Tacho's friends had built for that purpose. It might horrify international courts of law, but here in Tacho's back yard, everything was just fine.

Jaime was right. This was a wild-west country. And Marshall couldn't wait to do the numbers. You could hide in the numbers, they were cool and safe. Not wildly unpredictable, or crazy like Yelva Inez or Mattie.

"*Hijueputa!*" said the driver. "Son-of-a-bitch!" He stopped the car, put one foot out the door and stood to look down Roosevelt Avenue. Horns were honking, people were shouting. Something was stalled a block or two down the narrow main street.

A trickle of sweat ran down Marshall's neck. The driver hopped in and the taxi inched forward a foot, a foot and a half. Marshall looked at his watch. An hour, a little under, before he had his next appointment. Maybe Alfredo could take it and he could get started on this. Another piece of paper shot in the window and he shot it back out. More drivers were out of their cars, pounding the roofs and shouting. He'd never get back at this rate. He leaned forward and handed the driver a ten *córdoba* note and got out to walk.

Four blocks from the bank, a red Chevy pick-up with its hood up stood sideways, blocking the street. Dirty and rusting, it looked like it was missing a window as well as a driver. Kids, students probably, were on every corner. Others roved about passing the leaflets out with their heads turned back over their shoulders. Marshall brushed past them. If it weren't for the stalled pick-up, the police would have cleared all of them out by now.

"Mrs. Schimmer is waiting for you," said Fidelia when he stepped up onto the platform.

"Damn!" he said under his breath. He shoved his briefcase in the kneehole of his desk.

"I've put her in the conference room."

"Thanks, Fidelia."

Mattie sat at the far end of the table, silhouetted against the window. He came around to stand between her and the light.

She smiled up at him. "There didn't seem to be any other way, short of asking you for breakfast."

"I thought of that, too," he said and then regretted it. Her hair was loose and it hung down her back.

"Did you?"

"Yes." He sat down so that her eyes would no longer stare up at him. Her dress was blue, the same color as her eyes. Again he felt that mixture of excitement and fear, of being on the board and in play. Only this was a different board altogether.

From out in the street there came the sound of horns from behind the blockage.

"I saw you walk by the window," she said. "Just before you came in."

"It's some kind of demonstration. There's a pick-up stalled a few blocks up, so I walked."

There was a question in the soft knot above her eyebrows.

"The students are taking advantage of it," he said. "Handing out leaflets about the milk and gas price increases."

"I know." She laughed. "I got handed three before I could get inside the bank." She pulled one from her purse. "I don't understand all the Spanish, but it looks like a lot of rhetoric. Proletarian, I got that. And monopoly. Monopolies." She pointed to the words. Her fingernail was perfectly shaped and painted pink. He rubbed the back of his neck.

"*Lucha*," she said. "That means struggle, doesn't it?"

"Yes."

She looked up at him. "Julia speaks perfect Spanish, doesn't she?"

"She taught it."

"Oh?"

"In Cleveland. She was putting herself through graduate school."

"Graduate school? Is that where you met her?"

"No. She quit before she got the degree. She said she'd rather live the knowledge than get it from books."

"Good heavens. She gave up getting a graduate degree?"

"She got the first one, the Masters, but she quit the doctoral program after she finished all her course work." Marshall looked out the window. "She just didn't want to write the thesis." He looked back at Mattie and caught a smile that she quickly erased.

"I met her when she was teaching in Peru," he said.

It seemed both fitting and ludicrous that they should be talking about Julia. What else was there to talk about...that he'd screwed a peasant woman on a farm in the middle of nowhere; that maybe because of that, he'd just been placed on the biggest game board he'd ever been on, yet wasn't sure if he was a player or a pawn; that the whole thing was so big, so beyond his experience, that he wanted to forget it all, lay this woman here on the floor and rut his heart out? Or maybe he just wanted her to leave so he could lose himself in the numbers.

Unable to sit still, he got up and went to the window. She joined him immediately. There were more demonstrators now. The line stretched from the camera store across the street up to the corner. Some were women, ordinary women, the kind that sold stuff on the streets, only right now they were packing up. On the other corner, the shoeshine boys stood in a cluster, their boxes under their arms in case they had to run. One student collected leaflets from the ground and continued to pass them out. People walked in the street and looked back toward the place where the pickup blocked it.

"I don't understand it," she said. "Prices here are so low. How can they complain about a few pennies?"

He shook his head. "They don't understand. They've already got price controls. This is penny-ante stuff. If the government let the prices go to their natural level, it would take their breath away." His voice shook and it sounded harsh, even to his own ears. "As it is, the oil companies and the milk companies are suffering. It amounts to the government subsidizing…"

He stopped. Her face was turned up again, and she was listening, really listening, eyes wide, framed in long black lashes. The faint blue vein at the base of her throat jumped and he knew that the tip of his tongue would end there, on that blue thread, before slipping down… He took a deep breath and unlocked his shoulders. Somebody ran by the window. He heard sirens. Shouting. The crowd across the street broke and started running toward the lake, the vendor women and shoeshine boys following. He moved to the door of the conference room. From behind him came the sound of glass shattering and people screaming. Trucks roared down the street. The blockade had been broken.

"Fidelia," he called.

"I've got it," said Fidelia from the edge of the platform. Half the people on the bank floor were at the windows — customers, secretaries, clerks, even Alfredo. Across the way, the tellers craned their necks over their bulletproof glass barriers. The two security guards and the maintenance man were out the front door, slamming down the metal barriers that protected the huge plate glass windows, shutting out the light. Someone laughed and the bank floor took on a festive air.

A small shriek behind him made him turn back. Mattie stood sideways against the window, her hand over her mouth. He went to her. Up toward the barricade, a student lay in the middle of the street. The soldiers had several others and were bundling them up into a truck with dropped canvas sides. Two soldiers held a young woman by the arms. She kicked out wildly as two others went for her feet. In one motion they flipped her over and slammed her face down onto the pavement. One soldier thrust her arm up over her head at a grotesque angle and she went limp just as the metal barrier crackled down over the window and the conference room went dark.

"My God!" Mattie's voice was trembling. "How can they do that? Take such risks? Stupid, stupid, why did she fight?"

"It makes no sense." He felt sick. He concentrated on the sound the barrier had made as it went down, heavy and solid, but he couldn't tune out the shouting, doors slamming, truck engines roaring. Julia would've fought back. Fuck, she'd have been that ignorant.

Mattie was a dim shape in the light filtering through the curtains from the cracks in the metal louvers. "You're right," she said. Her voice was firmer now. "It's not sensible."

He opened his mouth to say something, anything, and then stopped as he felt her hand on his chest. It glowed in the dim light, each fingertip pointing upward like a flower that had taken root. The subtle echo of his heartbeat fed back into him as if she were his sounding board. He sought the sounds on the street, but there were none so he looked down again. Her face was exquisite, a delicate extension of that light touch that feathered down into his prick and beyond, into his butt.

The metal barrier rattled up outside the window and daylight flooded the room. Pedestrians walked past the window, cars moved down toward the lake. The woman with the plastic toys was setting up her stand again.

He stepped back to turn around and Mattie's hand fell to her side.

"You must love her very much," she said.

No! He felt the word explode inside him and was shocked. His muscles clenched against the smell of years of living together, of Julia lying in the bed beside him. He hated it. He hated himself. He'd struck a woman for the first time in his life; he'd fucked someone who had served him his lunch not fifteen minutes before, a woman who'd been served up to him on a platter by one of the country's upstanding businessmen. He'd just signed on to a business deal he didn't understand and didn't know if he was being blackmailed into it. And here, standing just inches away, was a gorgeous woman practically begging him to fuck her here and now.

And all he wanted was to close the door on everybody and work with numbers. Numbers didn't lie, they didn't have an agenda.

Mattie was saying something.

"I'm sorry. What did you say?"

"That's okay. I was just saying I should go." She looked toward the window. "I guess it's safe to go out."

"I guess so," he said, trying not to sound too eager. He held the door for her. "We'll be in touch."

She smiled. "I'm sure we will."

Chapter 13

José María put his hands high on the doorframe and leaned out into the street. Two houses down from Berfalia's, *doña* Hortensia hauled her rocker out, set it to the right of her door and eased herself down. It took her no more than three seconds to catch him watching her. She extended her hand and summoned him with bent fingers.

He checked the street. There was no one close by. Everyone was indoors, eating their suppers. He stepped out and went to her.

"And how may I serve thee, *doña?*" He carefully leaned his shoulder against her doorframe and smiled down at her. He'd known her all his life, at least the half before he'd gone to the States. He'd played with her grandkids, had even copped a few kisses from Migdalia when he was eight or nine, for which they'd both gotten a fierce dressing down, followed by a few good whacks when they couldn't stop giggling.

"You do a lot of leaning these days," she said quietly.

He was suddenly alert. "That's true."

"Not good for the spirit."

"I hadn't thought of that." He pushed away from the doorframe and pressed his lips together to keep from wincing.

"That's still hurting you?"

He frowned.

144

"You heard me, young man."

How could she know anything? Had Migdalia told her? No, he couldn't believe Migdalia would tell her grandmother. She'd sworn she wouldn't.

"Don't blame her, boy. Migdalia never said a word, but I don't miss much for an old lady with only one good eye. You should know that."

"I do," he said ruefully, remembering the countless times he, Migdalia and her brother Vicente were caught and scolded by her for things they'd committed on the other side of town. They'd arrive home an hour or so later and there'd she'd be, waiting for them, tongue sharpened and hands at the ready.

"I still don't know how you did it," he said. "It's like we wore signs on our foreheads."

"Something like that. You were good at keeping your mouths shut, but not a one of you knew how to school your faces. Now go inside. There's a jar on the table beside the stove with some salve I've fixed up for you. It's the clear green one. That should do for those wounds that are still oozing despite the good care Berfalia has given you. And no, she didn't tell me either. You know we never talk. Now go."

He groped his way through the dark house. He should never have told Migdalia where he'd been. She'd come upon him in a bad moment and conjured up an intimacy he hadn't felt in years. She, more than her twin, had been the strong one in their pack of three. Strong in ways it had taken him years to understand. Unlike her brother Vicente, she had no ambition for herself, just a fierce curiosity and the ability to read people. Just like her grandmother. And just like Hortensia. But it had all been cut short when she made the mistake of falling in love. That was a fuck-ass business anywhere, but here falling in love was an all-out disaster for most women. You keep a man down, pay him shit and he's one angry son-of-a-bitch with nowhere to vent his anger but on the ones who depend on him.

On this street alone there were many women who'd been beaten and left like Hortensia, or been raped at some god-awful young age like Hortensia's daughter, Juana. He didn't know where his own mother fit in this lineup, but thank God, his *tía* Berfalia and Migdalia had somehow managed to kick out the fathers of their children.

José María looked up and found he was standing near the little alcove where Migdalia's children slept. The little girl was sleeping, but the boy was sitting up, wide awake. Even in the darkness of the alcove, the child's eyes caught the light from the gap between roof and wall. José María put his finger to his lips and lifted up on tip-toe to soften the sound of his passing. The whistley breathing of clogged lungs followed him.

In the kitchen, a slanting ray of sunlight from the single back window lit up the hideous yellow-green goo in the jar. He snatched it up and turned back, hissing as his shirt tore at one of the scabs on his back. This place was haunted, filled with truculent gremlins: here a sharp pain, there a sad memory, and all around, the wheezing of a small child's junked-up lungs.

"The boy's up," he said as he came out onto the street.

"I know. It's the asthma. He sometimes spends hours like that. He's just waiting until I, or his mother, come to bed. He never says anything, just sits there and waits."

For once she didn't keep the resignation out of her voice and it made him anxious. He looked down at the jar in his hands. "This stuff looks poisonous."

"You know how it goes. The worse it looks, or tastes, or smells, the more healing it is."

He shrugged. "*Disque.*" He loved the word, its economy, its abruptness. 'So they say.' There was no single word like it in English and it never failed to end a conversation.

He lifted the paper covering on the jar and took a guarded sniff, then reached his pinkie finger down and ran a smear of the stuff over the tip of his tongue. His stomach gave a lurch and he gagged, coughed and spat furiously. When he came up for air, his eyes were streaming and the jar was sitting in Hortensia's lap.

"Jesus, God in heaven."

"I didn't tell you to taste it, fool."

He groaned as hiccups followed coughing. "If awful is healing…" He dissolved into gagging and back to hiccupping. Through tears he saw the jar being set on the ground. Her empty chair swayed back then forward. Run, he thought and screamed as she whacked him smartly just below the shoulder blades.

"Christ in heaven, woman…"

"Where he should be," she said and sat back down again. "They've stopped, haven't they?"

"Did you make it bleed again?"

"Your back? Not much, if I did."

He waved his finger at the jar. "How the hell did you come up with that? The smell alone would heal a herd of ailing buffalos."

"Buffalos." She bent over to pick up the jar. "Did you see buffalos while you were up there, boy? I thought they were all dead."

"There are some still left. In small herds. I guess they're safer that way." He squatted beside her chair and with a sigh he lowered his butt to the ground.

She stared off at the fading light in the western sky. Down the street, people had started coming out of their houses. A group of women stood near a door, their heads forward and bobbing up and

147

down. Beyond them, some children kicked an imaginary ball around in the middle of the street. Freed from reality, their movements grew grotesque, exaggerated, and their grunts turned to shouts.

Doña Hortensia leaned over and handed him the jar. "Dusk is always a hard time. Everything changes, water to steam, light to dark, silence to dust."

"Silence to dust?"

"Just keep your eyes open, José María," she said. "Bad things can happen at dusk. Now go home and put that stuff on you."

He turned to walk away, a knot in his belly.

She chuckled. "Good things can happen at dusk, too," she said. "Just don't miss them. And get a job."

Startled, he turned around and stared at her.

"You can't repair your aunt's refrigerator forever," she said.

"So you *have* been talking to her."

"Not exactly." She tapped her temple. "But we are from the same home town."

"Even though you never talk."

"*Disque,*" she said.

He chuckled as he waved goodbye.

She was right. Just sitting around here, he was of no use to anyone. He slipped into the house and immediately turned back to check the street again. Dusk had settled on the *barrio*. The children had moved farther away, urged along by badgering parents intent on their own conversations. On this side of the street, six or seven houses beyond Hortensia, a little boy was coming toward him, wearing almost nothing and dragging a stick along the sides of the houses as he walked. Hortensia had tipped her head back and closed her eyes. He was pretty sure she was faking it, and that when the child came abreast of her, she'd reach out and snatch him into her arms and they'd end in

148

a tangle of chucklings and gigglings. He wondered if he would ever be as good, as wise, or as observant as she was.

He shifted the jar from one hand to the other and set his shoulder against the doorframe, this time using his right side so he could watch the street coming from the city. Of course he had to get a job. What had he been thinking? That his comrades would welcome him back with open arms? Not when they had no idea what he might have said under torture. Or if the *guardia* were watching him.

They were probably just being cautious, but shit, for three days he'd worked on the refrigerator. The damned thing was more than thirty years old, as old as he was. The original motor was in good shape, all the old coils needed was refilling. The tubing was almost petrified. He'd replaced it, gotten a new wire and plug and painted the body the hideous purple his *tía* had fallen in love with.

Now, fully started on its tenth life, the refrigerator stood in Berfalia's kitchen, chugging and panting and wheezing and sweating buckets. A job that should have taken two, three hours, he'd lingered over for three days. Or, as Katherine would say, he'd malingered over it for three whole days.

A tenth life was impressive, especially since he hadn't fully started on his second. Unless you counted the second as ending with the Angel of Death. Which meant he was actually starting his third, in about the same shape as the old Victrola with its crackled finish, its articulated arm now permanently flexed backward as if caught hurling a stone. Of course he was back on pig slaughter detail. He'd been surprised at how quickly he'd fallen into it, and how sick it still made him.

José María closed his eyes, took a deep breath, and shifted his weight away from the doorframe. He thought again of the names on the walls of his cell underneath Tiscapa. He had no right to whine.

"*Adiós.*"

His eyes flew open. The child with the stick had stopped in front of him. He glanced up the street where Hortensia was still leaning back in her chair, her eyes still closed. He couldn't believe he'd missed the tussle between her and the boy. Or had she really fallen asleep? That worried him.

"*Hola*," he said to the boy.

The boy ran his forearm across his nose. He was wearing nothing but a shirt. "At least I'm not sick," he said.

The weight he gave the first three words, *por lo menos*, rolling the 'R' around his tongue, seemed to tell its own story. José María could almost hear the boy's mother in his voice.

"It's a good thing, too," he answered with equal gravity.

The child pointed down the street. "My sister is."

José María squatted down. "I'm sorry to hear that."

"She's going to die."

"I hope not."

The boy shrugged. "She'll go to heaven. She's pushy like that." He placed the tip of the stick on the edge of the door. "*Adiós.*" He walked up the street, dragging the stick along the wall of Berfalia's house, then along the wall of the next house.

"Polio," said his aunt Berfalia from the alcove off the front room where she slept.

"I thought you were asleep."

"That family's a disaster," she said.

She was in a filthy mood. They'd put the bite on the vendors at the market again. It was a new cop, she said, a jumped-up asshole shit, trained by the Yankees in the States or Panama or somewhere else the Yankees messed with. About the demonstration, she would say nothing. Which meant she probably knew a lot and just wouldn't tell him.

Or worse, it was possible he had become, after two weeks, an embarrassment, a burden. The thought chilled him and he turned into the darkened house. "Perhaps it would be well for me to move on."

The bed creaked. "It would be well for you to live. It would be well for all the fuckers to die. It would be well for the rains to come and for the sausage casings to be filled." Her voice moved toward the kitchen. "Don't give me your 'wells' and your 'would-be-well-fors'." The light in the kitchen came on.

He grinned. "Where's Andrés?" he called.

"Where's Andrés?" she echoed and slammed a pot down.

So that was it. "He'll come." And then because he'd said it, he leaned out of the house, expecting to see his cousin come shambling out of the dusk, his face full of what he'd seen during the day, his tongue lagging behind. Andrés, who loved everything and everyone, from the vultures that circled over the weekly pig slaughters to the ragged children who sometimes threw stones at him and sometimes took comfort in his arms. The fever had taken him when he was four years old and language was the major casualty.

"You'll see," José María called back into the house. "He probably took some child home to its *mamá*." The neighbors might dislike and even mistrust Berfalia for her abrupt ways and her refusal to gossip, but they trusted the shambling twenty-seven year old man-child who brought their children home from the battles of the street, pouring his broken word-gifts into their ears.

"Come and eat," Berfalia called.

He groped his way out to the kitchen and sat down at the narrow table.

"Don't wrinkle your nose like that. Food smells."

"It's just that…"

"I know. Your stomach hasn't settled yet." She set her own bowl across from him and sat down. "It will."

"I wonder if Maritonia got the *gringa*'s scholarship," he said.

She said nothing. He pushed the beans around his plate. Her response to his story of the *gringa* and her scholarship appointment with Antonio was predictable. "Good. Marry her and go back to the States where you'll be safe."

He moved his half-finished plate away and sat back, remembering the *gringa*'s determination to get past that pig. An appointment? In San Victorino? he'd been thinking when she turned toward him and he saw her gray eyes light up as though the sun shown from inside her. But then came the bruise, curving up and around the left eye. It was an obscenity and he'd wanted to erase her with her bruised eye and her *gringa* appointment. Just as he'd wanted to erase the ache in his back and the sad, empty homecoming with Luz and Antonio.

"You cannot move a mountain when you're standing on it," Berfalia said. It was one of her favorite sayings.

"No."

"Then why try?" She heaved up out of her chair and went to stand in front of the stove.

José María rubbed his forehead. Dammit, he'd had enough of being shut out. "So what is it this time?" he asked.

She shrugged. Her back was turned toward him. "The impenetrable wall," his cousin Miguel had called that stance.

She had raised José María and his sister as her own, dealing out the same rough justice, love, and mysterious aphorisms she meted out to her own two sons. And she'd done it alone. She had relatives in Boaco, and friends, or maybe only connections, in the marketplace, a whole network of people. She seldom talked about them, and she never talked about the father of her children; nor would she speak of his own father. In this home, fathers did not exist.

"I never found him, you know," he said.

She turned around to face him. "Who?"

"My father. I went looking for him once — you knew that?"

Her eyes closed. She didn't know, he realized. Or she didn't want to. So much for that.

He rubbed a thumb over the round knob at one side of his wrist. He wavered, partly because he loved her, and partly because the Angel was still there beneath Tiscapa, waiting for him. But he needed someone to know, someone he trusted. So he told her of that Missouri summer, of the heat and the dry, yellow fields, and the old cops who looked him over with their sad, assessing eyes. He told her about Katherine and about her last two years, her rage, and the silence at the end. How heavy and inert she had been.

"She cried at the end. I never saw her cry before. I thought her brain was gone, but then there were those tears, real tears, and she made these sounds..." He swallowed hard. "I kept seeing my mother, in the other room there, how you wouldn't let me go to her, and there was only the record player, and you kept playing one song over and over again to cover the noises she was making in her labor."

Berfalia was staring at the wall behind him, her eyes steady and unblinking.

"Then one day, when I got to work, Katherine was gone. Sergeant Eddie Brown said she'd passed early in the morning, before reveille. That's the way he put it, 'before reveille.' He was waiting at the gate to tell me, in bedroom slippers and an old coat thrown over his pajamas. And after he told me, he stood there like a soldier waiting to be dismissed." José María took a jagged breath and lowered his head.

"We were the only mourners at her funeral, me and Sergeant

Eddie. A punk kid and this crazy old coot who'd fought in every war in the last two hundred years. There was no one else. That was it. She was gone and we never found my father."

He felt a light touch on his hair, there and then gone before he could reach up and press it to his head.

"It was like he never was," he said. "Except I still have a button with an eagle on it, and there's that Victrola and some records."

His chair scraped the floor as he stood up. He went to stand in the patio door. She'd whitewashed both the pigpen and the outhouse while he was under the mountain, and they glowed in the deepening darkness.

"That Victrola…," he said. "I probably wouldn't have gone looking if he hadn't left it."

"You'd have gone." She went to the refrigerator.

"Yeah, but maybe not north to the States, maybe south or east."

The refrigerator door slammed. "You'd have gone north." She banged a pot down onto the stove. "You were going north the minute you were born. It works that way. The minute you asked who your father was, you were on your way."

"Well there, you see?"

She said nothing.

"Who was he?"

"What?"

"Who was my father?" He glanced over his shoulder at her.

"A Yankee. He called himself a *Marín*. We thought he was a sailor, but no, he was just a guard at the American Embassy."

"I know that. But why was he here? Did he fight Sandino?"

"No. I don't think so. But what does it matter? He was just a boy."

And then, when he turned to face her, she finally looked him in the eye. "Your mother washed laundry for the guards at the embassy."

154

"Ah."

She came and stood to the other side of the doorframe. "You thought it was worse. You thought he was one of the ones who killed Sandino?"

He was too tired to think. "You're right. What difference does it make? He came and he left." He shrugged. "He was what I made of him."

They were silent. The boy's stick scraped along the outside wall, going back in the other direction. There were voices and then a soft knocking. He looked at her. The Guard didn't bother to knock; he saw that she was thinking the same thing.

"*Pase*," he called out and went to the front room. It was too dark to see who stood in the doorway.

"Is that you?" said a husky voice.

"Augustín?" José María reached out to pull him in and Augustín stepped back. His breath was shallow and rapid.

"What's wrong?"asked José María.

"We need to talk," said Augustín.

"Come into the kitchen." José María led the way.

As they came out into the dim light, Berfalia stood up. The expression on her face made him turn around. Augustín was hunched over, one hand out before him. The skin on his face was the color of brick.

"*Hijuela!* Son-of-a-bitch!" José María reached out and guided Augustín toward the table. "What have they done to you?"

Augustín eased himself into the chair. He had shaved his moustache and his lips were clamped together so tightly that his chin and nose almost met over his mouth.

"Nothing," he said. "I've been running." He held his left hand pinched between his right arm and his ribs.

"And the others?" Berfalia asked. "Are we to expect whoever you were running from?"

"No, *doña.* I ran from myself."

"*Vaya!* Scarecrows," she jeered softly. "So now this is what the revolution has come to? Scarecrows?"

Augustín glanced at José María.

"We are waiting for Andrés," said José María.

Augustín looked up at Berfalia. "He was there, on the edges. He wasn't taken. Of that I'm sure."

Berfalia sat down with a thump; her chair creaked in protest. "He said he would go because this one couldn't." She mustered a weak glare for José María. "How do you know he wasn't taken?"

"I know who was." Augustín's mouth twisted. He put his head to one side.

"Why are you breathing that way?" asked José María.

"He's broken a rib," said his aunt. "More than one."

"The scarecrow comes to the witch," said Augustín and to José María's amazement, he began to cry, his face twisting grotesquely with each dry spasm.

"I can't." Augustín pressed his elbows tight against his sides and hunched over to allow the breath to enter his lungs.

"Yes, you can," said Berfalia.

Augustín looked down at the hastily constructed pack of melted ice on the table in front of him. "The ice was enough."

"No, it's not." Berfalia lifted his arms away from his skinny body. She nodded to José María, who took an elbow in each hand.

Anchoring one end under her thumb, Berfalia wound a wet, dripping cloth tightly around his chest and over his shoulder, once, twice, three times, then she tied the split ends into two knots on the side away from the break. Augustín was shivering. After she tightened the knots and tucked the ends in, she wrapped a blanket around both him and the back of the chair.

"If you don't move, that will set," she said, "and you might not puncture a lung."

"What makes you think he hasn't punctured one already?" said José María, sitting down next to Augustín.

"Because God watches over fools and drunks. And because he wouldn't have made it this far if he'd punctured a lung." She sat down across the table from them both. "Well, then," her tone softened, "who was taken?"

Augustín hung splinted against the chair. His breathing was still ragged. "Fourteen."

"And?" Berfalia demanded.

Augustín spoke in a whisper. "My sister, Sofía."

"Shit!" said José María.

"Bastards!" said his aunt.

Augustín tried to face José María but the blanket held him tight. "You would know. How can I get a message to her?"

"Me? I know fuck all. I was under the mountain." José María carried his chair around the table so that Augustín could face him without twisting. "Where did they take them?"

"The *Central*. We think."

"Do you want me to go?" asked José María.

"No. They'd simply take you in again. That would do none of us any good."

They both looked at Berfalia.

She shook her head. "If I go, they'll follow me here."

"Then I'll go," said Augustín.

157

José María stiffened. "And lose you both? You think you'll walk in there like the prize of the century and they'll let her go?"

"Shit!" Augustín leaned into the blanket. "I can't believe it. We have a demonstration for the prisoners and they fucking take fourteen more." He lowered his head and his shoulders shook. "Oh Christ, there's so much to do!"

"So let me do something." Jose Maria leaned forward, felt his aunt's hand on his arm. She shook her head.

Augustín kept his eyes on José María. "We need money, we need supplies, we need…Oh Christ, this was Sofía's first demonstration! She's only fifteen. She didn't even know when to run. I tried to get to her." His head turned from side to side. "I think they hurt her bad. Someone grabbed me and by the time I got away, they were gone." He dropped his head down. "I could kill the bastard who grabbed me."

"Instead, you broke your rib," said Berfalia.

"So? By taking her, they might as well have taken me."

"That was exactly what they wanted." Berfalia went to the stove and felt the bean pot with the palm of her hand.

"They wouldn't know who she was," said Augustín.

José María shook his head. "Don't kid yourself. They've got spies all over. They probably knew who she was the minute she hit town."

Augustín gave him a long, steady look.

"Ah. So that's it." Jose Maria laid a finger to the side of his nose. "You're thinking I turned, that I said too much."

Augustín's face screwed into a rictus. "No. I don't." He paused. "But there is always the possibility you said more than you think. That does happen."

"You really think they broke me without me knowing?"

"I'm not saying they did. " Augustín's voice dropped to a whisper. "But anything's possible."

"That's why you don't let me do anything except inks. Inks and mimeograph machines. Is that all I'm good for?"

"Well, you do make excellent flyers." Augustín winced as he sucked in air. "Christ, what a fucking ass you are, José. You're better than good." He gasped.

"Enough," said Berfalia. "Don't talk."

But there was no stopping Augustín now. "You have any idea how ordinary your face is? You could pass for anyone you want to be."

"Not any more."

"Yes, even now. I could stare at you for two weeks and not recognize you if you didn't want me to. That and the English. You've no idea what a treasure that is for us."

José María glanced up. "And you have no idea how smart they are at what they do. Christ, they already knew much more about the movement than I do now."

"Oh? And how do you know that?"

"Don't fuck with me. I knew from the questions they asked me. And they could tell I didn't know anything because they could see it on my face."

"Yeah, they left that alone, didn't they?"

"Pretty much. I wondered about that until they let me go. I think they didn't want me to look like I'd been down there."

Augustín opened his mouth but José María cut across him.

"Look, I can't say you aren't taking a risk using me. I mean they could be watching me, although I haven't caught them at it."

"Right, and we haven't either."

"No shit? Well I sure did miss that." José María looked at Augustín wryly. "So who knows what else I've missed?"

159

"We still need you."

"Oh yes, about my English that you thought would be so useful. When did you plan to use that?"

Berfalia brought the pot of beans to the table and dropped it with a thud. "There is nothing either of you can do tonight." She reached for a spoon. "The best thing you can do, Augustín, is rest. Eat this and stay the night here." It was an order.

"No."

She lifted an eyebrow and José María remembered Maggie Peters from Pittsburgh who was driving her silver airstream trailer down to Patagonia. This was how she must have treated her football players during World War Two. The lifted eyebrow, the give, and then the push, all the way to a city championship. Augustín didn't have a chance.

"You don't eat well," she said. "Or you wouldn't have broken that rib so easily."

"There was nothing easy about it, *Doña*. Besides, it's not good to have both of us under the same roof after a day like today."

"Then eat."

"I've already eaten."

"You have, have you?" She ladled beans, rice and a sausage on to a plate and set it down in front of him. "We are not so poor that we have nothing to spare."

She sat down before him and picked up a spoon. "And you, José, go and look for Andrés. And while you're at it, think of some way to get a message to Sofía."

José María nodded and said, "Don't wait up for us." As he left the room, he heard her say, "Now eat!"

Chapter 14

She could hear herself moaning as the dream slipped away.

"Julia!"

"What?" She tried to catch the tail end of the dream, but Marshall was up on his elbow and staring down at her.

"You were crying in your sleep," he said.

Still intent on the dream, she tried to roll away from him, but a sharp pain stabbed her left shoulder and she rolled back, face up, open to his gaze again. Go away, she wanted to scream. Please let me go back before it's over.

But it was over. Her mind was a blank and she wanted to cry. She looked at him through slit eyes. His lips twitched. What had he seen while she was sleeping?

"I shouldn't eat before I go to bed," she mumbled.

"I didn't know you had." He lay back down.

There were only three minutes left before the alarm went off. She gently massaged her collarbone and left shoulder. As if there wasn't enough loss already. There were her boots in the corner, and the rumpled britches, green-slimed from horse slobber, and the battered hard hat lying upside down. She closed her eyes. She hadn't told him about her fall yesterday, the second fall this week, nor that she had finally decided to quit riding after so many years chasing a dream born of burger grease and chipped nails in her father's diner after school. To gallop across an open field, unfettered and unafraid. For all her trying, she'd never been able to pull it off. Especially the unafraid part. But then she'd never told him about the dream to begin with, so how could she start at the end?

"What?" she whispered.

"I didn't say anything."

It had taken the fading beat of the horse galloping away and a ragged child in a cut-down communion dress, peering down at her from beneath a gallon can of water, for her to acknowledge there was no romance left in the fantasy. Here it ended. The horse long gone, a serious pain in her shoulder, and a small child toting water in a rusty can staring down at her.

She opened her eyes. Marshall was lying on his side, his face very close, watching her. Oh please, not yet, not another ending.

The bed dipped. She felt his breath on her cheek. Her chest rose in a silent wail.

"I'm sorry," he whispered, and kissed her lightly on the ear.

She blinked against the tears. "I am, too."

And that was it. There was nothing more to say. The dream had vanished. His arm slid under her shoulders. She rocked back then lumbered forward, an awkward jumble, into his arms.

When it was over, she lay still. If she moved, he would roll off her, and the moment was too fragile to sustain such a parting. No words, no movement. Her shoulder finally numb. Had she told him it was hurting, he would have stopped. Caught between 'no, please' and 'let's get it over with.' And therefore silent.

His head was down beside hers, his breathing even now. She could see the sharp curve where his head met his neck, his rumpled hair.

You wanted this, she told herself. You've always wanted this. Beyond the fantasy, despite the angry silence, down to the sadness, this was what she'd always wanted: to hold and to be held. So why, now, did she feel so hollow, so alone?

She took a breath, caught it up ragged, and he slid to the side, out and away.

He sat up, his back toward her, and reached for the box of tissues. "I had lunch with Tacho yesterday."

"Oh?" She tried to make sense of it: Somoza, lunch, this awkward coupling. She wanted to say something about the President, something that would show Marshall she cared. But words were unreliable, lies unacceptable.

An ache filled her belly. She grabbed for the first thought that came to her. "I fell off the horse again yesterday. I think I've had it with riding."

Chapter 15

Marshall dropped the pencil on the conference room table and switched the telephone receiver from one ear to the other.

"That's very generous of you, Jaime." *And totally off the wall,* Marshall thought.

Jaime Salazar chuckled. "It's just a ideas."

"Not a random one, I'm guessing," said Marshall to buy time. "You've been thinking about this for a while."

"For some time now," Jaime acknowledged. "Like I said, Beal Jackson is about finished, and I knew he was too proud to accept help from an old friend. I just didn't realize he was coming to you today."

And how did you find that out? "Yes, well he'll be pleased, I'm sure."

Marshall turned and swiped at the curtain to dislodge a crumpled piece of paper clinging to the rough fabric. The cloth cast yellow light across his arm, reminding him of Yelva Inez with her golden skin, the sunlight across her belly. Damn! What in God's name was wrong with him? He sat up and swung his knees under the table.

"There's one problem, Jaime. I don't think anything like this has been done before, so I'm not sure the bank would allow it."

There was a pause, pregnant with disbelief. He could almost hear Jaime thinking, *who cares? It would be off the books. An act of mercy should trump any rules. After all, it was between good friends. Besides, this was a bank in Nicaragua, not some rule-fettered Goliath in the States.*

"How would you see us going about it, Jaime?"

"You're the banker. I know I can rely on you to find the best way. Use your judgment. But if Beal has no other options, letting him know the source can't do any harms."

Marshall frowned down at the crumpled piece of paper now on the floor. *What the hell was the man up to? "Harms" to who? Himself? The bank?* He hoped Jaime's eccentric English didn't carry any added meaning. "I thought you didn't think he would take money from you." *Oh for God's sake,* thought Marshall. *You sound like a little old lady afraid to cross the street. This is Nicaragua. Here, there's always a way.*

"That's my point," said Jaime. "He won't, from me. But he'll take it if the bank is involved. It will gives him the respectables he needs."

"I suppose you're right. Certainly no one in their right mind would turn down an offer like this."

"Men who feel trapped sometime do strange things, my friend." Jaime paused. When he spoke again, his voice was deeper. "Beal's losses they are small to anyone but himself, yet dignity means a great deal to him. As it should. This way, he would be paying the banks back, not me, and the interest is all yours."

Marshall sat up. "Excuse me?"

"The bank's, Marshall. Who do you take me for?"

Smooth, thought Marshall. *Very smooth.* The man was a hell of a lot smoother than Tacho. Same bullshit, just a little more subtle.

"Marshall, it's a good deals."

"It's a great deal, Jaime." But he couldn't help wondering what Jaime was getting out of this. He forced a chuckle into his voice. "I'm wondering why you don't just buy stock in the bank?"

"I will, when you becomes President."

"Right." They both laughed. "I need to check with our head office first."

"Is that necessary?"

"Yes. But there shouldn't be a problem. You're one of our best clients."

"Oh well, whatever you decides, Marshall. I trust you. Beal's worth helping hands."

"That's certainly true."

"How is Fidelia doing with my foods deal?" asked Jaime.

"Great. You were right. She's sharper than a tack. You know, she's got the Montoya branch just about ready to open. I've put her name in to head office for a promotion. She should make officer in a month or so."

"A woman officer. That should raise eyebrows."

"It will. I'm looking forward to it."

"Well, let me know what happens with Jackson."

"Thanks, Jaime. I'll get back to you."

He replaced the receiver in its cradle. The more he dealt with Jaime, the less he understood the man. Hardheaded businessman, cowboy pilot, pimp, and now a philanthropist? In the end, Jaime might get Beal Jackson's land without having it go to auction, but he stood to gain nothing in the short run.

Marshall looked at his watch. Jackson would be here in twenty minutes. Good, now there was something to look forward to. And he needed it after the sour taste of this morning. He'd thought his apology to Julia would clear the air, but it hadn't. Not that it had backfired exactly, but what had it changed? They still operated in two different worlds.

He'd wanted to describe his lunch with Somoza, to laugh with her and let her know that maybe she was a little right after all, that there was something of the thug there. But she'd closed him down. She knew he didn't give a rat's ass about her horseback riding.

Later, in the shower, it hit him – sex had been better with Yelva Inez. There'd been that long, slow buildup, something he'd never experienced before, not even with Silla. And then that explosive release that seemed to go on and on like something inside her was squeezing him again and again. Christ, he could still feel it now. It had never been like that with Julia.

He bent over the arm of the chair and poked at the crumpled piece of paper now under the curtain. Julia and Mattie would be hunched over their art show plans this morning. What was it Julia was in charge of? Distribution? Something. It didn't matter. He zinged the paper pellet high against the wall, raised his arm behind his head and tried to catch it on the rebound. He was looking for where it landed on the carpet when Fidelia knocked on the door.

"Mr. Jackson is here, sir."

Fidelia came in ahead of Jackson, partially obscuring his face, and giving Marshall time to brace himself.

"Come on in, Beal. Come in and take a seat, I have some good news for you." Careful to use his own left hand, he reached for Jackson's undamaged hand and kept his eyes on the ruined face. Was it his imagination or had the scars gotten worse, more swollen, more grotesque? God, how could a man live in the world and walk around with so much ruin on his face.

"Shall I bring coffee?" asked Fidelia.

"Yes, thank you."

She turned to Jackson. "Black, sir — right?"

"Good memory." The voice was undamaged, but the lips threw the pronunciation off. "Thanks," he said softly and sat down.

She left the room, leaving a strained silence behind. Jackson's right eye squinted with something suspiciously like humor.

"A fine person," he said. "She reminds me of my wife."

Marshall's skin prickled. Not now, he thought. Jackson had never mentioned his wife before, nor the daughter, nor the plane crash.

"She would have been thirty-eight, today." His voice was mournful. "She was born in Rivas, July 22, 1932."

"Rivas?" *Come on Fidelia. Get that coffee here fast, for God's sake.* He knew the story. Everyone did. They said Jackson's daughter was conscious the whole time, and screaming, and he couldn't get at her. *Christ!*

"She didn't like to fly, you know." Jackson's head moved up and down as if he were the main audience to his own story.

The door opened and Fidelia came in with the coffee on a tray.

The room was quiet as she set each mug down. "Will that be all, sir?"

"Yes, thank you."

They watched her close the door behind her. "I have a piece of good news for you, Beal."

"That's what you said. What's up?"

Marshall cleared his throat. For a proud man there was no real way to soften the impact of an obvious charity. "I just received a call from Jaime Salazar, authorizing me to share with you certain confidential information about his account with — Whoa!"

They both jumped up as coffee spilled across the table. Jackson pushed his fallen mug away and began to mop at the flood with his handkerchief, splashing it onto the file.

"Don't worry about that," said Marshall. "I'll get it." He went to the door, called Fidelia, and turned back with his own handkerchief out.

It took five minutes to clear the table, wipe the file, and settle back down. Jackson was silent during the entire operation. The hands that had pulled the bodies of wife and child from a blazing inferno lay flat on the edge of the table, the one only slightly marred, the other twisted, mottled red and white, the two smaller fingers and half the thumb gone.

"Let me explain," said Marshall, settling back into his chair. "We've been holding the mortgages on two of Jaime Salazar's coffee farms in Jinotega as collateral for a larger loan. That loan has been partly paid off and one of the farms has now been released for Jaime's unconditional use. He's requested that the bank bind it over to you as collateral for a renegotiated loan on your cotton farm." He paused. *Was that anger on Beal's face?*

"The terms are simple. The mortgage is not to be held in your name but rather as bound collateral with your land for the term of ten years, after which it will revert to Jaime's use again. His farm, that is."

Beal turned his head and stared out the window.

"The bank will place an equity fund at your disposal for your running expenses, and begin to pull in interest only after your next crop is in…that is, the next crop after the drought. It's Jaime's wish…" *Christ, you sound like a goddamned lawyer reading a will.*

He plowed on. "Jaime wants the land to be bound in this way whether or not there's a need for it. In other words, should the drought end tomorrow…"

"Did Salazar say why?"

"Why what?"

Jackson turned to face him. "Why he's doing this?"

"I don't know. I assume it's because you're old friends. In fact, he said something of the sort."

"Right."

"For Christ's sake man, what's wrong? This is a chance to save yourself and you're asking why?"

"Wouldn't you?"

"No. Yes. Of course I would. But I don't see any strings attached to this one. You would be paying us, we would hold both mortgages, and, in the event of bankruptcy, your land would revert to us, not to Jaime. It's clean."

"No, thank you. I don't want it."

"What?"

"No." For once the man's head was not bobbing.

Marshall was stunned. He almost laughed out loud. *The man's crazy. What possible reason could he have to turn this down?*

Marshall took a moment, then began softly, "Let's look at it in a cold, clear light."

"That's what I've been doing, Marshall. For years."

Something about the wording caught at Marshall. He looked at the lattice of scars holding the man's face together, the weeping eyes, the lids that never closed completely. *Would he himself turn down an offer like this? No. Of course he'd take it. But not without thinking it over very carefully. From the start there were too many blind alleys, too many deviations from the norm.* He shifted in his seat and crossed his legs again. *But the question's irrelevant because he'd never let his business he owned go bust, period. Beal had to be crazy to let his estate come to this.*

No! The man's lost everything. He's a good man. He deserves better, certainly respect. If he doesn't want to explain turning down this deal, that's his business.

"Right." Marshall pulled the file toward him, flipped it open. "So...I want to be clear. You've run through the whole nine yards. There's nothing left."

"I understand."

170

"That's good — so you understand the bank is going to have to take your house, your car, your land, your farm machinery."

"My dog?" The man was smiling.

Marshall smiled back. "No, not your dog. But you must know you won't have enough left to go back home in a row boat."

"Nicaragua is my home."

Marshall sat back. "You'd stay in this…here?"

"This is my home, Marshall."

Not go back to the States where there were rules to protect you, where there was a system that made sense? Beal couldn't see that? "I'm sorry…It is your home, but…"

"You needn't apologize," said Beal. "Hell is an acquired taste."

Annoyed at the note of martyrdom, Marshall closed the useless folder.

"How long will it take?" asked Beal.

"What? The bankruptcy?"

"Signing everything over."

"I don't know exactly. There are a few steps first." Time, even thirty days, would give the man a chance to think over the deal, to live with his decision. Jaime had set no limits.

"We could file foreclosure papers today, but why not set a thirty day cap instead — get the paper work cleared up, get an accurate estimate of the value of your entire holdings…"

"I'm sure you already know the exact value."

"Be fair. We're a bank."

"Sorry. You're right. And a reasonably humane one, at that. I appreciate that, Marshall. Believe me, I do. What else?"

"We'll set a moratorium on the interest for the month." Jackson couldn't pay it anyway. Still, someone in head office was bound to squawk. Unless Jackson would see reason and take Jaime's offer. "It will give you time to see what you need."

Jackson burst into laughter. "You're like King Canute."

"Who?"

"King Canute. The one who sat on a beach on his throne and told the tide to stop coming in."

"Yeah, well, maybe it's worth trying for some people."

"Thanks, Marshall. I'll take your thirty days. I could use the time to get my things in order."

"You do that. I'll have Fidelia start the process." He shook his head. "Stopping the tide. I like that." He had a sudden image of himself and Yelva Inez in a small boat, hoisting sail, the wind speeding them through the surf and out into open sea. "Only I'd rather use the tide than try to stop it."

"Spoken like the excellent banker that you are," said Jackson.

Chapter 16

Julia turned the hatchback onto the bypass. Fifty feet in, a woman with a two gallon water can on her head turned to shield her two children from the dust. Juanita still stared straight ahead, her lower lip caught between her teeth. She'd barely spoken since Calixto had come to tell her that her granddaughter was very sick. Julia had offered her a ride on her way to Mattie Schimmer's meeting. If the child was so sick, it was likely Juanita would have to stay with her.

They hadn't even gotten to the bypass before Julia decided she would take Juanita straight to her door instead of dropping her off at the turnoff. She was in no mood to fritter away the morning in an art show meeting anyway. And she still felt bad about her blunder this morning with Marshall. Why hadn't she had the sense to show some interest in his luncheon with the President, instead of blubbering about her fall?

She sat up straight. That's it! She'd telephone Mattie to give her the list of artists she'd found. With Ninfa and now possibly Juanita gone, she'd have to stay home herself, for everyone knew that you never left the house unoccupied because thieves could clean the place out. It was a rule Julia loathed as *gringa* hype, but one she'd never had to cite as an excuse to miss something. Well now she could and no one would lift an eyebrow.

A cloud of yellow-red dust boiled over the road ahead and she plunged into it, honked and passed through to its source, a *La Perfecta* milk truck, its bottles jiggling and clinking loud enough to be heard over the wind and the burr of the Volkswagen's engine. She swung out and passed it, no mean feat on a road as winding and rough as this, then she rolled the window down, grateful for the cleaner air.

Juanita was looking more wretched by the minute.

"Surely they'd have sent for you earlier if the child was gravely ill," said Julia. Juanita just shook her head.

The milk truck clattered up beside them and the driver blew his horn. "Eat your own dust," she muttered, but he persisted and for a stretch they bounced along side by side. The air inside the Volkswagen turned yellow. Wind whipped her hair loose and she grabbed for the tie before it couldf fly out the window.

The truck driver shook his fist at her. His horn brayed.

You win, you son of a bitch. She rolled up her window, slowed the Volkswagen, and settled back into the dustcloud. She couldn't see anything and they were coming to the turn-off. She should just stop for the dust to clear and get her bearings. She was reaching for the gearshift when she heard a noise, like a whoop, a crash and the truck skidded to a halt. She slammed on the brake, swerved and stopped just in time as something hard hit the Volkswagen's windshield. The glass turned cloudy. Milk, a great splat of it shivering off in different directions.

"Shit!" she yelled as two figures tore across the road in front of her. Kids, and they were scooping up the unbroken bottles of milk without stopping. In seconds they disappeared into the heavy undergrowth on the left.

With a crunching of gears the truck ground forward. Julia's hand shook as she turned on the windshield wipers before the milk dried. They had passed the turnoff — she'd have to back up.

Juanita reached for the door handle.

"No, Juanita, I'll take you to your daughter's house."

Without waiting for an answer, she turned on the windshield wipers and then turned the car around.

"What in heaven's name was that back there?" Julia asked .

Juanita's hand was still on the door handle. "*Unos mal educados, señora.*"

"Rude? That's putting it mildly." Julia lowered her voice. "They did it just for the hell of it?"

"They did it for the milk, *Señora* Julia." Juanita's voice got stronger. "It's the demonstration against the rise in milk prices yesterday, and they're angry."

A rise in milk prices? thought Julia. And I didn't even know it. Milk was so cheap. A hair over fourteen cents U.S.

"So they're angry enough to steal?" She glanced over but Juanita had slumped back into her silence. Julia waited her out.

"Some were arrested, down on the Avenida Roosevelt," said Juanita finally.

"Avenida Roosevelt? How far down?"

"Close to the Plaza."

"That's where the bank is. The *señor* said nothing about it."

Juanita turned her head away and looked out the window. Julia stared ahead. He couldn't say anything about it because you cut him off, she thought.

She found the turnoff and slowed down to negotiate a maze of potholes. The street was fairly wide but the ruts were big enough to swallow the Volkswagen up. Straggling shacks turned into rows of small, adobe houses in faded colors. Finally Juanita pointed to an unpainted house and they drew up before it. Two naked children, their bodies the same color as the road, ran inside as a skinny woman with wild, white hair appeared in the doorway. A gaunt, desiccated creature with children swarming around her legs.

"*Gracias, Señora.*" Juanita stepped from the car. The two women plowed through the children, touched forearms, then walked back into the house. The children streamed in behind them.

Julia stared back over her shoulder, suddenly feeling marooned and alone. It was over so quickly. Nothing had been said about how long Juanita would stay. As long as she was needed, of course.

Three houses down, a woman walked out of her door and tossed a pan of dirty water into the street. The woman stared at her a moment, then disappeared back into the house.

Julia reached for the key in the ignition. There was a soft thump on the door and she stuck her head out the window. A small, grease-stained face peered up at her.

"I nearly knocked you over, little one," she said.

The child plumped down in the dirt and smiled up at her.

"*Permisito.* Excuse me, may I open the door?"

He patted the door.

"Okay. I'll go out this way." She crawled over the gear shift, climbed out the passenger side, and went around to squat beside him. He held up his hands and she took him into her arms.

He was warm and smooth, covered with a film of dust from his hair to his toes. His nose was running and he nuzzled it into her hair. She rose and bent her head. For all the dirt, he smelled surprisingly sweet. How light he was! And how long it had been since she'd held a child as small as this. Come to think of it, she'd never held the naked body of a little boy. She leaned back against the warm metal of the car and stared down in wonder at the bulging belly and the dusty little worm peeking out beneath it. "You're a boy," she said softly.

"Yes. That he is," said a voice in English.

She caught her breath. She didn't have to look up to know who it was. "My maid's daughter is ill," she said hurriedly, before he even asked. "Her granddaughter, I mean."

"That was your maid?" José María frowned and nodded toward the house behind them.

"Yes. So?"

He looked back at her, smiled, and spread his hands wide. "No, I didn't think you'd followed me here."

She laughed and caught it up on a little snort. "Of course you did."

He grinned and shrugged and her face went hot again, because of course she had, she'd followed him here straight out of her dream this morning. A bubble of laughter rose inside her. Dear God, it was him she'd been dreaming about when Marshall woke her up. She suddenly felt lighter than she had in months.

"Wait." His hand came up toward her face, the tips of his fingers touched under her jaw and his thumb pressed gently from the corner of her mouth downward. He held his thumb up.

"Jam," she said.

"Jam?"

"Jam with paprika. My daughter — she gave me a big Hollywood smooch this morning after breakfast."

"Of course." He nodded slowly. "Jam with paprika. Of course." He kept his eyes on his thumb, but his face went still. Then he came out of it with a twist of shoulders and torso, as if he were a dog shaking rain off his back. He straightened and put his hands behind his back.

Just like a policeman, she thought, getting ready to walk around your car, all the while figuring out how big a bribe he could get from you.

"Oh crumb!" She held the child away from her as he peed. The face had gone loose with pleasure. "You're right." Jose'Maria's face puckered up with suppressed laughter. "He is indeed a boy."

He could hardly believe it. Migdalia's mother was the *gringa's* maid?

Juana practically supported the entire family. It was either too good to be true or the worst thing that could happen. The sharp taste of disappointment dried his mouth; it was much too neat.

They'd given Migdalia two days to find out what she could about Sofía; any longer, she could come to grief herself. Maybe had already. They were running out of time, and who should show up? The golden trumpet flower with the gray eyes, a soft flush on her skin. Only a faint, yellowish stain remained of the bruise on her cheek. He held up the white ribbon and his hand shook. "This belongs to you?"

"Oh. I took it off in the car. It must have fallen when I got out." She started to swing her hair back over her shoulder but the child held it tight. She winced and José María found himself wanting to pry the small fist open and smooth back the hair. He wanted to stand behind her, gather up the mass of hair and then tie it with the ribbon. He wanted to tell her she smelled of strawberry jam. He wanted to blurt out, please, we need you. Yet he didn't know her — how could he?

"Strawberry jam?" he asked.

"That's right." She hitched the child up in her arms, then bent forward and to the side. "Could you?"

He closed his fingers over the ribbon, and he was prying the small fingers open after all, pulling the hair from them, thick hair, like golden honey touched here and there with fire.

"There." He stepped back. He had to get rid of her, before he did something he'd regret.

"Thank you." She smiled. "How are you?"

"Better, thank you. Much better."

"*Señora?*" Juana stood in the doorway of the house. She looked stunned. He could see Migdalia's news had hit her hard.

"*Sí?*" Julia walked around the car toward the woman. "*Que pasa?* What's happening, Juanita?"

He started forward, then stopped, not sure how to begin.

"I must stay here for a day or so, *señora.*"

"Of course. As long as you need. How is the child?"

Juanita's chin rose, she turned her face away. Not used to lying, José María thought.

Julia reached out and touched her shoulder. "She's not...."

Juanita shook her head. Hortensia appeared beside her and José María breathed a sigh of relief. He stepped back, away from the small huddle.

"*No doña,*" said Hortensia. "The child isn't dead. She's quite well. It's the child's mother."

He stiffened. Juanita looked appalled.

"Migdalia?" said Julia.

"Yes. She's in jail and someone needs to get her out." She stared hard at Julia.

Juanita let out a wail, turned and disappeared into the house. Julia pushed past Hortensia and followed her.

"What the hell!" whispered José María.

Hortensia raised her hand to silence him. Her thumb rubbed over her fingertips. More money? He'd already given her what the fine would be. Plus the bribe.

"Don't involve her," he whispered.

"Why not?"

"How do you know she can be trusted?"

Hortensia looked at him as if he were three years old. "Of course I trust her. You do."

"I don't."

"Don't be an asshole. Besides, she doesn't need to know everything." She held up a warning finger.

Julia came out of the house first. She gave José María a small smile and she spoke in Spanish. "Can you explain what it is I have to do there?"

"Go home," he said. "Let Migdalia's mother handle it." Julia shook her head and turned to Hortensia.

"Take Juanita to the central jail and ask for Migdalia's release," said Hortensia.

"It's as simple as that?"

"I didn't say it was simple. But for a North American *señora* and Migdalia's mother, it might work. We have the money for the fine," Hortensia fumbled in her blouse, "though they may ask for more. We can't be sure. *Una mordida?*" She looked up at Julia to see if she understood the word.

Julia nodded. A bribe. She glanced at José María, frowned, then her eyebrows rose and she said in English, "Something else is going on?"

"You don't know what you're getting into," he said.

"No, I don't. That's why I asked you."

When he said nothing, she shrugged. "Does this have something to do with the milk price and the demonstration?"

Fuck, but she was sharp. He could see she had caught his surprise.

"Right," she said. "But you won't tell me. So what you're saying is *Yanqui* go home and mind your own business."

180

"Please, *doña*, said Hortensia, offering her the bundle of bills they had so carefully gathered.

Juanita had come to the door and was watching the exchange. José María looked for signs of suspicion in her face, but it looked empty and broken. Maybe beyond repair, but there was no mistrust. If anything, she looked oddly comforted when Julia reached for her elbow and guided her to the car.

"Wait!"

Julia turned back. He gave a small inward sigh. All the cops would see was a beautiful *gringa* who could stare them down. The most important thing was to get Migdalia out with whatever information she had. And if Migdalia came up dry, than maybe — he glanced quickly at Hortensia, then back at Julia — could they trust her enough to ask for Sofía? It might work, as long as she didn't think too much and fuck it up.

"I'll come with you as far as the *Avenida* Roosevelt," he said.

Julia had started the car and was halfway through a broken U- turn when it hit her. What in God's name was she doing? Fear swelled from her chest into her armpits and she found herself wrestling with the small car's steering wheel. When she finally had the car heading back down the road, she glanced in the rear view mirror and saw exactly what she expected to see, the top of Juanita's head. No help there.

Beside her, José María was leaning back against the passenger door, watching her as he had that first day, his eyes narrowed, assessing, only this time there was something different, something stiff, almost as if he were angry.

And what do you have to be angry about, she wanted to say. "So," she stretched out the English vowel until she had a grip on herself.

"There is a risk, you're thinking, seeing as how I'm a foreigner and might get it all wrong."

He had the grace to smile, though she could see his mind was elsewhere.

"What am I to expect when I get there?" she asked.

"I don't know for sure. I've never actually been there."

She turned her head fast and he shook his head. "Not there," he said softly.

She nodded. "Then why do I get the feeling you've got something else on your mind?"

"Because I do." He levered himself around, leaned forward and addressed the dashboard. "Since you're so determined to go, I would like you to inquire about someone else in the jail."

"What?" She shifted down abruptly.

"Her name is Sofía."

"Sofía? Who is Sofía?"

When he didn't answer, she nodded. "You don't know if you can trust me enough for that."

He glanced up. Some of the tightness around his eyes eased. "Point taken. Her name is Sofía Alvarado. Take care of your maid's daughter first, but then ask to see Sofía, and if they will not let you see her, ask what her condition is. Say you understand she was injured when she was arrested."

"She was injured? What was she arrested for?"

"She was taken yesterday in a demonstration and they roughed her up."

"I knew it!" Julia smacked her balled fist against the steering wheel. "The milk prices. So that was what Migdalia was arrested for?"

"No, she was arrested for something else entirely. Something far more ordinary." His words were delivered slowly and his voice was a monotone.

She slowed to let a jeep turn into the back entrance of the Presidential Palace. "You sound as if you've had this rehearsed for days." The jeep bounced up over the rough curb-cut and shot up the concrete ramp.

"What? No. Actually, only for the last thirty seconds. Before that I didn't trust you. Remember?"

"What changed your mind?"

"You."

Talking with him was like looking into one of those mirrored balls with countless facets. "So what else am I supposed to do?"

But he was checking the side mirror, looking at something back at the Presidential Palace.

"Look, if I'm going to do this, I should know what I'm getting into. I feel like I've been given my marching orders and I have no idea what I'm walking into."

He smiled, "I hope I may never have to give you marching orders, *doña* Julia."

"So, I'm right."

"I'm sorry." He was serious again. "We are very worried."

"We?"

"If you do get to see Sofía, tell her that many people are praying for her."

"That's it?"

"It's a lot when you're in such a place. Besides, it's the best I can think of."

"And what if they ask me why I'm interested?"

"You're a friend."

"A friend! I don't know anything about her."

"Right. Okay – she's not quite sixteen, short, slender, dark hair…"

"Yes, but who is she? Presumably I'm supposed to know what she does. Is she a student?"

When she looked over again, his face had closed down. "Okay then, she's the daughter of my gardener."

"No. You mention anyone else, they'll want to know all about that person."

"And what will they want to know about me? My bra-size?"

He looked genuinely shocked.

"Sorry. Flight of fancy. I get it. I'm supposed to be immune, because I'm a *gringa*, right? And ignorance is my bliss… And you can wipe that shit-eating grin off your face."

"Maybe you interviewed her for a scholarship. No. Don't give them that. Don't give them anything. You're her friend, that's all they need to know. You are a woman of substance," he said in English. "You outrank them any day."

"And what if they foist someone else off on me? How do I know her when I see her?"

"She's got a little double scar on her chin, like two crosses. And she wears a crucifix her brother made for her, out of horn or wood or something. It's yellow, with a leather thong." He closed his eyes. "Just give them that lovely, cold eyeball of yours, *doña*." He started to laugh. "Act like you're entitled to know because you are who you are."

"Thanks."

"No. Seriously, if you act as if that's exactly what you expect, they'll be too busy reacting to that to ask any questions. He smiled. "You did it the other day. On the highway. Trust your instincts."

"My instincts? Afterwards you said what I did was stupid."

"But it worked."

He was right; she had trusted her instincts. But they came more from the sensation of those scars on his back than anything else. "What if what worked the other day is stupid today?"

"Stay strong. Men here make allowances for the stupidity of *gringas.*"

"Especcialy women *gringas.* Lovely. You really know your way to a woman's heart."

He got out two blocks east of the jail, came around the front of the car and squatted down on the curb so that his head was on a level with the window. "Do you have that clever knife with you?" he asked.

"Yes. I always carry it."

"Would you please give it to me? They'll only confiscate it at the door."

"Confiscate?"

"Don't worry. You're a *gringa.* They'll not be rough with you." He looked weary. "Remember, you are someone to reckon with."

"Look, I don't need you to patronize me. Not now."

"I'm sorry. You're worried. So am I." He pushed the knife into his trouser pocket. "Take the same route back. I'll catch up with you on the way."

Her voice rose. "I was supposed to be somewhere else this morning."

"So were we all."

Her foot hit the accelerator and the car jumped forward. In the mirror, she could see him squatting, one hand on the ground, his face turned toward her.

Chapter 17

The lobby of the jail was huge and freshly painted. It was lit by a pattern of openings incised into the wall above the entrance. Julia tried to ignore the sudden hush, the staring eyes, and the sick lump in her stomach as she and Juanita walked to the high counter at the back of the room.

"Excuse me, we've come to inquire about Migdalia Hernandez, who is being held here." Her voice rang out in the dense silence.

The officer behind the counter took several moments to realize she'd spoken in Spanish. Even as his eyes travelled from her face to her breasts and back again, his expression remained official and blank. She repeated her request again, very slowly. Two soldiers leaned over the counter for a better look.

"What is she in for?" said the officer.

She glanced down at Juanita. "We're not sure," she said, turning back to the officer.

"Then how do you know she's here?"

"We got a message this morning." That was true enough.

"Who sent you this message?"

It wasn't time yet for the eyeball, but she was sorely tempted. "I'm sure she's here, officer. Would you please check?"

"One moment, *señora*." He glared at the two soldiers eyeballing her tits and started toward a door at the back of the room, then turned back. "And your name is…?"

She hesitated. Marshall would be furious. She thought of the scars on José María's back. "Bennett. Julia Bennett." The officer nodded and disappeared.

She turned to face the room. Scores of people sat on benches that lined the walls. All stared at their feet or out the door. No one spoke. Fear tightened her chest and she turned to Juanita. But Juanita simply looked dazed.

"*Pastelitos,*"called a woman from the entrance. Someone called back and the woman lifted the broad, shallow basket from her head and settled the rim against her belly, selected a pastry, and wrapped it one-handed in a piece of torn paper.

"How much?" asked Julia.

"Fourteen cents," said the woman. "They're pineapple."

Julia bought two and passed one to Juanita, who held it loosely in her hand.

"*Doña?*" The officer lifted a section of the countertop. "Come this way, please." He held his hand up to stop Juanita. "Not you."

"Excuse me," said Julia. "Why not?"

"The Captain wishes it so." He smiled politely.

"I'm afraid that's not…" Juanita's arm brushed against hers. Ah, a sign of life. "Okay." Julia passed through the counter alone, gritting her teeth.

The corridor was long and poorly lit; the smell of disinfectant grew stronger as they walked along, the officer leading, Julia two steps behind. They turned a corner. One thing at a time, she told herself. First Migdalia for her ordinary crime, and then Sofía for the demonstration where she was injured. That's all they knew. How was she ever going to handle that? *Hello, I'm a friend of Sofía Alvarado, don't ask any questions, you oaf, just take my word for it because I'm a gringa.*

If only she'd left the house fifteen minutes earlier, she'd be on Mattie Schimmer's veranda now, eating coffee cake and planning an art show. And even as she thought it, she knew she was right where she should be.

Around a second turn in the corridor, the officer opened a door and stood aside for her to pass. Again she thought of those scars on José María's back, and of the monsters who would do that, and she stepped over the threshold on a surge of anger.

The room was empty. She hesitated. The green shag rug on the floor smelled of mold despite an air conditioner going full blast. Directly ahead, a bland painting of the Virgin in grays and browns simpered at her. To her right, a louvered glass window shimmered with the greens of a palm tree outside the glass. A large desk occupied the rest of that wall. Behind the desk was a high-backed, leather chair; in front of the desk, a wooden ladder-back chair awaited penitents.

She turned and reached for the door.

"There now." A short, thin man in an immaculate uniform stepped from behind a partition that she hadn't noticed, so well did it blend in with the surrounding walls. Reasonably good-looking, he had dark, straight hair, tired eyes and a firm handshake.

"*Capitán Baldizón* at your service." He gestured to the wooden chair, sat in the leather one behind the desk and held out a pack of cigarettes. She shook her head. He lit one himself, blew a long puff of smoke toward the window and sat back. "You have come to inquire about someone?" He glanced at a sheet of paper on the desk. "Migdalia Hernandez?"

"Yes."

"Well now." A wry smile curled up one corner of his mouth. "How interesting." He pressed the nearly unsmoked cigarette out in a glass ashtray.

"I don't suppose Migdalia thinks so."

His eyes narrowed, then widened. "You're probably right." He drew the word out until it contradicted itself, "...*probablemente. Y usted?*"

"Me?"

"You don't think it's interesting? Ah, I see you don't. You are indignant. And with good reason. One must consider the circumstances." He smiled as though he fully expected her to smile back and then frowned when she didn't. "What exactly is your relationship with Migdalia Hernandez."

"She is my maid's daughter."

He sat back and tapped the tips of his fingers together. "I see. Well, that too is interesting."

The air conditioner's condenser clicked off. From somewhere nearby came the watery thump of clothes being washed on a stone sink.

"Do you know what she was arrested for, *doña?*"

"Not entirely. Something ordinary, I suppose." It sounded so lame but that's what José María had said.

He made a little gasping sound. "Ordinary! Something ordinary?" For a second he looked like he was going to laugh, but he stopped himself. "Well then." He glanced down. "You may or may not know why the subject was brought in." The words lagged, as if he'd lost his place in the script and was looking for it.

"I don't know what she was arrested for if that's what you mean."

"Yes. Well, you see, it's quite serious, in view of what appears to be..." The top paper was lifted up but not proffered. "...the incorrigibility of the subject."

"Incorrigibility?"

He stood and went to the window. "Nicaragua is, after all, a moral nation, as is your own country. In cases such as these, it has been found that the stiffer the penalties, the less danger of repetition."

"Repetition of what? What are you talking about?"

He faced her. "Prostitution, *Señora* Bennett." He cocked his head to one side and almost smiled.

She froze. It was a slap in the face. Play it by ear, José María had said, knowing all the while what he was setting her up for.

"You didn't know that, did you?"

"No, I did not!"

He dropped the surprise and lifted one eyebrow.

Her cheeks turned hot. What did he think, that she was Migdalia's Madam? She opened her mouth to ask him but he held his hand up.

"I can see that you are as shocked as I am. This must be very difficult for you. Please, may I offer you some coffee?"

"No thank you. I just want to get Migdalia and go home."

He sighed. "I wish it were that simple. You see, there is a fine, a fairly substantial one in view of the subject's..."

"Incorrigibility. I know. How much?"

He looked pained. She was being indelicate. Such negotiations had rules.

"I don't set the fines, *señora*. The cashier can tell us." He picked up the phone, dialed two digits, waited, then spoke quietly into the mouthpiece, listened and hung up. "That will be one thousand *córdoba's, Señora* Bennett."

One thousand *córdobas*! Over three month's pay for Juanita. There was no way she could ever pay it back. Julia yanked her purse open and grabbed out her checkbook.

The officer held up his hand again. "No, *señora*. With your permission, I would like to suggest that you go to your husband's bank and bring the money in cash."

She stiffened. How did he know her husband was a banker?

"It is just that we do not handle checks," he said smoothly. "A matter of policy. I'm sure you understand."

Oh yes, she understood all right. She stepped out into the sun and crossed over to the other side of the street to gain the narrow strip of shade next to the buildings. A thousand *córdobas* in cash was a hell of a bribe for a maid to pay, or a prostitute, or whatever the hell Migdalia was. But all she could do was bite her tongue, because after this she had to ask the man about Sofía Alvarado, who was arrested and injured at a demonstration about the price of milk. Which was, she was sure, where the real shit would begin.

She turned north along Roosevelt, keeping close to the buildings. Now what was she going to do? A thousand *córdobas* was not a routine withdrawal. And she wouldn't get away with just going to the tellers' cages either. She'd be spotted by the formidable Fidelia and whisked into the conference room, with coffee and questions about the children while some lesser being scurried off to do her business. Then there would be questions from Marshall. She stopped for a moment. And there was no way in hell she was going to expose Juanita to more of his criticism. He could have his presidential lunch. He couldn't have Juanita.

In the end, he made no comment. He was on a call to Head Office. But as she stepped off the platform, having dispatched Fidelia with the story of Caley's jam and paprika on scrambled eggs, he put his hand over the mouthpiece and said, "I thought you were going to the art show meeting."

"I am. Later."

191

"The Schimmers want us to go out to the lake on Sunday." His lips tightened at one corner.

"You don't want to go?" she asked.

"Not especially."

"That's fine with me."

He nodded and went back to his call.

In less than half an hour she was back in the shaggy green office, handing over the money. She wished she had the courage to ask for a receipt. Instead she said, "Also, I would like to inquire about a woman named Sofía Alvarado."

"Sofía Alvarado?" His hands floated above the desk then landed, palm down, side by side. The precision and grace of the gesture spoke volumes. He must know about Sofía Alvarado.

"Yes."

Several seconds went by. "First it is Migdalia Hernandez who is your maid's daughter and a prostitute: now it is Sofía Alvarado who is…? What, *señora*, is your relationship with her?"

"I am a friend." She swallowed to clear her throat.

"A friend? No, I do not think so."

"I beg your pardon?"

"I am very sorry, *señora*, but I do not think Sofía Alvarado is your friend."

Oh shit! she thought. *God, bloody, dammit.* "She was arrested in a demonstration yesterday, and I understand she was injured. I want to know how, and where she is."

He smiled. "Ah, I see. She is a friend of your husband's."

"No! Why do you say that?"

"Was she not arrested in front of your husband's bank?"

Her head jerked up as if he he'd punched her. "I know nothing of that. I simply want to see her."

192

"See her?"

"Yes," she hissed.

He rose and she braced herself. "Please excuse me, *Señora* Bennett." He bowed and left the office.

She grabbed her purse, started for the door, turned instead and went to the window. What had she gotten herself into? This wasn't her problem.

Her shoulder throbbed where she'd fallen from the horse. She rubbed it, stretched her neck, laid her forehead against the windowpane.

How broken Juanita had looked when she came back out of Hortensia's house. Now it made sense. Her daughter was in jail for prostitution, a horror in itself. Given those scars on José María's back, who knew what could happen to Migdalia in a Nicaraguan jail? And it couldn't have made Juanita feel any better that they'd recruited her employer to get her daughter out of jail. Shame would be added to fear and heartbreak.

How much did a prostitute make each time she turned a trick? How much did Migdalia earn a month? Probably more than her mother. Juanita was paid 250 *córdobas* a month, almost thirty-six dollars, something Julia kept to herself. The Nicaraguans only paid one hundred *cords* a month and the *gringas* paid a hundred twenty to a hundred fifty.

No wonder there was a demonstration. She pressed her finger against the dusty windowpane and slowly wrote down the number 250 followed by the number 100. However you figured it, if milk went up even three cents a quart, it would add up to a sizeable chunk of money each month. Especially if you had small children.

The window's metal grill-work, all fancy curlicues, had been painted a glossy black, yet they were still bars, and beyond them, beyond the palm tree was a short stretch of concrete, another wall, behind which the invisible scrubber thumped away at her stone sink. To her right, another wing joined this one, forming a sharp angle against the window.

A small click sounded, metallic and precise like a latch shutting. She spun around. The room was empty.

She took a step toward the door, and then stepped back to where she could see behind the partition. It was a narrow alcove with some filing cabinets along the inner wall. Beyond them, there was a door at the far end, with a dark peephole a little below her line of sight. She walked toward it, her hand up, finger out. Suddenly, bright white light shone through the hole. Whoever it was, was gone. Damn, how she would have liked to poke the little turd in the eye.

As she turned, she saw another peephole on the wall to her right. Again just below her line of sight. But a convenient height for Captain Baldizón. It was set at an odd angle and, when she bent to look, she saw that it took in almost the entire office. And the area it didn't cover, the window she had been standing at a few moments before, the peephole on the inner door did.

She leaned out around the partition. The simpering Virgin hung on the office side of the partition. And there she found the lens of the peephole buried in the dark coloring of the robe near the Virgin's feet. So the little Captain had watched her come into the office without bending his neck. She felt a shiver race up her spine. She felt naked, just like she'd felt when Marshall had watched her this morning while she'd been dreaming.

Someplace, if not here, somewhere in this country, someone like the Captain had tortured José María. That same person, or another, could be tearing into Sofía Alvarado's back right now. Julia crossed her fists over her chest. It was just as José María had said, they would never hurt the *Gringa.* But they'd have no compunction about hurting a child. She wanted to scream.

Her hands dropped to her side. She owed Sofía something more than hysterics. She walked back to the window to stand with her back to it. She was entitled to this information, and the child was entitled. Entitled to have questions asked, entitled –– a cry rose up inside her and she clamped her arms around her belly again. I'm never going to ride a horse again, she thought. Nothing would ever be that simple again.

Without warning, the door to the corridor opened and the Captain entered. His face was flushed.

"What's happened?" she said before she could stop herself.

He shook his head and pushed the door closed behind him. There was a pause. "It is with real regret, *señora*..." He stuttered to a stop. His gaze was on her hands and stayed there as he came toward her. When he was a few feet away from her, he halted. "...that I must tell you –Sofía Alvarado is dead. She died this morning." He looked up at last, his eyes were moist; a tic under one pumped the soft flesh up over the iris. "Of natural causes."

"My God." Julia leaned against the windowsill for support. "How? She was only sixteen!"

"Sixteen. Yes." He turned to his desk, and she watched him stiffen into a military posture. "We're not at liberty to say more, *señora*. The next of kin must still be notified. Please take a seat."

As she let go of the sill behind her, something caught her eye in the alcove to her right. The peephole in the door was dark again. They were watching.

"*Señora* Bennett?" The Captain was standing with his right arm outstretched, pointing at the ladder-back chair.

She felt the heat rise up into her face. She could walk right up to

195

that door and hammer on it. Or she could go and punch the little fuck holding his arm out.

But this wasn't about her.

She took a deep breath and made her way slowly to the chair.

Once she was seated, he sat down. "We are trying to reach her family and perhaps you can help us there. I'm told she has a brother. Do you know where he is?"

"A brother? She never told me she had –– brother?" she finished lamely. "I had no idea."

"I see." He leaned forward and rested his fingertips on the blotter. "You are in fact just a friend."

"An aquaintance." Something crackled and she saw that she had crushed her purse to her chest. She lowered her arms. "I did not know her family."

"How strange," he said. "We are –– "

She cut across him. "How could I?"

"We are above all — "

She raised her voice. "How could I? She came from somewhere else, didn't she?"

He pounced. "And where would that be, *señora?*"

"She never said. What did she die of?" Pounce, counter-pounce.

"That we don't know. There will be an investigation." He laced his fingers together and pursed his lips; his fluster was gone, and with it, any indication of regret or compassion. "As I was saying, had you told me, *señora,* that you were planning to give Sofía Alvarado a scholarship to study in the United States, then...?" The unfinished sentence hung in the air.

"It appears you know much more about me than you are willing to tell me about, Captain." She stopped herself. He had not moved a muscle. He was waiting for her to make a mistake. If they knew about the scholarship program, they might know about her picking up José María after the interview with María Antonia. Were they after him and not Sofía's brother?

"I don't give scholarships," she said stiffly. "I interview people and I have never interviewed Sofía." Julia's lips tightened. Even if these bastards had never followed her before, they were likely to start now.

"Well then, in that case," he said at last, "I would not have such difficulty understanding how it is that you do not know her family. But, like the North Americans say, 'Some of my best friends...'" His English came up awkward, ugly in sound and intent.

She pushed up from the chair. "I think that's enough." Her voice sounded like a watery roaring in her ears, though she knew she was almost whispering. "My friend has died. You wish me to help you find some relative of hers. I can't help you. But I can help my maid's daughter. So, if you will excuse me..."

"Certainly, *señora*." He stood up, walked to the door and opened it for her. "*Ha sido un placer,*" he said and repeated himself in English, "it has been a pleasure." Looking very pleased with himself, he shook her hand.

"The pleasure has been mine," she simpered back in Spanish. She passed him, turned and walked back up the long corridor, her head high, her shoulders back, her buttocks tight. Look all you like you little prick, go ahead and look. She was about to turn the corner, when he called out. "Senora Bennett?"

She made herself turn slowly. "Yes?"

"We have a saying here in Nicaragua — "

She held up her hand to stop him. "Let me guess? 'You are known by the friends you keep?' Did your mother teach you that?" The look of shock on his face, that she referred to his mother in such a context,

197

was pure delight and she almost laughed out loud. "Good day, Captain."

He shook his head as if a bee had flown up his nose and now she did laugh. She had no idea what in God's name she thought she was doing, but something inside her had cracked or loosened and her legs felt weak with relief.

There was no laughter left by the time she and Juanita skirted the Campo Marcial, and turned up past the Intercontinental. Her hands were cold and slick on the steering wheel. She'd been a fool to mention the Captain's mother — his mother was the worst thing you could insult a son with. This was not a game. In the back seat Juanita held her daughter's hand. A fresh, ripe bruise swelled one of Migdalia's eyes shut and there was a scab on her swollen lip. They spoke in whispers, but Julia gathered that in order to earn the money for the child's medicine, she often worked a street too close to one of the brothels, and the Madam would turn her in to her cronies at the police station.

"*Que bruta,*" Migdalia said as if her own stupidity caused her more pain than the cops had. She spoke as though she wanted Julia to hear her. "*Ellos son salvajes.*"

"Those men are more than savages,"said Julia in Spanish. "They are evil, dangerous men." She glanced over her shoulder. "Maybe you should stay with Migdalia for a few days, Juanita."

"*Gracias, señora*"

There was very little traffic. An ambulance flew past on its way to the hospital. A white car, nearly a block behind her, seemed to be looking for an address. They passed a Popsicle man pushing his cart up the hill.

Julia wiped her hands, first one and then the other, on her skirt. Sofía was dead. She would have to tell a man who had scars like tree roots on his back, that his friend was dead, of natural causes, according to the Captain.

Half a kilometer into the bypass road, a single figure stood at the side of the road, sheltering under the high dirt shoulder. With a sigh of relief, she saw that it was José María. She took her foot off the accelerator and glanced in the rearview mirror. The white car now drove on the left of the road to avoid her dust trail. When she looked forward again, she gasped. He was gone!

A horn sounded to her left and she swerved. The white car had caught up and was passing. She glanced around wildly. José María was nowhere in sight. She jammed her foot on the gas pedal, then just as quickly released it. They had followed her. Oh Christ! No! Please, no!

Up ahead, the white car swerved to the side of the road and stopped. Both front doors opened, two men in khaki uniforms jumped out and scrambled up the high shoulder. A man in a tan suit stepped from the rear of the car.

The Volkswagen was still rolling, her foot hovering over the brake pedal. Migdalia and Juanita were two statues, facing forward.

"I'm sorry, I'm sorry, I'm sorry," she whispered. She had led the police right back to him! She yanked at the steering wheel, wanting to tear it out and jam it through the windshield.

The man in the suit held his hand up to stop her. She pressed the accelerator gently, held herself stiff, kept her eyes forward. She saw him out of the corner of her eye, at the side of the road watching as she went by, saw him in the rearview mirror, turning with her, watching until her dust tail swallowed him up.

In the rearview mirror Migdalia stared at her. "*Lo siento,*" said Julia softly. "I'm sorry. I didn't watch hard enough."

For someone who called herself a fool, Migdalia's one visible eye was exceptionally clear.

Julia spoke, the words tumbling out. "They said she was dead, Sofía Alvarado is dead."

"They said that?"

"Yes. She died this morning. They're looking for her brother to come in and identify her."

Migdalia stared out the window next to her. "Yes. Of course they would say that. And what did you say?"

"Why 'of course'? Oh shit! Nothing. I said nothing, but I led them right to him, and now who do I tell?"

"No one. You've told us. That's more than enough." Her tone was clipped, her lips tight against her teeth.

"But the brother..."

There was ice in Migdalia's eye. "Least of all the brother. Do you know him?" .

"No."

"Then it's none of your business."

There was a flutter from Juanita at the edge of the mirror.

"Thank you, *señora*, for all you've done on my behalf today," said Migdalia. "And for the fine wages you give my mother. You are certainly better than most. I would like to believe there is no malice in you."

"*Ay no! Migdalia!*" said her mother.

"Stop here!" ordered Migdalia.

Julia pulled the car to the side of the road. They were still a hundred yards away from the turnoff to San Judas.

"*Mamá?*" said Migdalia.

Juanita didn't move. Migdalia reached across her and opened the door. Her mother got out of the car. Migdalia stepped out and leaned back in. "I thank you, *señora*, but don't come back. It is too dangerous."

"I'm not afraid."

"You? Who's worried about you?"

"*Migdalia!*" Juanita snapped.

"*No mamá*. She doesn't understand. It's not you I'm concerned for, *señora*. It's us. And him." She jerked her head back over her shoulder. "And others. You can only cause trouble. So stay away. You don't belong here. And as for telling anyone, do not speak of anything that happened here."

Juanita grabbed her daughter's elbow. "*Migdalia, por díos!*"

"No Juanita, she's right." Julia stared ahead, her hands clenching the steering wheel to keep them from shaking. "Clearly, I know very little." She set the gearshift into first. "I will keep my mouth shut. I promise you." She bit her lower lip; each word was a separate little ache in her belly.

The car began to move. Juanita ran forward and called out, "I'll be back tomorrow, *señora*. I promise."

Chapter 18

José María threaded his way out of Acahualinca. He had a place to stay and work to do, good honest work. In the past three days, he had repaired Digna's decrepit mimeograph machine, collected paper and run off a flyer on home health issues. Though why that was needed in a country where women could diagnose a broken rib at fifty feet and splint it with starch and a wet sheet was beyond him.

The cathedral bells sounded noon, touching off a clamor of bells throughout the city and ending with the broken clank from the tiny chapel that served Acahualinca.

Spread out between the slaughter house to the south and the lake to the north, the *barrio* was a vast streetless place where all paths led to the city's garbage dump, a monstrous pile of refuse that oozed out into the lake, with hovels of every description roosting beneath its skirts.

Both a resource and a refuge, the dump served as central plaza and chief employer. Hot, dangerous work for gleaners and sorters, as well as the drivers of the small trucks that hauled the trash up the unstable, spiraling shelf that served as road and occasional executioner. Every day, the mountain grew and spread. Some said it was higher than most buildings in the city and, because of the laws of gravity, could go no higher. It could only spread outward, devouring it's nearest

202

children. Others talked about the tower of Babylon, and that times were bad enough for God to have another go at it.

Many families kept a stash of their most urgent necessities in the houses of friends or relatives farther away from the mountain. Digna, who herself had been forced out of her house a year ago, now kept three different families' emergency stashes. And though she was now nearly eight hundred yards away from the dump, she kept her own stash beneath her cot where she could grab it and run. This wasn't low-cost housing, Digna had told him once, it was no cost housing. And for good reason.

José María was about to cross the railroad tracks when he heard the clattering rumble of a landslide behind him. His fingers closed around the knife he'd taken from Julia. He looked back. Although more than a thousand yards away, he could hear the high-pitched screams of women and children as an avalanche of trash clattered down the mountain's sides.

In less than ten seconds it was over. A small slide with nobody hurt, it looked like. It happened at least twice a week and still the trucks kept coming, and the garbage pickers climbed through the rubble with their bags trailing behind them. How could anyone resist trash that was littered with treasures: a refrigerator that might still be made to work again, a sturdy table missing only one leg, thousands of knives, forks and spoons, gallon plastic bottles, and five-gallon metal containers. The makings of a working kitchen. Or a mimeograph machine!

Now he realized how wrong he'd been to think there was nothing he could do. There was enough material here to generate a million flyers: TB, polio, dysentery, typhus, alcoholism, influenza, babies dying of parasites, hunger, accidents. There were hundreds of ways to die right here in these few acres. Just about the only good thing here was that neither the police nor the army came into the *barrio* willingly. He felt safer here than he'd felt since he'd been released from that dark hole beneath Tiscapa.

He crossed over the railroad tracks near the slaughterhouse. Here there were remnants of real streets, some once paved, and tall poles that carried electricity. *Marengues* and *boleros* blared from tinny radios up and down the street. He could almost dance to them, but he still tired easily. The scars on his back were growing smooth and hard, though they were still sensitive; that had more to do with haunting than healing.

It still surprised him that he'd gotten away the day Julia brought the guard along behind her. He'd not run that fast since the days of Miguel's beatings. How could she let them follow her like that? Was it stupidity, ignorance, Yankee arrogance?

Now the police were trying to get Augustín to come in by saying Sofía was dead. And Julia had bought it. What an idiot he'd been to involve her. He shook his head. And yet, here he was, carrying the knife with him whenever he left the house, clutching it when something bad happened as though it could protect him.

The sidewalk had lost its curb and José María stepped out into the street. A car chugged along behind him, its mounted speaker blaring, "Yes, for the incredible price of twenty *córdobas*. Twenty *córdobas*, a mere pittance, a molecule, an atom…"

He grinned. The day was worthy of hyperbole. He was free and he had work to do. Molecules and atoms were the work of God. Acahualinca, ancient and sorrowing, was an altar to survival. He was glad he'd been sent here, where he could see more clearly just why the work was so important.

"Onions from Sébaco, one *córdoba*," called an onion seller in front of him. The basket on her head was loaded high. She held up a bundle of sweet onions tied by their green tails, and José María leaned toward her and sniffed appreciatively.

"Break open your piggy banks," crackled the loudspeaker, closer now. "You, *señor* shoemaker, you, too, *señora,* dog-cheap, nominal, a song…"

The onion seller's wide hips swayed and she put her bare feet down much as José María did, flat and with care. He walked along behind her. The sun rocketed off the paving blocks and set up a buzz in his head. Behind him a snow-cone man tinkled his bell, the wood seller called out, and transistor radios sliced at the air in endless, sweet disharmony.

"You, Madame Onion?" The rust-spotted, faded maroon car with the megaphone was almost level with them. "Young man," the voice paused and José María resisted the impulse to step back up on the sidewalk and walk into the nearest house. His hand closed around the little knife.

"Only twenty *córdobas,* a piece of paper printed by the national treasury for the sole purpose of enhancing your life with this miracle two-burner stove that lights in an instant! Especially when the gas is connected. Extremely cheap, too."

The voice dropped a tone as the car passed them. It was a dented 1956 Olds with the chrome gone and the suspension shot to hell. "The buy of the year. Lasts a lifetime!"

"If I die tomorrow," said the onion seller, who had herself stepped up onto the curb.

José María smiled at her and she rolled her eyes and grinned back.

The loudspeaker fell silent. The Olds pulled in and parked next to a remnant of curb. The driver's head was turned forward as though he were looking in the rearview mirror. Someone else sat in the passenger seat.

José María stopped. There were two people in the car. If he stayed on the street, they would have the advantage.

He glanced over his shoulder trying to remember what was behind him. An inviting row of dilapidated houses, hopefully with patios, and walls he could climb over. A few table-top stores.

The onion seller had moved on and was even with the Olds, her hips swaying from side to side, her feet still slapping down sound-lessly at this distance, what, twenty feet away? He started to turn.

The speaker clicked on, began to crackle. "In the words of Guillermo Chackispayaree," said the voice, a low murmur and horri-bly amplified, "to beee orrr not to beee."

Shit! José María pivoted. He walked up to the driver's window.

"Fuck you, man," he said. "You call this a cover?"

Mario's pockmarked, bellybutton of a face grinned up at him.

"*Moi, l'homme megaphone,*" he said in awful French. "I'm the mega-phone man," he repeated in Spanish. "The anonymous voice." He looked José María over from head to toe.

In the passenger seat beside him was a store window mannequin with silvery blond hair and a black negligee. A basket of green man-gos and a saltshaker sat on her up-tilted thighs. "You look like a piece of shit, Pepito,"

"Me?" José María straightened up and glanced up and down the street. "I'm okay. I'm on the mend." He ran his hand across the top of the car and whistled. "This is perfect!"

"Yes, you fuck-up. Wouldn't you just love to have it?"

"What would I do with a car?" Through the open window, he punched Mario's shoulder lightly. "So, bat-face, who's your friend?"

"This is Chiquita Banana. Here to serve you. Exquisitely."

It took them only a minute to transfer her loveliness into the back seat and set up the front seat for a real passenger.

"Real? Is that what you are now?" asked Mario as he got the Olds moving along the narrow street.

"I lost some things, but that's one thing I didn't lose."

"Ah." Mario nodded. "That's good to know."

"Does that mean you trust me?" The words came out before José María could stop them.

"Hey man, you do what's asked. You don't shirk. I like that."

"Well?"

"Listen. I trust you as much as I trust myself." Mario snorted. "In fact, I trust you as much as I trust anyone."

"Which means you don't trust anyone, not even yourself."

They both laughed.

"That's about it," said Mario. "I think we're all fucked one way or another, but we do the best we can, when we can." He shrugged. "Which, come to think of it, is pretty damn positive. I don't know about you, but it's way too easy to do the least we can." He thumped the steering wheel. "Hey man, what are you doing to me? All this philosophy — it rots the mind."

In answer, José María peeled the mango, cut a wedge, salted it and passed it to Mario.

"Nice knife," said Mario.

"Eat." José María jerked his head toward the traffic in front of them. "It passes the time." Ahead was a coal cart; behind them was a man with a wheelbarrow piled high with potatoes. The Olds was barely moving. On either side, foot peddlers sold threads, pins, pencils, erasers. A tray of plastic toys, a multicolored shimmer, floated by on the head of a little girl. Her slender brown arm was covered with the bleached patches of a fungus, some as big as a penny.

207

Mario hit the brakes to let a newspaper boy cut across in front of them. "You sure this trip is necessary?"

"Yes. You've never tasted sausages like these before," said José María.

"The long view at last. How reassuring." Mario eased out the clutch and the car inched forward. "How long have you been out?"

"Four weeks." In the back seat, Chiquita Banana listed into the pile of stoves. José María leaned back to straighten her.

"Leave her," said Mario. "She's tired. And I'm a jealous man."

"I'll bet." José María blew a kiss back at the huge doll with its up-bent knees and hostile surfaces framed in black. "Where did you find her?"

"Find her? God man, have you no delicacy? She came to me in the night…" Mario tried for a leer, but the mixture of rumpled muscles, twisted lips and pockmarked skin made his face look even fiercer than it was in repose.

"I see." José María passed over another piece of mango. "Who said passion has no place in the revolution?"

"I did," said Mario, his mouth full of mango.

"It's bullshit, you know."

"Bullshit?" Mario popped the last of the mango into his mouth and rubbed his hands together. "Passion and the revolution and…shit! What's he doing?"

Up ahead the coal cart tipped backward. The blackened hauler dragged a bag off the cart and lumbered into the maze of stalls.

"He's delivering," said José María. "Take it easy."

Mario rolled his eyes. "For a guy fresh out of the Big Man's Dream Rooms, you certainly are cool."

"Not so cool I didn't think you were a thug."

"In this piece of shit?" Mario buffed the bleached dashboard with

208

the palm of his hand. "They wouldn't be caught dead in a relic like this… I just hope we aren't either."

"Well, it's better than places I've known. It looks pretty good." José María gestured at the venetian blinds, open in the rear and drawn at the side windows, the green stoves, the tilting doll, her feet resting on a violent pink bathmat. It was a traveling storehouse to rival Digna's patio: clothes, sheets, bags of vitamins. "Where's it all headed?"

"To the mountain."

"You going soon?"

"Not yet." Mario rubbed his thumb and two fingers together. "We need money. Lots of it."

"Uh-huh. One of those."

"Something like that. A bank, maybe."

This was a surprise. Mario trusting him with this much information. And then he remembered that Julia's husband was a banker. Were they testing him? "Not much money in selling stoves, eh?" He jerked his thumb over his shoulder at the stoves. "You got a license to sell those?"

"Who me? I do everything within the law." He grinned, rummaged in a crevice in his seat cushion and brought out a stack of cards wrapped in a rubber band. "I made them myself."

José María removed the rubber band and thumbed through the collection of vendor permits, operators' licenses, and false IDs. A *Magnífica!* He whistled and rubbed the special card that opened doors, procured jobs, passports, licenses. You could only get one if you'd voted for Somoza. And then, of course, they had you by the balls.

"Good job!" he said. "Nice photograph."

"That's for starters. Then there's the cop down at the Chevron. He gets ten percent of all stove sales. The one the other side of this market only gets five. So I abide by the law, and the law is well served."

209

The coal man ducked under the pull bar, brought the cart to horizontal and began to move forward.

"I wonder how much that cart weighs," said José María.

"A ton." Mario looked over at him. "How bad was it?"

José María stared down at the feet of the people passing. "Passion is the revolution," he said.

"I'll buy that." Mario's tone was light and impersonal. "You've seen Digna?"

"Seen her? I'm staying…" He looked over at Mario, who shrugged. Jesus! José María dropped his head back on the seat. What a fucked up system when your friend couldn't know where you lived!

"I'm glad you're out," said Mario softly. "Fuck, you want to see passion?" He pointed to a cop who was caressing the hood of a car on the next corner. "That's my five percent friend."

"Is it?" José María sat up and squinted at the empty blue Volkswagen station wagon. Julia's car! She was here at the Boer market!

"Five percent, eh?" he murmured.

Mario nodded, "That's all he gets."

"A bargain." José María opened the door. "Given the rates a banker charges."

"Hey, where the hell are you going?" asked Mario.

"I already told you. I'm going to get some sausages for us." He gathered up the mango peel and got out. "Don't wait here for me." He leaned back in. "Or don't wait for me at all." He smiled to soften the words.

"You're not fooling me. Whose car is that blue Volkswagen?"

José María was shocked. "You don't miss a beat, do you?"

"In case you haven't noticed, José, that's what keeps us alive. And it's something you should have set in your bones by now."

José María wavered for a moment and almost got back into the car. Instead he closed the car door gently and stepped away.

"You're crazy," said Mario.

José María looked back into the car. "You're right, man. This is crazy. Look, don't wait for me. I'll be okay."

"You?" Mario thumbed back at the mannequin. "I'm worried for her. I've got plans for her. You think I'll stay around and watch you screw up?" His shoulders dropped, his mouth barely moved. "Who the hell are you fooling, José?"

"Only myself."

They stared at each other.

"I'll go down as far as the pharmacy and turn toward the lake," said Mario at last. "I'll wait for you there. I need a rest, anyhow."

"Thanks. But don't do that. Not with this load." He glanced meaningfully at the glove compartment where the forged ID cards were. "You take care, my friend."

Chapter 19

José María found her in the west building, the crafts section. He stopped in the lee of a hat seller's stall and watched Julia speak to a woman who sold clever weavings made of rags. She was examining a sample, and smiling. She seemed somehow fragile in the dark, dust-laden air, a white and honey-colored fantasy in a sea-green dress. Then, when she spoke, her hands floated and soared like seagulls.

She turned and walked out into the sunlight, shoulders back, head up, a loose, easy swing to her hips, stepping through the slime of cabbage leaves and onion skins as though she did this every day of her life, and he was pulled along like a fish in her wake, blinking, trying to make some coherent link between the words that would come out of his mouth and what the sight of her hair in the sunlight set up in his body.

He hadn't seen her at this distance before, on the move like that, unaware of being watched, unaware of him. He looked down. Of course, she wouldn't see him. He was just another Latino; and skinnier than most now.

"*Mierda!*" breathed a voice at his elbow. A dwarf with a goiter grinned up at him. "Nice to be inside that one, eh?" The little man's eyes closed; he cocked his hips once, twice and sighed. "Lottery?" he asked, holding up a sheet of tickets.

Obscene little prick. He could knock the little fuck over with one twist of the knee. The man's cheek and ear sank into the mound of the goiter as he fingered a ticket. "Your lucky number?" He winked. His eyelids were red and beaded with tiny yellow granules.

Dreams, thought José María. We're all up to our ears in dreams. "No, gracias," he said. "Not today."

"Missy, missy, can I carry your baskets," said a small boy at Julia's elbow.

"I have none." She stepped out of the crafts section and onto the street.

"Give me a *chelin*," he said, his pace slowing.

She shook her head. What a waste of time, she thought. She'd found no handicrafts worth exhibiting at the art show. The stuff at the Eastern Market was definitely better than here. But even they weren't anything special. She'd have to report in empty at the next meeting.

Up on the corner, the traffic cop who'd been fondling her car before was back again, one thumb in his belt, his other hand tapping the roof above the driver's seat. Annoyed, she cut across the street and into the food hall. The basket boy scampered along behind her.

She walked past the vegetable and fruit vendors, the fresh meat stalls, heading for the women who sold tortillas. She bought a *córdoba's* worth, pressing the hot package between her elbow and ribs as she walked past the giant pans of cooked rice and meat, past bubbling pots of stew, a thick tripe that smelled of basil and coriander. More men than women sat at the trestle tables. Metal spoons clinked against chipped enamel bowls. As she approached, a tiny silence rode with her — suspended spoons, suspended words — then the soft clink of metal on china again, and the conversations resumed after she passed.

I have a right to be here, she told herself. Her body felt awkward, and she made herself stop before an enormous woman who was frying sausages in a shallow pot filled with oil.

"Well then, your grandfather was a saint, peehole," the woman shouted toward the nearest table, startling Julia into stillness. "A fucking saint." There was a round of applause.

"*Viva!*" shouted a man in a battered yellow hardhat with a red ribbon taped to it. He lifted an eyebrow to Julia and tilted the hardhat up with his spoon handle.

Julia focused on the pile of hot sausages draining on the board beside the woman.

"And what does the lady want?" asked the woman. Julia looked up. "What?"

The woman spooned more sausages onto the pile. "The lady must want something." Her eyes were nearly covered by her round cheeks and she had a fleshy knob on the end of her nose.

"If she wants one, I'll take two more," shouted Yellow Hardhat.

Julia stiffened. "How much are they?" Her voice shook but at least they knew she could understand them.

"What'd she say?" muttered Hardhat.

"The lady wants to know how much the sausages are." The woman pulled raw sausages out of a plastic bucket and threw them in the oil. With fist on hip, her other hand probed the air with the spoon. "I'm told you have a graduated tax in *Gringolandia*, whereby the rich pay more than the poor."

"If that's so, what would you pay, *Gorda?*" called a different voice behind Julia.

The woman spooned up a sausage, then put it back into the oil. "So, while these good-for-nothings pay one *córdoba* for four sausages, the price for you will be four for one."

214

There was a burst of laughter, then a shushing. Julia was stunned and they could see it. She'd never been treated this way before in Nicaragua. When she spoke, her lips were stiff, and the words came out wobbly. *"La Buena educación no cuesta nada."*

"Que?" The woman raised an arm to quiet the table.

Julia repeated it clearly. "I said, good manners cost nothing." The silence stretched out for many long seconds.

"Is there something wrong, *señora?*" said someone just behind her.

Julia wheeled around. It was the cop who'd been fondling her car. She was reflected in his mirror sunglasses, and she knew from the motion of his head that he was moving his eyes up her body. The food hall had gone still.

"Absolutely nothing," she said. She could feel the power of the enormous woman behind her and she squared her shoulders. She turned back, saw the eyebrows lift, saw on the woman's face the same still, assessing look Migdalia had given her in the car that day.

"What spices do you put in your sausages?" Julia asked.

"Cumin," said the woman. "And garlic." She held up her cupped hand to indicate the whole garlic bulb. *"And ají, mucho ají, mucho chili."* She snapped a loose index finger against her linked thumb and middle finger to show how hot the chili pepper was.

"The small red?" asked Julia.

The cop leaned forward. *"Muy picante,"* he said. He repeated the woman's gesture. "Vedy hhhott!" He smiled and puffed out his chest.

"Yes, the small red one," said the woman.

"I learrrned eet een Forrrt Brraaag, my Eeenglish," he said. "Een *Nuevo* Carolina."

Yeah sure, she thought, *and with all that training, you're a beat cop?*

"Here, try one," said the woman. "The first is free." She held a sausage out to Julia on the end of a spoon.

"I haf also beeen eeen *el Panama*," said the cop.

Julia took a tortilla from her package and pulled the sausage from the spoon. Not since Peru had she eaten food from a street vendor; she would probably die of diarrhea.

"Eeen *el Panama*, many very hott, pregant weemans…Gracias." He accepted a sausage from the woman and a tortilla from Julia.

"It's delicious," said Julia. She could feel the tears come to her eyes.

The woman laughed. "No, keep your hands away from your eyes."

Julia wiped at her cheeks with the back of her wrist and took another bite. It was unusual for Nicaraguan cooking to be so hot.

"Many pregnant weemans all over," murmured the cop, his mouth full. "Aaaah," he sighed and tapped his belt buckle.

There was a shout out in the street. The cop half turned and made a gesture as though to make the noise go away. "Dees ees wan hell' hole," he said in a loud whisper. "Dees wan *desgraciado* contree." He waved his arm to include the entire country. "*Mucho troublis.*"

There was another shout. The cop reached out and stroked her upper arm with one finger. It took all her power not to hiss and step back. Instead she lifted her chin and stared down her nose at him. "I like Nicaragua."

Uh huh. Wrong move. He clasped his hands together, his cheeks chuckled up against his glasses and he rose to his full height. "Bravo. I go to keel dem. You wan I should keel dem?"

What in God's name…"No."

The sound of a jeep revving up brought him out of his trance, and, at another shout, he stuffed the rest of the sausage in his mouth and saluted.

"I am called," he mumbled in Spanish. "Goodbye, beautiful." He swallowed hard, then turned to the fat woman. "Treat this lady with respect, you hear!"

216

"Suck ass," muttered the woman as he marched away. She turned to Julia and they stared at each other.

"May I please have four raw sausages," said Julia. She handed the woman a twenty *córdoba* bill.

The woman put the bill in a pocket of her apron, wrapped four raw sausages in a piece of paper and handed them over. "You are wrong, *señora.*" She reached into another pocket and counted out a ten, a five and four ones. "Good manners can sometimes cost quite a lot."

Mierda! Nice to be inside that one. The words echoed in José María's head. They floated up into the blue white haze against the market roof, out over her bright green dress and trembled high above the three of them, tying them together, Julia, Berfalia, the cop, and from them to him. Something in him shivered, pulled at him, a light tug at the edge of things that he recognized from the prison. That moment each day when the air around him changed, thickened, grew charged, and he sensed far down the corridors, beyond any possible hearing, the soft footfall of his enemy. The waiting, the intimacy of that waiting, when all possibility began and could end in the next second. *Nice to be inside that one.*

"Do you intend to hatch that cabbage?" said a woman's voice behind him. José María jumped off the half open bag of cabbages.

The woman pointed to the top cabbage. "A little extra flavoring for the soup?" she asked.

He put his hand over his ribs. "It's my liver," he said. "I have a weak liver."

"Go on! That's a new kind of treatment. You hear that?" she called across to another woman who sold fruit. "He's got a weak liver, so he sits on cabbages."

"Of course," the other woman called back, "a suppository. Charge him for the visit."

José María backed away from them. The weaselly cop was on his way back now, his eyes darting this way and that. The two women fell silent as he came near; the cop scooped a mango up from the fruit seller's stall and winked at José María as he passed.

"Son-of-a-whore," muttered the cabbage vendor. She glanced up at José María. "Well? You want a cabbage?"

"Thank you, no. I think I'm cured."

"It's funny how shit cures," she said.

By the time he got away from them and worked his way around to get a clear look at Julia, she had picked up her package and Berfalia was actually smiling. The smoke from the stoves curled up through shafts of light from the holes in the roof. Berfalia's white apron glowed, Julia's face shone pale, her hand held the package close to her chest.

His knees felt weak. This was the woman who led the cops to him, he told himself. She was on the side of death. Death and all the white moneymen in their banks, the predators feeding on sick babies.

He told himself to go, to leave her, but his feet didn't move. If she were sick, she'd sure as hell have a hospital bed. She'd have a whole goddamned hospital. Her kids were probably vaccinated out of their perfect little skins and could read and write before they were born. They probably came out screaming "It's mine!" before they even knew how to gobble air.

She came toward him, her gaze focused on something over his shoulder. He held himself rigid. If he didn't move, she wouldn't see him. He was not so helpless this time; he was not in prison, nor so fresh out of it. The moment held nothing, no possibility. She had no part in his life. His mind was made up, his body was loose with the relief of making his decision, loose and vulnerable, and so his legs carried him forward into her path.

She shifted her eyes and saw him. Her mouth opened. She started to speak. But he stepped aside to let her pass; and her glance fell away as though the peppers in the stall beside him had caught her eye. But not before he had seen her face open in astonishment and then...pleasure?

The breath left him and he nearly stopped. She reached out with one finger and touched a pepper, delicately, then moved past, toward the open street. Slender, green and gold. Out into the sunlight, she broke into shimmering fragments of colored light.

When he turned back, his aunt was watching him.

Chapter 20

"I thought I'd find you here." Marshall slipped into the seat across from Lindstrom. "Do you mind?"

"Of course not. What's up?" The big Swede raised an arm to signal the waiter.

The table was partially shielded from the huge lobby by a potted palm tree. Lindstrom's chicken salad sat half eaten before him. He looked unhappy. "The meeting bothered you, too?" he asked.

"*Café negro*," Marshall told the waiter. He set his hands on the table. "Right. I don't understand what's going on here."

Lindstrom's smile was tight, difficult to read. "What? Golf clubs and cheap electricity? It's free trade, Bennett. Isn't that what's going on?"

"I mean this latest thing. Where's all that money going in the end? And why through us?"

"You don't like the way Tacho does business?"

"It's not that." Damn. This was a mistake coming here. Something in Lindstrom's eyes wasn't right. Not unfriendliness, but a kind of cold calculation. He'd forgotten how remote the guy could be.

Lindstrom was watching the waiter pour the coffee. Beyond the palm tree, a German couple with a baby were arguing about something.

The waiter offered Marshall a menu. He took it and put it down on the table. It didn't much matter what they ate, the food at the Grand Hotel wasn't great. It was the Bogart Casablanca movie atmosphere that drew people, the combination of huge courtyard as hotel lobby, the potted palms, ceiling fans two stories up, sunlight pouring down through an opening onto the miniscule swimming pool set within a three foot high platform in the center, and all the rest in mysterious shadow. A bazaar of shops lined the perimeter of the lobby and cushioned the wail of a siren out on the street.

"This country's hard on a man." Lindstrom pointed to Marshall's coffee. "I can't drink that stuff any more. My digestion's shot to hell since I came here."

"How long ago was that?"

"Four years. One more than you, Bennett. Your tolerance is still high."

Marshall took a sip of coffee. On closer inspection, the man looked like he was in pain. Shit, this wasn't going to end up as murky as Tacho's luncheon, was it? "I've always thought of you as cool," he said.

"Sure. Like a cucumber." Lindstrom used his fork to spear a cube of chicken out of the chopped celery and cucumbers. "Like I've been here forever. I know. It's easy when you don't have a wife and family, and you're blessed, or cursed, with an endless fascination with the workings of the devil."

"I don't follow."

Lindstrom offered that tight smile again. "It gives me an edge. So what's up?"

Marshall looked around, more to gain time than to follow any of the thoughts squirreling about in his head. The German woman was stomping through the Spanish words for fruit salad and French bread. Her husband supplied the gestures. A woman stepped from a gift shop and brushed past their table. Marshall waited until she was beyond earshot. "Look, I don't understand what's going on here? Do you?" He tried to keep his face from exposing how ignorant he felt.

"Not yet. Too many side deals, conflicting agendas, the stuff they don't want us to know. I wasn't being facetious though. What binds it all together is free trade, or rather, Tacho's brand of free trade. He wants profit. Lots of it. And so does everybody else around that table. And given that ultimately this country runs on an economy of scarcity, someone has to lose. Guess who?"

"The banks?"

"Hell no. We'll take in our share, and more. That's a given or we won't play, right? That's why you're here instead of back in, what is it — Ohio?"

"Good memory."

Lindstrom shrugged off the compliment. "I'm from Hartford. I didn't like insurance. Not as colorful."

"You call this colorful? The President wants to give away – " Marshall dropped his voice. " — to give away – "

"Sell."

"Okay. Sell almost a fifth of the country's territory for peanuts?"

"Five hundred million is hardly peanuts," said Lindstrom.

"It's not that much for a fifth of a country."

"It'll look like enough going through the banks."

Marshall shook his head. "On its way to where? Switzerland?"

Lindstrom held up his hand. "I'm taking it a step at a time. Tacho doesn't even have to use us. But he wants to look good Stateside, maintain his connections. He's got other irons in the fire."

"And they are...?"

"Well, you can bet they're not golf clubs. That's just a cover, probably for our benefit." Lindstrom shook his head. "No, it's something else. Something we don't even know about, and probably wouldn't want to know about. All we have to do is sit with this lolly for a while."

"You think it involves some sort of money laundering?" Their eyes swiveled around the room in tandem and Marshall lowered his voice again. "We're to clean up his act?"

"Not at all. But that's what he's supposed to think." Lindstrom sat back. "What we expect him to think. What he doesn't realize — " He leaned across the table and whispered, " — is that we have him by the short hairs, his greed, his insecurity, his monumental cupidity."

"And what's that supposed to mean?" Marshall said, and immediately wished he hadn't. "I mean why all this wooing? Lunch at the palace, then a high-level meeting behind closed doors."

"Aren't we all in the business of wooing, Marshall? We woo and the target buys?"

Marshall stiffened. "That's not how I see it."

"No, of course not. You don't show your hand if you're going to play the game. Look, we've just been waiting around for him to come up with a lucrative deal. And now he has."

"I see. He's wooing us."

"Yes, and Gualter is his chief romancer. The man with a gift for the turn of phrase. He's another bachelor, did you know that?"

"No. Is that relevant?"

"The shepherd of the President's affairs, a man of impeccable loyalty and concentration. Not even a family to pull his gaze away."

This was almost as bad as talking with Jaime Salazar. Marshall sighed. "I wouldn't know." He was hungry and the fruit plate looked good. "Mind if I order something?"

"Not at all." Lindstrom's heavy eyelids came down over his eyes.

"But don't dismiss people like Gualter, Marshall, or any of the people around the President. Each of them has his own fiefdom. They are each sitting at the end of their own gushing conduit. They can cut off the flow and call in their chits at any time."

Thanks for the lecture, thought Marshall. He waved the waiter over and pointed to the salad on the next table. "I'll have one of those. And a bottle of cold water, please."

The place was hot and still. The ceiling fan hardly stirred the air. Across the room, under the open skylight, someone jumped into the pool.

"So Tacho's going to let us in on his big scheme?" asked Marshall.

"Maybe, to a certain extent. We hold the bank, but he deals the cards."

"Aren't they usually one and the same?"

"Exactly. But we need him to think he's dealing the cards."

Shit. Did the man ever answer a question with a straight answer? He was even more Machiavelian than Jaime Salazar. And just as hard to understand.

"Is Salazar involved in Tacho's scheme?" Marshall asked.

"I wouldn't be surprised."

"He hasn't been around."

"That doesn't mean he's not in on it. Or he doesn't know about it. Tacho has two million hectares of the richest land in the country and Salazar has almost as much. How could he not know? Some of that land up there is his." Lindstrom leaned forward. "The person I wonder about, Marshall, is your friend, Valdés. He's come to both meetings, and he's not said a word about territory or electricity; he's only talked about golf clubs. Don't you find that strange? I mean, he's not exactly the court jester type."

"No, he's not." Marshall flashed back to that short conversation he'd had with Valdés after the second meeting. The hint of a job in Guatemala. Almost a casual hint, but none the less spoken aloud. He had a sudden flash of longing. Guatemala was full of mountains and forests. There was rain in Guatemala, and crops growing, and business humming along. Guatemala would be a wonderful place to live, full of Mayan ruins, and Indians who still wore native clothing. He would go tomorrow if he could just get Julia away from here.

The fruit salad came. Marshall laid the papaya aside and began to eat the pineapple. To his surprise Lindstrom reached across with his fork and speared a piece of papaya. Outside, another siren went by. The German couple's baby began to cry.

"You know," said Lindstrom, "if I didn't have head office hot on my ass for a deal like this, I wouldn't touch it with a ten foot pole."

"Oh?"

"Don't you smell it?"

"Smell what?"

"The odor of sulphur."

Shit! Marshall looked across at the mother who was bouncing the baby on her knee. There was something in the way the baby was crying, not cranky, just strange. High above, the ceiling fan had stopped turning.

"Damnedest thing," said Lindstrom. "Last night I went to the john, didn't turn on the light, and before I even parked myself, up from the bowl comes this iguana. Big bastard. Comes right at me. I guess it got in through the window louvers and was drinking the damned toilet water." He speared another piece of papaya. "It's a tough country."

"What'd you do?"

"I damned near killed it, trying to get it back out of the window without touching it." "

Marshall turned his head slightly, "You hear that?"

"What?"

Marshall was on his feet before the palm tree began to fall. He grabbed Lindstrom's arm, pulled him upward, then let go as the flag-stones under their feet began to shift. The baby shrieked, people were screaming. He reached around the palm, yanked the woman and the baby up and stumbled forward, shoving them ahead of him into the doorway of the gift shop.

"Stop, stay here!" he yelled, encompassing them in his arms.

The woman clung to him, shouted over his shoulder, the baby howled in his ear. The German man pushed in beside them. They were all breathing into each other's faces.

Realizing that the ground had stopped moving, Marshall dropped his arms. In the lobby, people were still running, some toward the street door, some toward the swimming pool. Clutches of people stood in doorways along the lobby's perimeter.

Far across the room, the man behind the front desk was looking at his watch, his elbow crooked at a high right angle. Marshall laughed at the outrageousness of the gesture. The German woman sighed and then she too laughed and they were all laughing.

They paid their bill quickly and left. Out on the street they listened for a moment to the high-pitched commentary around them, the nervous laughter.

Lindstrom smiled. "Thanks," he said, "I didn't hear a thing."

"When it's starting, an earthquake sounds like a train coming through a tunnel," said Marshall. They turned up toward Lindstrom's bank. "Thank God, this wasn't a big one."

"Probably somewhere else it was big. You've got good ears."

"Julia doesn't hear it either. Lots of people don't."

They said nothing more until they came to the bank.

"One more thing," said Marshall. "In this economy of scarcity, who is going to lose?"

Lindstrom looked as if he might shake Marshall's hand. And though the cool mask was back on his face, his tone was almost tentative. "Have you ever noticed, we're never so shocked by the devil himself, as we are by his servants?" He turned toward his bank's door, then turned back and said with a grin, "Neither so shocked, nor so fascinated. *"Que vaya con diós."* He waved and disappeared into the bank.

Marshall stared at the door swinging shut. Did Lindstrom ever answer a question straight? Not once. Everything was a riddle that just led to more questions and doubts. Like the sort of stuff Julia came up with. She'd probably have understood exactly what the man was saying.

It was a depressing thought. He shook his head. He couldn't believe there had been a time when he'd thought her wacky way of seeing things was fascinating.

He turned toward the bank. It had been a mistake seeking Lindstrom out. He'd have done far better if he'd just sat with the lolly in his own bank.

Chapter 21

Julia shoved the key into the ignition, then dropped her forehead onto the steering wheel. Marshall was angry again, and this time felt worse than the time he'd hit her.

He'd come home from the bank pissed off last night, and she'd been foolish enough to ask him why. When he'd remained silent and raised his open hand as though she were a fly hovering around his ear, she'd lost it and pushed her way into his study before he could close the door.

"Don't brush me off like that, Marshall. If you don't want to talk, have the courtesy to tell me so."

"Courtesy?" His lips jutted out and went back in, something he did when he was going to say something he really didn't want to say. "Courtesy?" he repeated. "Not too long ago it was honor."

"Honor?"

"Yes, when you said Clara Valdés had no honor –" He stuck his fingers up and mimed quotation marks. "– because she'd tried to sell her fur coat to some beggars."

"Yes. You're right. I did. And you know why?"

He rolled his eyes up.

"Because she thinks it's funny to treat a beggar like somebody sub-human. Where's the honor in that?"

"Christ, these are clients of the bank."

"Oh right, the bank. The bank is the arbiter. And what you're telling me is that if they're clients of the bank, anything they do or say is fine. Banks don't give a shit about honor."

"Jesus, Julia, can you hear yourself? You are so judgmental." He turned away then turned right back around. "You know, there's just no living with you," he said softly. He flung his arms out in a wide circle. "You fill up all the space with your holier then thou judgments and there's no air left to breathe."

Shaking his head, he walked into the bathroom and slammed the door.

By this morning, he was fully launched on his usual post-argument silence. Which wouldn't end, if it ended at all, until she came to him and apologized.

There's no living with you, he'd said. No living with you, no air left. It was like a curse, one that you refused to acknowledge in case it might come true.

Airless, yes. Neither of them could breathe. And this was to go on until they died? She remembered reading that a person could live three weeks without eating, three days without water, but only three minutes without air.

Can't stay here, she thought. Go! She started the car.

At the highway, she set off south toward Granada, got as far as Masaya then turned back. She'd go into Managua instead and let the crazy streets tell her when and where to turn.

Two hours and a gas station later, she parked the car just south of the railroad tracks that separated Acahualinca from the city of Managua. She got out of the car to stretch her legs. The wind was coming from the west, bringing a sickly rotting smell. Holy shit! Of course —

the garbage dump was somewhere down here. How could she have forgotten that? The heat was intense, but no worse than the stink.

"Missy, Missy...*Doña*!" A small crowd of children spilled out from between the houses and came running over the railroad tracks. At least a dozen of them.

"The footprints, the footprints, you've come to see the million year old footprints," they yelled as they surrounded her. She couldn't help but laugh. "The footprints," they shouted. "We'll take you to see them." One little girl caught her right hand and pulled. Two girls fought over her left hand and her purse fell off her shoulder and hit the ground. Julia bent over, hooked it up and slipped the strap over her head so that it was anchored across her chest. When she straightened up, she saw that there were even more children running toward her.

"Thank you for your offer, but I've not come to see the million year old footprints."

They were shocked. Not see the footprints? How could she not want to see these wondrous footprints, one of the thirty-seven wonders of the world? One boy plunged an imaginary knife into his chest and three girls followed suit.

"Well then, what have you come here to do?" asked a girl who was taller than the others.

"I've come to find a woman who works for me, Ninfa Campos."

"What's her second last name?" asked the girl.

Julia was embarrassed. "I don't know, but she has two children, a boy and a girl."

After a brief conference they decided there were two or three such Ninfas. There was Ninfa Campos Hernandez who was only twelve and was too snooty to talk to anyone because she was in the third grade of a real school. And there was Ninfa Campos Sanchez who did have kids but the children couldn't agree on how many, maybe seven, maybe a dozen.

Amidst a lot of elbow poking they came up with a third woman, but surely the *Doña* wouldn't want to see her.

"Why not?" asked Julia.

They looked around at each other and shrugged their shoulders.

"Because," said one of the bigger boys, "she killed her husband and she ran away with the kids and she ended up here. And besides…"

"And besides…?" said Julia, but the boy was rolling his eyes and shaking his head.

"Because she's crazy," yelled someone out at the fringes of the mob.

The boy looked around at the other kids who nodded and circled their ears with their fingers. "She doesn't have a second last name," the boy added. "She said she'd never take a man's name ever again."

"She's a witch," called a tall girl from the back of the crowd.

Another boy swiped his finger across both eyebrows.

Julia burst out laughing. "Yes, that's her." She drew Ninfa's single eyebrow across her own forehead. "That's the one. Can you take me to her, please?"

The children cheered, laughed, jumped up and down. Who cared about some old million year footprints when they could see a murderous lunatic witch with a single black eyebrow confront her ex-boss right in front of them?

"What's your name?" she asked the bigger boy as they started off.

"Hector Baldos Lozano," he said, and saluted her.

"That's an excellent second last name."

And suddenly, they were all sounding out their second last names in one loud cacophony, out of which she could only discern a few: Gomez, Gutierrez, Torres, Rivera…by now there were at least eighteen children. Did any of them go to school?

"Listen, listen," yelled Hector. "I've got it, we're going to see Ninfa Campos No Name."

"No Name, No Name," they chorused.

She turned to Hector. "You have a mean streak, Hector Baldos Lozano."

He frowned, clearly puzzled by this. His silence spread to the others and they crowded close. What was happening? What had he said to make this stranger angry?

Christ, Julia, who do you think you are? The ache in her gut bloomed again. She wiped the sweat off her forehead even as a drop fell from her nose onto her chest.

They were waiting. She took a deep breath. The stink had diminished somewhat, or she was getting used to it.

"I was wrong, Hector, and I am sorry."

More confusion. What was the *señora* saying?

"Let's get going," she said. And everybody seemed happy with that. There were no streets here, just paths that meandered from house to house, sometimes circling a house in its entirety and doubling back to make a figure eight. If the children left her, she would never be able to find her way back to the car.

They were heading west, that much she knew, toward the garbage dump because the sound of the dump trucks was getting louder.

The houses were very basic. One room, a front door and a back door seemed the most frequent design. Some were made of thick cardboard wrapped in thin, plastic sheets, others of tent material. Still other houses were made of sheets of zinc or tin, or huge metal cans flattened and pieced together. The roofs were mostly corrugated tin.

They came upon a house that was made of stones piled up as neatly as a New England fence and topped with a thick straw roof.

"That's a pretty substantial house," she said.

232

"It doesn't matter," said Hector. "When the garbage comes this way, it will go under just like all the others."

A garbage dump that traveled? Julia wondered if she was dreaming. With that stench of overheated garbage?

Two young boys ran out of a house to join them, and now there were twenty children.

They turned a corner and there it was, a few hundred yards away. Managua's garbage dump rose hundreds of feet above the flood plain. Its sides seemed to heave as the trucks at the top backed to the edge and dropped their loads, causing landslides of refuse to tumble away into a sludge of brown water and dust at its base. The noise of their falling and the thick, foaming splashes sounded so close she expected to feel its spray. Parked around the base of the garbage mountain were several rusting cranes, one with its bucket dangling loose. Another was buried up to its knees in garbage that had rolled down from above.

The field between the base of the dump and where they were standing was empty save for a few small piles of trash.

"Were there houses here?" Julia asked.

"Oh yes," said Hector, "hundreds of houses." He shrugged, "They took them all down and built them again back there." He waved back the way they had come.

So the garbage did move, thought Julia and that was how the stone house would be buried eventually. The thought made her shiver. Where would it stop?

As though she had spoken aloud, the tall girl answered. "It's going to cover the whole world."

"But we get to play futbol here," said Hector. "At least for a while. Come on, let's go to Ninfa Campos, the assassin."

As she stumbled along, the noise of the children, the trucks and the grinding, heaving mountain, faded away. Go see Acahualinca, he had said. All that talking, about her hair and eyes and laugh lines, it had sounded like a casual invitation, just something to see. Only it hadn't been a casual suggestion. It had been a challenge and she'd fallen for it, as he probably knew she would. She felt small and useless and ridiculous in the face of all this horror, and that was what he wanted. The shit had decided she needed educating! She wanted to be angry, but she had no energy for it. It was all too much to take in.

The children pulled her back to the sun and heat. "We're there, *Doña*. Almost there," they yelled and made her turn around. Her little teachers, a whole army of them.

She trudged on until they yelled, "We're here!"

And there was Ninfa with her single eyebrow stretching from temple to temple, standing in her doorway, waiting with her arms crossed over her chest.

Some of the children stayed to watch what would happen between the two women. Some of them left Julia to join a group crouching over something on the ground. Ninfa held a hand up to shield her eyes from the sun. "Stop that!" she yelled at them.

"*Uno, dos, cinco, seis,*" they counted, one, two, five, six… "No, it's three, five six." A scrawny girl with mud colored hair knocked another girl over; there was a scream and a melee of bare feet and arms, rags tearing.

"How are your children?" yelled Julia.

"Ana María's better. That's her." Ninfa pointed to the child that had knocked the other one over. "The little one's sick now. My boy."

"Your boy?"

Ninfa tilted her head to one side and grinned. "As I've told you before, I have a son, *doña* Julia.

"I'm sorry to hear he's sick. Is there anything I can do?"

Ninfa puffed her lips up and blew out a raspberry. Julia flushed and forced herself not to step back. It was the same look the sausage woman at the market had favored her with. And Migdalia, when Julia had driven her home from the jail.

"I believe you left without collecting your pay, Ninfa." Julia fumbled in her purse and came up with the whole amount for a month and handed it over. She had rounded it up to 250 *córdobas*.

"Thank you." Ninfa's eyes traveled from the money to Julia and Julia felt herself flush again.

"You can have your job back whenever you want it, Ninfa," she said, hating the sound of her own voice. She felt a sick shame, with anger fluttering around the edges, which only made her more angry.

"I didn't know I'd lost it," said Ninfa, pinching the money between her thumb and forefinger.

"But you..." A child screamed and Julia looked down. The children were actually enlarging a hole in the dirt. One boy, smaller than the rest, straight-armed Ninfa's scrappy little daughter. "Little fucker, it's seventy-twelve," he shouted in her face.

Ninfa put her foot out and sent the boy sprawling. "Mind your manners before the *señora*." The boy gave a perfunctory howl.

"Show her how you can count, Tadeo," said Ninfa. She looked up at Julia, "They learn by counting the flies that crawl up out of the hole." She rolled the bills into a cylinder and slipped them down the front of her dress. "I don't want your job, *doña*. I have other ways to live. Besides, I need to be here with my children. But I thank you for coming." She went back into the house and let the sheet of cloth that was the door roll down to the ground.

Julia was astonished. Why was the woman so angry and bitter?

"Psssst!" One of the larger boys tugged on her arm. "Come and see the farm."

Numbly, she let him lead her away. The other children gathered behind them as he took her around the house.

A farm? she wondered. In this nightmare? More likely the footprints again. She shook her head at them, she didn't want to see the goddamned footprints. "I must go," she said weakly.

"Not yet. Look there." The boy stopped at the edge of a wet patch. "There. Look at that."

Footprints crisscrossed the mud, and refuse clogged the meager dribble of water — bottles, cans, a shoe with no sole, and what looked like a desiccated Kotex pad. Disgusted, she turned to leave and her thong got sucked off in the mud. Without bending over, she jammed her foot back into it to drag it out. She would throw up if she let her skin touch that water.

"See there!" Hector pointed to a rough wooden container at the edge of the dribbling water. It was half filled with some indefinable thing and covered with a light cloth that rippled in a stray current of air. She took a step closer, saw that the "cloth" was made of thousands of creamy white maggots tumbling over each other. She pulled away but Hector tugged again.

"See," he said. "Look what she does." He actually seemed proud as he pointed back to Ninfa's house, then to an empty jar with a lid, and then at another. He grinned up at her and waited. Finally, he made an impatient gesture toward his mouth and chewed.

Eat them? Julia's legs buckled and she went down on her knees.

The children scattered as the hot bile rushed up her throat and her breakfast followed. Her knees and her fingers had sunk into the mud. She blinked away tears, then closed her eyes.

"Lies," came the children's panicky voices, "He lied, she doesn't eat them. Lies, *señora*. Water, she needs water."

Trying to check her sobs, Julia grit her teeth. It was José María who'd lied. Maybe to show the *gringa* what really happened here in his country, or maybe for another reason. Then another thought took over. Perhaps he was even now looking on.

She groaned and pushed herself up. The children retreated. She turned and bolted through the pack with no thought of where she was going. She felt the children closing in around her. Panic filled her. Hector, or was it another boy, bounced in front of her and laughed, pointed at his temple; the others called to her to wait, they would lead her. She ran faster, turning first one way and then retracing her steps to go another way. Lake Managua was just to the north of Acahualinca, but she had no idea where north was. Sweat ran into her eyes. Her thigh muscles cramped. She slipped on something and staggered. A fly buzzed her cheek, her hair, her ear. She swatted at it and she was sure she could hear it laugh.

Terrified, she stopped. She was lost. The children clustered together ten yards back and waited.

Somewhere up ahead, beyond the jumbled houses, were the railroad tracks, the slaughter house, and her car. If she could just get to the railroad tracks she could walk in either direction and find it.

A house made of rusty metal plates stood across her path and she thought of walking straight in the front door and out the back. Her body felt massive, as if she could, by merely passing through these insubstantial houses, smash them out of existence.

Forcing her feet to bend with the path, she skirted the house and came to a rain barrel. Down in its depths, her own face stared up at her, red and swollen. A tiny moan curled up out of her belly. She slid down the side of the barrel and huddled at its base, her head against her drawn-up knees.

What a fool she'd been. She felt anger, then grief, and then again anger. Goddamn all the arrogant sons-of-bitches who thought they knew what she needed in order to be a real person. First Marshall and now this. Goddamn herself for being so stupid as to listen.

A hand came down on her shoulder, large and black with dirt. She jerked her head up and banged it against the rain barrel. Someone stood above her, black against the sun. "No!" she screamed and came up swinging. "You fuckers! You bastards!" She kicked, swung her shoulders, butted with her head as arms came around her, pinning her arms against her torso. By his strength, a man; her face was squashed against his neck She opened her mouth to scream and instead bit into the muscle that bound neck to shoulder. The man yelped and turned his face into her ear.

"Stop it," he said in English, "Stop it, Julia!"

She opened her mouth and let go. His breath whistled past her ear. "Oh God," she sobbed. "Goddamn you. Goddamn you," she whispered.

José María sensed Julia's legs giving way, and he went with her, trying to soften her fall. *Son-of-a bitch*, he thought. *She's strong!*

As they landed, he on one knee, the other leg sprawled out, he managed to get his arm around her and bring her around so that her back rested against his chest. Hesitantly, he reached up with his free hand and smoothed her golden hair. Seeing the broad smudge of mimeograph ink he'd transferred to her hair, he bit his lip and quickly wiped his hand on his trousers. Then he swiveled around her and propped her back against the barrel. She came up boneless and loose like a rag doll. This close, he thought he could hear her heart beat. He wanted to feel it with the palm of his hand. Instead, with one hand, he unbuttoned his shirt and began to wipe her forehead with its tail.

"Sorry, that's even worse," he said. But he didn't stop. She opened her eyes; the whites were tinged red. She'd been crying and, from the smell of it, she'd been sick to her stomach as well.

"I didn't think you would take me up on it," he said. *Liar!* he thought. The last thing he should ever have done was tell her to come here.

Her eyelids drooped and she shut him out again. When she spoke, her voice was low and he had to lean forward and grab the barrel's rim to keep from falling into her lap. He watched her lips form the words, "The police, they followed me that day. I'm sorry, I'm so sorry. I should have known. I should have watched more carefully."

"But you didn't. What's done is done." Cradling her jaw with his fingers, he ran his thumb from the corner of her lips out to the midpoint of her cheek. Her eyes flew open.

"Sorry," he said. "There was ink there." He held up his blackened thumb. Well, now there was, a dark narrow stain, like someone had opened a crack on her cheek. And the ink was still wet enough to look like drying blood.

"Thank God you got away," she said. "Did they tell you? Sofia Alvarado is dead."

He settled back onto his haunches. Maybe, maybe not, he thought.

"They didn't tell you?"

"They did."

She frowned. "You don't believe it?"

He shook his head. "I'm not sure."

He saw her glance down at his bare chest, then up at his hand resting on the side of the water barrel. With one hand, she lifted his hand away and looked at it. "What have you been doing?"

"Screwing up."

She sighed. "It's easy to do, isn't it?"

He pushed his head back to get a better look. "I don't always screw up, though you'd have no way of knowing that, would you?"

She took a breath that collapsed into a shudder. "No. I wouldn't." She turned his hand over. "It's ink, isn't it?" She traced a line across his palm from the base of the fingers to the heel of the thumb. Her touch shot through him, brought him up rigid against his jeans. He kept his eyes on hers, willing her not to look down. He took a ragged breath and was about to close his fingers over hers, but she slipped her finger away and brought it under her nose.

"Mimeograph ink. I remember that from college."

"College?" The word made no sense here. He looked into her eyes. Shining brown and gold, like her hair.

"Yes, college." Her mouth tilted into a smile that wobbled between anger and tears and he waited, hardly breathing, to see which won out.

"I worked my way through college, Mr. Simon Pure from the masses." Anger. Plain, simple anger. He grinned then quickly forced his face to become solemn.

She threw a hand out to take in everything around them. "You knew what I was going to see here, you with the 'hair like the trumpet flowers, and what beautiful children you must have, you should go see Acahualinca.' All such shit!"

"It's my home, Julia." Part of him was tickled that she'd remembered his exact words.

"Do you have any idea how pompous you sound?" Her face came close, her fingers slid up over his shoulder and touched the topmost scar on his back. Wary of her pity, he shrugged her hand away, then regretted losing it.

"You wanted to teach me a lesson, didn't you? Whether I'd paid for it or not."

"Seeing isn't paying, my dear friend."

Her head snapped back and the barrel gave a hollow bong. "What you mean is it's not payment enough. It'll never be enough." She rolled away and huddled over her knees. He couldn't make out what she was saying and he hitched forward, but she stopped as he got close and turned her head to the side. One blood shot eye stared at him.

"Julia?" He bent over her; his back and thighs grew tense. He had no idea what he would say, or could say. "*Te quiero*," he whispered at last, "I love you." He was shocked. Where did that come from?

"Maggots," she said, and her face crumpled.

She felt his arms go around her and pull her up. She tried to orient herself. The children stood at a distance, their bare feet and skinny legs nearly swallowed up by the dust they kicked up.

"Enough!" he called out to them. "You have better things to do than stand and stare." But his voice was tender and they vanished without a word.

She stepped back from the circle of his arms to see his face more clearly and lost her balance. In an instant his arm came around her shoulders and she stared stupidly at that same hand now cupping her opposite shoulder.

She opened her mouth to speak but lost the thread altogether as he led her around the house, through a narrow door into a hot, dim room. He pulled aside a curtain hung on a string, sat her on a cot, and went away. In a minute he was back with her purse and a tin mug of water. "I think it's all there. It got dumped out." He reached above her to a shelf and handed her a clean rag. "I'm just going up to the tracks to get more water. I'll be right back."

She held the rag awkwardly in one hand, the mug in the other, and tried to steady her breathing. A radio blared away in the house next door. There were no windows in this house and apart from the two doors, the one she'd come through and one in the opposite wall, the room's main source of light came through the foot-wide gap between the top of the walls and the overhang of the metal roof. Above her, there were only two holes in the roof, and she followed the shafts of light down, one onto the bed and one onto the floor. She saw dust motes spiraling up and down within each one, just like they did at the market. Such busy little worlds, visible only when the light hit them and then so beautiful, and so very insubstantial.

Heat radiated from the walls and off the mimeograph machine. A fly buzzed over the remains of rice and beans on a plate next to the machine. The plate was the only object in the room that was out of place.

She rose unsteadily and stretched her arms out. The room was a little more than half again their length from finger tip to finger tip, maybe six, eight feet wide and what? Fifteen feet in length, front to back? As she turned to check that out, some of the water in the mug slopped onto the floor. It beaded up into rounded blobs, and was suddenly gone. A dirt floor then, but so smoothed and polished with use that she'd taken it for wood or polished stone.

Her mouth was sour, her skin sticky, and there were stains down the front of her dress. Somewhere along the way, the tie had loosened and the dress was open to her waist. When had that happened?

She undid the knot and pulled the panels out to the sides to let the hot air get at her sticky skin. The fabric around the armholes was dark with sweat and smelled like cat piss.

There was a scuffle of footsteps and something clanged against the wall next to the bed. She whipped the dress closed and fumbled with the tie. A sudden surge in the music next door beat a counterpoint against the sound of water falling into the barrel. A lot of water it seemed, and yet the sounds of both music and water died in less then a minute. Only the sound of retreating footsteps and the thudding of her heart were left.

There was no mirror among the items laid out on the wooden crossbeam above the bed. A neat pile of clean rags, squared and folded, sat between a statue of the Virgin and a tin box marked 'salt' in crude block letters. An unframed photograph of a woman standing in a doorway was taped to the wall beside the Virgin, who gazed upward in ecstasy, her arms open to the world. In the photo, the tired woman in the doorway wore no shoes and looked like she simply wanted to disappear into the darkness behind her.

Julia lifted her eyes up to the gap between the roof and the wall. *And you have shoes on your feet and a dress you've had the leisure to sew yourself while other women made your bed, cleaned your house, and made dinner for your family.*

Julia crossed to the door at the back of the room and looked out on a patio no bigger than the room behind her. The patio was filled with broken furniture, plastic bottles, glass bottles, cans and other metal objects, some rusty, some quite shiny. All from the garbage mountain, she was sure, but unlike the dump, everything was in order and didn't stink. Someone had spent some thought in organizing it. There was a pile almost as tall as she was of metal containers of every shape and size. Another pile consisted of plastic jugs and bottles. Newspapers had been bundled and tied and the bundles were balanced one on top of the other under a rickety palm shelter. Along the back wall, there was a pile of glass bottles, a pile of clay pottery, and even a pile of broken ceramic pieces. The wooden furniture had been neatly chopped into legs, seats, backs, and tabletops, all more or less of equal length, and each component was laid among its own kind.

A narrow path wound through the maze to the back wall, where a whitewashed outhouse stood in the right hand corner, a pot of red flowers nailed to its door. Well done, she thought and was sure there would be toilet paper in there. As welcoming as it looked, she didn't want to be caught in there when he came back, so she quickly filled her mouth with water from the mug, swilled it around, and spit it into the dirt behind the plastic bottles. She poured the remainder over her hands, wiping them with the rag he had given her. There was nothing left for her armpits or her sticky skin.

Something thudded against the wall of the house. She fled back to the cot and sat, her hands clasped in her lap, her knees together as another cacophony of thuds and bumps and watery splashes played itself out. Then he was standing in the doorway, grinning down at her.

"Sorry about that. It's like being inside a drum, isn't it?"

She nodded. From her perch on the cot, she watched him set two buckets of water inside the door, then come to the center of the room.

Neither of them spoke. Without the music, the far off whine of the garbage trucks sifted into the silence. A silence that seemed to stretch on forever. She could not take her eyes from his. She had never seen such a naked face before, could never have imagined one. On a bubble of panic she tried to think of something to say, but there were only little slivers of thought. In desperation, she opened her mouth to force something out and heard herself say, "It is a far, far better place that I go to than…."

She clapped her hands over her mouth as he continued on his own, "than I have ever known," and he was laughing and kneeling down to take her hands in his. "No, no," he said. "Don't do that." There were tears in his eyes. She remembered the scars on his back.

He's like a mirror, she thought, seeing there her own fear and hurt and wonder. She, too, wanted to laugh. But she hurt too much.

He reached over, dragged one of the buckets next to the cot, then sat back on his heels. There was a red mark on his cheek where she must have hit him. She touched it and he brought his hand up and held hers there, his eyes suddenly wary, questioning. At last he turned his face and moved his lips against her palm. She stifled a tiny cry.

He rose on his knees, took up the cloth, dipped it into the bucket and, with one hand cradling the back of her head, he began to wash her face. His touch was gentle.

She took the cloth from him and rubbed the black mark on his forehead. His head wobbled like a small child submitting himself to be washed.

"How old are you?" he asked.

"I think I'm sixteen. And you?"

"Eighteen." He reached up for more rags and washed the hollows behind her ears, the back of her neck, the line of her jaw and chin. And with each touch, each hesitation, a pause here to draw a ring around a mole just below the corner of her mouth, or there, where the pad of his thumb stroked the hollow at the base of her throat, she felt herself opening, falling.

She took the cloth away again and bent forward until she could feel his breath on her lips. There she paused, felt his arms go around her, his body rise to gather her up until they stood facing each other. They were nose to nose, eyes wide open. And yet he had not moved, she was sure of it.

"Yes," she whispered, and watched as his hand floated toward the tie at the front of her dress.

At the last minute, slipping her hand up inside his, she pulled on the tie herself and it came undone.

245

Book Three

Chapter 22

"They're not eaten," José María murmured, "at least not raw. It's because they're almost pure protein, and when they're dried and ground up, they enrich the flour." His voice was tender and sleepy, his lips so close to her ear, so soft, that he might have been whispering poetry instead of talking about maggots.

Julia held her breath; her body felt distant, flung loose and floating against the bare branches, against the blue sky. Somewhere, a long distance away, her knee and the flesh of her thigh hovered against his, and somewhere beyond that, light years away, beyond the curve of the earth, their feet lay entangled.

They were in a small amphitheater, a natural hollow between the roots of a *guanacaste* tree. Big enough to hold them, deep enough to hide them from the fields and from the road beyond.

She let her breath out slowly. Each time she was with him was a small miracle. They had no set way of meeting. Today it was a note under her windshield wiper at the marketplace. Once she found a note in her purse, and the outrageousness of it had only filled her with more longing: that he should be so close and not touch her or speak because of who she was, or who was with her. It seemed he knew better than she did when the time was right.

There was a deftness in him that belied his raggedy-ass demeanor.

And his irony masked a gentleness she had never experienced before. Used to the sharp edge of cynicism that wove through most conversation, she had been unprepared for the ease of simply telling the truth without fear of being ridiculed. For him, ridicule was just a nasty form of self-protection.

"Why dump your own shit on someone else?" he'd said. "All it does is make someone else feel bad. Is that what you need to make yourself feel better?"

Of course there were things about which he never spoke. Nor did she ask. The scars on his back, the ridges and ropes her fingertips had begun to know by heart, were enough to silence her.

When they were together, the world was filled with wonders. A single butterfly moving from leaf to leaf with apparent unconcern that two giants were watching her every move. Or the afternoon Julia taught him how to whistle on a blade of saw-grass, a lovely hour-long process, because they couldn't stop laughing, and laughing led to other things. They'd also shared the sadness of watching a wounded yellow-jacket slowly disappear beneath a swarm of tiny red ants that had come to feed on him.

But when they were apart, the world came crashing down on her. At night she would lie awake beside Marshall, dry-eyed and horrified. What in the world was she doing? What was she thinking? She was surely going to destroy the very things she had so painstakingly crafted for herself and the children to make a world that worked for all of them.

There were very few happy marriages in the world, but at least she and Marshall had managed to forge a decent home for Becka and Caley. Both were happy and healthy. Marshall was dependable. He loved his children. Other women put their husband's needs first. So why couldn't she?

The very thought drove a knife through her gut and she'd quietly slip out to the back yard to pace. The movement and the cool dew on the grass soothed her, and after a while she would go to the back fence and call to Serafina and the horse would amble over to nuzzle the cyclone fence and console her.

"What a fine animal you are." Julia poked her fingers through the fence to caress the velvety flesh around Serafina's nostrils. To have been saved from slaughter just before she was sacrificed, Serafina was due her honor and more.

"I am so happy to know you," she whispered one night as her finger met the even softer flesh of the nostril's edge and Serafina blew a puff of warm breath out in welcome. That moment, the feel of that warmth, the creature alive and well before her when it could so easily have gone another way, had filled her with wonder.

Just as being beside José María did. A feeling that she was bigger than herself, and better, would inhabit her whole being. No doubts, no self-recriminations. No anger tucked away in hidden corners ready to jump out at her for unperceived lapses.

Another time, Serafina lifted her head and blew her grassy breath on Julia's face. Julia laid her forehead against the cyclone fence and let exhaustion claim her. Then, with a bustle and rustle of his three straggly feathers, Fernando, the ex-fighting cock, landed on Serafina's rump and began to crow.

"It's fucking three in the morning, you rude shit-bag," she hissed up at him.

Delighted with her response, Fernando puffed himself up like a huge, misshapen pumpkin and began to crow his heart out. And Serafina, as deadpan as Eeyore, huffed and puffed and ambled away, the cock urging him on.

"Thanks a lot, you two." Julia whispered, "I'm going back to bed."

And oddly enough their conversation would have eased her pain, and she would fall asleep the minute her head hit the pillow.

Julia admired a dapple of sunlight that brought out the gold in José María's eyes. Then he lifted the eyebrow and closed that eye and she sighed. "What?" she said.

His eye opened. "Are you going to answer my question?"

"What question?"

"Any question. Pick one and answer it."

She laughed and fell back against him. "I was thinking about silence, and how some silences can feel wrong, and others feel peaceful and kindly."

Now his eyes were truly closed.

Don't go there, she thought. "I know there are things you can't talk about. There always will be. And that's fine. I see that as discretion. Or privacy."

"More discretion. Privacy is a rich man's right."

"Oh, come on. Everyone has the right to privacy."

"Think about it, Julia. If you lived twelve people in one room, not counting the babies, then privacy is not an option. Look at us here. The two of us. Do you think we're the only ones who've made love and slept here?"

"Yes, you're right." That ten or twelve people living in one room would preclude privacy should have been obvious. That she didn't know it as a fact of life was the issue. *Is it just ignorance? Willful blindness?* Her face turned hot. "I'm sorry, I didn't think about it at all. I thought we're just very lucky to be together."

She came up onto her elbow. His bones were set so neatly under the smooth skin; a small breeze riffled the hairs on his chest.

252

"José María,"she drew the syllables out, testing them, "*el cuñado*, the brother-in-law."

"Ah yes, my brother-in-law." He squinted up at her and she moved her head so that it shaded his face from the sun.

"No, don't do that," he whispered. He curled his fingers in her hair and pulled her head down to his shoulder. Then he settled back on the leaves.

"Shall I tell you another story?" he asked.

"Yes."

"It's something that happened to me a couple of days before you came to Pochomil for your interview with María Antonia. I was thumbing my way down there from the South Highway to my wonderful brother-in-law when along comes this woman hauling a silver Airstream trailer and she gave me a ride. Her name was Maggie Peters and she was driving all the way down to Patagonia and back."

"Oh my gosh. I'd love to do that."

He chuckled. "Why am I not surprised? Anyway, she must've been seventy, a retired school teacher with this wild head of white hair." His hands encircled his head.

"You sure that wasn't a halo?"

"Maybe it was — although she wasn't exactly angelic. She kept telling me how tough she was. During the war, she'd coached a high school football team because the men were all away. Her team won a city championship. She actually stuck her arm out and dared me to pinch up any flab."

"Did you pinch her?"

"Of course. And she was right, there wasn't any."

"What made you think of her now?"

"I don't know. First I met her, and now I've met you — and it's like a connection... Maggie Peters. She was kind."

"In a flabless sort of way."

"That's it. Exactly."

"Does that mean that I'll probably take off for Patagonia in my old age?"

"You probably would. It'd be more fun if we did that together." He curled his fingers in her hair and drew her head down to his shoulder, then settled back into the leaves.

"He's a bastard, my brother-in-law."

She was startled at the shift in conversation.

"*Un hijo de puta*, a son of a bitch." He raised a hand as though to pull something from the air, and instead opened his fingers and let it spill out. So much for his brother-in-law.

"How did your parents die?" he asked.

"In a car crash."

"Was it hard?"

"Yes. But it's fourteen years now. And you? Do you think about your mother's death?"

"Sometimes. I never knew her. She died giving birth to my sister."

"And your father?" she asked.

He didn't answer. His hand was floating again.

"What?" she prompted.

"My father?" He rolled onto his side, facing her. "He was a marine at the U.S. Embassy… It's why I went to the States. I wanted to find him. Instead, I found Katherine. Or she found me."

"Your mentor. The one who got you off the streets in San Francisco."

"That's right."

"How old were you."

"Eleven, I think. She was the best thing that could have happened to me there." His finger traced a line from her temple, along her jaw

254

and up to her mouth, one long tickle of hairs rising to meet him; warmth from his thumb and fingertips slid back up along her cheeks and across her eyes. "Oh yes," he said. "Like I told you, she civilized me. Or at least she tried."

She closed her eyes. "Who else mentored you," she asked.

"Andrés, my cousin."

"The one who was injured at birth? Who cannot talk?"

"Oh, he can make himself understood alright. And I've never known a man as kind as he is. And there's my *tía* Berfalia."

"The Queen of the sausage stall? She didn't seem to have much milk of human kindness when I met her."

"Who said milk had anything to do with kindness or mentoring? My aunt is not about milk of any kind. She is the place we call home, the roof over our heads, and the floor beneath our feet. We are strange, we human beings, aren't we? We make do with what we have, or try to make it better."

"Yes, that's better than just making do," she said. "We can even make art out of old cow patties."

He laughed and rolled onto his back again. "And then there's my sister Luz Alba María. I used to tease her terribly. About everything, about her nose, about her belly-button, about the pigs. And she took it all, whatever I dished out." He sighed. "Now she takes it from my brother-in-law."

"Why doesn't he like you?"

"It's because I bring him nothing. He would have me lay marble floors for him; instead I patch his zinc roof." He dug his chin into his shoulder and looked at her sideways. "I'll bet you have marble floors."

She held herself very still to hide the hurt. "I certainly didn't read him correctly that day of the interview. And on the way home, you told me I was a *gringa* and therefore I couldn't understand him."

"Was I that brutal?"

"Well, no. But it did puncture my conceit."

"About?"

"I don't know. I guess I thought I was less a *gringa* than I really was."

He snorted and she laughed. "That does sound arrogant, doesn't it?"

"No, it's honest. I thought I knew everything there was to know about the States until Katherine died. Now I think I don't know how to be in either place."

They stared up into the *guanacaste* with its wildly curving branches.

"You hear that?" he asked.

"What?"

"Thunder. Or an earthquake."

"The sky is clear."

"An earthquake then." He drew her closer. "It never seems quite over."

"What?"

When he didn't answer, she sat up and pulled her blouse down over her head. A dried leaf, hidden inside, scraped against her breast and she tried to pull it out.

"Let me." He reached up, slid his hand around the curve of her breast so that his roughened palm cradled it. He stared up at her. A spasm gripped her vagina and the warm, sweet, slippery liquid followed. A bird called out and was answered by another. His fingers straightened, stretched and gently pulled the leaf out and she felt the long pulling of her vagina, as if it were being drawn toward him. The muscles of her thighs trembled as she balanced herself, swung her leg over his hips, knelt over him and hovered, tilting her pelvis forward in soft strokes, lightly brushing his penis till it rose up against her and then into her.

She drew the ties of her skirt around and together, tied them and rose to her feet. Her body was light, urgent with energy. Lifting up on her toes, she swung one foot, then the other up, back, down, circled slowly around him, small steps, steps that fluttered leaves up against him. She reached down and pulled him up and together they danced around the small hollow, holding hands and circling each other.

A shadow came and they paused to watch a small white cloud dither across the sun until they were looking at the sun again. She forced her feet to begin the dance again. Only now it was a mourning dance, their steps cut in half, slowing to a stop.

Above them, a root sprawled along the rim of the hollow. Beyond was the field, a thicket of bare trees and then the narrow dirt road, with the car edged off into a dry stream bed.

"It is very private," she said. "There must have been centuries of children conceived here."

"Yes."

Yes and again, yes. That she didn't know it as a fact of life was the issue. And that she knew a mourning dance even before a death had occurred seemed like only a beginning.

Chapter 23

They drove into Masaya, past the main square and she said, "Is this all right?" She nodded toward the National Guard quarters on the other side of the park.

"Worse yet, up the mountain, there's *Coyatepe*, the infamous Citadel." He smiled as though he hadn't a care in the world.

"Infamous?" she said.

His smile disappeared. "For the hospitality of its dungeons."

She parked her car across the street from the marketplace.

"Hey," he said.

With her hand on the door handle, she looked over at him.

"I trust you," he said, and then because he always took back a little when he had given, she reached out and laid a finger across his lips.

His fingers closed on her wrist and he lifted it to his mouth. "And I'm afraid," he whispered around it, then drew her to him, and kissed the hair above her ear. "I'm afraid I'll go away, and I won't remember that I trust you."

Stunned, she pulled away. His eyes were wide, the lids trembling as though he were fighting to keep them open. His pupils were tiny black dots. He's gone, she thought. He's already left. She let her breath out slowly, afraid to make it true by speaking. In silence, they got out of the car and walked toward the market.

"Well, son-of-a-bitch," he drawled, looking beyond her. "Look who's here."

There was a small crowd milling in front of the great stone entrance to the marketplace.

"How's that for timing?" He touched her elbow. "Come, I want you to meet someone." With a light touch, he steered her across the street into the crowd.

A shell game was in progress, a blind lottery vendor shuffled by, riffling papers in the air and, next to the gray stone wall, a street performer was telling a story to the delight of a small crowd. Beside him, a small child danced out the actions of his words.

José María stopped at the edge of the crowd. His arm came around her waist and she could feel his excitement. The knot in her belly began to ease.

The man looked drunk but there was no slurring or histrionics. His Spanish was beautiful, pitched low, tender — the Spanish that so often undid her. She wondered anew what brought this sweet, answering echo up from her belly whenever she heard Spanish spoken freshly. What shivering prickle of memory sent her pelting along its rhythms, heart racing, breath undone, to meet and touch, and know everything around her. It was as if long ago all awareness began within its sounds and only now could she begin to gather that long ago world around herself.

The story was about shoemakers, many of whom were dying all over the country. But there was one who caused himself to disappear. The speaker's hands flew wide and everyone looked around to see where the shoemaker had gone. Was he behind them, above them, down the street, up the street? But no, he was nowhere to be seen.

The little shadow grabbed at the speaker's trousers and pointed to an empty spot on the paving stones.

"There?' the speaker mimed, then shook his head. There was nothing there.

The boy went to the exact same spot and plucked a small square of leather stuck through with a big needle out of nowhere. The speaker looked at his audience, shook his head, then waved the boy away.

Again the boy bent and drew forth a tiny leather shoe. He held it up for everyone to see.

There was shock and dismay. The shoemaker's very own, decidedly tattered shoe.

"That's his," said someone. People rolled their eyes and shook their heads remembering how the shoemaker had so much business he never had time to mend his own shoes.

"Yes! That's our shoemaker," said the storyteller. "Look how he's invisible!" He went over to shake the invisible shoemaker's invisible hand and then led him here and there in a victory parade.

Julia found herself waving and smiling along with the rest. José María tightened his arm around her waist and chuckled into her ear.

But then the speaker suddenly whisked the invisible shoemaker behind his back. "Just one moment," he said. "Of what possible use is an invisible shoemaker?"

Anxious titters broke into open laughter.

"Well then, tell me what an invisible man can do."

"Check on who the wife talks to," said one man.

Laughter greeted this statement.

"Listen to what mischief the kids are up to," said a woman eyeballing one particular boy of the many who carried the shoppers' baskets. In a wink, the boy disappeared behind the wall of the market entrance.

Off to her left, Julia saw a couple of *guardia* walking toward the group.

"He can check out what the big guys are planning," someone said in a voice barely above a whisper.

"Don't forget the little guys," muttered an old man.

"He can keep watch without being seen," said a young boy whose back was toward the approaching *guardia.*

"Rescue disappearing shoemakers," said the young girl at his side.

At last the speaker spotted the *guardia.* "That's a lot of listening," he said. He glanced over to a skinny young man who promptly yelled, "He can stop a thief before he steals your eggs." To emphasize his point, the boy grabbed at his scrotum to see if it was still there. There were howls of laughter and one or two "for shames."

Now being close enough to have heard, the two guards laughed as well.

The speaker bowed to the audience and thanked everyone for their participation and their appreciation. He turned to the boy and bowed to him. The little imp bowed, people cheered. The boy pulled a red baseball cap from under his shirt and started circulating through the crowd for coins.

"Hey, Miguel," yelled José María.

The speaker turned, did a double take and plowed through the crowd. "Son of bitch." He grabbed José María around the neck. "Where the hell have you been?"

"Around." José María pounded him on the back and shoulders. "My cousin," he told Julia. "This is my cousin, Miguel." Julia held out her hand.

Miguel gave it a brief shake and acknowledged her with the barest of nods before turning to José María. "Come," he said. "Let's eat." He took a handful of coins from the red cap and gave them to the boy.

"Wait," he said, scanning the crowd. He spotted the boy with the anxious scrotum and tossed him a coin.

"That's it," he said and set off up a side street, shouting to them to follow.

Miguel's house was the last one in a row of houses that ran from the marketplace up to the top of a hill. It stood out from the others because it had clearly not received its annual Easter painting for many years. Instead of the pinks and yellows and blues of the other houses, Miguel's house was that wonderful color the English called puce, which Julia had dubbed "puke" from her Georgette Heyer regency romance days. In this case it veered from the classic greenish brown with hints of moldy purple to patches of black turned gray, where in former rainy seasons the mold had grown up from the dirt.

She was still lost in a mixture of wonder and nostalgia when Miguel's shout drew her into the house.

"Mujer," he yelled as he pushed through the door, "we want food and drink, we are thirsty."

After the brilliant sun, the house was dark. Julia stopped to let her eyes adjust before she moved farther into the room. The welcoming smell of simmering corn dough filled the air. And something else that she couldn't put her finger on. Bread? Yeast?

A woman came in from the patio beyond the front room. Tall and gaunt and stunningly beautiful, she wiped her hands on her apron and walked directly over to Julia, bypassing Miguel altogether.

"Clothilde, señora, mucho gusto. It is a great pleasure to meet you,"she said in Spanish.

A little surprised at the woman's directness, Julia stuck out her hand for a real handshake. No flaccid lady handshake this. Clothilde's hand was muscular, the skin rough.

"A pleasure to meet you," Julia replied. Behind her, José María chuckled.

The woman was older than she'd first thought. Clothilde's warm brown eyes were widely spaced and her nose was just crooked enough to make her beauty haunting. Her skin was a lovely caramel color. It was the harsh creases that flared at the corners of her mouth and the red and roughened skin of her hands that aged her.

"Please, consider our house yours."

"Thank you," said Julia.

"Hello, cousin." José María slid his arm around Clothilde's shoulders and gave her a hug.

"I'm glad you have brought your friend, José."

"I am, too." He turned to Julia, "Clothilde is the sane person in this home."

Julia didn't know whether to laugh or to protest. Before she could do either, Miguel poked his head between José María and Clothilde.

"Food?" he murmured. Again he was ignored.

Julia waved at the large dented pot on the stove. "You are making *tamales*? They smell wonderful."

"That's laundry. The *nacatamales,* I've just taken off the stove." She pointed to a trestle table where an equally dented pot sat. "My neighbor's daughter is getting married tomorrow."

"Oh dear. Laundry and *tamales.*" Julia turned to José María. "Have we come at a bad time?"

"Are you kidding?" Again he hugged Clothilde. "And miss the best food in Masaya?"

"No *nacatamales* today, Joseph. Those are spoken for. I've got rice and beans and *tortillas*. And the pickles."

"Nonsense," yelled Miguel, suddenly recovering his voice. "José is family. What can you be thinking?" He turned to Julia. "It's a small wedding, just family and a few neighbors." He shrugged. "Besides, she is three months pregnant and – "

"*Basta!* Enough!"said Clothilde. Beneath the frown there was a hint of laughter in her eyes. "Do you want me to tell Clarita that her promised *nacatamales* were eaten by you, over my objections? And that your excuse is that because she's a loose woman she doesn't deserve them? May I remind you — "

"No you may not," said Miguel hastily. "But..." He shrugged his shoulders and whispered, "...you can always make more."

Clothilde pushed him away. "Only if you paint the house this afternoon."

"Ah." He released her. "I disappear," he announced and backed away into the inner patio.

"Works every time." Clothilde turned to Julia and gestured to a table against the wall opposite the stove. "Please have a seat." She turned back to her stove. "And you too, José."

Instead of sitting down, Julia followed Clothilde back to the stove. She had never seen anything like it. Made of clay, it was shaped like an enormous hollowed out pig. The whole thing rested on a heavy board laid across four saw-horses. The wood fire inside was fed by branches and logs shoved into one end of the beast. A metal tray at the other end had a little hillock of ashes already scooped from within. Three round openings on the top were the burners. It was amazing.

Clothilde was smiling. "You are curious about the stove?"

"Yes, it's ingenious. It seems wonderfully efficient, too."

"It is that." Clothilde was stirring a pot of beans on the middle burner. "I've had it for years. There have been stoves like these for centuries here. My father used to make them in San José. And my grandfather before him."

"San José?"

"Costa Rica."

"Ah." Julia moved her hand along the side of the stove, a few inches from the surface. She glanced up at the space between the top of the walls and the overlapping roof. "So that's why there's so little smoke."

"Yes. Those spaces serve as our light and our ventilation and they grant us safety from prying eyes. Windows make a house weaker."

"Of course. I've just never thought of it that way. Coming from the north where there is much less sunlight for half the year, we put windows all over the house."

"Yes." Clothilde looked Julia straight on, one eyebrow lifted. "I suppose when the people make the laws, they are more likely to obey them."

Holy cow! thought Julia. It was a quantum leap from sunlight to politics. Here was a woman who thought about government and actually talked about it. She hadn't realized how hungry she was for a conversation like this. She had to slow herself down to even understand what she wanted to say, how to make sense of thoughts she hadn't let herself speak of for years. This wasn't a hawk, diving for every scrap of edible flesh; this was a woman who was interested in what Julia had to say.

"I'm not so sure it's that simple," Julia said slowly. "If you have a stake in crafting the laws, are you more likely to follow them? It has the ring of truth. It's certainly what I grew up believing. And still believe today. But is it true?"

"You only guess?" said Clothilde.

"Well..." It was as though her tongue had gone rusty from disuse. "I'm not saying this well, I know, but I've always thought that governments that entrust the people with their own welfare...no." This was like trying to herd cats.

She started again. "The thing that makes democracy so wonderful is the same thing that make it fragile. Every person has a voice in what happens. In an election the majority rules, and if some power-hungry person comes along convincing enough…"

"A demagogue?" asked Clothilde. "We've had our fill of those down here." Clothilde hefted the pot of laundry onto the table with the *tamales*, then turned back. "But you have a constitution. We studied it in school. So even if your democracy is fragile, your legislators have learned to compromise, to give a little and take a little, so that everyone has a voice."

Clothilde's voice dropped to a whisper. "Here there is no such thing as compromise. There is no 'everyone' to be considered. Here there is only one voice, only one person that governs. All the rest must serve his needs and wishes or be done away with."

Her voice dropped even lower and Julia was reduced to lip-reading. "Here, to live freely, with dignity, we must be willing to… We must be willing to bleed."

"So what are we going to eat?" said Miguel coming up quietly behind Clothilde.

"Sit down and wait!" Clothilde turned back to Julia. "Would you like some coffee?"

"Sí," said both men at once.

"Yes, thank you," said Julia. "And may I use your bathroom?"

Clothilde led Julia out to the patio and pulled aside one of the many sheets hung up to dry.

"Over there, beyond the sheets and behind that wall. There is water in the tank." She pointed to the big unpainted stone tank with its attached scrubbing board. "And a bucket beside the toilet. The paper is in a basket."

Still bemused by their conversation, Julia followed the directions and sat. She took a deep breath and looked around her. Despite the crude technology, the toilet was spotless and everything was in its place. The toilet itself was of gray molded cement and sat above a cement waste tank. Something had been added to the tank to tamp down the smell.

There was no door to the toilet and from here she had a full view of the patio. She tried to count all the sheets hanging on the sagging lines. A dozen at least, and most of them folded once in order to fit them all on the rope that was available.

A dozen sheets, plus what was in that huge pot on the stove. Clothilde was doing laundry for others, as well as making *tamales* for a neighbor. It was Clothilde who held this house together, keeping it clean, shopping, cooking, and responding to the needs and whims of her husband, the Great Orator, all without modern conveniences.

This was a different world than any she had come across down here. One she knew next to nothing about. She'd thought she knew who she was, where she was and what she wanted. She had prided herself, above all else, at adapting to everything down here. Why, when it was clear that her 'everything' had encompassed so little? Because she spoke the language fluently? Because she had a degree? Because she drove around the countryside on her own and interviewed kids for scholarships?

"Beer and skittles" — the words flew in and laid themselves alongside "puke." Julia grunted, half in laughter and half in despair. Three years and only now, today, had she glimpsed the depths of her ignorance.

Clothilde was literate because almost everyone in Costa Rica was literate. And that was because the government paid for education down there and not for an army. But she was also well-spoken and straightforward, traits that only she herself had formed. How many thousands of women, perhaps hundreds of thousands like Clothilde, lived here? None that she knew. She had been too busy mocking the silliness of women like the ones at the swimming pool. Or the ones who came to their dinner parties.

Julia spread two sheets of thin toilet paper over her knees and found herself looking down at a beautiful woman with red lips, glossy dark hair and huge dark eyes. She turned the sheet over. Clothilde's toilet paper had been torn from a women's magazine printed in Panama.

When she got back to the front room, the coffee was on the table along with a nicked bowl of raw sugar and three spoons. Clothilde was bending sideways to push the branches further into the stove. That done, she checked the contents of the pots. "Ready," she announced. She handed Julia a cloth-covered basket of warm *tortillas*, then carried the two pots to the table.

Julia sat eating rice and beans as the talk at the table swirled around her. From the jar of hot peppers, onions and vinegar on the table, she dribbled some of the juice over her beans. The new flavor scathed her tongue.

"This is delicious," she told Clothilde

"Thank you." Clothilde handed Julia a cup filled with something brownish yellow that smelled strongly of yeast. Julia's stomach lurched. It was *chicha*. How was she going to get out of this? She looked up and smiled.

Clothilde nodded at the cup and smiled back.

Julia held the cup with both hands. All she knew about *chicha* was that it was made of corn softened in a mixture of water and lime, then chewed, usually by the women of the house; then the chewed corn was allowed to ferment. Not too long ago, it had been outlawed in Nicaragua for hygienic reasons, but no one could stop it being made in people's homes.

She took a sip, and found it had a strong, yeasty, fermented taste.

She couldn't stop the slight gag that rose in her throat. She set the cup down carefully and smiled, and all three of them burst out laughing. She shook her head. "*Lo siento.* I'm sorry."

José María rubbed her back. "It takes some getting used to," he whispered. His touch made her chest and throat ache.

She felt completely undone. A stove of the sort that had been made for centuries, two dented aluminum pots, and a spotless dirt floor that shone like marble — could she ever make a house as home-like as this on her own? Stop it! she silently screamed at herself. Stop your whining! She sat up straight. Miguel was holding forth, something about dying. It took her a moment to catch the thread of the conversation.

"Haven't you ever noticed, José, how everything you do has to do with trying not to die here in Nicaragua?" Up went his cup, a dribble trickled down his chin. Miguel wiped it with the back of his hand and nodded his head in what appeared to be total satisfaction with himself.

"*Jodido!* Fuck, cousin." José María laughed. "So that's what it was all about?"

"What?"

"All those beatings?"

Miguel thought for a moment. "That was my gift to you. My Art."

"Your art? My ass. So how was it you never left any artistic bruises for our aunt to see? No. You just loved a good punching bag."

"Because I loved you, cousin, better than anyone else."

"What am I missing here?"

"You're not listening. I loved you better than anyone else, and you went away."

"Thank God. If I'd stayed I'd have probably ended up a brain damaged lump from all your loving attention."

No one spoke. No one moved. Until now, it had all seemed part of a forever conversation. Everybody talking and no one thinking, just being together. Now there was something beneath the words that Julia couldn't make out. Something so vivid and painful it didn't need words or thought to bind the three others into one whole.

Julia stared up at the underside of the corrugated roof. They trusted each other. The hard ache of tears pushed up into her chest again. 'I'm afraid I'll go away,' he'd said 'and I won't remember that I trust you.' And she'd only focused on the first part of the sentence.

"Okay, cousin," said José María. "You once told me that the stories were simpler here in Nicaragua, and the dying easier. Tell me, just how is it easier?"

"If you haven't noticed how easy it is to die here, then you're in more trouble than I thought." Miguel held his cup out to Clotilde.

José María frowned. "Ah... not an easy death, but a death too easily come by. Point taken."

Miguel looked spectacularly pleased with himself. Then he switched his attention to Julia. "And you. Do you have a story to tell?"

Startled, she shook her head.

"Don't." Clothilde put a hand on Miguel's arm.

Julia smiled. "It's alright. I think everyone has a story to tell. Some are better than others. Some shorter than others."

"That's it," said Miguel. "Mine are the better kind. They are my Art. A little long perhaps, but I work on that."

"I thought beating up on me was your Art, cousin."

"I have a multiplicity of talents, José. But you wouldn't know that, having lived so many years in the great white paradise up north."

Clothilde poked Miguel's shoulder.

"Knock it off," said José María. He turned to Julia. "Watch out.

Every time he changes the subject it's because he's hiding something."

Julia smiled, hearing that simple 'watch out' as a hope of things to come.

"Aha!" Miguel jumped up. "A story! And I thought you'd never ask." With his hand over his heart, he took a deep breath.

"No!" all three shouted, then fell to laughing.

Undaunted, Miguel turned to Julia, "As I was saying, I once made a story up, a story that came straight from my heart…" His voice faded away. He glanced at his cousin. "Must an artist explain his art?"

Something passed between them.

José María smiled sadly. "Is that really the question you want to ask?"

Clothilde was looking at her hands, resting one on top of the other on the worn boards.

The silence deepened. Julia felt it full of unspoken things, ideas, feelings, history. Like those shafts of sunlight piercing the holes in the marketplace roof. Straight as arrows they fell onto the pavement, the tables, the people. And within each shaft, thousands of little floaters swirling in constant motion, up and down and all around. This one a thought, that one a dream, or a memory, a smell, a taste, a voice. And all of them part of one luminous world, one family. And then there were the millions of specks that filled the rest of the hall and went unseen without the sunlight.

Julia sat back. A trickle of sweat ran down between her breasts and she poked the cloth of her shirt in to sop it up.

"Should," she said out of nothing. "I think the word is 'should', not 'must' you explain your art."

José María look confused. But not Miguel.

"Me?" he said. "Never. 'Shoulds' are not my style." He frowned.

"Well, perhaps, but only sometimes. The truth is that I'm the animal who loses his skin and drags himself away — what are the right words for that?" He glanced at his cousin.

"He moults," said Julia. "And then he slithers away."

"Yes," José María grinned. "That's it, you are moulting, cousin. And walking away."

"I like slither better," said Clothilde. With a wry smile, she rose, grabbed a towel, picked up the pot of boiled clothes and carried it out to the patio. Water splashed, a spigot was turned on full force, followed by the sound of vigorous scrubbing and a full-throated song.

Miguel nodded. "So you will not catch me out. I just moult and then I slither away, away, too far away." He swept his hand out and stared beyond it into the distance.

Julia couldn't help but laugh. "Point taken."

"Thank you. You are kind. It is very hard work to slither for long distances, as you may well imagine. And because you are a wise woman, I would like to be counted among your list of people who tell stories that are not too long."

Julia laughed out loud. What a complicated man. He was rude, loud, and silly. But he was certainly not the fool that she had taken him for when they entered the house. He had the same crazy humor that José María had, only much less coherent. But the light was there. It worked for him.

And it seemed to work for Clothilde as well. She was certainly not his slave, not with that scrubbing and singing coming from the patio. There was so much energy and rhythm there you could dance to it. The word "trust" came to her again. Or was it acceptance? It was more like that they were good friends, getting closer every moment of their lives.

José María touched her wrist. "What do you think?"

"I'm sorry. I wasn't paying attention. What did you say?"

He smiled. "You were 'gathering the wool'," he said in English. It was a phrase he had learned from her.

"Actually I was trying to knit something out of the wool," she answered in English. "And I've lost one of my knitting needles."

"Speak in couth," said Miguel, pouring himself another cup of *chicha*.

José María switched back into Spanish. "I was telling Miguel where you and I met."

Julia laughed. "Actually, I think we met twice that day. Once at your brother-in-law's house and later, on the road."

José María shook his head. "She actually thumbed her nose at a jeep full of the *guardia*."

"She what?"

Julia felt her face heat up. She touched José María's shoulder. "It was the scars...I knew they had done that to him and I wanted to distract them..."

"Scars? What scars?" Miguel jumped up and balled his fists.

"Oh no you don't," said José María standing up and backing away. "You stay away."

"You bastard, you never told me." Miguel started around the table but Clothilde, who had just come back in from the patio, grabbed his arm.

José María started to laugh. "What? So you could jump me and add some of your own?"

Miguel skidded to a halt, bent over and slapped his thighs. Julia chuckled as the two men roared. Clothilde simply shook her head and rolled her eyes in what looked like loving resignation.

The sound faded away, leaving behind a ringing echo. The room was yellow-dim and filled with heat and the sharp, yeast smell of the *chicha.* The roof overhead crackled underneath the sun. A fly hovered over the jar with the pickles.

José María's finger touched her back. She reached back and held it against her, held her breath, held on until the moment passed.

They said goodbye. Clothilde gave her a little hug. She came to the door with them and they stood for a moment, an uncertain group, hovering at the edge of the fierce, white sun-glare.

"I'll come part of the way with you," said Miguel.

"Good," said José María, and as if it were a signal, they started down the street. "When were you last up north?" he asked Miguel.

Julia turned and waved at Clothilde who was still in the doorway.

"How far north do you want?" said Miguel.

José María pursed his lips. "To the mountains?"

"Months."

José María sighed and Julia wondered why — the question seemed so innocuous. Like flames licking at wood, she understood the surface of things, then a glimmer of what lay beneath, then only the sound.

She stopped and frowned.

"What?" asked José María.

"Marble floors and zinc roofs."

"Of course," he said. Though he spoke in English, his tone caused Miguel to laugh. And so she did, too. Then, to hide her frustration, she bent and picked up a stone and flipped it underhand into an empty lot.

"Do that again," said José María.

"What?"

"Throw something."

She picked up another stone and threw it, this time overhand.

"Did you see that?" he said to his cousin.

274

"I did." Miguel scooped up three stones, handed them around.

"That tree over there, the *mango*," he said. Without any further explanation, they lined up.

"You first," said Julia. She slipped the strap of her purse over her neck and across her chest, settling it at the small of her back. Her stone had a nice heft; it was a good inch and a half in diameter and smooth.

Miguel wound up and hit the tree solidly. José María missed. Julia hit a glancing blow off one of the lower branches. They lined up again and this time Julia missed but the other two hit their mark. On the third round they all hit the tree.

"Where did you learn that?" asked José María.

"I played ball as a kid. Hardball." She stretched her hands up over her head then, laughing, flung them wide. She bent to pick up a stone, pointed to a fence post half again as far as the trees and hit it. Miguel loped around the *mango*, bending as he ran. He lobbed a stone at José María, who flipped it to Julia. She popped one up for Miguel. He fired it back and they were off and running. Her purse flapped against the small of her back, and her hands stung even though she gave with the catches. If she kept moving, she didn't notice the sting so much. José María threw softly, but Miguel had no such compunction. She was up against a fence when she saw a stone coming too fast. She ducked and raced after it as it bounced away. She ran out into a cross street, bent to scoop it up, and ran full tilt at someone standing there. She threw out her arms to try to stop but it was too late. She collided with a grunt, going down in a tangle of arms and legs.

"*Ay diós!*" she said. "*Perdone.* Oh god, I'm sorry."

"I'm very sorry," said a voice in English. To her horror, Julia was looking down at Mattie Schimmer.

"Oh shit." Julia scrambled up. "What are you doing here?"

Mattie struggled up onto her elbows. She said nothing.

"I'm sorry. Are you alright?" Julia reached a hand down to help her up, but Mattie was looking past her at José María and Miguel, who were holding each other up in a fit of laughter.

"Here, I'll help you up," said Julia.

"No thanks." Mattie sat up, knelt, then rose. The men dropped into silence and stared at her red hair like two small boys. Mattie turned away and scanned the ground.

"What are you looking for?" asked Julia.

"My shoe." Mattie's bare foot was tiny and white, with pale pink-enameled toenails, and she dragged her big toe as she pivoted.

"Ees dees eet?" José María held out a white sandal.

Mattie took it and looked up at his face. "You speak English?"

He shrugged, held his palms up and shook his head.

Mattie turned to Julia, not bothering to hide a look of contempt. Julia had a glimpse of what lay ahead. Was this where it ended, where it all stopped?

Mattie nodded down the street. "I was seeing about a pair of rocking chairs I'm having made." There was a lift to the sentence that asked for a like comment from Julia.

"That's nice," said Julia. "I've never gotten a Masaya rocker." She bit her lip to keep from babbling lies, or worse, the truth.

"For the patio," said Mattie.

"What?"

"The rocking chairs."

"Oh, I see." Julia looked around. José María was twisting his base-ball cap in his hand as though he had to go to the bathroom and was waiting for permission. Miguel shuffled his feet and looked down. Dusty and deplorable looking, the both of them. She could hear as clearly as Mattie must have, the sounds their voices had made, all three of them, as they played. Wild laughter and swearing in Spanish, like kids who'd known each other all their lives.

A tiny squirt of joy filled her. Whatever it was they were doing, however foolish and dangerous it was, the men were only trying to cover for her. She turned back around and made a sweeping gesture with her arm. "This is my refrigerator repairman, Juan Ordoñez. And that is his brother, Mario." She hesitated, then catching a glint in José María's eye, she jerked a thumb toward Miguel. "Mario's amazing. He can lift a refrigerator all by himself. Just amazing."

Miguel lifted his head like a dog hearing its name. José María gazed at Mattie with a blinding smile, all the while twisting away at his cap. It was a gift, that smile, a perfect gift, but how could Mattie know that?

"Nice," said Mattie. "That's certainly interesting." And she looked José María over like he was a cold pork chop. "Does he make house calls?"

Julia felt her face stiffen and for a moment she couldn't speak. "Of course." She kept her voice steady, light. "Unless Mario comes and collects it."

Miguel raised a hand above his head, twisted beneath it in a semicircle and began to declaim poetry at a *nancito* tree hanging over a fence. José María slapped his pockets, first in his shirt, then in his trousers. He looked under his arm, down his back as he slapped his rear. "Tell her," he said in Spanish, "I want to give her my card."

"What'd he say?" asked Mattie.

"He says he wants to give you his card."

He drew out a jumble of tattered paper and the stub of a pencil.

"That's okay, no, that's okay. I don't need it. Besides, I can always call you if I need his number." Mattie backed away and bent to put her sandal on. "Shit," she said.

"What?"

"It's broken."

"Oh, I'm sorry. I'll fix it," said Julia.

"With your permission, give it to me," José María said in Spanish. He held his hand out for the shoe, another blinding smile on his face.

"No!" said Mattie sharply. She straightened quickly. Her face was flushed and her mouth worked without a sound. For an instant she was startlingly ugly and then the look was gone and she was smiling. "Oh, for heaven's sake, why not?" She handed the shoe to him. "Do you think it can be fixed? *Regalo?*" she said, mixing up the words for gift and fix.

He dropped his eyes and Julia could see that he desperately wanted to laugh at this gift of one broken shoe. Please, don't make it worse, she thought. But he kept his eyes down and his lips tight as he turned the shoe over in his hand. At last he glanced up at Mattie shyly. "Tell her I think I can fix it," he said in Spanish. Taking the Swiss Army knife out of his pocket, he turned back to Mattie and said with a note of triumph, "I feex!"

He plucked Miguel from his poetry, and together they squatted over the shoe, mumbling away in Spanish.

"Amazing," said Mattie. "You'll be coming to the meeting next week, won't you? At my house?"

Julia scanned the sky. She'd forgotten. Christ, these days she forgot everything but when she would see him next.

"Aren't you?"

"Yes, of course."

"*Aqui!*" shouted José María. "Look!" Waving the shoe, he came back to Mattie. He presented it to her with a self-effacing smile.

"How'd he do that?" Mattie slid her foot into the shoe. "Perfect. Will it last?"

Julia translated.

"*Quizas.* Maybe." He shrugged. The joke seemed to have run out on him. He looked sad and weary.

"Well thanks," said Mattie. "*Gracias. Hhhasta la veesta,*" she said to José María.

"I'm sorry," said Julia.

"That's okay. All's well that ends well."

They watched in silence as she walked away.

"How did you do that?" asked Julia without turning to look at José María.

"What? Fix the shoe?"

She turned. "How did you manage to look so dilapidated. So…"

"Nicaraguan?" he said softly. "How would you have wanted it to be? Was there any other way to make it better?"

"No. You're right, I suppose."

He touched her wrist, stroked it. "As you said before, *mi amor,* marble floors and zinc roofs."

Unable to speak, she looked at his finger. Under his stroking, she opened her hand.

"Can you live in that house with the marble floors and a zinc roof?" he asked.

She looked up and saw her own pain reflected in his face. And something of the fear. Fighting back tears, she shook her head.

His voice broke and came out ragged. "Neither can I, my dearest love."

Chapter 24

The electricity was off again and the streets were dark. A milky haze drew a ring around the moon. The air was still and hot, cloaking the houses with the sour smell of urine and garbage. Odors he only noticed when he was returning to Acahualinca.

José María stopped at the pump, more to steady himself than to take a drink. But the water had already been turned off and he only managed to catch a few drops to wipe his face. He stared at the grayish blur of his palms as though they belonged to someone else, not that person who had sat under Clothilde's roof, listening to family talk and alive to the feel of Julia beside him, knee and thigh and hipbone separated only by their sweat-soaked clothes. So close even the tiniest current of air was like a cool finger drawn across their skin, leaving a trail of goose-bumps in its wake.

The pain cut into his belly and lungs; he squatted and rested his forehead on his knees and waited for it to pass. Miguel's voice like honey, as it always was when Clothilde was there.

He shivered and forced himself to stand. The moon wandered into a curtain of cloud then reappeared only to plunge into another. It was dizzying, all that movement up there and none down here. He turned slowly and listened. No sound at all, not even the wind. He cocked his head. What was he missing?

Nothing, he told himself. Ghosts. Still, he plotted a zig-zag course home, stopping at each turn to assess what lay ahead. It was a slow process and, halfway there, he stumbled on a stone, came down hard on one knee. He rocked to one side and fumbled in the dirt. A stone with sharp, gritty edges. He tightened his fingers around it wishing it were alive and he could squeeze the life out of it. Pain gripped his gut. Only now he knew its source, had known it for hours: he would never sit at a table with her, lean back and laugh, just laugh for the sheer joy of seeing her laugh. They would never lie curled up against each other through an entire night.

It took all his strength to stand up and start walking. All he wanted to do was sleep, forget, do nothing beyond the simple act of breathing. Digna's house wasn't that far away. Maybe she was already asleep.

Her front door was open, not just open but stirring with the wind. There was no light on inside. He stopped and backed away. A raid? Some disaster while he was gone? The rest of the street was dark except for a small light that glowed through the cardboard walls of the house opposite Digna's. But that was nothing new. With five children, one was sick just about every day. He took another step backward, turned and slowly walked past the water barrel. Then around to the back of the house. It was way too quiet.

Getting over the wall and down into the patio took forever. He crouched behind the outhouse and listened, then moved quickly into the house.

"José?"

"It's me."

They were sitting on the bed. Digna and someone else. Oh shit. They knew about Julia. They were going to cut him off.

"*Pase*," she said.

281

"Augustín? Is that you?"

He knelt before them. "What is it?" He held his hand out but neither of them took it.

Christ, he didn't know if he could bear losing both Julia and his work. He was shivering.

"It's Sofía," said Digna. "They've found her."

"Where? Augustín, what happened? For Christ's sake!"

"The South Highway." Augustín's voice cracked. "This morning."

"Was she...?" whispered José María.

"Dead."

He rocked back on his heels. "Oh Christ!"

"She'd been dead a day at most."

"But that's impossible. It's almost nine weeks since they said she was..." Fuck! What was he thinking?

Augustín had to clear his throat before he spoke, "She died sometime yesterday or last night." Again his voice broke. "If I'd gone to her when they first told us, she'd be..."

"You'd both be dead," said José María.

"That's what I've been telling him," said Digna. She was holding on to Augustín's arm, half supporting him, half restraining him.

"Right," said Jose Maria, "They wanted you. The moment they found out who she was, they thought they had you."

"You think I don't know that? But she'd be alive; they'd have traded her for me."

"Man, come on, you know better."

"The bastards had her for nine weeks, José! Every day she was hoping I would come and every day they were telling her I didn't want to come."

"How was she...?"

"Tortured. Worse than you."

Digna cut across him, "We haven't seen her body."

"Who has?"

"People," said Augustín. "Some people passing by."

"Ah." For their own safety, nothing more would be said about them. Eyes that looked, hands and feet that helped, all were at risk.

Digna's voice hardened. "Now they're saying *la guerilla* killed her, that we tortured her ourselves. That we're fighting amongst ourselves. And in the meantime, they're out there waiting for Augustín to come and get her body."

"You're sure it's her?" asked José María.

"Yes. She still had the crucifix."

"What crucifix? A lot of people wear crucifixes."

"Not like this one." Augustín held something up and Jose Maria's fingers closed around it. It was light and smooth. He slid his thumb over it and found that the cross pieces were twisted upwards like the two arms of a **Y**.

"You made it?" he asked.

"Yes. For her first communion. One for her and one for me."

"So this is yours?" There was a thickening along the shaft and the arms, the merest hint of the body of Christ. "And someone had the guts to go close enough to see for himself that she wore a crucifix. That took courage."

"A little boy climbed a tree."

"But they had to be watching." The ache in his throat made his voice hoarse. "They want you to know it was her."

Their silence was answer enough.

"So what'll happen?" asked José María.

"My mother will come and take her back to Boaco," said Augustín. "What's left of her."

No one spoke. José María glimpsed the flicker of the candles in the house across the way. Had Sofía been in the same cell he'd been in? Had she managed to write her name down? Had they killed her by accident, just gone too far? Now they were waiting for Augustín to come get her body. Would they leave her mother alone?

"One other thing," said Digna. "The people who saw her body are pretty sure she was in Tiscapa. They found her just off the South Highway, right where you were. Her wrists were tied together with palm fiber, not the metal ones they use in town."

"Jesus!"

"Jesus?" growled Augustín. "If Jesus were around, my sister would be alive."

"Don't," said Digna.

"Fuck that." Augustín pried his arm loose from Digna's. The entire leadership is in prison, thank you Jesus."

"We'll get them out."

"How? Demonstrations? Prayer vigils? Some graffiti maybe? We don't even have the money for paint. That's what we really need – money. Lots of it. For guns, not paint."

Jose María's knees ached. He sank to the ground. "You're right. We're getting nowhere this way."

Digna sighed. The cot creaked as she rose and went out. The door to the outhouse closed, the bolt snicked across, sounding loud in the silence.

José María stared into the darkness. He could almost feel how lumpy the mattress was where he had first made love to Julia. He wondered if he would ever be able to sit there again. As if their loving were a betrayal of Sofía. Of Augustín, of all of them. With a silent wail he pushed himself up and dropped down beside Augustín. He could hardly breathe.

"There is to be an expropriation, José."

"What?"

"An expropriation."

"You're deciding this now?"

"Not just me and not just now. It was already in the works." There was a lag to his words. "We didn't make the final plans until yesterday."

We? Another meeting without him. He'd probably end up a messenger boy again. And he didn't give a shit. He deserved it. "What kind of expropriation?"

"A bank."

"Which one?"

"We were thinking either the Chicago bank or New York. Chicago's better, but we need to check them both out. That's where you come in."

"Oh?"

"Yes. We think you'd be the right man to check out which one has the better layout. You know, fast in, faster out, the tellers, the vault, the exits, the guards — everything."

José María suppressed a sigh of relief. So they didn't know about Julia after all. Or they wouldn't risk sending him. Still, he could almost picture himself walking into the bank, asking for an appointment with Julia's husband, and getting it.Are you crazy, you dumb shit? he thought. Tell them! He could feel himself start to sweat.

"With your English," Augustín was saying, "you could pass as a business man. At least get yourself beyond the tellers, and speak to one of the managers."

"You've got to be kidding."

"Oh? Why's that?"

He almost blurted out, Because it's fucking crazy, you ass! "You did say both banks?"

"You've got a problem with that, José?"

"Well, there is a slight conflict of interest."

"We know about that."

"And you still think I'm the one to go in?"

"Yes."

That was it. Nothing more.

The silence stretched out and José María began to wonder if Digna had died in the outhouse. Or was she staying out of this discussion on purpose? "So you were just waiting for me to say it?"

Augustin grunted his assent. "That's right."

"So now what? I'm out?"

"No."

"I'm in because that way you can keep an eye on me."

"Cut the crap, José. You've got a shitload of good stuff. You're light on your feet, you've got imagination, you see things others don't, you care — "

"How come I can hear a 'but' in there?"

"No one doubts your commitment, you've proven that."

"How?"

"There are people who know you better than you know yourself." Berfalia, he thought.

"And you didn't spill anything when you were inside."

"How do you know that?"

"We've got ears."

"Inside?"

Augustín didn't answer. José María lost patience. "Then how come they didn't give us any information about Sofía?"

"We work on the same system the *Guardia* does. Apart from a small group of people, no one person has the whole picture. The fewer contacts the better. You know that."

"Goddamn!" José María shot up off the bed. "For every little bit of information, you've got a different person? That's a lot of people."

"I wish." Augustín sagged back against the wall.

The grief and weariness in the man were so profound that José María stifled an angry retort. "Where the hell is Digna?" he muttered, and then a little louder, "She could've had a heart attack by now."

"She'll be back."

The lights in the house across the way went out at last. The darkness became a physical presence, crowding everything else out. Would to God he could stay in it forever.

Chapter 25

Fidelia handed Marshall Beal Jackson's file.

"Do you know what he's going to decide?" asked Marshall.

She shook her head. She looked tired.

Well, here we go, he thought; here at least was some good news. "Please sit down, Fidelia."

She lowered herself into a chair, smoothed her skirt over her knees. She folded her hands together and waited. Formidable, Jaime had said of her. And so she was, he thought, formidable enough to turn back the tide, but shrewd enough not to try.

"I want to thank you for the work you've done on the Montoya branch. It couldn't have been done without your efforts."

She nodded, and cocked her head to one side.

He smiled. "I just heard from Chicago today on your promotion. It came through."

She raised one eyebrow, the other followed slowly. A woman officer!

Was that a gleam in her eyes? He grinned. "Congratulations. Can I get you a cup of coffee?"

"Oh no, ah...no, thank you, sir. When do I start?"

"You already have." He tapped Jackson's file. "In fact..." He reached inside a manila envelope waiting on the table and handed her the brass nameplate.

Her freckles merged in a hectic flush, and now she did smile. "You ordered that without me knowing?"

"Yep."

"It's beautiful." As she held it up, the brass caught the light from the window. "Thank you." She pursed her lips in that strange way she had when she was trying out a new phrase. "You really went to bat for me…WENT to bat!" She laughed and shook her head.

"Your work convinced them. That was what counted."

She laid the nameplate down. "Maybe I shouldn't put it up until Alfredo goes to the Montoya branch."

"I can handle Alfredo. He won't have time to complain." If Marshall had his druthers, Fidelia would go to the Montoya branch instead of Alfredo; she was a much better banker. But there was little hope of pulling that one off. Maybe when he went on leave, he wouldn't get a replacement in from Chicago and she could fill in for him here , where the action was.

He leaned back in his chair. "You have the talent to be a first-rate international banker. I think you should consider spending some time in Chicago and then moving on to other countries."

Up went the eyebrow again. Of all people, she would know it was a test. Locals generally hated to leave their own countries, particularly women with children. Which Fidelia didn't have, but she did have a very large family.

"That's certainly worth thinking about," she said.

"What? Shocking Alfredo or becoming an international banker?"

She smiled. "The two are not mutually exclusive. Who do you want as your assistant?"

He shrugged, disappointed at how quickly the back patting was over, "You'd have a better idea than I, since you've trained them all."

"Right." She rose. "Well, thank you very much." She paused at the door. "I have learned very much from you, and look forward to learning much more." She closed the door softly behind her, but not before he glimpsed a broad smile on her face. A funny woman. More like a man, which is probably what made her such a good banker. He trusted her. Which was more than could be said about most people he'd worked with.

Maybe, if he could swing it, he'd go to Guatemala and take over when Axelen went on his home leave. It was unorthodox, but why not? Alfredo here, Fidelia in Montoya. He'd have two months in Guatemala, where he'd always wanted to go. With or without Julia.

He stopped halfway up from his seat and sat again. His body felt heavy and awkward. He wasn't sleeping well. Julia had taken to sleeping in the living room and, though he didn't see how that should interrupt his sleep, it had. There were dreams now too, a lot of them, where he went looking for something he could never find, dreams that went on and on until he woke up exhausted.

Hell, maybe it was a good thing to be alone in the bedroom. It was peaceful. He could get used to being alone. Going to Guatemala by himself didn't sound bad, except for leaving the kids behind.

He rose and went to the window. The woman who sold trinkets had moved in under the shade of the concrete overhang. This close, he could see the small gap where her zipper had pulled loose and a patch of flesh showed through. It made him think of the holes in Yelva Inez's dress, those shadowed patches of bare flesh, the stray hair curving up close to the nipple.

But then the trinket woman bent over a small boy and the spot of flesh squeezed up like mustard out of a bun and he turned away.

290

Why had he agreed to meet Mattie for lunch today? He didn't need another complication. Still, something needed to be said, if for no other reason than to ease any awkwardness when they met socially. The fact that Mattie had called him instead of the other way around made it easier. It was she who had sought him out. It made it seem more like a business lunch.

Fidelia opened the door and said, "Mr. Jackson, sir."

Marshall rose. "Beal, good to see you. Come in." He locked onto Jackson's good eye and shook his left hand. "Sit down. Take a seat."

Jackson pulled up a chair and lowered himself into it. He looked worse than usual. Clearly, accepting Jaime's offer had been a bitter pill. Why? What was that about?

Marshall sat down. "How've you been?"

"So-so." Jackson made a wing-dip motion with his left hand.

"Sorry to hear that." Marshall paused to soften the business at hand. He'd hate to be someone's charity case. "What have you — "

Before he could finish the sentence, Beal said, "The answer is no."

"What?"

"I'm not taking the offer."

A truck backfired in the street. "You can't be serious."

"Never more so."

"Beal, this drought can't last forever. It could be over in days."

"If it rains tomorrow Marshall, my crop's still gone." Jackson spoke without strain. As though this was all a simple transaction and the outcome meant nothing.

"But without Jaime, there's no way we can continue to cover you."

"I don't expect you to."

"What are you going to do?" Marshall fought to keep his voice down. "You'll have nothing." He felt his face flush. He hadn't meant to be so blunt.

Jackson offered his ghastly grin. "That's correct. But I still won't take the offer."

"You're crazy."

"Really?"

"No, I'm sorry, I didn't mean that."

"Of course you didn't. I know how hard you've worked on this, you and Fidelia. But it's done, it's over."

"Beal, for Godsakes!"

"Believe me, not even for Him." Beal leaned forward. Marshall tried not to back away.

"Listen, I may not look it," said Beal, "but this feels great. For the first time in a very long time, I feel free." Jackson patted the table. "I suppose I should thank Jaime for that." He shook his head. "Unbelievable, eh?"

Unbelievable? It was crazy. Marshall punched the buzzer. What was going on? Where the hell was Fidelia?

There was a knock on the door. Fidelia came in with the coffee tray. "There's a gentleman here from…" She looked at a card on the tray. "…from Enterprising Enterprises, Inc."

"Never heard of them," said Marshall.

"I haven't, either. He's in molded plastics, I believe." There was a ghost of a smile on her face.

"Thanks, tell him I'll see him in twenty minutes. "

"Shall I offer him coffee, then?"

Jackson stood up. "No Marshall. Let the man in." He nodded to Fidelia. "I'm sure Fidelia and I can work out the details of…what is it, going into receivership? I'll set up an appointment for tomorrow. Today, I have other things to do." As he spoke, he moved toward the door. Marshall had to hustle to catch up with him.

"Don't worry about me," said Jackson, "I'll be okay. You take care of Mr. Molded Plastics." He started across the platform.

Marshall followed. He felt sad. The Plastics man was sitting in the chair beside his desk and craning his neck to get a look at the pictures of the children. A skinny guy in a well-cut suit and a shirt with a collar that was too big. Nosey little creep!

"I'll be right with you," said Marshall.

"Sure." The man stood, turned then nodded. "I'm not going -- " His eyes slid past Marshall to Jackson and widened fractionally.

Cool customer, thought Marshall, revising his opinion upward a notch. Jackson looked as if he were going to speak, but he only nodded at the man and made for Fidelia. Reluctant to let him go, Marshall followed and waited while they made their appointment, then walked Jackson across the bank floor. "What are you going to do now?"

"Well, to be honest, my dog and I are going to the beach."

"Oh?"

"Yes. I'm not kidding." Beal chuckled. "I'm going to sit myself down and take comfort in the waves. It's okay. I won't do anything foolish." He bumped Marshall's arm with his twisted hand, walked off and melted into the flow of vendors, shoeshine boys and ordinary people walking in the bright sunlight. Here and there eyes glanced in horror or fear that such destruction could be visited on a living human being. Once he had passed, a woman lifted her hand to her breast and made a sign against the evil eye.

On the platform, the Enterprising Inc. man was talking to Fidelia. Marshall started across the bank floor; this would take no more than a minute. After Jackson, it would take even less. And then maybe he could get to some real work.

José María saw the two men pause at the door to speak to each other. Their shadows were mirrored on the bank's marble floor.

He had no idea what he was saying to the woman. Something about smoking, his words bubbling out while the sweat grew cold on his palms and behind his ears.

The last warm thing he'd touched was the gleaming brass plate on the glass door before he stepped inside and crossed those acres of marble, making a mental list as he went. One guard at the door; a platform ahead with three desks on it; teller's cages along the wall to the left of the door, with waist high brass poles and velvet cords to keep the customers in line.

The width of the passage behind the tellers and the outside structural wall indicated a vault at the far right. Which was odd, even to his unpracticed eye. A vault up against an outside wall? It made no sense.

Ahead was a raised platform with the three desks, a mezzanine above it, and a door behind and to the left of the desks. To the right, the platform ended more than halfway across the back wall allowing for an alcove but no visible exit.

With every step, the chill inside him grew. He sensed eyes staring at him from behind. Stop now, he kept saying to himself, the layout was unworkable. There were those nightmare velvet cords to stumble over as Mario, or Augustín or whoever it was backed away from the tellers' cages. With no visible second exit and the mystery behind that door in the back of the platform, there were too many negatives.

Turn around and go, he told himself. But he kept on walking and only stopped after he'd stepped up onto the platform. He took a slow, deep breath. Two more steps and he was in front of a huge, empty desk with the brass plate that read, Marshall G. Bennett, Associate Vice-President.

He wasn't surprised. Julia had never actually said what his title was. Vice-President. What else had he expected? Illusion had never been a part of the picture; it had been everything.

"May I help you?" A woman's voice, slightly irritated tone. He turned and stared down into a pair of yellow-brown eyes surrounded by freckles. A grim face with no hint of accommodation. The sign on her desk said, Fidelia something.

"My name is Alejandro Lacayo," he said and handed over the card Mario had so carefully designed. She glanced at it, laid it on the center of her blotter and waited.

Damn! His fear turned to anger. You crazy, dumb fuck, ask her a question and get out now. "I'd like to speak with Mr. Bennett."

She gestured toward the man at the desk behind her, a Nica with a pompadour and a tight collar.

"No. It's Mr. Bennett I'm supposed to see." And he was, pulling another card out of his breast pocket and pretending to read, "Marshall Bennett, Assistant Vice-President." Before she could reach for it, he slipped it back into his pocket and smiled. There was a clean ashtray on her desk. He would have given anything for a long, slow drag on a cigarette.

"I'm sorry," she said. "Without an appointment…"

He felt pressure behind his eyes; his ears were ringing; he opened his mouth. "Surely Mr. Bennett is more creative than that." It was so outrageous, he suddenly felt nothing. He was floating, completely unencumbered. He smiled. And her lips twitched. She had a mouth that was wide and full and made to smile.

The latches on the briefcase clacked as he drove his thumbs under them. The Yo-Yo filled his hand, a firm, sweet shape. He slipped the loop up past the knuckles of his finger. She tilted her head to one side. Almost reluctantly, her eyes slid away from his face and down to his hand and then on to the shimmering green disk spinning across the floor.

It was all in how you kept your distance, Mario's friend the Yo-Yo man had said, making the thing appear to walk up Digna's wall. "You're watching the Yo-Yo, so you don't see my hand." And they had all laughed at the political significance of the statement.

"I have in here thirteen different models, including one with genuine rhinestones,"said José María. "And hundreds of tricks." It had taken him an entire day to just master twenty-three of them.

"This one's called 'walking the baby.' Look how she skips."

Her eyes widened.

My, my, he thought and took a stab in the dark. "How could any child resist this?" He slid the Yo-Yo down the length of his arm and let it spin on the end of the string, then using his other hand to fashion a cradle out of the string, he made the Yo-yo appear to rest inside and rocked it back and forth. "The baby's in the cradle — nighty-night!"

A smile lit up her face and she looked up at José María with delight.

A buzzer sounded nearby. Still smiling, she lifted her hands in surrender. "I'll speak to Mr. Bennett," she said, and carried the card away with her.

His knees unlocked. His head was pounding again, and his hands and feet prickled. Around him, the sounds of business resumed. He pocketed the Yo-Yo, picked up the briefcase and went to the chair next to Bennett's desk, carefully looking up at the mezzanine before he sat down. From up there, one could take in everything on the banking floor except what was directly underneath. There would be a stairway, maybe leading up from the room the woman had gone into. Even worse was the fact that the next building was laid smack up against this one. There was no sign of a second exit. Which defied all logic.

He settled into the chair and set the briefcase between his feet. The Nica with the pompadour gave him a snotty look. José María smiled and turned his back on the man. The desk stretched away at his elbow and he looked it over as casually as he could: there was a letter opener squared evenly with the marble pen stand, an empty in-box, an equally empty out-box, the gold letters MGB initialed on the leather blotter holder. All his research and he didn't know what the 'G' stood for.

At the top of the desk, turned slightly away from him, were two picture frames, their glass opaque at this angle. He leaned forward. They were beautiful girls, blonde with big, light eyes. The older one had a heart-breaking smile, and the younger one grinned like the devil. Both smiles he'd seen on Julia. He half rose in his seat and stared at the other picture. Julia, leaning against a stone wall, her hair tied back, her hands behind her, and on her face that same heart-breaking smile. He glanced out onto the banking floor, one quick swipe and he'd have it in his pocket.

"I'll be right with you," said a voice directly behind him. He shot up, turned. There were two of them! He hadn't even heard them coming.

"Sure," he said, amazed he had a voice at all, then surprised he'd spoken in English when Bennett had spoken in Spanish. He tried to shrug, heard himself say, "I'm not going — " He stopped short as the man behind Bennett came into focus. That scarred face — the man with the dog. Icarus!

Icarus looked up, started forward, his hand rising, the one good eye leveled at him in recognition. He was going to speak!

297

José María gave a tiny shake with his head and forced the muscles of his face to form a polite smile.

The man's hand rose and pressed an invisible pen into his jacket pocket. He smoothed the jacket as he turned away and continued on behind Bennett. Outside, a siren wailed; behind him, the woman's typewriter clacked into life. José María sat down. He shivered. Had she been typing this whole time?

The two men walked to the front door. Julia's husband and the man who'd once offered him a *rosquilla*. He was sure the woman with the freckles was staring at him. He looked back and caught the tail end of something on her face — worry, speculation maybe, suspicion?

"Have you ever tried to give up smoking?" he asked her, pointing to the ashtray on her desk.

She looked bewildered, then shook her head 'no.'

"It's very, very hard." He proceeded to tell her just how hard it was. Icarus drifted off into the sunlight and the banker was on his way back.

"That's four times, and this will make my fifth." He patted an imaginary pack in his breast pocket and waited until she looked up and he knew the man was standing behind him. He turned, stood, and put his hand out. "Alejandro Lacayo," he said in English. "Pleased to meet you."

"Marshall Bennett." The man's hand was warm. His tone of voice was not exactly bored, but something close. His eyelids drooped halfway down over the eyes. He sat down heavily at his desk and tapped Mario's small white card on the blotter.

"Plastics?" he inquired.

"Toys," said José María. The blood was rushing back to his hands and feet with a vengeance. His hands tingled, and without looking at them, he knew they were red and swollen.

"Look," said Bennett in a tired voice, "With a weak economy and a drought as serious as this one, I don't think toys are a good investment right now."

José María nodded. That was it, time to quit. He picked up the briefcase and smiled, then heard himself saying, "bread and circuses."

"Pardon?"

"You know. Playing takes the mind off hard times." His thumbs slid beneath the clasps again and opened up the briefcase. He brought out a box of *Topo Gigos* and another of Yo-Yos and spilled them out onto the desk. The man winced and José María opened his mouth to apologize. Instead he nearly laughed out loud. This was crazy, it was fucking terrifying, like he'd just whizzed down the steepest pitch on a roller coaster with no restraint whatsoever, and now he was soaring up the other side. And he wasn't dead, he wasn't being dragged away, he had all his toes and fingers still. He smiled at the man behind the desk.

"These are selling — how do you say it? Like hotcakes? In fact," he pulled Mario's financial sheet from the samples case and handed it over. "We have orders into January of next year."

"January?" Bennett stared down at the shimmering colors. He picked up a neon green Yo-Yo, pulled the loop over his finger, held his arm out and let the Yo-Yo fall away. It gave a weak bounce up and rolled back down, coming to rest just off the floor.

"Bob your hand as it reaches the bottom."

Bennett's mouth quirked up on one side. He was winding the string around the Yo-Yo. "Like this?" he said and ran the thing out quickly.

"Yes, that's it. You learn fast."

Bennett stood up, took a step away from the desk and snapped the Yo-Yo out at an angle, hitching his wrist as it reached its furthest extension, so that the disc swung in a full three hundred and sixty degree wheel, once, twice, whistling mournfully. Through its blur José María could see the startled face of Fidelia, and behind her the pompadour. With a sharp slap, the Yo-Yo snapped back into Bennett's hand and he looked up. "It's like riding a bicycle," he said.

José María whistled softly. "And I thought I was good." He shook his head. "You'd make a great hustler, you know."

Bennett grinned. "Hadn't thought of it that way. Who knows?"

"Goodness!" a woman said from below the platform. A low laugh sent a shock through José María.

"That was marvelous, Marshall. Could you do it again?"

"Hi there, Mattie. Come on up."

That voice, soft and filled with subtle intimacy, almost directly behind him now. He couldn't turn, couldn't move. With a sick dread, he waited for her to come around and see his face.

"If I remember correctly," said Bennett, "it's called 'Around the World'." He stepped back and ran the trick again.

As casually as he could, José María glanced around and there she was, the woman with the red hair and the devastating eyes, the one Julia ran over in Masaya. Dressed to kill and gorgeous, she was watching Bennett, her lips parted. Nothing ugly about her now.

"That's wonderful, Marshall," she said. "Where'd you learn that?"

"When I was a kid in Hamilton. Yo-Yo's were big there." He pulled the string from his finger and handed the toy to José María. "Not bad. It's a fine Yo-Yo."

"Thanks."

"Oh! Hello. Don't I know you from somewhere?" She moved directly in front of him. "It's Ordoñez, isn't it? Refrigerators?"

He rose and tried for a puzzled smile. "Refrigerators? No. I'm afraid you've got the wrong person." He held out his hand. "My name is

Lacayo." Bitch, he wanted to shout, don't you remember I couldn't speak English then?

"This is Alejandro Lacayo, Mattie. He has a plastics factory out in Tipitapa."

"Mattie Schimmer," she said. Her hand, too, was warm. "Plastics?" She shook her head. "I could have sworn I met you somewhere else."

He offered her a courteous bow. "I'm sure I would have remembered."

"Yes." She took her hand away. "And I thought I had." She turned to Marshall. "This is amazing. I apologize for jumping the gun and meeting you here, but I wouldn't have missed this for the world." She laughed again. Low and sultry. If spiders could laugh, he thought, they would sound like that.

"Thank you for coming in, Mr. Lacayo." Bennett handed him the financial statement. For an instant, José María just stared at it. How had it ended up in Bennett's hands? He was sure he'd put it back in the briefcase.

"You've given me a lift, but I'm afraid, hustling aside, I'll have to say no."

"I'm sorry." José María began to gather up the toys from the desk.

"They're beautiful." Mattie Schimmer reached down and picked up a pale blue *Topo Gigo*. "May I keep this?" She held it up and, one eye closed, sighted at him through the clear plastic.

No! He wanted to snatch it back, knock her down, run. "Yes, of course. It would be my pleasure."

She rubbed the little beast's ears. "It's very well made. It's supposed to be a mole, isn't it?"

"Of a sort." He had the toys back in the case, the clasps closed. He reached across to shake Bennett's hand. "Thanks for giving me your time." He nodded at the *gringa* bitch, then at Fidelia, who smiled back.

He hesitated as he stepped off the platform, afraid he would stumble. He could feel their eyes on him. His timing was off and he was moving too fast. It wasn't until he was halfway across to the door that he felt fully in charge of his body. Forget the back stairs, or another exit, he had screwed with the plan and gotten caught. And he'd put everyone at risk, even Julia.

The sun and heat nailed him as he went out the door. He felt his control begin to slip. There would be no way back to her now.

Chapter 26

In the dim candlelight of the restaurant, Mattie's hair framed her face like a fiery cloud, and the hollow at the base of her throat had a little pulse. Yet he felt nothing. He didn't get it. After Beal Jackson and the skinny guy with the Yo-Yos, she should have been a delight to look at. He brought a spoonful of beans up to his mouth and blew on it.

She'd ordered a glass of wine, but she hadn't touched it. Nor was she eating. Instead, she propped her elbow on the table, cupped her perfect chin in her hand, and said, "It couldn't be more simple, Marshall. I want to make love with you."

The mouthful of hot beans roared down his gullet like a claw hammer. He coughed, drank water, coughed again, wiped his eyes and opened his mouth to speak.

"Don't," she said and her hand found his. Her fingers curled over and around his, pulling them up as though she were pulling him up inside her. A slow, sensual tug left him gasping. Before he could stop himself, he snatched his hand out from under hers, and then tried to soften the gesture by turning it over to rest palm down on the gleaming tablecloth.

Oh yeah? You felt nothing?

Mattie's fingers with those orange nails lay in a crumpled mound where he had left them. He looked up at her, hoping he didn't look as desperate as he felt.

She gazed back steadily, one eyebrow raised and her lips pressed together. Then she smiled. Her signature Mattie smile. "Think about it," she said. "I'm a patient woman."

He started coughing again and held his hand up. "I have. Believe me, I have."

How in God's name had he gotten here? "Look Mattie, we're friends. I mean Garv's not only my friend, he's my business colleague. Christ, I play golf with him."

"Oh?" She looked amused. "Garv doesn't mind."

"Of course he would." A beat too late he picked up on the tense. "But he loves you," he blurted out.

"That doesn't mean he minds. We have a very clear understanding. We're not possessive." She'd stopped just short of saying, "We're adults," but he could read it on her face, in the small inward curve at one corner of her mouth. And then she did laugh. "Why should that surprise you? We're consenting adults. Believe me, Garv won't mind. And Julia certainly won't either."

"What?" He straightened up.

"Oh come on," she said. "Don't you see it ? Garv has had the hots for Julia for years."

He felt his jaw go slack. "No. I don't. See it, I mean." Julia would have seen it, and being Julia, she'd have made no bones about telling him. He could thank her for that, at least. He glanced around the room. If he could just get up, thread his way around those two empty tables and the three men at the table nearest the door, he could walk out. No, he had to pay the bill.

She dipped her fork into her beans and twirled it. He hoped they burned her, too.

"So how do you mean, 'Julia won't mind'?" he finally asked.

Her eyes narrowed. She laid the fork down. "Marshall, it's not that I don't like Julia. If anything, I admire her tremendously. She's beautiful and she's terribly smart..." Her voice trailed off. She picked up the glass of wine, took a sip, then looked at him over the rim. "I feel like an idiot next to her. You know, that way she has of showing how clever she is, all those questions about whether the way things are means something more? I feel like I'm somehow in the wrong, or I stand for the wrong things, or I have the wrong friends." She shook her head. "Like I'm a lightweight."

Each sentence was like a blow between his eyes. Christ, Julia did that to others, not just to him. He caught himself leaning forward, and sat back abruptly.

"Why should you think you're less than...?" he asked.

"You know, this going native thing of hers?"

"You tell me," he said, but she sailed right on, ignoring his sarcasm.

"You know, her Spanish? And then she's all over the place; you meet her in the oddest places. There's nothing she can't do. Or maybe wouldn't do. Maybe that's it." She shrugged, an exaggerated gesture that showed off her long neck. It made him think of turtles. And of Jaime, and the east coast turtles he would have to go and see sometime soon, and the goddamned dinner party with that awful hamburger pastry Julia served.

"Like it doesn't matter what she does," Mattie was saying. "She's the great Julia Bennett." Mattie twirled her fork again and he wanted to grab it from her and shout, shut up and eat your food.

"The truth is that I feel stupid around her. Inadequate."

He snorted. "Inadequate? You?"

"There! I can see you feel that, too. I can see it in your eyes. She's cold."

"Excuse me?"

"No. I'm right and you're too honorable to admit it."

"Julia's a good person." He hated himself for even saying it. This was crazy. Was Mattie just propositioning him because she felt jealous of Julia? Putting Julia down because she felt inferior? And here he was defending Julia, when what he really wanted to do was to throttle her.

Mattie put a finger to her lip as if to shush him up. "That's exactly what I'm saying. Julia's a good person, but she's cold and acts like she's always right. Don't you think you deserve more than just common decency? You deserve warmth and passion. And compassion."

Compassion, the word hit him hard. It was a word he'd never have used himself. But, with a terrible sinking feeling, he knew it was exactly what he wanted. And passion. Simple and uncomplicated, without the awkward embarrassment he had with Julia. But certainly not this ugly thing of Mattie's. He wanted something simple, free and uncomplicated. Two people comfortable with each other, not judging each other, not coming up short all the time.

He tried to keep his voice steady. "Mattie, I'm sorry. It just won't work."

"Why? Because you'll hurt Julia? Surely you know it won't."

"There you go again. What do you mean by that?"

"Come on, Marshall. Think about it."

"About what? What is it you're trying to say? Just say it, for God's sake."

"Oh come on, what do you think she does when she's off doing her scholarship stuff?"

"Excuse me?" Why was he even listening to her? Why didn't he get up and leave?

"When she goes off in her car for hours by herself?"

306

"I don't want to hear this."

Mattie sat back and crossed her arms over her chest. The repulsive orange nails went into hiding. "I guess you don't." She pursed her lips as if she were trying to decide something.

He knew he wasn't going to believe whatever she might say. He wouldn't believe her for one minute. She was spiteful and mean and not very bright.

She sighed. "I'm sorry. I was out of line. Just put it down to wishful thinking. Let's drop it for now. I don't want to lose you as a friend. You're one of the few men I've known that I really admire and I would never dream of offending you."

"Thanks." He signaled to the waiter to bring the bill. "I'm sorry too, Mattie. Really sorry."

Marshall lay on the bed in his study and pondered just how it wouldn't work. How having sex with Mattie was a bad idea. Especially after the blow up he'd just had with Julia.

When they'd walked out of the restaurant, he saw that Mattie was wearing sandals and that her toenails were orange too, and once again he was repelled. But here, lying on the bed, he could picture those very toes flexing as her ankles wrapped around his back, her thighs...

He reared up and sat on the edge of the bed. He could picture it all. And he knew that his anger at Julia was fueling the fantasy.

Obviously it hadn't been the best time to talk to Julia about going to Guatemala. He probably should've gone straight to the shower and waited for a better time. But it seemed there never was a better time. Not with Beal Jackson, or Mattie, or the land deal with Somoza, whatever that was about. When he'd called Jaime back to tell him about Jackson's refusal, he'd come away feeling like it was his fault.

Jaime's cool tone, that bogus retreat into quaint Spanglish, the slight accent, "Eet's time to apply *de breques*, no?" That was certainly not the friendly, debonaire Jaime, the perfect host, complete with thrills and chills in the sky, iced champagne, afternoon fucks on the ground. And fucks that were better than anything he could dream up about Mattie, much less about Julia.

He stood, crossed to his desk, pulled out the chair and sat. It didn't help that on the drive home, a tire had gone flat, and the lugs were frozen on the bolts, and by the time a kid came along and spit on them and beat them with a stone and got them loose, both of them were so dirty and sweaty, the flies were all over them. No wonder that by the time he got home, all he could think of was getting out of Nicaragua.

And why shouldn't he want to get out of here? Wasn't moving on to a better place what it was all about? After all, it was his work that supported her and the kids. She knew what being married to an international banker meant. The travel, the entertaining. Organizing their new home. She loved that — new country, new house, new schools for the kids. She'd even enjoyed managing the packers. She enjoyed it so much he'd sometimes wondered if she'd married him so she could travel the world. A free ride. Maids to do the work so she could do whatever she damn well pleased.

Unable to sit still, he stood up. Goddammit, if they ever moved back to the States, he'd make sure she did all the work herself. And he wasn't going to let her make maids out the children just so she wouldn't have to work.

He had the urge to chug a martini, which shocked him a little. He never drank before his shower. And didn't intend to, now. But Goddammit, marriage was about working together and knowing the ground rules. She knew that.

There was a soft knock on the door. It opened and Becka peered in. "Mother says you're supposed to be at the Helgars by seven-thirty."

"Right." He went to the window. When he didn't hear her leave, he looked back over his shoulder. "It's okay honey, come on in."

She came and stood beside him, first looking out, then up at his face. She looked worried. He patted her shoulder. She'd probably heard it all. Damn Julia, dammit.

"How are you doing?" he asked.

She frowned. "Are we going away, Daddy?"

"Would you like that?"

She shrugged.

"Does that mean 'no'?"

She shrugged again. He reached and ruffled her hair.

"How was your day?" she asked in exactly the same tone Julia used.

"Whoops! And how old are you?"

She stiffened and he patted her quickly. "I'm sorry. You sounded so grown up." He leaned his forehead against the louvers. This calm, steady child. Some day she'd be big, she would be gone, and he would never really have known her. "My day was shitty," he said.

He heard the little intake of breath. He never swore in front of them. He put his arm around her shoulder. Well, he couldn't tell her about Mattie, and he didn't want to tell her about Guatemala, not just yet.

"Today I had to be hard on a good man." He paused, started again, upgrading the language. "I had to foreclose on a man I admire. Tell him the bank could no longer wait for him to pay us back. He owes the bank a lot of money, and now we're going to have to take everything he owns away from him."

She was looking up, her eyes wide. "Why?"

"Why what?"

"Can't you just…" She seemed to be hunting for a word.

"Forget about it? No. There are rules. If people don't pay back what they borrow, then there's nothing left for other people to borrow when they need it."

"What'll happen to the man now?"

Again he was startled. "That's a good question. I don't know. I didn't like doing it." He gave her hair a gentle tug. "Seven-thirty, you say? I think I'd better take a nap before this big 'do' tonight, don't you?"

"Yes," she deadpanned. "Seeing how it's been a shitty day."

Chapter 27

Mattie's driveway was chockablock with cars, the line ending three feet from the highway. Julia eased her Volkswagon onto the shoulder above the highway at the tail end of the line and set the brake. Easier to escape, she thought. She cracked the windows and climbed out. It was times like these she missed Carol and Madelen the most. Not only would they have arrived on time, but she'd have had someone to bitch with as the meeting dragged on. Over time, they had worked out a set of gestures that kept them alive and chuckling through even the most interminable meetings.

Someone up near the house was gunning an engine, that peculiar wang-wong sound a car made when it was caught in mud or sand. An early drop-out? The lucky shit. Her throat ached and she looked up at the sky to stretch her neck and let the pain roll back down. It had been two weeks without José María.

You can turn around and flee, Julia; this far away, no one at the house can see you. This art show meeting isn't that important. But she couldn't give herself that much leeway. She couldn't even let herself imagine giving up. José María hadn't given up when they had nearly flayed him alive.

She took the bundle of records off the passenger seat, put them on top of the car and was locking the door when a horn howled and

Garv's jeep hurtled around the bend in reverse, half on and half off the same steep shoulder she was on. She plastered herself against the car door and closed her eyes. For an instant the howl of the jeep's engine went silent and then the jeep hit the roadbed with the crunch of metal against stone. By the time she got herself turned around, Garv had straightened out from a three-point turn and was pulling up beside her.

"Oh God, Julia, I'm sorry. I didn't mean to scare you." He got out of the jeep and pointed at her car. "Jesus, I did that?"

"What? Oh shit!" She turned and slammed her hand down on the fliers, but it was too late. More than half of them were twisting up into a funnel of wind. Garv took off across the highway to the screech of brakes and a braying bus horn. Once he was across, she turned back to find only a few fliers left anywhere near the car.

After ten minutes of scurrying about, tripping over each other and giggling uncontrollably, they managed to corral nineteen of the original sixty. The rest were nesting in the trees or soaring even higher. They sat on the shoulder above the drive and laughed until tears fell.

"What in God's name was that all about?" she finally said.

"You wouldn't believe it; it's a damned parking lot back there. It took me half an hour shuffling cars just to get the jeep clear."

"The ladies didn't help?"

"No. They were deep into who knows what..." He shook his head. "They just gave me their car keys."

"You had to do it all? That's crappy."

He grinned. "I know. If you'd been there, you'd have marched them all to their cars and directed the traffic."

"Am I that bad?"

"No. You're that good. I don't think you'd have sat on your bum and given me your keys."

"What in heaven's name was so important they couldn't take...?" her voice trailed off.

"I don't know. They stopped talking when I came in." He flushed.

Oh shit! she thought. Mattie's told everyone about José María.

With a grunt, Garv pushed himself up and reached out a hand.

"I'll tell you this Julia, I'll be glad when this show is over. It's like the goddamned house is under siege." He glanced up the driveway. When he looked back at her, his smile was gone. "I hear you're up for a transfer."

"That's news to me." She tried to laugh. "You know how it is, after two years in a place you begin to wonder where you're going next. And if you don't, other people'll do it for you."

"Well, I hope you stay as long as you want. You're a good woman to have around." He reached for his door handle. "Don't let anybody tell you different."

She stifled the tears that started up from somewhere deep in her chest. "Mattie told you about the refrigerator repairman?"

His hand fell away from the handle. "Look, Julia, not everything Mattie says is true. I mean, like yesterday — "

"It's true, Garv."

"I mean she was... " He stopped and shook his head.

"I'm sorry," she said softly.

"No. There's no reason you should apologize. It's us. No, it's me. I never realized she was so bored. We've got so much. This house, the beach place, travel whenever she likes, the art show...how can she be bored? She does whatever she wants, whenever she wants." His shoulders sagged. "And I do pretty much whatever she wants."

"Garv, listen — it's not boredom. Mattie didn't make it up." A crow called out overhead. Julia looked up to draw back the tears that had finally made it to her eyes.

"No, whatever's going on with you, or you and Marshall, or you and whoever, I know what I'm talking about here." His voice was so low she had to lean forward to hear him. "Mattie's got many fine qualities, but she's bored, and she's smart. And that's a bad combination."

He sat down in the driver's seat, his legs still outside the car. "Be careful," he said, his voice now clear. "Sometimes Mattie hurts people more than she realizes."

I doubt that, thought Julia, remembering the look on Mattie's face when she realized that Julia was actually playing with those dilapidated peasants. "Thanks, Garv."

"Hey, it's okay. Listen, any time you want to put a phone patch through, just give me a buzz."

"I'll do that. Thanks."

"Altogether that's 217 catalogued items." Julia cleared her throat. "There's certainly enough wall space at the Ruben Darío for them all. There's certainly enough wall space for the paintings, and the theater has in storage more than fifty bench boxes to put the rest on."

The room felt airless, the eyes too many, the faces so still. "But that's nine more objects than we thought we had." There were frowns from the few women who were still awake.

Again she cleared her throat. "That'll mean an extra page for the program. We can avoid that by cutting back on the size of the logo in the centerfold."

There was a very long moment of silence before bright smiles broke out with a chorus of, "Great, that's fine, good work."

"And thanks to you, Julia," said Mattie. "Now Amy has the schedule worked out for the cataloguing and setting up, so I'll just hand the meeting over to her."

Julia nodded, too tired to smile, and headed for the dining room.

There were two pieces of coffee cake left and she lifted out the corner piece with the crusty brown caramelized top and ate it without benefit of a fork or plate, licking her fingers afterwards. Her eyes glazed in a rush of tears at the feel of her tongue against her finger. Please, please keep him well, she thought. Don't let them do that to him again. She snatched up the last piece of cake and carried it away to the veranda.

The air outside was still and a haze high up in the sky bleached away the blue but gave no relief from the heat. She walked to the railing overlooking the swimming pool and devoured the cake, then licked her fingers again.

So word was going around that they were moving. Which was strange because the war at home about a possible move to Guatemala had fallen into a deep silence.

"Are you all right?"

Julia whirled around.

"Sorry," said Mattie. "I didn't mean to startle you."

Julia looked down at Mattie's toenails. This month they were orange.

Mattie put her hands on the railing and they stood side by side like two passengers on a ship, watching the wake roll out from beneath their feet.

"It's called Cool Papaya," said Mattie. "I got it in Miami in the airport."

"What?"

"The nail polish." Mattie turned sideways and leaned an elbow against the railing. "Marshall liked the color. I saw him yesterday. I told him I ran into you — or actually how you ran into me."

For a moment, Julia couldn't breathe. A parrot squawked from the kitchen wing. She looked at Mattie. "Oh?" she said softly.

Mattie laughed. "Do you ever get upset, Julia?"

"Only under fire."

"Then now is no time to worry."

She actually sounds relieved, thought Julia. "I don't understand."

"Because he didn't believe me."

"What?" Julia turned to face her. "What didn't he believe?"

Mattie frowned.

"Come on, Mattie, what are you really trying to tell me?"

"Just that I've had lunch with Marshall a number of times. Didn't he tell you?"

"No? Should he have?"

"You know, he's nowhere near as cool as you are, Julia. The man has passion…I asked him to go to bed with me."

What the fuck? It was so ludicrous Julia laughed. "Is that how you do it?"

"He turned me down," said Mattie. "He actually blushed. You know how he blushes?"

Blush? Marshall? Julia almost said yes, of course, what woman hasn't seen her husband blush? Too hurt to speak, she just shook her head.

"No?"

"No. Only when he's angry."

"Really?" Mattie frowned, then sailed on. "So I suggested we all play."

Julia's breath came back in a rush. "What in God's name are you talking about?"

"Don't be coy, Julia, all four of us. Garv isn't so unattractive, is he?"

Julia shook her head, more to clear it than to agree.

"No?" Mattie ducked her head back like a goose. "He's not attractive?"

"Does — does Garv know about this?"

"Of course. Did you think the phone patches were an entirely innocent offer?"

Fuck! Who were these people? *She does whatever she wants when she wants it,* Garv had said, *and I do whatever she wants.*

"Oh, I see." Julia snapped her fingers. "This time Mattie doesn't get what she wants when she wants it."

Mattie flushed. "Maybe so, but not for long."

Julia started across the veranda, but Mattie blocked her way.

"You think you're so much better than the rest of us, Julia. But you have no idea. The truth is I can report your so-called refrigerator repairman to the National Guard."

"You what?"

"You heard me. Your refrigerator repairman, Juan Ordoñez? That *was* his name, wasn't it? Juan Something? I met him again, yesterday."

Stunned, Julia backed up to the railing to steady herself. Alive, oh God, he's still alive!

"I thought that would interest you. It certainly did me. I was surprised. Finding him sitting there with Marshall. Oh dear — now that does bother you, doesn't it?" She ran a finger down Julia's arm. "Poor Julia."

"Don't touch me," Julia whispered.

Mattie stepped back. "Why do you think he was in the bank? Was he really trying to sell Marshall plastic toys from his factory in Tipitapa? And why do you suppose his name was Alejandro Lacayo yesterday, instead of Juan something or other? Oh yes. It was him alright. A little scar here," Mattie pointed to her hairline, "hazel eyes, overlapping front teeth with a chip in one. Yes, it was him. Oh and he'd shaved and was wearing a snappy suit, a little too big for him, but I'm sure it was him."

"No. That's impossible."

"And guess what? He speaks flawless English. But of course you knew that, didn't you?"

Julia couldn't move. Only yesterday? What time yesterday? Where was she when he was smiling at them? At the market? Back in the kitchen, sorting through the baskets? And he was at the bank with Marshall? And...

"By the way — I checked. There are no plastics factories in Tipitapa. Now why do you suppose a man would take on a new identity to go to a bank? To get a look at his girlfriend's husband? I don't think the National Guard would think so. But I do think the man really knows how to play people."

Playing her? No! Had he been using her all along?

Mattie held up a small, pale blue object for Julia to see. "This was one of his toys, made in his Tipitapa factory that doesn't exist."

Julia raised her hand.

"No you don't. It's mine." Mattie held it against her chest. "He gave it to me."

"My God, who are you? Can you hear yourself? You sound like some cartoon wicked witch."

"And oh yes, he had Yo-Yos too, and he had Marshall slinging one around like a pro."

"You're crazy."

There were voices, a rustle of women standing up in the living room.

Mattie spoke in a rush. "Don't you wish? He knew I recognized him. He was surprised I didn't turn him in. Was that a mistake?"

"What are you two talking about out there?" someone asked from the veranda door.

"Nothing," said Mattie over her shoulder. "Meeting over?" She turned back to Julia. "Tell me it wasn't a mistake."

Julia was sick to her stomach. She shook her head, unable to speak.

"Fine," said Mattie.

Chapter 28

They were Marshall's sort of fashionably late, though you wouldn't know it by the expression on his face. Julia snapped the thread with her fingers, smoothed the gold frog closure against her knee and started to push the needle into the dashboard, remembering only at the last minute how he hated that. He was already angry, and getting more so in the absence of a parking space.

She'd gotten home late from the theater, aching with fatigue after a day setting up the show with Mattie and the ladies. Another day on a sagging tight rope.

It had ended in a standoff. Mattie had said nothing more about José María and Julia hadn't asked. But she couldn't stop thinking that he was out there, that he'd been to the bank, to case the joint if she were to believe Mattie. After weeks of imagining, nothing else made sense.

"There's one!" Julia pointed to an empty parking space near the plaza.

Marshall nosed the car into it and they were instantly surrounded by a small army of boys. Ordinarily, he would stop to banter with them, but tonight he flipped a coin to the smallest, most ragged one and promised the second coin later should the car still be intact when they returned.

"*Va, pues!*" The boy caught the coin and jumped onto the fender. "I take care of it, meester." He patted the car tenderly and glared at the other boys.

She'd seen this a hundred times, but tonight the small ritual caught her attention in a new way. Take care of my car while I'm gone, it went, keep an eye on my baskets, watch my house, keep me safe from the depredations of little people.

Marshall was already half-way across the plaza and she ran to catch up, took his arm and saw him grit his teeth. In his tuxedo, he was the Gothic hero, the remote and self-contained master of his world. A world that was as removed from her as the Wicked Witch of the West. How quickly knowledge erased illusion.

She looked back over her shoulder and stumbled. He gripped her arm.

"For God's sake, watch where you're going," he growled.

This place had always filled her with awe — the two bridges over the railroad tracks like flying buttresses, the National Theater's windowless flanks so enormous they dwarfed the people who walked beside them, the huge columns around the corner facing the lake. All set in acres of white flagstones. Yet, she knew it was in fact a white stone monstrosity, built next to a stinking lake by a President with the power and the will to squash anybody who got in his way.

A warm wind blew steadily off the lake, chopping the moon's reflection up into a shimmering sparkle, plucking at her hair and her dress. The gold frog at her knee was loose. She eased herself free of his grip, shortened her pace to ease the pressure on the frog, and fell behind.

A piece of paper blew across their path, another hit her arm and she almost caught it before it peeled off and flew away. She turned the corner and stopped short. The plaza was filled with people, hundreds of them, all facing the theater, watching the guests as they gathered in front of the building.

Marshall stopped and waited for her to catch up.

"A lot of people," she said.

"So? Just shows you did your publicity right."

There were more than the usual number of people, but then Art Show posters had been plastered on every streetlamp in the city, and also the President was coming, usually a big draw. At least Mattie was hoping it would be.

Still, something didn't feel right. The crowd was too quiet, all bunched together with that empty space between the crowd and the theater. Standing near the theater's entrance was the U.S. Ambassador and his wife, with Mattie, Garv, and dozens of other people, all waiting for the President, who usually arrived last.

The wind veered as Julia took the first step of two up to the marble portico. Another paper caught at her skirt. This time she caught it before it flew away. Turning back to see where it came from, she saw José María a few rows back in the crowd, his body half obscured by a woman with a baby, his face turned toward her. Her breath caught at the haggard look on his face. Even at this distance, twenty yards perhaps, she was sure she could see the greenish brown of his eyes, and feel the shape of his shoulders in her arms.

Marshall was tugging at her arm. "What is it?" he said.

"Nothing." She glanced up. His expression stopped her. He was looking over her head straight at José María. Dear God, Mattie was right, he had been at the bank. Almost without thought, she swung around as if to walk toward the entrance. "Damn," she said, slapping her hand down over her dress. "Now look what I've done."

"What?"

"The damned thing's come away again." She flapped the skirt open and the flat loops of the frog dangled loose on one side.

"You just sewed it on!" He pulled on her arm and she jerked away. "Where're you going?" he asked.

"Look. If I walk in there with the bottom frog torn, the ones above are going to go and it'll be my crotch on view."

"Jesus, Julia, he's here! The President's here!"

"Oh." Only now did she hear the car doors slamming. To her right, behind a cordon of bodyguards, a heavy figure in a black tuxedo emerged from a limousine, followed by a slender woman in a flame-colored dress, then Jaime and Catalina Salazar.

She glanced around and saw that José María was weaving his way out of the crowd toward the far right. Where was he going? In a panic, she said to Marshall, "I'll be right back. Just say I had an accident." She hurried along the side of the theater, back toward the plaza.

The boy jumped down off the car. "See. Good job."

She shook her head, turned away and peered into the darkness. To her right the theater rose up, hiding the lake. By now they'd have formed the reception line; soon they'd be in the theater, filing along behind the President, nodding, smiling. There'd be speeches, and tiny canapés and California champagne, and the warm feeling of a job well done, of having participated in an important event.

Here, the plaza was almost silent, shadowy. She paced around the car. Maybe she'd made a mistake, and José María wasn't coming, he'd stayed there with the onlookers. She pictured him moving through the crowd as she'd silently tried to call him to her. She was almost sure he'd looked back at her, and then she remembered his expression. Something in her chest exploded as she realized he hadn't been looking at her at all. He'd been looking at the President. Acid flooded the back of her mouth.

Oh dear God! He hadn't come for her. He'd come for the President! The thought flung her away from the car. She stumbled, snatched at her high heels, hopping desperately on one foot, then the other as she tore them off and started running back toward the theater. Oh please God, don't, don't, don't!

José María looked back over his shoulder and saw her disappear around the far corner of the building. Yes! She was heading for the street behind.

Just before the end of the building he turned back to face the crowd. Here was a perfect wind tunnel. From here a lot of the flyers would end up at the entrance, and some might even make it inside. He leaned against a palm tree, drew out the second package and saw that his hands were shaking. You're a fool, he told himself as he tore the wrapping off and started to slide the top flyer off. When it didn't come easily, he looked down and swore. Goddamn shit! They'd tied a string around the whole package and fucking knotted it! There was no way he would be able to untie it with his hands shaking so badly, and Julia was on the other side of the building.

He started to laugh and swallowed hard against the sudden spurt of saliva that flooded his mouth. It was such a ridiculous little package to carry so much freight. The string wound around all four sides and then was tied with a double knot plus a neat little bow made from the string ends. Someone had taken pains with it. It spoke of their concern. They were telling him to stay cool and do his job, take care of himself, and them. They were telling him he was no longer a stranger. He let his breath out. His shoulders dropped and the tightness drained away, leaving him empty and drunk with love.

For them, but most of all for the woman who was waiting for him behind the theater.

It took less than a minute to loosen the strings and slide them off. The top fliers riffled in the wind, making a satisfying, rapid-fire popping noise. He pressed his thumbs down on the top sheet, edged it up until it clattered wildly, then eased the pressure on his thumbs and the flier was gone, soaring over the heads of the onlookers, up high above the entrance until it caught a downdraft, folded over on itself and floated down toward the doors. Perfect.

He looked down at the rest, four hundred and ninety-nine sheets, the best work he'd done yet, clean, good copy. His heart was pounding as he held them up and let them go, in one long, wonderful burst, like a flock of birds pouring from his hands, rising and swooping away to join the ones floating down over the heads of all those people. A blizzard of single sheets slapping into bodies, swooping down around heads, to be caught and read as she had done. *Literacy is Art, Literacy is Justice.* All this he saw moments before he turned and fled, north and then west, running easily, with no pain, and now no thought but to see her.

He made a wide circle behind the cathedral, the government palace and then across the plaza, hoping against all reason that she would still be there. And when she came out of the darkness, her hair streaming, her shoes in her hands, her mouth open, bare legs flashing through the long skirt, he opened his arms in a wide, welcoming embrace.

At first she didn't see him, and he called out softly. She swerved with a muffled cry, as if he were a snake in her path, then stumbled and went down on her knees. Her face was white, her eyes, staring up at him, were huge.

He crouched before her, not daring to touch her. "What is it?" he said, and then in Spanish, "*Que te pasa, mi vida?*" His life, his love.

She didn't speak, and he watched as relief replaced her fear. He could feel both in his own body and he knew immediately what she had feared. Reaching out, he rose, pulling her up with him, held her, lightly, carefully. "*Mi vida, mi amor,* my life, my love. You thought I had come to kill him."

Still trying to catch her breath, she nodded.

"Julia." He brushed her hair with the palm of his hand, her cheek, her lips. "Don't cry," he said, and then remembering her that first day in Acahualinca, when she came at him with her fists and her teeth, he blurted out, "no, of course, yes, cry." They laughed, an instant of crazy laughter, muffled quickly and then she was crying again.

"You were coming to stop me?"

She shook her head, rested it against his shoulder. "I was afraid."

He put his finger under her chin and brought her face up. "No, Julia." He gestured with his head back toward the theater. "If I have anything to do with it, the son of a bitch won't be assassinated. He'll run away terrified, knowing exactly who and what he's running from, and why." From all of us, he thought, alive and dead, from Sofía, and himself, from Augustín, from our collective nightmare. And from our strength.

"It was your face," she said.

"What?"

"In front of the theater. Your expression was so awful."

He nodded. "I'm sure it was." He'd been caught out by the sight of them together, arm in arm. He was used to looking straight into her eyes, but he saw that she had to look up into her husband's face, that she'd had to do so for all the years she'd been with him, and for an instant he had hated them both.

He stroked her cheek, then rested his own against hers. "No, my soul," he whispered, "I didn't come to kill him. I came to tell you I love you." He moved his lips against her hair. "And to say good-bye."

"You're going away?"

"Yes. No, don't ask."

She shook her head. "You're safe," she said at last.

"Yes."

"For now."

She rubbed her thumb from the side of his nose across his cheek as though making sure he was real. For now.

One of the flyers skittered by and, keeping one hand on her hip, he bent to scoop it up.

"What is it?"

He held it up for her to read. "Literacy?"

"Yes."

"That's why you're here?"

"*Mi vida.*" The paper crackled as he wrapped his arms around her again and gave himself up to her scent. He would carry her with him somehow, in his heart, in his head, in his skin and tongue and lips.

She leaned back in his arms. "She told me, you know."

"What?"

"Alejandro Lacayo."

"Ah." He watched her expression — sorrow, anger and fear again. "Did you think I used you?"

"For a minute, no more. No, that's not true. You had every right to. But Mattie would turn you in if she could."

"Can she?" he asked.

"I don't think so. She doesn't know your name. But you're taking a big risk." She gestured toward the theater.

"One I will not share with you again."

"No!" she moaned. "It's not fair!"

"You're just finding that out?"

"I don't need your sarcasm. Not now."

"No, of course not. That's not what anyone needs for a journey."

"What journey?" There was a startled look of hope on her face.

"Go home, Julia."

"No," she whispered.

"Go back to Ohio, *mi amor*." He watched the tears slide up over the edges of her eyes and felt his own face wet. "When it's over, I'll come and bring you back." Oh God, that he should promise such a thing, that he could possibly come out of this alive and go to her. He pulled her to him and they clung together, teetering like a top coming to a stop.

They fell from the sky as if a tornado had gone slack, and automatically, Marshall snatched a flyer out of the air. An ordinary piece of white paper, with black print: *Literacy is Art, Literacy is Justice.* He turned to look out at the crowd and the man wasn't there. Lacayo, that was his name. Alejandro Lacayo.

What did Julia have to do with Alejandro Lacayo?

The ceremonial greeting had ended and the President was being hustled inside. Several men in dark suits wove through the crowd looking for the source of the flyers. Some people backed away. Others stood in their path and were knocked out of the way.

"Where's Julia?" asked Mattie. "What's wrong?"

Marshall blinked. The faces around him were a blur. He couldn't remember what he'd said to the President. Or to Hope, his wife. He hadn't heard a thing. He'd been thinking of Julia, seeing again the look on her face.

Mattie put her hand on his arm. He shook it off and turned away;

her small gasp registered only as he reached the corner of the building.

They were standing a little distance from the car, their arms around each other, their foreheads touching. A blinding pain shot through Marshall's head and he could see nothing. Someone tugged on his sleeve and he jerked his arm up. It was Mattie, pulling at him, shaking her head. "Don't," she whispered, "please," and the sound of her voice set him free. He yanked his arm away and yelled, "No!"

Like puppets, they sprang apart and turned to face him. Mattie shouted something he couldn't hear. Lacayo spoke to Julia and her face twisted into a grimace. Chattering and giggling children swarmed in front of Marshall, their fists against their foreheads, index fingers pointing up. He swept them aside like tenpins and dove. Lacayo stepped in front of Julia, twisted his body so that his shoulder caught Marshall in the chest and they both went down. Marshall struggled to hold on as they rolled on the ground. The back of his head slammed into the curb and for a second he couldn't see.

Quick as a cat, the man was on top of him, his breath in Marshall's face, in his mouth, then hot on his neck. For a brief moment, Marshall had the man in a headlock, lost it, caught an arm and rammed it upward. Lacayo grunted, his body went limp. Marshall struggled to his knees, found himself staring into the other man's eyes. "You bastard," he whispered. "I'll give you fucking Yo-yos."

"You whore — ," taunted Lacayo between gasps, " — go fuck Tacho." He blew the last word up into Marshall's face, grabbed his balls and squeezed.

Marshall gasped, doubled over, rolled onto his side and clutched at his balls. He sensed Lacayo scrambling up, tried to stop him, even managed to get onto his knees, but Julia was in his way and he couldn't bear to bring both hands away from his groin.

"Go!" she shouted.

"Bitch," Marshall screamed, but it came out a whimper. Nausea rolled up through the pain, toppled him over on his hands and knees, and he vomited into the gutter.

"Here!" said Julia.

Marshall opened his eyes. She held out a handkerchief. Mattie stood there, her arms hanging at her sides, her mouth open.

Fucking bitch! Both of them, fucking bitches!

"*Está bolo,*" said one of the kids.

"He no drunk," said another. *Está loco.* "

"*Sí,* horns do dat."

There were sniggering laughs as the little shits ventured closer.

"Are you all right, Marshall?" said Mattie.

"Here," said Julia again as she bent to wipe his mouth.

That simple gesture drove him upward. Ignoring them both, he staggered to the car. The key slid into the lock on the first try and he opened the door.

"Hey, mister," said the littlest boy, grabbing at the door. "I took good care of it. I did a good job."

Marshall reached for his wallet. Julia was at the passenger side of the car, her hand on the door handle. Did she actually expect him to let her in?

He grabbed out a twenty *cord* note and tossed it to the small boy.

In the sudden melee that followed, he got behind the wheel, slammed the door, rammed the key into the ignition and started the engine. He backed the car up, scattering a bunch of kids and, with the tires screeching, he drove off. In the rearview mirror, Julia and Mattie were staring at him. The little shit was tearing across the plaza, with the other kids hard on his heels.

330

By the time Julia came home, he'd packed a large suitcase and was throwing all his important papers into his briefcase.

"Where are you going?"

He pushed past her and went to the bathroom to get his toothbrush and shaving kit.

"Where?" she shouted.

"None of your...." His mouth filled with spit and the words caught in his throat. He slammed the door shut and leaned back against it, trying to catch his breath.

"No!" she screamed. "You can't." She pounded on the door so hard he could feel it through the wood. Let her her pound her hands to pulp.

She stopped abruptly. He cocked his head. Was she walking away? Just walking away? He yanked the door open and shouted, "Oh yes I can, bitch!" He snapped his mouth shut and stared down at Becka gaping up at him, her rumpled nightgown hiked up above her knees, her flower print suitcase clutched in both hands.

"What the hell are you doing?" he roared.

She hunched her shoulders up around her ears. "I'm going with you."

"No!" yelled Julia, suddenly there again. She reached out, but Becka ducked into the bathroom and crowded up against his back, the little suitcase squashed between them.

"You can't take her with you."

"What the hell do you know?"

"I'm already packed," said Becka.

He glanced back at her. Her eyes were round. She was terrified. She ducked behind him again and he could feel her forehead come to rest against the small of his back.

"You're not going anywhere, Becka," said Julia. "Give me that suitcase."

Marshall put up his hand. "Don't touch her. If she wants to go, she can."

"No!" Julia yelled. "You can't!"

"Oh, but I can," he said. "I can take them both, remember?" The power of being right, of being supported by something greater than himself, warmed him. "We're in Latin America. And I'm the father." That got to her, he could see it in her face, suddenly drained of color.

He turned to Becka. "Are you sure, honey?"

With a gasp, Julia came to life. "You can't. I won't let you."

Pushing Julia aside, he pulled Becka into his study and sat her on the couch. When he turned around, Julia was right there, red-faced and screaming. He grabbed her and shoved her out of the room, slammed the door and locked it. Julia pounded on the door. Good, let her know what it felt like.

He sat down beside Becka and put his arm around her. "I'm sorry, Becka. I know this is hard for you. But are you sure?"

"I packed." Her eyes were still huge.

He made his voice soft. "When did you pack?"

"Yesterday."

"How the hell did you...What about Caley?"

"She's hiding. She doesn't want to go."

He felt relief. Two would be much harder. "Where's she hiding?" Becka shook her head.

"Is she safe?"

She nodded and set her suitcase down at her feet.

"All right, honey. We'll stay at the hotel tonight. Tomorrow we'll fly out." He gave her a quick hug.

"Where?"

"To Guatemala."

She swallowed hard and nodded.

He looked at her small, fierce features, her mother's huge grayish eyes, and his heart sank. Christ! What the hell was he doing? He couldn't take her with him.

Julia's hammering had stopped.

"You sure you have everything?" he whispered. "Your toothbrush, underwear?"

"Can I take my school uniform?" she asked. When he hesitated, she whispered, "Don't make me stay here."

He felt heavy, his anger compromised. She was a kid — what would he do with her there?

"Please?"

He patted her head, gave her chin a little push with his finger. The ache inside him eased. "Okay, honey. We'll go together."

Chapter 29

The plane was called twenty minutes late. Marshall watched Becka turn from her vigil at the window and grab up his briefcase before he could reach for it. Without looking back, she headed across the waiting room. This after she'd been staring down the highway for nearly an hour, hoping that someone would come save them from their folly. He shook his head, picked up her ridiculously flowered carry-on and followed her out into the sunlight.

The hot tarmac gave off a wave of mid-morning heat that caught him off guard. To the south, the low bulk of Santiago Volcano and its riding cloud of steam punctuated the horizon. At the foot of the ramp, Becka bashed his briefcase against the bottom step, stood back, hiked it up and rammed it against the next step.

"Here, I'll take that," said a man in Spanish. "Let me help you."

"No, *gracias*," she said and struggled on. The man stepped up ahead of her and looked back at Marshall, then away as if embarrassed by what he saw. Marshall sensed the other passengers bunching up behind him. Waiting.

"Becka," he said between gritted teeth. To grab the briefcase from her, he would have to lunge and he'd only look like a bigger shit. He lunged anyway. She stepped up at the last minute and he went down hard on one knee. He hauled up her carry-on and took the steps two at a time, reaching her just as she got to the top. He raised his free hand to grab for the briefcase.

"*Buenos días*," said the stewardess, smiling at them. Marshall paused in mid-grab and tried to smile while Becka marched into the plane past another stewardess and the co-pilot and banged her way down the aisle.

"It's here, it's up front." He waved the boarding passes. "Come back."

She kept going, past two, three, four sets of seats before she finally came to a halt. "What number?" she called without turning around.

"Four C and D."

She backed up and, still with her back to him, slid in to take the window seat. She shoved the briefcase under the seat in front of her, then sat down and looked out the window.

He slid Becka's carry-on under the second seat and sat down hard. "May I remind you," he growled, "that you were the one who asked to come along."

Without turning around, she groped for his hand, caught it and held it in her own. Her hand was very cold, her fingers so small.

He ordered a bottle of Chivas Regal at the duty-free shop in San Salvador airport and paid the bill in dollars. Then they found two seats together in the crowded waiting area.

It had taken him three days to get everything together: to get Becka's school assignments, to work with Fidelia on the details of the Montoya Branch opening, and to whip Alfredo into shape to handle the everyday business at the main branch, with telephone consultation for major problems. Tomorrow, Bart Axelen was leaving the branch in Guatemala for a two-month home leave. Even after a month of lobbying upper management, it had taken three calls to Chicago to make subbing for Bart actually happen. He had no idea whose toes he was stepping on in Guatemala, but he'd cross that bridge when he came to it. Meanwhile, eight weeks would be enough time to figure out what to do next. Certainly enough to explore Rafael Valdés' offer of a permanent job in Guatemala.

Becka tugged at his arm. "The plane," she said, jerking her head toward the gate. "They made the announcement again — they're boarding."

"Again? Why didn't you tell me?"

"I did," she said. "You didn't hear me."

"Your duty-free package, sir." The stewardess held up the bag as they reached the top of the boarding ramp.

"Thanks." He peeked inside. "This isn't it. Mine was Chivas Regal."

"I think this is yours," said a soft voice behind him.

He turned. "Thank you." His voice trailed off as he stared down at the slight man with the very thick glasses and the empty sleeve pinned to his shoulder. Horse — yes, Faustino Horse, the bookkeeper at Jaime Salazar's farm. Yelva Inez's husband.

The man looked exhausted. His eyes flickered past Marshall, then he bowed his head, the plastic duty free bag dangling in his outstretched hand. Behind him, Yelva Inez stepped up onto the platform wearing a dress that was too tight and too short, its mustard color making her skin look like wood glue. Her hair had been cut short and her face emerged round and Indian and very frightened. The rough-soled feet that had danced toward him in that magical gold-barred room were covered with a brand new pair of squat clunkers with shoelaces. He felt a wave of embarrassed pity and self-loathing as he exchanged packages with the man.

"You are traveling to Guatemala City, also?" asked Horse, in English.

"Yes." Marshall glanced down at Becka. "Yes, we are." He smiled and gave a formal nod to each of them, then, one hand on Becka's shoulder, he steered her to their seats. Horse and his wife made their way past him to the back of the plane.

All during the ascent, Marshall faced forward. But when he felt the plane change altitude and begin to rock downward again, he jumped up and went back to the lavatory. Horse and his wife were sitting on the port side, the woman next to the window. Neither of them looked up.

When he came out, she was there, waiting to get in, braced as if trying not to fall. When he made room for her, she squeezed past, and stopped. "*Señor?*" Even in a whisper, her voice was harsh. Perhaps she was unused to speaking. He didn't remember that from before, didn't recall if she'd even spoken a word.

"*Sí?*" The plane gave a small lurch and she clutched at the doorframe of the lavatory. Her wide face, made wider by the dreadful haircut, was shiny with sweat. Her hand on the doorframe was clean, the fingers long and slender, the knuckles white. The sound of the landing gear engaging shot her back out into the aisle. "It's okay," he said, pointing to the seatbelt sign. "They want us to sit down." He indicated the aisle where the stewardess was bustling toward them. Yelva Inez said something he didn't understand and then, with a sudden motion that was astonishingly graceful, she kicked off her shoes and leaped up the aisle toward her husband and safety.

Marshall stared down at the shoes. They were truly ugly, wide in front and even wider in back. As the stewardess began to scold him back to his seat, he bent, picked them up and carried them down the aisle to her.

337

Chapter 30

It was the same every day. Julia and Caley got up, dressed, and discussed the whys of going to Kinder.

"I don't see why I have to go. Why can't you teach me here?"

Why indeed? "I'm not a teacher," she said.

"Is Becka going to school?"

"I'm sure she is."

"Where?"

"In Guatemala City."

"I don't like Mrs. Ferris. And Tara sits on my statue every day and flattens it. And Jeremy has snot hanging out of his nose."

Each day, Julia took her to school, gave her a Kleenex for Jeremy and a mango for her snack and pushed her out of the car.

Caley had begun to wear the lavender terrycloth lining of Julia's old shower cap again. One day she pulled it down over her eyes, turned to face her and leaned back against the car window. "What if there's an earthquake," she whispered, "and you're out here and I'm in there? All alone." She raised the hat and squinted into the back seat as if she were looking for Becka.

Julia held her breath. The losses were so great they never talked about them, yet half their days were spent conjuring up ghosts. Becka! She felt an aching rage that Marshall had taken her, and yet she was glad he had her. He would be missing Caley, he would be hurting, too, and it was her fault. At least that was what Marshall thought, and what everyone else would think.

And then last night, a moth had invaded Caley's bed, and she'd ended up sleeping with Julia. Just this once, Julia had told her, knowing it was already set in stone.

"There hasn't been a quake in a long time," she said finally. "Not even a tremor. I'll be back at twelve to pick you up."

Caley's shoulders fell. She walked down the path, dropped the Kleenex in the dust, stepped on it and went into the small, yellow school. In a moment, Mrs. Ferris came out. Julia waved, then quickly backed the car out of the driveway.

She had no idea what people were saying. She'd seen no one since the night of the art show. She had been dumbfounded when Mattie had offered to find a taxi for her that night. And even more surprised that Mattie'd apologized for not driving Julia home herself. Beth, from down the street, had come to see her twice, Catalina once, and to both Juanita had said Julia was sick.

"Go back to Ohio, *mi vida*," José María had said. Go back to Ohio. But it wasn't an option, not with the kids split up and everything at loose ends. When she'd checked with Fidelia, she'd found out that the rent was paid for two months, and Marshall had left enough money in the checking account to last several months. No, she couldn't leave Nicaragua, not without Becka.

"Damn!" Becka's voice resounded from her bathroom.

Marshall flapped the newspaper down. "What is it now?" he called.

"My toothbrush broke."

"Your new one?"

Becka didn't answer.

"Your new toothbrush?" he yelled.

She mumbled something and he heard the bathroom door close.

He dropped the newspaper on the bed, swung his feet to the floor and strode into her room. "Becka? Answer me when I ask a question!"

Her bathroom door opened a crack and she peered up at him. "It's okay," she said in a soothing voice. "It's early. Go back to bed."

He gaped, unable to find words to answer.

"It's okay," she said again.

He pushed the door open and she leapt backwards. "Daddy! This is my bathroom!"

"No. It's the hotel's bathroom. And I pay for it. Where's the toothbrush?"

The toothbrush head lay in the sink, broken along the bottom row of holes. He turned around. The handle was clutched in Becka's hand. "That's not a new toothbrush; look at those bristles. I told you to pack a new toothbrush."

"No you didn't."

"Yes I did!"

"You didn't! Mother did."

It was the first time she'd mentioned Julia since the night they'd left the house, and it felt like she'd punched him in the gut.

With a flick of her wrist, she threw the toothbrush handle into the sink. "You didn't say anything!" She leaned against the doorjamb, crossed her arms over her chest and stuck her chin up. It began to tremble.

"Ah, honey." He sat down on the toilet seat. "Don't."

She stared up at the showerhead and slowly her face smoothed out.

"You didn't get another toothbrush, then," he said. "What were you doing in the closet that long?"

"Listening," she whispered. Her gray eyes filled with tears.

"Oh."

"Daddy…" She spoke in a very small voice and he could hardly hear her. "…this isn't working."

Oh God, no. He couldn't leave now, not when he'd stepped on so many toes to get here. And what about the job Rafael Valdés was hinting at?

She was waiting. "Do you want to go back, honey?" He felt sick even saying it.

She looked at him a moment longer, then turned and walked back into her room.

He slumped back against the toilet tank. It wasn't her fault. She was trying very hard. He was the idiot, blowing up like that. He had to control what came out of his mouth. She wasn't Julia.

Becka came to the bathroom door. "I'll meet you downstairs in the lobby." Her smile was small and mournful.

"Okay honey. I'll be down in a minute."

He heard the door click shut and he got up and went to his room. She was right, it wasn't working, but he had no idea what to do about it, short of going back.

Downstairs, Becka sat on a couch, holding his copy of the Wall Street Journal as though she were reading it. Scuffed knees, awful oxfords, chewed down fingernails were all he could see of her. These days she looked more like an American child than the proper little *Nica* she was back home.

"Come on," he said. "Let's have breakfast."

She folded the newspaper, put it under her arm and followed him into the breakfast room.

"The trouble with you," she said, when he refused to taste her papaya, "is that you decide ahead of time you won't like something and you won't even try it."

He swallowed his mouthful of scrambled eggs and managed to put his fork down on his plate without slamming it. "Becka," he said softly, "you are not your mother. You have no idea what I like and don't like. So please stop it."

She chewed her papaya slowly, her eyes fixed on a spot beyond his right shoulder. He knew she was struggling to keep from crying. Again.

"Look at that," she said finally, pointing out the window.

He turned to see a boy out on the sidewalk, swinging a Yo-Yo in broad circles, drawing it into his hand like the tail end of a line drive, than walking it around the doorman like Charlie Chaplin with a cane. A kid with kinky, blond hair and a face powdered with freckles. Just a street kid, he told himself, with no shoelaces and his shirt hanging out. Just a kid.

"He's good," said Becka.

"Yes." Marshall jabbed his fork down through his eggs. "He's very good."

Chapter 31

On the day Caley discovered invisibility, Mrs. Ferris called Julia.

"It's her new solution," said Julia.

"I beg your pardon?"

"If she hides behind a door, she's not there. She's invisible."

"Invisible?"

"Oh, she's there all right. I make sure of that."

"That may be so, but she can't learn anything if she sits all day with her eyes closed."

"Ah." Julia didn't know whether to laugh or to cry. Wasn't invisible better than punching the other kids? She sighed. "You're right, Mrs. Ferris, I'll be right down to get her."

And that was that. No more Kinder.

Still, the next day, and every morning after that, Caley went behind the door, just in case. Sometimes, when she thought Julia wasn't there, she talked to Becka behind the door.

The rustlings, the muffled whispers, the pauses when an invisible Becka spoke were too much for Julia. "Come on," she said, squatting down before the door one morning. "We're going to the beach." And in a flash, Caley materialized.

By the time they made it to the turn-off to Pochomil, the thick, dark clouds that had teased them for the last three days without dropping any rain were rolling up from the west. The President's sugar crop was nearly hip high, testimony to the virtues of irrigation. A quarter of a mile in from the road, a crop duster flew low. None of which delighted Caley as much as seeing the *pijules* poking at cow shit for undigested seeds. Without her sister, Caley could be as loud as she wanted to be about those *gro-tis-cue* birds. Julia laughed and forbore to correct her pronunciation of "grotesque."

They passed the turnoff to San Victorino, where she had first seen José María over the back of that enormous pig with her piglets. A slender man with hooded eyes that had laughed at her when she finally stepped onto the porch. She sat up straight to ease the enormous cramp that took over her chest and upper arms.

She parked the car off the road and led Caley down the path to the beach. The clouds covered all but a patch of blue to the northeast. The beach, the water, the thatched shelters near the dunes were all in shades of gray, except for a woman in a faded red dress who was carrying sea water up from the beach, one bucket on her head, one on each end of a yoke strapped across her shoulders. The woman paused at the bottom of the path and squinted up at them. Julia waved her forward and stepped aside to wait for her to pass. She could hear the unmistakable sound of a jeep spinning its wheels in the sand. The high-pitched whine of back and forth. The woman's eyes moved in that direction and the corners of her mouth drew down. Julia nodded, unsure whether she and Caley were welcome.

"*Buenos dias,*" murmured the woman as she passed.

"*Buenos dias.*"

"And God be with you, little one," the woman said, though Caley was hidden behind Julia. Caley snaked a hand around Julia's hips and waggled her fingers.

Once down on the beach, Caley kicked off her sandals, pulled the lavender shower cap over her ears and ran down to the water.

"Don't go in," shouted Julia. She threw her bag under one of the shelters, slipped out of her sandals and jumper and sprinted down toward the water. Something flashed at her feet, and she twisted out of the way. A bottle. She bent and picked it up, half expecting to see a message inside. Disappointed, she flung it away, snatched up Caley's hand and they plowed into the water.

Not until their fingers were wrinkled and pruney did they finally head for the shade and lunch. The beach was still deserted; there was no sign of the jeep. They attacked their peanut butter and banana sandwiches, already limp and gooey from the heat and humidity, and all the better for it. Before she had even finished a half of her sandwich, Caley thrust her hand into the bag of brownies.

"Caley, get out of there – now!"

Caley held up a hand oozing with chocolate.

"Put that back, we're eating lunch first." Julia snatched what was left of the brownie, wrapped it in a napkin and dropped it back into the bag. She handed Caley a towel. "Here, wipe your hands with this. No, Honey, go down and get it wet, then wash your hands. And don't go into the water."

Caley got up and walked down to the water, kicking up sand all the way. Julia turned to reach for the bag and froze, her hand suspended mid-air. Something red had caught her eye. She squinted at a long, low shape in the sand two shelters over. A body? She squeezed her eyes shut and shook her head. Half buried in the sand? She looked again. Dead? The air exploded from her lungs. Her heart pounded. How had she missed seeing it before?

Caley! Julia sat up on her knees, half turned and breathed a sigh of relief. Caley was squatting over something in the sand a good ten feet from the water. Julia made herself look back at the neighboring shelter. She squinted, saw a minute fracture in the sand covering the chest close and open and close again. Alive, thank God. And judging from all the empty bottles lying around, it had to be a man. Outside the cocktail circuit, she'd never seen a Nicaraguan woman even tipsy.

A breeze rattled the banana leaves overhead. Down at the water's edge, Caley was making friends with a big yellow dog. A hefty dog, better fed than most of the ones that ran loose. Just as a wave came in, the dog would jump back and go down on its forepaws as if to bow, and Caley would crouch down. Every third or fourth wave, the dog would rear back on its hind legs, then prance between Caley and the rising tide and bow to Caley's curtsey.

Damn, thought Julia, he was herding her away from the water. How brilliant!

At a point several feet away from the water, the dog stopped his dance and lifted his nose, and Julia became aware of the whine of an engine. She looked toward the sound and saw a jeep bumping steadily along toward them.

Caley stopped, the dog crowded up against her, turned and sat at her feet. The Jeep was still a distance away but coming too fast for Caley to make it back. Julia rose and sprinted down to stand beside them.

The jeep slowed down as it passed. Two soldiers in green fatigues, their sleeves rolled up above their elbows, stared out at them. The driver's cap was pulled so low that his sunglasses didn't reflect any light. Beneath them, deep grooves flanked his nose and mouth. His passenger wore his hat tipped far back. One hand held a rifle; the other lifted a bottle to his mouth then raised it to Caley and Julia. He brought it back down then faced forward.

Enough, thought Julia. A drunk passed out nearby and two drunk Guards cruising the beach — it was time to go.

Something cold touched her palm. The dog drew his head back and stared up at her. He thumped his tail down into the water. Only then did she realize the three of them were standing in the water. Caley had wrapped her arms around Julia's thighs and was pushing her face into Julia's hip. The jeep had gone beyond the path to the settlement and was fast disappearing.

"It's alright, honey, you can come out now," she told Caley. "Come on, let's go." They headed toward the shelter, Caley clutching Julia's hand, the dog scrambling to either side in herding mode. They were several feet from the shelter when the dog left them and went to sit beside the drunk in the sand. Ah. The drunk owned the dog, or the dog owned the drunk. Either way, this smart and loyal dog was offering a good reference, so she felt a little better. She would rest awhile, instead of leaving right away.

Her face smudged with chocolate, Caley lay curled up against Julia's hip. Julia was propped up on her elbows, her legs stretched out in the warm sand.

She'd had no calls from the scholarship program in a long time, no interviews in months. The very last time was that day she'd met José María. The day the trap door had dropped open beneath her. And there it was again, the pain in her gut and shoulders, with the thought that nearly always followed: my God, what have you done?

Julia lay back and stared up at the woven roof above her, dirty straw turned golden by a sudden shaft of sunlight. She closed her eyes. Yes, it was the silence in the house. And the sense that there was nothing she could do. The loneliness without Becka, and the chatter between the girls. Of Marshall what could she say? That she didn't miss him? That he was a decent man and he didn't deserve this? That there could be wholeness without him? Yes, to all three. But more than anything else, she missed being with José María. She was hurt, angry that he'd told her to go back to Ohio, and she was terrified that they would hurt him again or even kill him. Yet she knew without having had it spelled out that his real life, the work he did, the risks he took, were what mattered most to him. This tiny country with its battered history might be a mongrel to others, a joke, but it was his home and he would give up everything for it.

She opened her eyes and saw that the slice of sunlight had moved down to the edge of the straw thatch and would soon fall off to the ground. The breeze was gentle, the swish of the waves was comforting. A gull cried out, and Caley nestled in even closer.

God forgive me, thought Julia, then let go, dozed, felt his arms around her, bobbed her head up as a wave smacked down on the beach, dozed again. And when she felt the slight shift of sand somewhere out beyond their shelter, she opened her eyes just enough to see the back of the drunk from two shelters over now sitting only a few feet from her shelter, his legs stretched out like hers toward the water, his near hand scooping up sand and letting it slide through his fingers. And there was the dog, resting his muzzle across the man's knees and watching her.

There was no reason for the man to leave the shelter of his cabana and sit in the sun, fitful though it was. She snorted and the dog lifted his head and cocked it to one side. If it weren't for you, she thought, I'd be long gone. And I don't even know your name. Dog, she decided, whose tongue was lolling, his eyes laughing, she could swear. And so she lay unmoving, half hypnotized as she watched the man's hand pick up the sand and let it fall, over and over again. It was some moments before she saw the scars, the three bundled fingers, two almost hidden behind what looked like a melted candle. "Mr. Jackson?" she said softly. "Beal Jackson?"

He turned around, nodded and said, "Hello, Mrs. Bennett."

He remembered her name. Startled, she swung herself up to a sitting position. To a man who'd lived here most of his adult life, she must have been just another come-and-go face, here for a year or two, then gone. So many of the long-term ex-pats didn't have the time to spend on such people. Even Mattie, with her *gringo* directories, art shows, international nights, plays and charities, had not drawn them out.

Without waking, Caley rolled over and settled into another position against Julia's thigh. Beal Jackson was watching them with something like a smile on his scarred face. "Of course I remember you," he said as though she'd spoken aloud. He lifted his hand toward his face and the smile widened, revealing a beautiful set of white teeth. "Not easy to forget my name. Yours is equally memorable."

"Oh?" She cocked her head. What was it that Mattie had said at one of the art show meetings? That Jackson had lost his land?

"Is that your dog?"

"We've been friends for a long time." There was something about him that reminded her of José María. Against the stiff monkey horror of his face, there was his voice, low and musical. She'd never noticed that before. You were always trying too hard to look him in the eye, she thought.

"Do you come here often?" she asked.

"I practically live here. I love this place."

She glanced around. "I know; it's beautiful." She took in the empty bottles. Was it possible that he actually did live here? Had they taken his house as well? Then it struck her — had Marshall had anything to do with this? Was Bank of Chicago the bank that had taken his home?

"I mean the whole country," he said. "I've always loved Nicaragua."

"Yes," she murmured and looked out at the water, not trusting her voice.

He started scooping up the sand again.

"I'm sorry about your land," she said and cursed herself for the tremor in her voice.

"I came here with nothing. I will not leave empty-handed." A smile touched his eyes. It didn't seem so hard to look at his face. "Indeed," he said, "it would be impossible to leave this land empty-handed."

"You're leaving?"

"No, not yet," he said, shaking his head.

A small figure zigzagged along the beach, a child perhaps, coming steadily toward them. Sun shone through a hole in the clouds, picking out something red at the distant figure's waist.

"Your husband tried to help," he said. "Did he tell you?"

"No. He doesn't talk to me about business."

Jackson's hand paused in its sand-sifting.

Probably doesn't believe me, she thought. "Marshall talks about ideas, theories. Not about people."

"Of which he has little understanding?" The hand started scooping again.

"Pardon?" When he didn't answer, she asked, "Was that a question?"

"Probably not." He shrugged and shook his head. "I don't think he can put himself in another person's place."

"Excuse me?"

"Which is probably wise in a banker."

"True." The falling sand had begun to annoy her; some blew across her thighs.

Jackson looked around. "This place once seemed like a paradise. Peaceful, enough for everyone, easy living, even kind..." His eyes found hers. "That's how I saw it before."

"Before? Your accident?" She was shocked that she'd said it.

"Accident?" He spat the word out.

"I....I mean the plane crash."

"That was no accident." His words were muffled behind clenched teeth.

"It wasn't?" Maybe he was drunk after all.

He leaned forward and watched the child who was closer now, a boy, maybe eight or nine, wearing a man's sawed off jeans tied at the waist with a red rag, and two fiber bags hung across his chest like *bandoleros*. Bending, straightening, dropping things in one bag or the other, he moved steadily toward them, zigzagging as the waves lapped up. When he was directly below them, he stopped and looked up. His skin was dark, his hair a dull, sugared-honey color.

Jackson waved and the boy waved back. The dog rose, went to the boy and dropped onto his forepaws in the same little bow he had given Caley.

"She sleeps soundly," said Jackson, nodding at Caley. The shower cap had rolled to one side and Caley's hair was glued to her temple and forehead with sweat.

"She certainly does," said Julia. A grinding hum brought her head up. The jeep was coming back up the beach, bucking along the water's edge at tremendous speed, wet sand flying up behind it. The driver crouched down over the wheel; the passenger hung on to the rollover bar and swayed wildly.

351

"Oh my God!" she said. "They're going for that boy!"

Jackson was up and shouting. The boy ran toward them and the sandbank behind them. The dog raced with him, sprinting from one side to another and barking as if to encourage him to run faster. Something landed at Julia's feet as the boy tore past. The dog skidded to a halt beside Jackson as the boy hit the sandbank, scrambled up and disappeared over the top.

"Run!" yelled Jackson, giving Julia's shoulder a push.

Where? she thought as she crouched over Caley.

"No! Don't stop. Run!"

The jeep was closer now, and from the sound, was heading straight for them. Julia scooped Caley up into her arms and took off for the sandbank with Caley screaming in her ear. Julia huddled at the bottom, pushed Caley behind her, then turned back to face the oncoming Jeep. It was close enough now to see the grin on the face of the man clinging to the rollover bar. With a wild cry he flung something in a high arc above their heads. It caught the sun dazzle as it rose. There was a shot, like a throttled thunderclap.

"No!" she screamed, twisting around and falling to cover Caley. Jackson thudded down beside her. She lay still, trying to breathe. There was the sound of wood snapping, then laughter, more shots and finally the dying sound of the jeep heading up the beach.

A high, thin wail came from Caley. Julia let herself go limp. And there was the dog, breathing into her ear. She turned her head; his tongue licked her nose.

"Stop!" She opened her eyes and sat up.

Jackson was once again under what was left of the shelter, on his knees, staring up at the sand bank behind them.

"What the hell was that?" she said. He shook his head.

Caley whimpered. "Caley? You're okay."

Caley squeezed her elbows tight against her knees and gave a small, desolate sob. Bending close, Julia smelled the thin, sharp odor of urine.

"Oh honey, we can wash it off. Look. They're gone and we have the whole ocean to wash in."

Beal Jackson touched her arm. She looked up; he pointed down at Caley, then toward his face as he started to move away. She caught his hand and shook her head. She let go of Jackson, lifted Caley up and held her close.

"Honey, here is a friend. This is Mr. Jackson. He helped keep us safe." But Caley struggled silently to be put down. Back on her own feet, she tugged Julia toward the water. Julia gestured to Mr. Jackson to follow and, to her surprise, he did.

As they stepped around a mass of banana leaves, he bent and picked up an empty *Flor de Caña* rum bottle and held it up. "They won't be coming back," he said, and tossed it away.

Caley dropped down into the water and paddled around behind Julia's legs.

"That was it?" Julia said softly. "They were just drunk?"

"No, Mrs. Bennett, nothing is that simple here." His mouth twisted into what may have been a smile. "That may have looked like two drunks on a lark. But it wasn't. They've gone inland now to see if they can pick the boy up there."

"But he's only a little boy!"

"A little boy maybe a hundred years old. Like so many others." Caley paddled in close and brought her head between Julia's legs. She glanced up, then stuck her head in the water and blew bubbles.

"But, in the state they're in," said Jackson, "I think the boy will be okay. For now."

"Why did they come after us, then?"

He shrugged. "To scare us – make sure we don't get any ideas." This appeared to amuse him. "You got any ideas, Mrs. Bennett?"

"No. They sure succeeded in scaring any coherent thought I may have had out of me."

"Exactly."

She was still shaking as they collected their things from the remains of the shelter. And getting angrier by the minute.

"Do you want these?" She held up the bananas. The tremor was back in her voice.

"Thanks."

Caley waited in the curve of the bank, huddled under the yellow towel, her eyes closed. Julia had never seen her this stoic. Jeeps, scary faces, and mortification were part of the beach now; all Caley wanted was to go home, and yet she waited.

"What's this?" Julia held up a small leather pouch. "Oh dear. It's that boy's. I must have kicked it under the sand when I ran."

"I'll take it," he said, a little too quickly. "I know where it's going." She looked at him. "So it's dangerous, isn't it?"

"Yes." He slung the pouch over his shoulder. "But worse for him if I don't take it."

"What's in it?"

He glanced at Caley, shook his head.

Enough of this, she thought. "You said it wasn't an accident, your...that plane crash. What did you mean?"

Something in the way he turned his face away and stared up the beach where the jeep had disappeared forced her on. "Mr. Jackson, they might have been going after that little boy, but they almost ran over my daughter and me. They deliberately attacked us. They shot at us, for God's sake!"

354

"We were just handy."

"Oh, I see. They were shooting off their frustration at not getting the boy."

He nodded.

"I guess that makes it okay."

"Of course not. It's not safe to know too much, Mrs. Bennett."

"I'm sorry, but it doesn't feel safe not knowing anything. And..." She tried to stop herself. "I'm just so fucking tired of all the secrets. I know I've — " Her mouth filled with saliva and she had difficulty swallowing. "I know I've kept secrets and — " She held her hand up as she swallowed again. "I know when the shit hits the fan, it's the secrets that mess us up. Oh I get it, this is a country where you have to keep secrets or you might get killed or others could die. But I know, or at least I feel, that if you don't understand the situation, the context..." it was one of José María's favorite words and it gave her more confidence. "Without knowing that, you can get killed, too."

"That makes some sense."

Some sense?

He moved toward the water. She followed and they stopped when the water was above their ankles, not so far that Caley would follow, yet far enough so she would not hear them. For some moments they watched the waves roll in, a slow, oily surging and receding, leaving behind a snarled thread of white bubbles and black seaweed tendrils.

"I saw something once, Mrs. Bennett..." He was talking quickly, his voice so low, she had to come up close to hear him. "I saw a man thrown from a plane. It was before my crash, months before...I was flying up over the crater of Santiago, and there they were." He shook his head. "I was behind them, and this thing — this big ball, came out — and it opened up into a man." He bent swiftly, gathered up a handful of sand and threw it out toward the water. "His arms were waving wildly and his legs were kicking — he was alive!"

Julia was too horrified to speak.

"I got out of there fast, thought maybe they hadn't seen me, maybe it was okay, maybe if I kept my mouth shut…. And I did, but I kept seeing that ball opening up like some huge bug, and I kept feeling what it must be like to fall like that."

He wasn't telling her this, she told herself. Things like this didn't happen. But they did. There were José María's scars. "Did you go to the police?"

"These guys were the police. They were bigger than the police."

"How — how could you know that?"

He sucked air up through his nose. "Because it's a fucking fraternity up there!" He put his scarred hand out. "I'm sorry, Mrs. Bennett, excuse me. You just don't know. Everyone up there knows everyone else, the planes, their call signs, who the pilots are. It's a small country, I knew whose plane that was. And no, I didn't tell a soul."

That's enough, she thought, don't tell me any more. She took a step away from him.

"You asked, Mrs. Bennett." It was almost a cry of despair. "You were the one who asked…"

She turned back and waited.

"I never flew again without looking over my shoulder. But then nothing happened, and the man acted like nothing was wrong…"

"The man?"

"The pilot. I knew him socially. I began to feel safe. Not good, but safe."

A gull cried out overhead and they both looked back toward the small mound of yellow towel, topped by the purple shower cap.

"She's invisible," said Julia.

"Of course." He nodded. "She's very beautiful," he said and turned back. For a while he didn't speak and she thought it was over, that he would go no further. She would respect that.

"About seven months later," he said, "it was Zenita's sixth birthday, and she'd been talking about going on a plane ride with her mother and me for months and I couldn't say no. So I checked out the plane, went over it with a fine-tooth comb. I was so sure I knew what I was doing, God help me."

He was shaking now. "I thought I knew what I was doing, Mrs. Bennett," his voice grew softer, became a thread, "but we blew up in the air."

"My God," she whispered.

"That's right. Two explosions, small ones, one up front, the other in the tail. They went off simultaneously. There was no possible reason for it to go like that except explosives. The bastard put bombs..." He covered his face with his hands, pressed his fingers up into his scalp. "My wife died in the blast, but Zenita was alive, she was screaming...and I couldn't get her out."

She touched his arm. He took a deep breath. "Later, when I was in the hospital, the bastard's wife came to visit me...a kind person, a good person...at least I think she is; she came to tell me how sorry she was. She told me her husband had offered to fly me to the States for skin grafts! I couldn't believe it — I was half unconscious with the pain and here this killer was offering to fly me to the States, and I knew if I took him up on it I'd probably end up in a crater. Or somewhere out in the ocean.

"It felt like she stayed for hours and I wanted to babble everything to her, I wanted to tell her to run. And of course, I didn't know if she knew everything already. I hope to God she didn't."

Far out to sea, a rain squall sailed slowly by, its gray column dark against the lighter gray of the sky.

Julia felt sick. "Why hasn't he come after you since then?"

"I think he's changed his mind. I think it pleases him to see me like this. It pleases him to think I am suffering every day. This — " He waved a hand toward his face. " — this is my life insurance."

"Motherrr," a high whine issued out of the mounded towel. "When are we going to goooo?"

"I'm coming, honey." She turned back to Jackson. "Who was he?"

"No, Mrs. Bennett, I've never told anyone. Before Adelia and Zenita died, I was afraid for them. Then, all I could think of was killing him."

Caley began to emerge from the towel and now he spoke quickly. "But then I realized someone else would just take his place and it could be even worse. I would be the mess someone else would have to clean up. It's not one man, Mrs. Bennett, it's the whole corrupt system. Even that little boy knows that." He took her hand in his good one. "I should never have told you this, but after today you're no longer an innocent. Please, for your own safety, don't ever tell anyone what I've told you. Not until you're out of this place for good. Then, there will be time for speaking. Indeed, then you must."

"But what about you, are you safe?"

"As long as he thinks I'm suffering, I'm safe." He gave a low, dry chuckle and reached down to pat the dog. "There are more important things than safety, Mrs. Bennett."

On the ride back, Caley wanted to sit in Julia's lap.

"No, honey. It's not safe. And besides, the car's too small."

"I hate this car," Caley said and pounded on the dashboard with her fist.

358

"Look at the birds, honey." But Caley didn't want to look and neither did Julia, so she sped up again, away from the sugar fields, the humpish cattle, the shit-eating birds. She felt sure the jeep was following her, would scream around a bend behind her or block her way ahead.

She saw the man falling from the plane, his legs flailing, saw Beal Jackson trying to reach his wife, his daughter screaming inside the flames.

She touched Caley's shower cap where it met the yellow towel. "You okay, honey?"

"Mmmm."

"It was pretty scary."

The purple shower cap nodded slowly.

The air grew cooler as they drove up through the hills. At an intersecting dirt road, Julia heard the whine of an engine. She lifted her foot off the accelerator. The jeep! She started to back up, then hit the accelerator. It wasn't a jeep after all, it was a plane! Caley's hand came out from under the towel and grabbed Julia's skirt.

The plane flew out from behind a stand of bamboo crowded up close to the road, twenty, thirty feet up, a dark, howling shape, spewing a cloud of white poison from its nozzles. Julia stopped the car and frantically tried to close both windows.

The plane turned at the end of the field, rose and headed back.

Her temples pounded. She let out her breath. "Look Caley! It's the fumigator plane!"

"Don't want to look."

Julia tried to breath normally. She shifted into first. Nausea filled her stomach. Her skin was greasy with fright. The plane, further away now, moved parallel to the road. Two butterflies flew out of the bamboo stand. Pale yellow, they flopped over each other, just above the windshield, gaining altitude with each circle. Several more flew out. There were ten at least. Then twenty.

"Oh honey, look. Oh my!" Julia's voice caught. There were hundreds of butterflies rolling out of the bamboo stand. Clouds of pale yellow butterflies. Light, like sun drops against the green of the field, the gray clouds.

Caley raised her head enough to see over the dashboard. "Ohh," she breathed.

The yellow cloud moved across the field, heading for another bamboo stand. Bright, tumbling mass, caught up in itself. Halfway across, one or two fell onto the ground. And then more fell. Still, more than half made it across and into the bamboo. A bark of shrill laughter burst from her and then she was crying, crying as she shifted gears and drove up the road. Caley was crying too, hard throat- tearing sounds, with her head up and wailing, snot sliding past her lip.

The first raindrops made big, powdery impacts on the windshield, like squashed bugs pushing the dust aside. Then there were more, until finally the rain was crashing down all around them and Julia turned on the windshield wipers. They stuck their arms out the windows and, still crying, drove up through the first rain of the season.

Chapter 32

Andrés met him at the entrance to San Judás. José María swiped at the water dripping off his nose and smiled at the sight of the short figure hopping over the puddles in the road, holding a broken sheet of zinc roofing over his head. A welcome committee of one.

There had been no way for Andrés to know that he was coming and yet here he was with his zinc roofing, like so many times before, guided by a sixth sense, an intuition about his people.

"Aha! Good man!" José María tapped lightly on the sheet of metal as it bobbed around him. The metal rose and was offered as a shared shelter. José María held one end of it against the top of his head and extended the other out over his cousin's small head. Andrés stared at his own freed hands as if they were about to speak, then grabbed the opposite edge of the metal. Fever had taken most of his speech from him when he was a child; now he had no connectives and few verbs. Andrés did verbs with his body.

"What is it?" said José María. The rain pounding against the metal ran his words together.

"Miguel!" shouted Andrés.

"Miguel is here?"

Andrés nodded emphatically. A big, near-toothless grin formed and then disappeared as he tipped his thumb toward his mouth, his baby finger extended upward.

"Drinking again?" Not good. Still, it would be good to see him, to have all the family together once more. "How is *tia?* he asked.

Up went a thumb.

"Good." He needed some of Berfalia's strength now.

The grayness of the day made the houses of San Judas look more than ordinarily bleak. Still, these were palaces compared to the sieves in Acahualinca. At least Digna's house wasn't down close enough to the lake to float away, although another move farther away from the garbage mountain would be due soon with these rains.

The street where Berfalia lived had turned into a mire and he and Andrés had to part ways in order to negotiate the narrow path that constituted high ground. A brief tussle over who would give up the sheet of zinc was resolved when Andrés bounded ahead without it. José María picked his way along, slipping and sliding and cursing the rain. The sheet of roofing had become a sail, tossing him this way and that. He passed Hortensia's house at a stumbling run, dropped the zinc sheet and splashed straight into Berfalia's arms.

"*Jodido!*" She managed to push him away and give him a hug at the same time. "You're soaking wet. You're shivering."

"*Tia!*" He made a quick grab and was rewarded with a poke in his chest and the smallest of smiles. "Ah, home at last," he said. He rubbed his chest and laughed.

"Okay, man!" Miguel's voice came out of the dimness to his left. He felt a blow on his shoulder and turning, he grabbed his cousin and pounded him on the back. They stopped just short of wrestling each other to the ground. Andrés had been right, Miguel was thoroughly ripe.

"How's it going?" Miguel shouted. His cousin's breath was heavy with *chicha*.

"Well enough."

"You were always a terrible liar."

José María grinned. "That's because I was scared shitless."

"Of me! No. Never. A liar you may have been, but scared you never were. He drew José María closer and whispered, "But now you are."

José María rolled up his eyes, stepped back and took the towel Berfalia offered. "He been giving you shit too, *tia*?" he asked.

She shrugged and walked back to the kitchen. "No more than usual."

"*Mamá!*" roared Miguel. "When have I ever given you trouble? Have I ever abandoned you?" He turned in place, stumbled, then recovered and spoke to the wall. "Have I ever gone away and left us to our own devices? Have I ever been secretive and sly and — " He pointed at José María. " – duplicitous?"

"Yes," said his mother from the kitchen doorway.

"Oh." Miguel dropped his arm to his side. "I have?"

"Every time you drink that poison."

Miguel leaned close to José María and grinned. "Oh well, it takes one to know one, eh?"

"Right, you shiftless, prosy bastard," said José María. "Who do you think I learned it from?"

José María set his elbows on the table. A can, placed to his left to catch a rain leak, was nearly full and a wreath of splash surrounded it. Before he could move, Berfalia switched the can for an empty one and brushed the wreath down onto the dirt. The water plopped loudly on the bottom of the can. He grit his teeth and counted. About one drop a second. She'd need a bigger can to get through the night.

She set a plate of sausages and rice down before him. They were hot and he ate them with relish, aware she was watching.

Miguel shoveled in a mouthful of rice and continued with his tale. "And so, cousin, coming through Somoto, I see it again. They walk into a town, pick up somebody, anybody, a vendor, a shoemaker, they like shoemakers, they think shoemakers are all Sandinistas. What?" His eyes widened at their combined protest. Even Andrés had joined in.

"So you're all the experts now, here in your safe little house." When no one said a word, he shrugged. "So they take this shoemaker off for questioning, just like that." He waved his fork in a circle next to his ear. "One minute there, the next minute gone. And they don't ever come back, these shoemakers." He stared down at his plate. "Before we know it, we'll be a country of barefoot people."

"We'll know it," said Berfalia.

"We know it already," said José María.

"Food!" yelled Andrés and he gave his mother a hug as she passed by.

"Leave off, and eat," she said.

"Home!" He waved at José María and Miguel, then burst into laughter.

They stared at each other.

"Well *doggonnit*, Andres, you're right again," said José María. "It's the first time we've all been here together in a long time."

Andrés jumped up and danced around the table. "Dawgant, dawgant, dawgaaaaant," he sang the only word he knew in English, then buried his head in Berfalia's bosom.

"Twenty-one months and three weeks," said Berfalia. "Now eat. I don't cook table decorations."

"Long time home." Andrés' voice turned sad. "Long time."

"Cheer up, brother," said Miguel. "We'll all be here again, shoeless, maybe, but together."

"Shoeless! Since when have you started spouting this stuff?" said Berfalia.

"In memory," Miguel said.

"You make no sense, fool."

"That's the point, mamá. Fools get to make perfect sense. Fools and artists."

"So that gives you a double dose?" asked José María.

As Miguel swung around, he knocked over the glass of *chicha* at his elbow. Both Berfalia and Andrés jumped to mop it up but Miguel stared at José María, then leaned to one side and whispered, "Where is she?"

"Who?"

"*La gringa. La beisbolera.*"

"Gone."

"Liar."

"Gone home, and thanks," said Berfalia as she refilled Miguel's glass.

Miguel drank it down in one long pull and lifted the empty glass to his cousin. "You know what I think, cousin? I think you're going to need eyes in the back of your head. And still – " Without looking at his glass, he held it out to be filled again. " — it's not going to help." He set the full glass down before José María. "Drink!"

"What do you know?" said José María.

"Nothing."

"Exactly. So shut up." He took a gulp of the beery drink. He was shocked at how hard it was to hear Julia spoken of around this table. Most of the time he kept her somewhere between his breathing and his bones, automatic and unconscious and all through him. Still, when he'd passed Hortensia's, he'd felt the beginnings of a shiver: Julia with a baby in her arms and he holding her jaw steady with his fingers and with his thumb, wiping a kiss of strawberry jam and paprika from the corner of her mouth. He stared down at his thumb, longing to raise it to his lips. That very first touch, a child's straw-berry-jam kiss.

It was too quiet, and when he looked up, everyone had their eyes down, watching their forks rise and fall. A mixture of laughter and pain twisted his gut. Tomorrow he would disappear. To prepare, they had said. And soon, the bank job would be over. That's all he knew for sure. He did not have a good feeling about it, but as Miguel had said, the bastards were mopping up all the shoemakers and some-thing had to be done about it.

The rain can was nearly a third full and the noise of the water falling had softened. When he looked back across the table, Miguel was watching him. Miguel pushed his plate back and leaned forward.

"Speaking of fools, do you know cousin, on the day they took the shoemaker away in Somoto, there was a lunatic in the town, a crazy man who thought he was a story teller. This man stood in the plaza and told his story over and over again…"

It's the same story Miguel had started when Julia was there, thought José María. The sound of the rain falling and the rhythm of his cousin's words brought her back and he could feel her thigh against his, her arm, and he could reach up and touch her back, so smooth, so unprotected…

"…the same story again and again until all the people in the town had heard it, and those who had come from all around had heard it.

366

And when the sun went down and the people went home, this crazy lunatic kept on long into the night. Until at last, the ghost of the shoemaker came back."

Miguel held up his hands, then brought them down and stared at them. "He knew it was the shoemaker's ghost because the man's throat was slit and his hands had been torn away and he had only one foot and that was bare. So the lunatic told his story once more and this time the shoemaker's ghost picked up the beat and together they built on it, telling it again, and then again, until it was a thing of great beauty and the whole town echoed with it and the earth and the sky sang it back and there was nothing left of the long dark night but the silence in the cool, gray dawn."

Miguel looked at Berfalia, then back at José María. "Fools," he said sadly, "sometimes make sense."

José María rested a moment in the story's silent dawn. Miguel, his comforter, afflicter, fool and mentor. He wanted to thank his cousin, but only nodded.

"You do?" said Miguel.

He nodded again. A lie was as good as an embrace sometimes. "As you say, cousin, it'll be all right." Even as he said it, he felt the horror of Sofía's last hours, and of knowing himself just how awful it was.

He looked around at the darkened room, the old refrigerator, the stone washbasin, this rough table. Somewhere out there was a bank and a gun and a plan, and tomorrow they would begin to come together. And all he wanted was to be here. He opened his mouth to say something, anything, but the rain gave a sudden surge and the roof shuddered and filled the room with a deafening roar. As the others looked up, he looked at each of them, Andrés, Berfalia, Miguel. They were his family, and yet his hold on them seemed so slight.

Where he was going now, he'd be alone. As he had been forever. And now, what was now?

Chapter 33

The timer rang. With her hand raised high above her head, Julia slammed the dough down against the counter one last time and stood back, letting the muscles of her arms and shoulders go limp. Ten solid minutes of slamming the strudel dough down had raised her spirits a bit.

It had been a morning of ups and downs. On their daily tour around the back yard, she and Caley had found that once again the *lulo* plant had recovered from this year's attack of the ants and was flourishing. There were so many fuzzy, bluish purple leaves they had lost count somewhere past forty and Caley was so excited she wanted Becka to know. But the phone lines were down because of floods and mudslides.

A crestfallen Caley had stripped down and gone out to bum- slide back and forth on the marble patio, and Julia had decided to make a strudel.

Everything about making a strudel was fun. Just pounding the dough against the kitchen counter for ten minutes until it relaxed gave her a high. Stretching it out paper thin was another form of victory. But the final step, picking up the floured sheet and letting the dough and filling roll up on itself until it came to rest at the other end of the table, a very fat snake, that was pure accomplishment.

After she put the strudel in the oven, Julia headed for the bedroom and a shower to wash off the flour and butter and filling that had gotten caught under her fingernails. She'd barely gotten her dress up over her head when she heard a car door slam out front. Then the doorbell rang. What now? she thought. Anybody who'd come in a car had stopped coming long ago. Except, oh shit, the landlord! She poked her head out the bedroom door to tell Juanita to say she wasn't in, but she was too late. Juanita had already opened the door.

Julia threw the dress back on, tore out of the bedroom and there he was, turning into the living room. She met him halfway.

"*Buenos dias, doctor Medina,*" she warbled. "And how are you today?"

"Good morning, *doña* Julia."

So it was Julia now. She wondered how long it would be before he dropped the *doña*.

"I have come to see if you have had any more flooding." He pointed to a white patch between the wood paneling and the ceiling. "I see there is some damage there, not too bad, but," he chuckled, "children will be children, won't they?"

It was so bogus, Julia almost laughed. "That is not water damage, Doctor; that's a spider's egg nest."

"A spider's nest? And you don't get rid of it?"

"No, I don't."

"Why not?"

"Because spiders have eight legs and they kill other bugs."

"Eight legs?" He looked at her with suspicion.

"Eight eyes, too. Although there are some that have none." She started to edge toward the patio doors. "But we have no flooding in this house, Doctor; spiders yes, but no floods. I would have called you if there had been any."

"What are you…ah yes, I see." He tried to smile. "You are playing with me, Julia, no?"

"No, *señor* Medina." It was an effort to keep her voice from rising. "I am decidedly not playing. Had you called me before you came, I would have told you that we have no water damage and no flooding."

"I tried to call you, but the phones are out." He bent forward and his tone changed. "I understand Mr. Bennett is in Guatemala and I was concerned for your safety."

O dear Lord. "Thank you, Mr. Medina, we are perfectly fine." She took another step toward the patio.

"Well, that's good — very good. Will you be going to join him soon?" His smile glazed over. "You see, I have been to the bank, and they told me someone might possibly be wanting this house soon."

What? "Who at the bank would say such a thing to you?" He flipped his wrist up as though the question were irrelevant. "No, Mr. Medina, I will be staying in this house. I am in it. And we have a contract." She glanced down at his belt but he wasn't wearing a gun today. Maybe it was out in the car.

"But not staying for long?"

It was a question, and she took heart. "I have no idea how long."

She had made it to the patio doors, but there she stopped, suddenly reluctant to let him see Caley.

"Repairs," he said. "Repairs will have to be made."

"Repairs? I'm still here, Mr. Medina. And everything is working just fine."

"Oh you need not worry. I myself will supervise the workers so that you will not have to deal with strangers."

Strangers I can handle, she thought. She turned and faced the patio. Caley gave a wave as she whizzed by and Julia wiggled her fingers back at her and turned around. The man was a belly width away from her. Jesus!

She twisted sideways and walked around him. "Look, Mr. Medina, I know the rent has been paid in advance. And I am still in residence."

"That's only part of the contract," he murmured. "Of course be assured I will be here every day during the work. I know it will not be too much of an inconvenience for you."

The thought made her sick. She shook her head.

He sighed. "It's difficult not having a man around. There are needs unmet…" He moved closer.

"Mr. Medina, please have the goodness to step away from me. I can't breathe. And get this straight. Just because *señor* Bennett isn't here… *señor* Medina, there's a child out there — get away from me!" She fumbled for the patio door latch. Where the hell was Juanita?

His belly nudged hers.

"Back off!" she whispered down at him. To her surprise, his hand rose to touch her face.

She jerked her head away. "Are you listening, you shitfaced, asshole pig," she yelled. "I would no more dream of fucking you, than fucking a….a walrus!"

There was a popping sound, his face seemed to swell and a wet bellow slapped her in the face. He fumbled at his belt. She finally lifted the latch and slid the patio door open. One step through, she nearly collided with Caley.

Caley took one look at Medina and screamed. Then she was paddling backward toward the door to Juanita's quarters.

Medina's mouth had fallen open and his eyes had glazed over. He gave a sudden massive shiver, shot past her and barreled across to the open flagstones. There he twirled, lifted up on his toes, buried his hands in the trumpet vine and hauled at it. A long stretch of the vine tumbled down, showering him with water. Almost instantly his floppy breasts showed pink through his white shirt. He looked down, his eyes following hers and he grinned hugely. Another pirouette, another vicious tug and a whole blanket of vines tumbled down. A roof tile fell and shattered on the paving stones.

Medina looked at the pieces, then up at her. "And I would rather fuck a sick donkey than fuck you, you whore." He waggled his hips forward and backward. "Yes. That's what everyone's saying about you."

"Get out! Get out of my house!"

"*Señora?*" Juanita's voice quavered from the doorway.

"My house!" he howled. "It's my house and you're ruining it."

"The rent's paid. It's mine as long as the rent's paid. Now get out!"

"You stupid woman, in Nicaragua things are managed very differently. I could have you out of here by tomorrow."

The doorbell rang. He glanced at Juanita, then at her. "*Coño!*" he yelled and waddled back into the house, his huge buttocks working against each other beneath his wet trousers. Julia followed at a distance. The doorbell rang again just as he flung the door open. A figure in white jumped back. Oh shit, Catalina Salazar! What could be worse?

For an instant Medina and Catalina faced each other, then he stepped around the tiny woman and rushed to his car.

"Anibal!" Catalina called out.

Julia stepped out onto the porch. "Stop him. He's got a gun in the car."

"Anibal, stop this minute!"

Medina skidded to a halt.

"Anibal, whatever are you doing?" said Catalina in a mournful voice.

"*Doña* Catalina…" His words came out constricted and hoarse. "Lamentably, I very much fear that you shall be known by the company you keep."

"Yes indeed," she said. "And how is your dear mother?"

In the act of wrenching his car door open, he stopped and stared at her over the roof of the car. "She's fine," he said. "Now I am — "

"And your wife? I hear she is not well."

"My wife – " his voice cracked into a falsetto and he swallowed, " — yes, my wife who is the finest woman on this earth, may soon be called to her blessed reward long before her time because of the evil, malarial air of Bolonia, when she should be up here, in this far more salubrious house which is falling apart because this," he pointed to Julia, "this whore dishonors it with her very presence and her evil filth!" He ducked, the car rocked, the door slammed and, with a screech of tires, it roared away.

"Goodness!" Catalina turned to Julia with a big grin. "What was that all about? No, don't tell me, I know. He finally discovered you are here alone."

"Yes."

Caley barreled out of the house and threw her arms around Julia.

"It's okay, honey, the bad man's gone. Let's put some clothes on."

"I'll take her," said Juanita. "Here, little one, come with me."

Julia turned back to Catalina and shook her head.

Catalina nodded. "And he just dropped in to see what he could do."

"Yes."

"Enough said. The man's a scoundrel of the worst sort."

"Come in." Julia hiccupped and started to laugh. "Oh God, I called him a walrus." Again she hiccupped. "I didn't even know I knew the word in Spanish. Or did I say whale? *Ballena?*"

"Yes! A little less droopy, but a lot bigger." Catalina held her arms out wide and they both laughed.

They sat down on the couch and the laughter drained away. "It's even worse." Julia struggled not to cry.

"Oh, my dear." Catalina hitched over to Julia and put her arm around her. "*Ay diós mio, mi amor*…there, there."

The gentle touch and the soft Spanish was too much, and in a second Julia was pouring out everything: Medina, Mrs. Ferris, the attack on the beach. She didn't mention Beal Jackson, that wasn't her story to tell. But oh how good it felt to talk to someone other than Caley and Juanita, or the women at the market.

"*Diós mio,*"said Catalina, when Julia finally ran out of steam. "What a lot of nightmares. It sounds to me like you need a rest. And it certainly sounds like you shouldn't stay here."

"I can't leave."

"I don't mean Nicaragua. I mean here in this house."

"Where can I go?"

"Let me think….not here. Not in Managua. Some place where it's peaceful. She snapped her fingers. "The farm!"

"The farm?"

"Yes, the one Jaime gave me when we were married. It's perfect. It's an old coffee farm up in the mountains, out beyond Yalí. Oh Julia, it is so beautiful. And peaceful." Catalina scooted forward on the edge of the couch her arms working like propellers. "You will love it. You could take Caley and I could drive you there in the jeep."

Catalina patted Julia on the knee. Julia had never seen her so vibrant.

"We need a four-wheel drive to get there," said Catalina. "Especially now with the rains. But that just makes it all the more fun. Out in the country everyone is friendly and when things go wrong, people just appear out of nowhere to help." She smiled and switched into English. "They just come out of the wood." She tilted her head and frowned. "Is that right, they come out of the wood?"

"Woodwork, I think. Things come out of the woodwork. But woods is fine, people come out of the woods."

"Woods. Woodworks." Catalina shrugged and shifted back to Spanish. "But don't worry. It is all mine and nobody goes there without my permission. So you would be alone. Just think — no electricity, no phone, and no crazy landlords."

"Alone?"

"Not exactly. There will be Tatiana, the caretaker, she will be there. But yes, you may as well be alone absolutely. I think it's what we all want sometimes, what we all need. Time to be alone, totally and completely alone. That is, except for Tatiana, but she is a ghost."

"Totally? I — I don't know, what if — "

"Ah. I see it. You worry Becka will come home and you will not be here. Yes. Of course. But there is the shortwave. We'll take it with us, all charged up. I will give Juanita my telephone number so if anything happens, I can raise you on the radio." She made a winding gesture as though she were starting an antique car. "Or if something goes wrong up there you can raise us on the radio."

"You wouldn't stay?"

"Oh no. I have too much to do here. There is my Ernestina's fifteenth birthday, and a reception. But do not worry, Julia. If you need to come back, or if I hear anything you need to know, I will come or one of Jaime's drivers will come to get you. No, no, shhh." Catalina lifted her finger. "And what's even better, Jaime has a *helicoptero*." She twirled her fingers, then grinned and shook her head. "I know, you laugh, and I do, too. It is crazy, but he does have a helicopter. He thinks it was for him the wheel was invented. But a helicopter means from the farm you are in your home in less than an hour. Oh Julia, please say you will go. You need some time for yourself. And I would love to take you there."

Julia took Catalina's small brown hand in her own. "You once told me that God keeps his eyes on your hands, do you remember that?"

"I did? Goodness, how boastful of me. That was the convent school."

"Yes. That was it." Julia felt a quickening of excitement. "You, Catalina, have blessed hands. And a heart to match."

Chapter 34

"When will you be back?" asked Becka. She popped the Yo-Yo up and down nonchalantly, eyeing her reflection in the plate glass doors of the hotel entrance. Marshall could see two taxi drivers reflected in the window. Both were silently smoking in front of their respective cabs. Neither spoke nor even looked at the other.

"Late. Don't wait up for me."

"I won't. I never do."

And so far she hadn't. In fact she slept too much. She was either sleeping, hanging out with Patrick, Mr. Prepubescent Yo-Yo Boy himself, or showing off some new Yo-Yo trick to the chambermaid. "With all the sleep you get, you sure look tired," he said.

"I'm not tired." She went into a fair imitation of Patrick's Charlie Chaplin waddle.

"You've learned that well. How about your school work?"

"Same boring stuff. I better go do it, before it gets too late." She made the Yo-Yo skip across the pavement. "The nuns in Managua were better," she said as she went through the doors.

"The nuns played with Yo-Yos?" he called out.

She popped her head back out and rolled her eyes. "No, Silly, the nuns taught; it's Patrick who does the tricks with the Yo-Yo." She backed up and closed the door between them, then cut across the lobby and disappeared into the elevators. He suddenly felt lonely. No goodnight hug. Caley would have been all over him, he thought sadly. Damn Julia!

"Mr. Bennett?" said a voice in English.

Marshall pivoted around. Dammit to Hell! Horse! The very last person he wanted to see.

"Good evening, Mr. Bennett." Faustino Horse stood a little back from the curb, his shoulders hunched up around his ears.

Marshall caught himself looking around for Yelva Inez, but she was nowhere in sight and he breathed a sigh of relief. "Yes?"

"I was wondering, Mr. Bennett, if I might speak with you."

Marshall bit back a decided "no." The man's suit was rumpled, the empty sleeve was pinned to the shoulder carelessly, and the thick glasses were spotty. His shirt was clean and his face was so recently shaved there was a tiny nick under the left corner of his mouth, with a speck of toilet paper stuck to it.

"I'm just on my way somewhere," said Marshall.

"Perhaps I can accompany you part of the way." Horse raised his hand. "Just for a very short while."

"Can you tell me what this is about?" No, maybe he didn't want to hear what it was about here on the street in front of the hotel. "Just for the trip then." He beckoned the driver of the first cab.

"*Si, señor*," said the driver, pinching off his cigarette and tucking the stub into his shirt pocket. Marshall yanked open the door of the taxi and climbed in first. He wondered how long Horse had been waiting here for him.

Horse asked the driver to turn on the radio, then waited until the man seemed engaged in negotiating the narrow streets, before he began whispering in his heavily accented English. It took Marshall a minute or two to decipher the content, given Horse's accent. When he did, he was aghast. "What?" he barked.

Horse winced. Marshall cleared his throat and tried to modulate his tone. "What are you saying?"

The taxi took a corner too fast. Marshall put his hand on the back of the front seat to keep from falling into Horse. "Come on, man, out with it."

Marshall felt the man's hot breath in his ear. "Jaime Salazar," he whispered.

Marshall jerked his head away and turned around to face the man. "Cut the crap. You're telling me that Salazar is that dangerous?"

Horse gave a little nod. His mouth clamped shut and he looked like he was going to cry.

"Dangerous to me? To you? To your wife? To the economy?" Marshall stopped, then plowed on. "You want money, don't you? And you think I'll give it to you if you feed me some crap about Salazar?"

The man sat up straight. "Not everybody wants money from a banker, Mr. Bennett," he said, enunciating each word carefully.

"Bullshit! You have no other connection with me than through my banking connection with Salazar." He thought of Yelva Inez. Christ! Blackmail? "Listen to me! Jaime Salazar is a respectable businessman. He's been to my house. I know his wife." Horse's eyes went round. "Socially," he barked. "I know her socially."

Horse brushed this aside. "You think a man who owns property can't be dangerous?"

"I'm saying I don't entertain thugs in my home."

Horse faced forward and spoke rapidly, his eyes on the street ahead of the taxi. "Mr. Bennett, I know no one in Guatemala, we are alone here. Mr. Salazar, on the other hand, has many connections. He knows that I know much about him. Too much. He would not hesitate to...." He blinked rapidly.

It was so bizarre, Marshall wanted to laugh. But there was no question but that the man was serious. Marshall could almost smell the fear rolling off him. What the hell?

"Already I have seen them following me," said Horse.

"You what?" The fear tipped over into anger. "If it's so dangerous, why did you come here in the first place?"

Horse closed his eyes. He shook his head and the shaking persisted, a small, sideways tremor. "Mr. Bennett, please help me."

There was something about the man's repeated use of his name, the odd accent. "What's your real name? Horse isn't a name." Maybe he was a Nazi in hiding.

"Mr. Bennett, are you listening? I need your help."

"Why me?"

Horse turned away and spoke to the window, his tone dropping with each phrase. "I think you are an honest man. A man of conscience. Not like the others. You have..." the last words were inaudible.

Marshall turned away. Neither spoke as the taxi moved down one block and then another. A man of conscience? Not like the others? And there was Yelva Inez, naked, the bars of sunlight playing across her skin as she moved. Where had this poor bastard been that afternoon on the ranch? Waiting somewhere for it to be over? How many times had he had to wait through afternoons like that?

The taxi cleared the city traffic and wound through tree-lined residential streets. Single lanterns lit up the white walls and carved wooden gateways hiding what must be huge houses.

Horse finally spoke. "She is a child, a savage. Innocent. He owns her."

"Don't be ridiculous. She's Indian and he's white, like you."

"She is not his child. She is his property. As am I."

"For godsakes, slavery went out a hundred years ago!"

"There are many ways to own a person," said Horse. "He gave her to me. She is my wife. There was a child, but he died. He gives her to others. Now he says he will give her away."

Jesus, the man was a lunatic. "What are you saying? How? Why?"

"Because he can."

Marshall couldn't breathe. He tried to open his window but the handle flipped around without making a connection. He glared down at his hand. "What did the baby die of?" he finally asked.

"We don't know. The doctor took the baby away. Now that I have taken my wife away, he will do anything to get her back. To him, she is property."

No. This was crazy. Jaime Salazar? Urbane, thoughtful, educated. This man was a lunatic. A liar. It was crazy even listening to him.

"I am aware, that I look less respectable than Mr. Salazar, and for that reason you may find it hard to believe me. But he is a…he is a murderer."

Fuck! Marshall pounded on the back of the front seat. "*Pare!*"he roared. "Stop!" The taxi whipped toward the curb. "Get the hell out of here, you creep. I don't know what your game is, but I'm having none of it." Horse was huddled against the far door. "I don't know what's with your wife, but you can't expect me to believe Salazar is a murderer. Might as well tell me I'm a murderer. You think I don't know what you're up to? You want money!"

"Mr. Bennett, Mr. Bennett…" There was anguish in the man's voice. With his good hand, he reached for Marshall's flailing arm, the stump on the other side bobbing in obscene echo. "I'm saying I'm in danger — my wife is in danger — here in this city. We do need money to leave."

"And how do I know that's what you'll use it for? That this isn't some bullshit story? Get out!" Marshall reached around him and found the door handle; he jerked it, but it failed to release. "Goddammit, look at that!" he bellowed. "And you expect me to believe Salazar would follow you all the way here and kill you? There's not a single Latin-American that's that organized. Or that persistent." He yanked the door handle to no avail and pounded the seat back in frustration. "Driver!"

"Mr. Bennett...my wife."

Marshall flipped the handle on his own side and the door actually opened. He backed out of the car. The driver stared up at him, moonfaced. For a moment, Marshall thought to pay him off and walk, but he didn't know the way and the taxi was his.

He marched around the taxi and yanked open Horse's door. Horse emerged back and shoulders first, his hand clinging to the roof of the car. At last he stood up and turned around to face Marshall. The speck of paper had fallen off and blood trickled down his chin. "There is no one else. No one," he whispered.

Marshall slammed the door. "That's too damned bad, mister. Too goddamned, bloody damned bad!" He threw himself into the front seat, slammed the door, turned toward the driver and jabbed his finger toward the windshield, unable to get another sound out.

The whiskey no longer burned going down his throat. He watched Valdés' wife move from guest to guest. She was beautiful, talking and smiling like that. Catalina was her name. No, that was Jaime's wife, this one's Clara. Was she the one who sold her fur coat to the beggar? No, Julia, had exaggerated, if not lied, to make her point. Clara was a good hostess, moving from guest to guest like that; he wanted her to touch him on the arm and smile at him. His glass was warm in his hand. A waiter took it and gave him whisky.

He decided he would go slower with this one and even as he was thinking it, he gulped a mouthful. What kind of whisky didn't burn going down? Good whisky. Good people, polite people. People who knew good whisky...the wife passed by, glancing up at him through her eyelashes. But then she passed by him without giving him a pat on the arm. He looked around to see if anybody had noticed. But nobody was looking at him. And he couldn't tell if that was good or bad. Probably good. He didn't know how many drinks he'd had, but he wasn't sure his mouth could form words now. Not and make sense.

It was finally raining in Nicaragua, the fat man in the corner had said, a Nicaraguan, standing there eating his soggy *canapé*, probably wishing he had a piece of *chicharrón* now. But the whiskey was good, the whiskey was smooth.

There were too many paintings along the walls, and the colors hurt his eyes; he didn't know if he wanted to work for a man that had that many paintings; it was ostentatious. When he'd asked Valdés if he did business with Jaime Salazar, Valdés had laughed and he'd remembered that Valdés and Jaime were married to cousins, cousins marrying cousins like they did down here — was that the other woman, the Nica, the one with the fur coat? And Catalina was from Colombia, so she wasn't a cousin, not in Nicaragua.

He gazed across at the Nicaraguan in the corner. He was probably married, too. And where the hell was Julia, his lying wife? She was good at working the crowd. No, not true, she was bad. And he didn't want her here.

He stared at the picture of a fat woman on the wall and tried to get things straight. Valdés' wife was Clara; Valdés had a steel mill here in Guatemala; Jaime's wife was Catalina, who came from Colombia; Jaime had a cotton farm, and Jaime was a murderer. Shit, fuck, damn! That just wasn't true. Except that he could still see Horse wilting on the curb as the cab pulled away.

The room tilted.

"Would you like some coffee?" said Valdés, suddenly appearing beside him.

"Thank you, but I think I'd better go home." But it wasn't a home. It wasn't his home. Marshall felt his head turn away from Valdés as if of its own volition. Shouldn't cry here. Not here.

"Of course," said Valdés. "Drink the coffee and I'll have my driver take you."

The hotel lobby was nearly empty. Dead for this time of night; still, not that late. Marshall stepped across the carpet carefully, thinking he shouldn't have drunk that much. Hardly ever drank – tonight, a little too much. He jabbed at the elevator button. It didn't take much, two, three drinks? Something about that struck him as funny.

The elevator doors slid shut, closing him in. He felt his knees give as the floor came up to meet him. He rose up on his toes and bounced, lifted off as if he were going to make a bank shot, touched the ceiling and landed. The car lurched. Not bad. How many floors? Ten? How old was the elevator? If it fell, then he would just jump up at the last minute and he'd be in the air when it crashed.

At the sixth, his floor, he punched the button again and the elevator cranked to the top floor slowly, ponderously, and was still jiggling when he jumped. He remembered it had an automatic return. He would race it down to the sixth floor and get there first. As the doors slid open, he bounded through the blurred image of two startled people springing apart. Their shocked faces, mouths open, hands still groping toward each other, followed him as he tore down the stairwell laughing until his knees were weak, his body so light he had to hold on to the banister to keep from floating away. Then he was on the sixth floor hallway, listening to the echo of his own descent, the sound of his own breathing, a hollow, empty sound.

The overhead lights were off in the hall and only a few wall lamps were lit. The window at the end of the hall gave some light from the street below; the red light over the stairwell door and the blue bulb over the linen closet door were on. Above the elevator, the indicator showed that the elevator was just arriving at the sixth floor.

Well, shit, he was good. He walked down the hall to the window and stared down at the lights across the city. Pain, hard and sharp, cut through him; the lights below blurred and he pictured Faustino Horse on the curb where he'd left him, infinitely small and vulnerable. How much did Horse know? Certainly more than he did. That land deal, cooked up in the President's fancy dining room; he'd never gotten it straight. Golf clubs and electricity? All a chimera, a magic show. And yes, greed. The word sliced through him. And he and Lindstrom were the hired audience, or possible accomplices.

Something behind him made him turn, a noise or a movement, but the corridor was empty. He walked to the other end of it. Whatever it was, it had come from up here, near the linen closet where Becka's chambermaid friends had their headquarters.

The door was ajar and he gave it a push. The closet was dark. Leaning inside, he listened. The scent of clean linen washed over him, and there was something else, a faint intake of breath. His own? No, someone was there.

He reached in and felt along the wall for a switch. There was none. He turned his head up and listened. Whoever it was, was perfectly silent now, still there, but quiet. He stepped inside, swung his arm in an arc through the air above his head, connected with a string and pulled. White light sprang at him. The small space was filled with it and it took him a moment to realize that a sea of sheets lay on the floor.

His heart was pounding; it was as if an entire wall of sheets had toppled down and were washing toward him, threatening to push him out into the corridor. Then, as he watched, they moved, broke up and settled again.

Sliding his feet forward into the mass, he bent and pulled at the sheets and she rose up out of them in one movement, much as she had shot up the aisle of the plane, with surprising grace. Yelva Inez!

Her dark hair fell almost to her shoulders, down over the ugly blouse that had come unbuttoned in two places. She was breathing hard, her mouth open. She was frightened and he could almost feel her shaking inside him. She was caught. He had caught her and he must take care of her. Horse had said to, he had said…Marshall felt the sheet slip from his fingers, saw his hand rise and reach out — Horse had said, what…? Didn't matter.

Her skin was smooth, smooth along the jaw and up over the cheek, smooth behind her ear where his fingers entered her hair and bent to fit the curve of her head. He pulled gently and she came. Until her face was directly beneath his. His left hand grazed the side of her cheek, her neck, down to the buttons, the top one, and then the middle one and then with the palm of his hand against her breast, he slid the blouse away.

Chapter 35

The farmhouse was perched on a hillside and the porch hung out over the valley like the front of a ghost ship. With twenty-seven paces in length and almost eight paces from the railing to the wall of the house, there was room to walk for miles. Now, after three days, Julia reckoned she had covered at least five miles. More if you counted that walk she'd taken down into the valley yesterday.

Just thinking about it made her shiver, so she swung her old cardigan around her shoulders. One minute she was cold, and the next she was hot. She was sure she'd picked up some kind of bug down there.

From up here, everything was silver with rain and fog, and gold when the sun broke through. When the wind blew, the tops of the yellow-green palm trees rolled in waves. The silvery gray-green eucalyptus had a different sway, much of it stiff and out of rhythm. As for coffee, it was only when she took her walk yesterday that she was able to see the few coffee plants that were left after years of neglect. According to Tatiana, housekeeper and cook, many years ago the farm had produced its own coffee, with plenty left over to sell.

A formidable woman Tatiana, with fierce black eyes, a shovel jaw, and hair standing out from her head in a white halo. From the moment they'd arrived, Tatiana had mesmerized Caley, who instantly became her slave. Julia was left with the very mixed pleasure of having time on her own to think.

On the ride up to the farm, Catalina had told Julia about Tatiana. Back in the late twenties, Tatiana and her husband had worked a small farm in the next valley. But she was unable to have children and her husband beat her and so she left him and came to work for Jaime's father. Her husband took another woman, a *"pura india"* from the jungles of Zelaya, and had seven children by her. He also took to drinking, and from time to time, he would appear at the farm to demand of Tatiana his conjugal rights. Until one night when she dragged out a machete from under her cot and whacked his arm off, or as near to that as counted, for it became gangrenous and had to be amputated. Within a few months, he sickened altogether and died, and his woman and their children left the valley and were not heard of again.

Tatiana was shunned. After all, her husband had only wanted what was his under the laws of man and God; you didn't just do a good man in because you felt like it. Some in the valley thought Jaime's father should have handed her over to the courts.

Which made Catalina laugh. "Of course he wouldn't take her to the law. He was the law on his own land...Yes, I know, it was appalling," Catalina had said when she saw Julia's expression. "But it makes wonderful telling at dinner parties."

There was so often a kind of casual cruelty in the stories people told here. They took a story of pain and hardship and painted it over with humor. Was it a way to endure hard times, a way to cope? Julia had also seen it as a literary device. She'd wanted to write a paper about it in graduate school, but she'd been talked out of it by her advisor, who was himself a Costa Rican and didn't see anything negative about it. But Julia had.

"Aren't you being a little judgmental?" he'd asked. For him it was an elegant way to cope that required intelligence and wit.

It wasn't until she met José María that she came to see it as so much more than a literary device. For him, it was cruelty. And there was nothing casual about it.

"When you're rich," he'd said, "you feel you have the right to be nasty and call it clever. It's a way of saying I am superior and that gives me the right to make an ass out of myself and call it wit."

Julia stopped at the railing to stare down at the forest canopy.

"It's a jungle, Julia, not a forest," Catalina had corrected her on that first evening on this porch.

Here and there, Julia could see thin columns of smoke rising above the trees. From houses, Catalina had said. Julia couldn't help but wonder about the people who lived down there? How did they manage in this constant rain? And what was it like to live in a green world?

"Those are homes, Julia. They live a simple life here. Jaime calls them subsistence farmers, because they grow just enough for themselves."

Subsistence farmers? That was what Marshall had called small landholders. He believed it was far better for all that land to be taken over by a competent landowner who really knew how to farm. The farm would be managed better and the former landholders would be paid to work the land. They'd have a steady income and security.

Which was bullshit, José María had said. The farmers got paid pennies for their land, got paid even less for their labor, and were often not paid at all when the harvest was bad.

Julia had said nothing of this to Marshall, nor had she told Catalina what José María believed. By now she knew better than to commingle her worlds.

The trip up from Managua had been amazing. The higher they'd climbed, the worse the roads got. There were washouts that had been scantily repaired. Mud slides that had been pushed aside or over the side. They'd gotten stuck four times and each time, just as Catalina had promised, whole villages had descended on the jeep to help pull it out.

That had probably been the best part of this whole trip, getting to know Catalina. And to admire her grit, and her ease with people. Those men who'd hauled and heaved and had pulled her jeep out of the sinkholes had seemed delighted with their *doña* Catalina.

Great-great granddaughter of a slave in Cartagena, daughter of a millionaire, orphaned when she was five and raised in convent schools, Catalina told Julia how she had met Jaime when he was going to Georgetown University and she was visiting a cousin and considering going to college in Washington. "But then I met Jaime and we got married. He was like a prince, gentle and courteous. He still is. I have been fortunate. Though back with the nuns, I didn't think so."

Catalina had radioed ahead and, by the time they'd reached the farmhouse, Tatiana had prepared a feast of spiced venison and beans and baked plantains. That whole day had been beautiful.

A wave of rain forced Julia back from the railing. She leaned against the wall of the house and slid down until she was crouched over her aching knees. Aching knees, aching thighs, aching back, not to mention her shoulders and elbows and wrists.

It had been a horrible mistake to go down to the valley yesterday. She'd been lonely with Catalina gone, and Caley making puddings with Tatiana. She'd tried not to think of Becka with Marshall. She couldn't sit still, and in a moment when the sun came out and the sky had a few blue patches, she'd headed down the path, stopping every dozen feet or so to knock giant balls of mud off her boots.

If everything looked green above the canopy, everything beneath it was stained a strange muted yellow and brown, like the outer edges of an iodine stain. Yellow and brown, and a greenish gold when the sun knifed through the trees. Steam rose from pools of still water. Everything dripped. Then came the mosquitos in their thousands, and the crumbling houses, abandoned, she thought, until she saw a woman sitting outside one, combing a child's few hairs. Both of them had the unmistakable reddish hair, gray skin and distended bellies of malnourishment. A little girl, she thought, but wasn't sure.

The sharp, sour stink of wood smoke and decay hung over everything; a pesticide can had been placed to collect rain water dripping from the broken roof tiles. Julia couldn't hide the shock on her face and the woman turned away. Dismayed at the despair and hopelessness written across that woman's face, and feeling even as she turned away that somehow she was implicated in that woman's story, Julia had fled back to the farmhouse and sat out the rest of the afternoon in paralyzing grief.

Was that what happened to most subsistence farmers? How many years had she lived down here alongside such poverty without doing anything about it, without even letting herself see it, much less know about it? She'd made a couple of attempts to disagree with Marshall about the fate of subsistence farmers, but she'd been forced to admit that in fact she knew very little about the matter because she hadn't seen those people, and he'd said he had. Well, now she had, too, and what she'd seen down in the valley had nothing to do with philosophical arguments. It was more like an open wound without a scab.

My God, she'd thought she'd seen the very worst of poverty in Acahualinca, but there the children were lively. There were people like José María who were organizing against the dictatorship. Ninfa wasn't hopeless, she was angry. She actually produced maggot flour to feed her kids. But that woman down in the jungle seemed to be just waiting for life to be over.

Julia pressed her fingers against her temples. Her head throbbed and she felt queasy. She rose and once again leaned her elbows on the veranda railing and tried to breathe the pain away.

Rain came across the valley and up the hill in sheets. The shade palms covering the coffee plants bent with each wave, then popped up again like fingers plucking at the fruit beneath. It made her seasick to watch them.

On the outside of the house, the wood had soaked up so much water it was turning black. She'd already seen the mold starting to bloom in the corners of the bedroom where she and Caley slept. But she couldn't stop seeing the despair in that woman's face. How little she knew about herself or about anyone else. How shallow was her knowledge. She who so loved living in these beautiful countries, each one more fascinating than the other. Each one a treasure to explore, to enjoy, a place where she felt at home because she willed it so. She had relished the fact that she was a stranger in a strange place. Where she could appear to fit in beautifully. But never really had to. Not fully.

She closed her eyes. No. Not fully. She had never truly invested herself, that part of herself that she had always held back from friends whom she loved until she left town and then forgot. That part of her had not wanted to see this.

Stop! She couldn't separate herself into such neatly zippered compartments. See, folks, the rest of me is clean. No, she was one whole person. But she'd never wanted to see something like that. Why? Because if she saw it, she'd have to do something about it?

This was just what José María was fighting to change.

Julia pushed back from the railing and sat down again. She was no better than the tourists for whom each country was another pelt for their collection back home. There would be pictures to take, music to listen to, sunsets to view. Important people they could say they'd seen at a distance. After all these years, her own list was quite fabulous and she was sure she'd be able to dine out on every bit of it for years if she wanted to. The President of Nicaragua? Oh you mean the dictator Tacho and his beautiful wife — well let me tell you...

Oh God, stop this! She pushed up and walked unsteadily to the kitchen. There she found Tatiana feeding tree limbs into one end of the huge clay cooker. Big metal pots were boiling on two of the three openings. Flames leapt up through the third. At the other end of the cooker, Caley was raking ashes into a large metal garbage bin.

Neither Caley nor Tatiana looked up from their work. Julia slipped away unnoticed.

The day drew on. At one point, Julia went into the bedroom and took off all her clothes. Then she put them right back on because she was cold. There were spells when she lost track of time, hours or minutes when she sat within José María's arms, rested her head against his neck, breathed in his scent. Each time she woke up, it was worse. Her back hurt all the way up into her skull and down into her legs. Pain moved from one site to another, this shoulder, that ankle, but always the head and back. No position was comfortable. Bonebreaker, that was the word, but she couldn't think of the medical term. The thing that Ninfa's child had had. Mosquitos. Malaria? No, something else.

By nightfall, she couldn't eat. She sat with Caley on the veranda steps. The sun had set and the big house rode into the darkness above the valley. Cricket screams pierced her ears and fireflies sparked inside her eyes. Caley couldn't sit still. She moaned and scratched her bottom where chiggers chewed the flesh beneath the elastic bands of her underpants.

"Stop it, Sweetie."

More moans, half pleasure, half pain. "Can't."

"Come, let's go get your jeans on,"

Julia started up with Caley hanging on to her knees. "I'll bring them out, then."

"No!" Caley wrapped her arms tighter.

"Come on, dammit, let me go!"

Caley sprang back, her lower lip trembled. Julia scrambled up. She was shaking so hard she was sure she would fall off the veranda straight down into that nightmare valley. She made her way through the darkened house, Caley right behind her. Above the kitchen patio, a thin crescent moon coming up over the roof was unbearably bright. Julia smacked open the door to their room and stood still on the threshold. Three days of occupation and the room stank. Only mold and sweaty human flesh could survive in there.

Caley bumped into her from behind. Julia grit her teeth, took a step forward and froze. No, not just a smell. Someone was in the room. Without moving her head, she peered through the towering mosquito nets and saw that one of the window shutters was slightly open. Seconds crept by. There was no sound, simply the sense of a presence, something solid in the air to her right, near the open shutter. She pushed Caley back through the door, took a step backwards and listened so hard her teeth ached. Nothing.

She'd imagined it. She was sick. She would find Tatiana, go back in with a lamp. She groped for Caley's hand and they tip-toed through the kitchen and out into the back patio where a lantern hung from one of the laundry poles. Tatiana sat on a low stool, her hands deep into a bowl of cotton fluff. Feathers. Chicken feathers.

"I think there's someone in my room," Julia whispered.

Tatiana shook her hands over the bowl and the white stuff fell away, some floating off onto the dirt patio. Without a word, she walked back toward the bedroom, with Julia and Caley stumbling behind.

God, it hurt to move. Halfway there, it came to her. An open window and silence? It was José María! He was waiting for her, and wouldn't come out when Caley was there. She turned, bumped into Caley, turned again. Fireflies were all around. The moon lifted free of the roof, its two prongs floating together to form a ring rolling above the roof's edge…a sign he was waiting for her! She sprang forward.

Tatiana had reached the bedroom door. Julia wanted to cry out, but she needed all her strength to gain the covered walkway. Again she stumbled and this time lost her balance and went down. "Wait!" she called, scrabbling around, trying to get up. But Tatiana was gone.

Inside! He must be inside the room. "Wait! Help!" Julia crawled to the bedroom. There he was, beside the window. She climbed onto the bed. Behind her there was a scratching noise. "No!" she shrieked and dove off the bed toward him. Pain shot up her hands and arms as the wall exploded against her. "No!" she cried and slid down the wall. "Oh no! He's gone, you scared him away."

She managed to turn herself around toward the light. "Please bring him back." She squinted at the light from a glass lantern swinging on its hook. And José María was coming toward her, arms out, hands gleaming with tiny white feathers. He crouched down, slid one magical hand around the back of her head, pulled her toward him and held her so close it hurt.

Chapter 36

Marshall punched the elevator button and the door opened immediately. The elevator was empty. Late afternoon, and the entire hotel seemed empty. Once the door slid shut, he leaned against the back wall. He still had a hangover. And lunch with Valdés hadn't gone well either. They'd talked about the steel mill and the lumber business and it seemed Valdés was indeed leading up to a job offer. But just when Marshall was thinking Latin America was not the place for him after all, not after last night's incident with Horse's wife, Valdés asked, "Do you know a man named Holst?"

"Horse?" It slipped out before he could stop himself.

"Yes, that's it. Claus von Holst. An accountant. The man's a little crazy, but he's a genius with numbers."

Horse! Valdés knew him as Von Holst! The name wasn't some crazy nickname after all. Marshall made himself look Valdés in the face. "No, I'm sorry," he said, "I don't know any von Holst. Is he your accountant?"

"No. I just thought you might have heard of him."

And there it was left. Valdés said nothing more on the subject, and nothing at all about a job offer.

Marshall stepped out of the elevator. The door to the linen closet was closed, thank God. He stepped hastily across the hall, and knocked on Becka's door.

No answer.

"Becka?"

He opened his door and walked through into her room. She wasn't there, and her bed wasn't made.

He hesitated, then went to the linen closet and knocked. Nothing. He resisted the temptation to look inside to see what condition it was in. He checked on the floor above and the one below. The maid on the seventh floor, a face he hadn't seen before, told him she hadn't seen a little girl, and the maid from his floor hadn't reported in. The woman who worked on the floor below his just shook her head. Probably indigenous from the mountains and didn't speak Spanish.

He went back to the sixth floor and, after checking their rooms again, he forced himself to open the door to the linen closet and turn on the light. No one there, and not a thing out of place. One wall of shelves was filled with precisely folded sheets. The other one was nearly empty. Presumably at the laundry or on the beds. Then why weren't the beds in their rooms made?

He went down to the lobby, asked at the desk, checked the coffee shop, the gift shop, the travel agency, even the beauty parlor. She wasn't anywhere in the hotel.

Damn the girl, she was probably out with that little Yo-Yo creep. He hurried through the lobby and stepped outside. No, whatever Becka and Yo-Yo boy were up to, they weren't in front of the hotel. Shaking his head in frustration, he went back into the lobby.

"There is someone waiting for you, sir," said the doorman.

Marshall followed the man's gaze to a couch across the lobby and thought for a minute he was going to throw up. Yelva Inez. What now? He turned back to the doorman, but there was a slight glint in the man's eyes. Screw you, he thought as he turned and walked across the lobby.

She wore a black shawl over the same clothes she'd worn the night before. Her blouse hung out of the skirt on one side, her stockings were wrinkled, and the buckle on one of the shoes was missing. Her eyes were red and swollen and her mouth was contorted into a grimace. He wondered why they even let her in the hotel.

She struggled to stand.

"Please sit." He took a seat at the other end of the couch.

At first he couldn't make sense of what she said, then he picked out the words, "gone," and, "they took him." Her right hand sprang up and slapped her face. "They took him," she sobbed.

The couple on the next sofa over stopped talking.

"Who? Who took him?" Marshall murmured.

"Men. He's dead. I know he's dead." Her voice rose.

"Stop it!" He pitched his voice low but it brought her up short. The couple weren't looking, but they weren't talking either. The doorman stood watching from just inside the door.

"Why me?" Marshall whispered.

She stared at him.

"I mean, why come to me?" He remembered her naked body and he closed his eyes. "I can't help you," he said.

"He didn't come back," she whispered. "I've looked all over for him."

"When? Last night? Today?"

"He didn't come back," she whispered again. "And he would."

Yes, he would. The man's fear for his wife, his desperate urgency had been obvious. They knew no one here, he'd said.

"Do you want money?"

"My baby," she moaned.

Baby? What the hell? He scooted an inch or so toward her and articulated precisely. "Do you need money?"

She said nothing. Oh God, what if she didn't want money? What if she wanted him to take care of her? Last night was insane. Of course, she would come to him.

He stood up, sat down. Perspective, he needed to think. Maybe it was a scam. Maybe Horse was hanging out there somewhere and they'd cooked this whole thing up together.

Well, he'd not make the offer again. He'd just wait to see what she'd say.

She was looking at the young couple, or through them, tears streaming down her face. "They took him," she said.

"Horse?"

She nodded.

"Who did?"

When she didn't answer, he said, "Who? What did the men look like?"

"In a car. Where we stayed. They were waiting."

"Where?"

"El Superior."

The couple shifted to the near end of their couch. Marshall frowned at them. He checked his watch; it was still early. If he sent her back to her place, maybe he could think of something. He couldn't make a decision with her here right in front of him. But if he stuck her in a taxi, what was to keep her from coming back? If he went with her, maybe she'd be satisfied that he knew where she lived, and then she'd agree to stay put and wait.

Wait for what? Damn! Now he'd have to leave a message for Becka when she came in, tell her to wait on dinner. Or eat alone. Christ!

"Come," he said brusquely. "I'll take you there."

To his horror, she clutched his wrist and knelt before him. "*Gracias.*" She bowed her head.

"*Ya, basta,*" he said. "Enough!" The couple were plainly ogling now. Their eyes sparkled. Clearly this was the best show in town and they were composing what they were going to say to their friends. The crazy *gringo,* and the even crazier Indian. *La India.* With all its pejorative meaning here in the Capitol.

Goddamn them all! He helped Yelva Inez up, took her elbow, and ushered her across the lobby as if she were the bank's most important client.

El Superior was a grim little hotel, a block away from the Central Market and down a side street. The narrow, dirty entry hall widened only slightly to accommodate a registration desk and two ancient chairs. Everything was bathed in a sickly glow from a single bulb, painted green, that hung directly over the desk.

At one end of the desk there was a battered coffee maker and a tray of upside-down coffee cups and stacked saucers.

Yelva Inez clapped her hands and a tall, stooped man, hitherto invisible, rose from behind the desk. He reached for a key from the wall-case behind him. Marshall counted swiftly; there were twelve cubbies, none of them with a room number.

Yelva Inez nodded her thanks and walked down a long corridor filled with the odors of mold and urine overlaid with Lysol. A door opened on their right and a man stood yawning in his undershirt and trousers. Someone spoke from inside and the man closed the door.

She turned a corner and, hurrying to follow, he nearly collided with her. She was staring at a large stain on the threadbare carpet in front of a door. He prodded with the toe of his shoe; it gave with a wet, sopping sound.

She unlocked the door, opened it, gave a startled cry. He looked in

401

past her, then closed his eyes. He wasn't really seeing this. It was like a bad movie. Illicit sex, bad lines, bad scenes. A steady hissing sound came from somewhere further inside. He felt her move into the room away from him. He'd have to open his eyes and see if it was real. He stepped forward.

The room was large, with a very high ceiling. A double bed, or what was left of it, stood in the middle of the room at an angle. Its stuffing was strewn over the floor. The drawers from two small chests had been flung about and the contents made a bizarre pathway to another door. She ran to it and he followed. His shoes squished on the carpet.

A bare bulb lit up the plastered walls and concrete floor of a large bathroom. An unenclosed showerhead in one corner ran in a steady stream onto a pile of wet towels. A small sink overflowed in another corner. Water covered the floor; a set of underwear floated near the toilet. The top of the toilet tank had been removed, the ball float was twisted up at an angle and water poured down the tank's sides.

Marshall stepped around the woman, grimacing as his socks got soaked. A rag had been stuffed down the drain of the sink. He pushed back his sleeve and drew it out, then turned off the water. He ducked under the toilet tank and turned the valve. He straightened, hoping she would turn off the shower herself, but she hadn't moved from the doorway. Damn, he'd be wet through.

He eased behind the stream of water and turned the faucet off. In the sudden silence, water dripped loudly .

She came across the room, her shoes splashing, her eyes staring as though she were in a trance. He bent to pick up the pile of towels that blocked the drain at his feet. There were three of them, heavy with water. He jumped as the last towel gave a gentle tug and something started to roll out of it, something heavy. The thing slipped into the water without a splash and lay there, a white, rubbery, fungus-like thing. Marshall grabbed at the wall to steady himself and tried to make sense of it. It was only when he looked away that he could be sure what he'd seen. A human hand, swollen and grayish-white, lay on its back, the fingers curling up toward him. It was a left hand.

She barreled into him, her head knocking the wind out of him. His hands involuntarily caught at her but she twisted away, her fists beating at him until she was completely free then she came at him again. He raised his arms to ward her off, slipped and lost his footing, sat down hard in the water. He gasped and tried to catch his breath.

He watched her disappear out the door and he couldn't move a muscle to stop her. He heard a low wail coming from his own throat, tried to stifle it, tried not to think that a human hand, one he himself had shaken, floated beside him, closer, then slowing in a stasis between opposite pulls, and finally giving in to ride the last of the water gurgling down the drain.

Clinging to a cold, slimy wall, he forced himself up. Once on his feet, he wiped his hands against his wet trousers, then looked down at his hands. With a cry he lunged toward the sink, slammed open the faucet and held his right hand under the water until nothing but clear water was disappearing down the drain. He hung on to the edge of the sink, then turned and looked back at the wall next to the shower head.

Red stains twisted down the wall, braiding together, then apart, and ending in a flat horizontal line where the water had risen to meet it, then receded. He felt the man's hand on his arm. "I look less respectable than Mr. Salazar, nevertheless..." An empty sleeve seemed to bob in the air. "I think you are a man of conscience, Mr. Bennett...there are many ways to own a person."

He stumbled across the bathroom and into the bedroom. The

woman was neither there nor out in the hall. An open door at the end of the hall led onto a concrete patio.

The air was cold. His trousers and jacket were wet, and he shivered. He wanted to vomit, but the remains of his lunch were long gone and he could only lean against the building and blink at the garbage cans that lined the wall, the rusted hulk of a bus. Behind the bus was an alley that seemed to lead to the street. Was it through here they'd taken out what was left of Horse?

He started down the alley, his footsteps loud on the concrete. When he looked back, no one was there. He was almost to the street when he thought of Becka and began to run.

Chapter 37

Marshall glared at the doorman, a different one this time. Becka wasn't in her room. He hurried back to the lobby, but this uniformed jerk hadn't seen her since she left in the morning with Patricio to go to school.

"Patricio?" He heard his voice rising. "Who the hell is that? Patrick? The Yo-Yo boy?"

"*Si, señor.*" The doorman kept his eyes on the street.

"Well where the heck is Patricio?"

"He doesn't live in the hotel, *señor.*"

"I know. But where does he live?"

The man shook his head. His face pronounced severe judgment on Marshall's ignorance and bad manners.

Furious, Marshall swung away. The man was right. What had he been thinking of all these weeks? He'd never really checked in at the school after registering her that first day. He'd never asked her where Patrick lived. He'd been crazy! Negligent!

"Please, mister." Marshall felt a tug on his jacket. "I know where they are."

It was the kid who'd polished his shoes for the last several weeks. Marshall swooped into a crouch. "Where?" he yelled, but the boy gave a squeal and took off down the street. Marshall lumbered after him. "Come back, I'm sorry, I didn't mean to scare you." Halfway down the block, the kid stopped and began walking backward, away from him, his box held up before him.

"Please come back."

The boy came to a stop. "I didn't do nothing."

"I know. I didn't say you did. You want money?"

The kid shrugged his shoulder against his cheek and took another step backward.

Marshall grit his teeth. Goddamn, goddamn, goddamn. Come back here you little shit. PLEASE! He glanced toward the hotel where the doorman was inspecting the sole of his shoe. When he looked back, the kid had taken off and the sidewalk was empty.

The lobby seemed vast, a wasteland of chrome and glass and carpeting. It rushed at him and slid away as he answered the two policemen's questions and then answered them again, yes and no, and here, and there, numb to it all. This time he wouldn't yell, he wouldn't lose it. He took them to her room and there noted with them that she'd taken no particular possessions. And none were taken from his room either. They followed him around and nodded as each drawer was opened.

He was a *gringo*, rich enough to stay in this hotel, so they treated him with respect; and yet they, like the doorman, seemed to have pronounced judgment on him. He could see it in the way they shifted their eyes to the side, as if afraid to make eye contact with each other. He had lost his daughter. He was a bad father.

He kept his voice smooth and still, tried to summon the right tone. Find her, just find her, he screamed silently, and all the while he kept seeing the floating, dead hand and the blood in the shower. But he couldn't tell them about that; they'd say he did it and put him in jail and then he'd never find Becka. The two things weren't connected. Oh God, please don't connect them!

Age, weight, height, identifying features, here, right here in the passport. He gave them Becka's gestures, expressions, words, an endless supply of details he'd never realized he had. They gathered them all up and finally took everything of Becka's away with them. And when they left he went over and over everything he could remember: the broken toothbrush, her leading him to the airplane in San Salvador, her wading in the tractor tire, and the tirade at Caley for wearing her school uniform with jam-stained hands. He sat down on his bed and wept.

He woke up with a cry. The room was dark. The street six floors below was silent. He lifted his head and listened. The door to her room was a shadow with a faint glint where the knob protruded.

He rolled over and reached for the telephone. The operator put him through to Managua immediately, but he laid the receiver down in its cradle after two rings. What could he say? That he'd lost their daughter? Had screwed up so totally he'd lost Becka?

He got up and stared down into the empty street. A man with a laden mule walked under a streetlamp, lit for a moment in color, then became a shadow swaying into deeper darkness. At this distance, there was no sound. Yelva Inez and Horse, they were shadows now, and yet he knew, just as he knew the mule and the man existed beyond his field of vision, that they were there. And would always be there. He had betrayed them both. He had done to them what he despised. And there was Jaime Salazar, and Horse's accusations, and Valdés, who knew Horse as von Holst, and had seen through his lie about not knowing Horse. Who was Valdés, after all? A crook?

No! He didn't believe it. Didn't want to believe it. These were men of substance, respected in their worlds, landowners and collectors of

407

art. You didn't become a person of such standing if you were a criminal.

But now that sounded stale to him.

Marshall saw himself reflected in the window. There was nothing he could recognize in the face that stared back at him. "Bastard," he said softly, and the glass misted over.

There! He turned. Definitely a noise. He started across the room and stopped. The doorknob moved.

"Becka?"

The door slowly swung open and she came out of its shadow.

"Honey!" He knelt to gather her up. "Oh, Becka." He held her away, felt a second's rage that she had scared him so, then he grabbed her back. "Are you okay? Where have you been?"

He felt the top of her head against his jaw, first a nod, then a shake. "It's okay," he said, and it was. She didn't have to tell him; just the feel of her, safe, alive, in his arms was enough. His eyes stung.

She took a deep breath and held it. She was crying.

"Shhh. It's okay, it's okay honey, you're back, that's what's important."

"Patrick took me to meet his mother."

Marshall almost laughed at the images that conjured up, of engagement rings and wedding plans. "Was she nice?"

"Yes. She sells fruit at the marketplace. They live there."

"In the marketplace?"

"Yes." Her voice dropped to a whisper. "They sleep on the floor next to the fruit."

That skinny kid with the big grin and the fabulous Yo-Yo tricks? "But doesn't Patrick speak English?"

"Yes. His father came from Nebraska and they lived in a house. But he died and now they live in the marketplace."

"But he's always so cheerful."

"Yes, he is."

There was something more on her mind, he could tell. He could feel the tension in her shoulders, the way she was sitting. He waited with his arm around her.

"Daddy?" she said at last.

"Yes?"

"Are you going to die?"

Me, he almost yelped, of course not! But he didn't want to brush her off like that. "Yes, honey, but not for many, many years. You'll be old and have children of your own before that happens."

"How do you know?"

"Because I'm very healthy and I don't want to die and miss all the wonderful things you're going to do." He didn't know where the words came from; they sounded like something Julia might say.

"And Mother?"

It was like an echo and it took him by surprise. How could he answer such a question here in a strange hotel in another country?

"I'm guessing your mother feels the same way I do."

She waited, but what more could he say?

He saw himself packing them all up and taking them home to some place simple, a place with a Fourth of July parade, and leaves they could rake in the fall, and snow on which they could go sledding. A place where they would all be safe.

He carried her into her room and set her on her bed. When he settled beside her, his arm around her shoulder, he could finally say it. "I think it's time we went home."

Chapter 38

The little VW headed out and their dilapidated Ford had the parking lot to itself. José María checked his watch: twelve twenty-five, only five minutes to closing time. The armored car had left fifteen minutes ago. Three blocks away, the second escape car was in place and, by now, Daniel had cut the barbed wire into the empty lot behind the bank and was waiting to be let in. Everything was ready and waiting for Enrique, five kilometers away. But Enrique was late and Augustín wasn't going to let them leave the car until he actually heard the blast. A trickle of sweat ran down José María's neck under the ridiculous beard; he wiped it away, shivering at the iciness in his fingers. Come on, let's go! he thought. The blast would have to be from an atom bomb to be heard at this distance.

"They'll close up if we wait any longer," he said.

Augustín, his face muffled up to the eyes by the flame red beard, nodded and reached for the door handle. "Fuck Enrique," he said, as if longer odds didn't matter. The car shook as he stepped out, shook again as Pepe followed. Mario huddled over the steering wheel and stared down the street the *guardia* would come up if something went wrong. He hadn't been happy with the role of getaway driver. José María punched him on the shoulder. "You okay?"

"Yeah, sure. I got a trick or two up my sleeve." His thumb punched back over his shoulder.

That sounded ominous, but there was no time to challenge it. "Don't we all?" said José María, and he followed the others. They were on their way, only twenty seconds behind schedule.

They caught the bank guard in the act of closing down the metal screens for the lunch hour. Pepe clipped him behind the ear, shoved him inside and clamped him to the chair with the handcuffs just as the two tellers looked up. By the time they understood what was happening, Augustín was up on the counter. "*Arriba los manos!*" he shouted, pointing a gun down at them. "Up, up, high above your heads!"

There were two figures seated on the platform. José María was almost on top of them before he recognized the woman from the main branch. Her eyes were fixed on his gun, her hands were flat on the blotter; the freckles stood out on her pale skin like a disfiguring disease. Damn Mario! He'd never mentioned the freckles. She was bound to recognize the former Yo-Yo salesman despite his beard and glasses.

The man in the chair beside her had turned and was staring, too. A well-dressed son-of-a-bitch, even calmer than the woman. His eyes crossed just a little to take in the tip of the gun just inches from his nose, but he did nothing more than shift backward in his seat and look up inquiringly.

José María gestured for him to stand. "Take her hand," he said, motioning for the woman to rise as well. "No, right hand to right hand."

Pepe hit the platform and José María tossed him the handcuffs. Without waiting to watch them go on, he took out his knife, got down on his knees and slashed at the carpet under the desk. Thank

God the alarm had been too far for her to reach without shifting her position and giving it away.

"There's no need to be rough with the lady," the man said to Pepe. José María's head came up so sharply it hit the underside of the desk. That voice! He could feel it buzzing through his body. His back began to burn. The piece of carpet came away in his hand and he stared at it blankly. For a moment his hands were dead and he couldn't make them move.

"*Jodido!* What's taking you so long?" hissed Pepe.

"Coming." José María tried to keep the panic out of his voice. He worked on the wires feverishly. His fingers were like stumps and he nearly kicked off the alarm. By the time he disconnected it, he was soaked with sweat. Still he hesitated before he backed out of the narrow cubbyhole. He had never actually seen the Angel's face. But the Angel surely knew his face.

His hand brushed the gun he'd laid aside to work on the wires. No killing, they'd said. Not unless the safety of the team depended on it. No deaths to be laid at the Movement's door. He wiped his hand on the carpet, picked up the gun, and rose slowly. This would be an execution. Justified! For hundreds, maybe thousands!

"What the hell have you been doing down there?" said Pepe. He slapped the guard's gun into José María's hand and took off to let Daniel in.

So now he had two guns and standing before him was the man who knew every cell of his body and its response to agony, the man who night after night had brought him home to nothingness. Slight and neat he was, the man who'd torn the skin off his back; he was almost of equal height. His right arm hung loosely across his body, right wrist attached to the woman's right wrist. They were so close together the Angel's left arm was invisible.

412

José María raised the gun in his right hand and gently pushed it against the man's left shoulder. The woman was saying something and he transferred his gaze to her and then to the clock above the tellers' cages. Twelve thirty-six. Augustín had dropped the first bag of money onto the floor outside the cages; inside, one of the tellers was filling the second bag. The guard was still unconscious in the chair beside the door.

José María looked back and saw that he had turned the Angel around and that his gun was inches away from the soft place where the man's spine fled into the skull.

Try not to die. Miguel, who loved him, had said. I am perishable and dying, Miguel, and the first is irrelevant. The second is life.

Dimly he heard a groan and connected the vibration in his chest with the sound. The mouth of his gun moved down to the Angel's back. The woman was looking at his face and he saw that she had recognized him. He wanted to speak to her, to say something, anything, to tell her about the scars on his back and the blackness down under the mountain, of the needle scratching through his life, lifting and then dropping, lifting and then dropping, and the songs from the Victrola.

He prodded the Angel toward the vault; the woman turned and followed, obedient to the handcuff. Her shoulder brushed his and for an instant they were locked together, the three of them, moving as a unit. Her free hand rose; she pointed at the man's left shoulder. Before José María could react, the man stumbled, twisting to the right. The motion pulled her across in front of José María, and she threw her hand out to catch herself. José María jumped aside and brought the gun in his right hand down, catching the Angel's temple and his right eye as he came around. The Angel's head snapped to the side, a gun

413

flew out of his free hand and he fell, jerking the woman down on top of him.

With a cry, José María pushed her away and kicked out at the man's shoulder, at his chest, again and again. The body jerked with each blow and gave nothing back and he found himself sobbing.

"Jesus!" yelled Pepe. "What the fuck are you doing?" He grabbed the guard's gun from José María's hand and tossed it to Daniel. "You haven't even started on the goddamed vault!" Pepe scolded.

José María stared down at the two figures on the floor and said, "I forgot to frisk him." He saw again the woman's pointed finger; she'd tried to warn him!

"Fuck!" Pepe yanked the woman up. She came readily enough, but her wrist was still anchored and the man didn't move. "You asshole!" said Pepe. "You knocked him out! Here, give me the key." He jerked the handcuffs up and down. "Give me the key!" he yelled.

José María shifted his gun to his left hand and fumbled in his pocket, but Pepe had lost patience and was hauling the man's body toward the vault with one hand while the woman staggered along behind. José María started after them. A shout from the bank floor made him look back in time to see the bank guard lunge toward the wall beside the glass doors, dragging the chair behind him.

"The alarm!" yelled Daniel. Both he and Augustín raised their guns and the man exploded against the wall.

The guard hung there forever, until his legs gave way and he slid down the wall and fell face down, the chair clattering down on top of him.

A teller screamed. Augustín jumped down into the cage, brought both women onto the bank floor and pushed them toward the guard. "Help him!"

They approached slowly. As the younger one lifted the chair, the man's arm came with it, still cuffed to the chair back. The guard was trembling, vibrating like a rattle, his breath coming in gasps, his forehead pressing against the marble. And then it was over.

The older of the two tellers turned toward the wall and vomited. The younger one carefully lifted the chair back in place on top of the dead man and crossed herself.

José María grabbed for the handcuff that bound the Angel to the freckle-faced woman. He thrust the key into the lock, twisted it, and took the cuff off the woman. She rubbed her wrist and looked up at the window.

"Fuckin' open the vault, bitch!" said Pepe. Slowly, she turned away from the window.

"Do it!" he shrieked.

She's hearing something else, thought José María. But all he could hear was his own ragged breathing and the anger still ringing in his ears. Pepe kept up his tirade and that, too, drowned out the sound. But at last there was no mistaking the thin, hot sound of a siren. More than one.

"Come on," shouted Augustín from the bank floor. "We've got enough. Everybody out!" He grabbed one of the bags and was running toward the plate glass doors when he stopped in his tracks as though he'd been shot. The bag flew forward with his momentum and threw him off balance just as the doors blew inward and Mario dove into the bank, ahead of a wall of flame.

"There she goes!" yelled Mario. "*Adios compañera!*"

The doors swung shut and the flames backed up and swung outward, revealing a twisted body, a woman lying on her back, arms raised, legs arching out obscenely. The flames had already burned her clothes away. The two tellers started to scream.

Mario turned Augustín bodily and pushed him toward the platform, waving for the others to follow. "The Guard! We can't go out that way, they're almost here." He crossed the platform ahead of the others and opened the door to the back corridor. His face twisted as he looked back toward the entrance. "She'll hold them off, God bless her," he said.

Augustín went first. Daniel and Pepe followed, each carrying a bag. José María was last. He picked up the Angel's gun. The woman with the freckles stood by the vault, watching him, that same calm look in her eyes. If it was she who'd somehow set off the alarm, she'd also warned him of the Angel's gun. He raised his hand to her as he passed by.

Mario waited until he was through the door and then ran ahead. José María swung back to close the door. Dense black smoke swirled up against the glass doors, obscuring for a moment the figure in the flames. The heat cracked one of the doors with a report like a pistol shot. As if on signal, a gust of wind scooped away the flames and smoke, and there, in the momentary clearing lay the once perfect form of *Chiquita Banana*.

"Goodbye," he whispered as he ran down the corridor.

Chapter 39

She slept. Woke. Shadows around the bed billowed and squeaked through the mosquito netting, then fled out into the darkness. One shuttered window rattled and the rain pounded on the roof, waves of rain, constant rain and darkness. She lifted her head and pain stamped down each vertebrae like a furious teenager. Her head throbbed and her bones scraped against each other.

She tried not to move. Was too spent to weep.

Caley lay curled against her legs. Gritting her teeth against the pain, Julia reached down to stroke the soft hair.

When she woke again, the shutters were open and the sun was shining. She tried to turn her head to look, but the pain behind her eyes was so terrible it all disappeared.

Again, she felt the warm bundle curled into her bent knees shift and settle. Caley. And Becka? Where was Becka? She began to cry. Pressure against her thighs, a movement, a sticky finger smelling of sugared ginger stroked her cheek, and she slid back into sleep.

Again and then again, a rooster punctuating her dreams — a butterfly sewn to the palm of her hand struggled to free itself. Her father scraping the diner griddle and talking about the new Pontiac, the one she knew now would be his coffin. And through it all, the woman with the wild white hair changed her sheets and brought trays of food she couldn't swallow. Tatiana, her face set in a frown of concentration

"Mommy?"

It was Caley standing somewhere between her and the window.

"Yes?"

"Tatiana says you have the dengue."

"Oh." Fever, headaches, bones grinding against each other. Mosquito borne dengue.

"Mommy?"

"Yes?"

"Can I sing you a song? Tatiana says I should sing a song."

"Yes, please, I'd like that."

Caley's little frog voice, scrape, scrape, up and down. Marshall couldn't hold a tune, either. *"Estas son las mañanitas, que cantaba el rey David."* She was singing the Happy Birthday song: *These are the dawn songs that king David sang to the beautiful girls, that we now sing to you...*

"Whose birthday is it?" Julia asked.

No answer.

"Caley! You told Tatiana it was your birthday?"

Again no answer. Finally, "She made me a ginger cake. And she gave me this." A tiny square of cloth, a letter 'C' woven into it, was held up to Julia's face. "She made it from an old shawl."

"But your birthday's months – "

"Shhhhh." The finger touched Julia's lips. Caley lifted her face up into Julia's line of vision, a scowl and then a smile almost too fast to register. "It could be your birthday, too; we could have another cake." Her lower lip began to tremble.

"Oh, Sweetie." Julia reached out to pull her down, stifling a groan at the pain. "Shhhh, shhhh. It's okay. We'll have a birthday party, I promise."

She slept, and woke, and slept again. Someone was at the front door. Julia tried to stop Juanita before she answered it, but she was too late and people poured into the hallway, each one carrying a present. There was the doctor from next door with a headless Barbie doll, and Dr. Medina carrying a hornet's nest with live hornets inside, and he was going to open it. "You fucking walrus," she yelled, but no sound came out and when she tried again he shoved the whole nest into her mouth and she woke to a blinding headache and for a moment she couldn't breathe.

Yes, she had called him a walrus. She could still see him hauling away at the vine, his shirt getting wetter and wetter until his pinky-brown tits showed through the cloth and he was panting. She had a sudden image of Marshall's pale, naked body flying out of the shower as she jumped into it on their wedding night.

"Are you okay, Mommy?"

Julia let her breath out slowly. "Yes, Sweetheart. Could you ask Tatiana for some chamomile tea?"

"I can make it myself." Caley slipped under the mosquito net and ran off, leaving Julia to stare up at the knot where the mosquito net had been tied to a single ring screwed into the ceiling. Her throat felt as tight as that knot and she had to force herself to breathe slowly. Deeply was not an option because her chest hurt.

Yes, that was their wedding night. And when she'd run out of the bathroom, he was standing on the other side of the bed with a towel covering him from his nipples on down. And his face! His nostrils flared and his lips twitched as though he'd smelled something rotting.

"Don't *ever* do that again," he'd said, his voice barely above a whisper. "The naked body is never attractive."

She'd stood frozen as a wave of hot shame engulfed her. Followed by an agonized need to cover herself up, and her refusal to do so.

419

What she couldn't remember was how long she'd held out before she'd finally reached down and hauled up the heavy bedspread.

That was when she should have cut and run. Why hadn't she told him he was full of shit, that he had a lot to learn, that she was in no mood to teach him, there were far better things for her to do. But she hadn't. The thought had never even occurred to her. She'd simply shut down. Never again had she seen Marshall fully naked. Just that flash of bum disappearing around the shower curtain on their wedding night.

"Mommy! What's wrong?" Caley wriggled up under the mosquito net. "You're crying."

"Yes, I am." Julia opened her eyes. Caley was leaning over her, her face a picture of misery.

"Why are you crying?"

Julia tried to shake her head. "Because I'm hurting."

"Why?"

"I just want to go home."

"Me, too." And Caley started to cry.

Catalina appeared without warning. It was a blowy, silver and gold day, with almost more sunshine than rain, and Catalina came with spatters of mud on her cheeks, her braid loose and hanging down her back.

"You came by yourself?" Julia dangled her feet over the edge of the bed. She was weak but she could get up and even take little steps without that blinding pain.

"Of course." There was a note of impatience in Catalina's voice.

"I'm sorry," said Julia. She touched Caley's hair, then her shoulder, wanting to draw her in and hold her tight.

"Sorry? For what? I came because I wanted to." Catalina went to look out the window.

"What's wrong?" asked Julia.

"Nothing."

"Is Becka all right?"

"Yes, she's fine. It's nothing serious." Catalina turned around. "In fact, it's good, I think."

"They're back home."

Catalina's eyebrows flew up. "Yes, as a matter of fact they are."

"Marshall wouldn't come here?"

"It wasn't an issue. I offered to come and he accepted."

"I see." So he wouldn't come himself. And why should he? He was the one who'd been wronged.

"Are you okay?" said Catalina.

"Oh. Yes. Fine. The fever's gone. I sleep a lot, but at least I don't have nightmares." She waved her hand in front of her face, then shook her head tiredly. "How soon are we leaving?"

"Soon. But only if you're ready."

Julia's mouth went dry. "There's something else — isn't there?" A hot wire threaded through her gut. José María! But no. How could Catalina know anything about José María? Unless Mattie...

The silence stretched out, Caley whimpered and Julia realized she was squeezing Caley's hand. She eased the pressure and brought the damp fingertips up to her lips.

"Yes there is." Catalina glanced over her shoulder. "But it has nothing to do with you."

Julia winced. Was she being shut out or was she being let off the hook? She felt raw and vulnerable, longed to lie down and disappear. Instead, she stood up so that she could turn around more comfortably.

"Jaime's had an accident," said Catalina. "I will have to go back to Managua immediately. And I'm not sure you are well enough to travel."

"Oh I can travel — especially if I can have a thermos of that wonderful painkilling tea that Tatiana makes." She tried for a smile. "What happened to Jaime? Is he all right?"

"I don't know what happened. It came over the radio just as I got here. Jaime doesn't tell me these things. Especially not over the radio." She laughed abruptly. "We women are fragile creatures, you know. He would be livid if he knew I'd come up here alone."

He doesn't know how dauntless you are? thought Julia. Suddenly the image of the hovel down at the foot of the hill came to her, the woman combing her child's hair in the dripping fog, and Becka's cool gray eyes, José María's finger against her back, stroking. She sat down abruptly and drew Caley close, resting her forehead on Caley's hair. In a flash Caley's arms were around her, and Catalina was beside her.

"You are weak, my dear. You must rest."

"No I'm not. I'm just woozy, and a little crazy." She sobbed, "Oh Catalina, I just want to go home. It's time we went home."

Chapter 40

It was nearly 10:00 p.m. when Catalina turned the Land Rover into the driveway. Becka catapulted through the door and leapt on Julia before she could get her feet down onto the driveway. Julia held the long thin body close, shocked at how easily the remembered shape fit into her arms, how awkward her daughter's body was, and how beautiful. Both of them were laughing and crying. They were together, they were home! "Oh honey," Julia whispered.

At last Becka dropped to the ground and stood back. The sudden distance caught Julia off balance; her feet hit the ground, she staggered and only then was she aware of the pain in her legs and back. "I'm so glad to see you." She dropped back onto the passenger seat.

Becka gulped, a noisy, rasping sound. "Where's Caley?" she said.

"Here!" Caley popped forward from the back seat and hung her head over Julia's shoulder like a colt peering over a gate.

"Hi," said Becka.

"Hi," said Caley.

Becka tilted her head to one side. "I have something to show you."

Caley clambered over Julia and down to the driveway. "What? Something good?"

"Come see." Becka grabbed Caley's hand and together they raced into the house, leaving Julia recovering in the Land Rover.

Catalina touched her shoulder. "Do you want me to come in with you?"

Julia shook her head. "You've done so much already. I don't know what I would have done without you." She reached back into the jeep for her bag. Behind her, the door opened. She took a deep breath and turned around. It was Juanita.

"*Señora*." Juanita's bare feet scraped on the driveway. "I'm glad you're here."

"So am I, Juanita."

Juanita reached into the back to pull out the suitcase.

"*Gracias*, Juanita." Julia turned back to thank Catalina, but she was looking over Julia's shoulder.

"Is he there?" whispered Julia.

"No. No one's there."

"I don't know whether to be grateful or not."

"I'll be glad to come in with you, Julia. There is something to be said for the first words spoken."

"No. Thanks anyway. But I'll keep that in mind." She shook her head. "I guess my accounts are coming due."

"Do not grovel, Julia. Never grovel." Catalina smiled, a crooked little smile. "You are better than that."

He stood in the door to the children's room. His eyes flicked toward her, then away. Home again, thud, she thought.

She stood beside him and looked into the room. Her heart gave a thump.

"So she got a Yo-Yo," she said at last.

"Yes. She's got a Yo-Yo."

"She's good."

Again he gave her a quick, sidelong glance.

There it was, in his face, in the sudden flush. He was remembering something. The bank? Or the scene outside the theater?

"When did you get back?" she asked.

"Yesterday."

A day and a half they'd been here, waiting.

Her purse was slipping. She headed for the bedroom. A tendril of the trumpet vine had poked its way through the window next to the bathroom. A survivor.

Across the room, there was a rumpled depression on his side of the bed, as though he hadn't moved at all last night. God forbid he should touch her side. She dumped the purse in the middle of the bed and went to the window. Becka with a Yo-Yo! Was it chance, or divine retribution?

"You were sick?" he said from the doorway.

"Yes. Dengue."

"Is it contagious?"

"No. It's mosquito borne." She turned to face him and saw that he'd stopped listening. "Up at the farm, Caley didn't get it," she went on. "Actually she got chiggers. But I went down into the valley and I must have picked it up there."

He stayed in the doorway, his expression blank. No, she told herself, not blank, just absent. It was his expression when he listened to her mother talk.

Julia shook her head. Whatever had made her think she could ever plumb this man's secrets? Just talking with him was like trying to siphon gas out of an empty tank, all fumes and a bad taste. She wrapped her arms around her belly. Dammit, Julia, be fair. At least he hasn't snatched up Caley and barred the door.

He came to the foot of the bed and sat down on the cedar chest.

His face was haggard, his voice hoarse and low. "I'm leaving, Julia. With the children."

She gaped at him, the wind gone out of her. Just stay on your feet, she told herself. Don't grovel.

"With you, if you want to come," he added.

The banjo clock ticked in the front hallway; the hum of crickets sifted in through the open window.

"That's what you want?" she asked.

"I don't know." He looked up at last. "Do you know what you want?"

"No. I don't." And then the kids came tumbling in only to halt and stand still as if they too did not know what to say.

"What?" she asked. They lay side by side in the darkness.

"I didn't say anything."

"Oh."

The air conditioner shifted up a tone, a languid, dragging whine.

"I don't know," she said, a little louder.

"What don't you know?" Each word came out separately.

"If we can do it."

"It? Be specific, Julia."

She clamped her mouth shut until she could keep her voice steady. "Go through life not talking...."

He cut across her. "Is that your decision?"

"Shouldn't we talk things over a little, first?"

He was silent.

How could they be lying together in the same bed like two corpses and still be alive? A void, filled only with her guilt and his justified anger. The implacable equation. Years of it, seeping into everything, every move, every thought. How could Becka and Caley possibly thrive in such a world? There was something so fundamentally wrong with that equation. But no matter how she tried, she could not break through the hard justice it was wrapped around. Hers, the guilt. And his, the justice.

Don't grovel, Julia. She pushed herself up against the headboard.

"What?" he said.

"Nothing."

It was as though his specific gravity was so much greater than hers that she could only end by disappearing altogether within it. Her hands were freezing and yet her neck and head were hot. How could she even think with him lying there?She had to get out of here. But where? The pool? The stables? She could grab a horse and gallop forever. The sudden image of her actually breaking into a gallop made her laugh. In all these years, she'd never been able to go from a canter to a gallop without falling off.

"What's so funny?"

"Nothing." There was nothing funny in any of this. The dream was gone, along with so much else. The perfect life, the perfect wife, the perfect children, the perfect love affair. She turned to face him and folded her legs beneath her.

"What are you doing?" He turned on the bedside lamp, sat up and swung his legs over the side of the bed so that his back was to her.

"I don't know if we can to do this," she said.

"Do what?" he said to the windows.

"Live together without ever saying what's happened. Or what we feel about it."

He stood up and turned to face her. "I've wanted to talk for years, Julia. About a lot of things. Simple things. The children, the house, what we do each day. Is that so hard?"

"Yes, if that's all we talk about."

"Christ!" The arm was out, the hand chopping at the air. "Can't you see? I can't...I *won't* talk about what I'm thinking, what I'm feeling. I'm not even always sure what I'm feeling. And I won't wallow in it."

"How can you wallow in something that doesn't exist?" she blurted out before she could stop herself. "I'm sorry." The bed felt suddenly huge. "Maybe counseling?" she started, then clipped the word off before she could finish it. Counseling? What was she thinking? After years of hoping they would get counseling, the very thought of it now made her sick to her stomach. Sitting in a room with some third person, each waiting for the other to speak. It would be unbearable. Like cutting away a rotting limb, slice by gangrenous slice, only to discover it wasn't attached to anything.

In a sudden panic, she rolled off the bed and stood trembling, gripping her wrist with her other hand. An arm rotted through from years of misery, falling away, and she trying to catch it, fumbling...

"Did you hear me?" He had come around the bed and was standing inches away.

"What? No, I didn't. I'm sorry. What did you say?"

"I said no. Absolutely not. No counselling."

She plopped down on the bed. "Oh God, yes!"

"No. Are you listening?" He raised his hand again and made a single chop at the air.

"No, I mean yes, I agree with you. It's not an option. And it's never been an option."

"What?" He faltered.

"You've been right all along."

"What does that mean? For years you've been...shit, Julia, what are you trying to say?"

"I'm just saying you were right, it won't work. Counseling can't possibly work. Not when neither of us want it."

"What? All these years you've been nagging…Wait. What does that mean? That it's over?"

"No, Marshall, it means I have no idea how to make this work. How to raise the children together, live together and respect each other all in the same space."

"So, you're giving up."

"I didn't say that. It means we have to find something we share, some common place to begin again. And take it one step at a time."

"One step at a time? Start all over again?" His hand started chopping. "You can't be serious. I don't want any new beginnings. Christ, if I had to begin all over again, it wouldn't be with — " He stopped abruptly.

"With me? That's right for both of us, Marshall. It means for starters, my decision won't be based on the hope that we could change each other, or even live together without problems."

He was silent. Then just as she took a breath to speak, he said, "I know what you're doing. You want your cake and eat it, too. You want the kids. Well, you just remember, we're in Nicaragua. And here the man has – "

"We're Americans, Marshall."

"We're here!" he yelled. "And here a woman can't even take her children on an airplane without her husband's permission. His written permission."

"For Christ's sake! Can you even hear how you sound?"

"What?" He looked startled.

"I didn't say I was leaving."

"Then what are you saying?" he yelled and then glanced toward the door. "Get back to your room, you two."

By the time she turned around, they were gone, their door closing quietly.

"I'm saying I don't know." She flipped on her bedside lamp. "How did you get to be so perfect, Marshall? Have you never done anything wrong? Have you never thought about another woman?"

"Good God!" He chugged back around the bed again, sat down and pushed himself up against the headboard. There were dark circles under his eyes. "Look, Julia, you're smart, you're a good mother, the kids need you. Just come with us."

"What changed your mind?"

"I haven't changed my mind. It's just that it's impossible to think of the kids without you." He turned his head away. "So maybe it will work."

To her, it sounded like a death sentence.

"You heard about Jaime Salazar?" he asked.

"Catalina said he'd had an accident."

"An accident? It was no accident. It was a bank robbery. He was hurt when the bank was robbed. An 'expropriation,' they called it."

"Who called it?"

"The bank robbers, when the money's stolen for a particular purpose. Jaime was at the new branch talking with Fidelia. And some thug beat him over the head and kicked him. Shit! Kicked him! And they killed a guard, too. "

"An expropriation?"

"That's what it's called. At least that's what Jaime said they called it."

"Jaime told you about it?"

"Of course he did. What did you think?"

"He didn't tell Catalina?"

"Yes he did. Catalina was up in Matagalpa and Jaime called her. It was he who told her to pick you up before she came home."

"Jaime?" No, that couldn't be right. Catalina had said Jaime would be livid if he knew she went to the farm alone. "You didn't ask her to pick me up?"

"Indirectly," said Marshall. "But it was Jaime's idea. What does it matter?"

He was right. It didn't matter. Except that Catalina had lied. A lie that seemed to hold no meaning or purpose.

"When did this robbery happen?"

"Yesterday. I got back after three and the thing happened at the noon closing. The place was a mess, bullet holes all over, tellers in shock, the National Guard everywhere; they cordoned off the entire neighborhood, and were going through it, arresting people right and left."

Every word hit her in the gut. She sat down carefully, each hand firmly on the bed to keep her from sliding onto the floor.

"Jaime, he was cool as a cucumber. They shot the guard, Julia, and they kicked Jaime and laid his head open for twenty-six stitches! Terrible, really terrible."

Julia nodded. Mattie had said she saw her refrigerator repairman at the bank. He was selling something. Yo-Yos. Oh Christ, fucking shit.

"Julia, this man Alejandro Lacayo — tell me the truth, would he have had anything to do with it?"

Alejandro Lacayo? That was the name Mattie had told her. Julia pressed her feet hard onto the floor and managed to stand up. There was no sense in pretending. She opened her eyes wide hoping he wouldn't see the tears. There was nothing left to lose. "I don't know, Marshall. I'm not sure…I think I understood what he believed…" She

431

shrugged. "I think he would certainly support stealing from the rich to give to the poor. I remember – "

Marshall stiffened. His lips went tight. He inhaled through his nose as he prepared to speak.

Julia raised her hand to stop him. "Wait! I'm not saying that's right. I remember Mattie telling me she saw him one day at the bank trying to sell some toys. He could have been looking over the bank as a possibility." She swallowed. "As to whether he was using me — " She stopped. She couldn't get the words out. Nor would she.

Chapter 41

The paper blurred before him. The sweet smell of coconut candy cooking in the next house drifted into the room along with the soft rhythm of the candy maker's spoon thumping against the pot. José María dropped his head down onto his folded arms, letting sleep wash over him. Through the gentle rhythm, he saw Julia, her arm raised over the pot, her feet planted square, her head thrown slightly back. He tiptoed up to her and buried his face in her hair as it fell down her back. He saw her cross the room carrying a basket of sweets, and he helped to swing it up onto her head, then bent underneath to kiss her, to pass the basket onto his head. But he couldn't see her face.

A shadow moved just beyond his vision. He snapped awake. The Angel! Standing in the doorway to the patio. He reached for the gun at his belt. Stopped. It was the child, standing at a safe distance, holding out the fat alarm clock.

José María took it and smiled. In four days Gabriel Lenín had taken the broken alarm clock apart and put it back together again in working order; pretty good for a boy of six, who didn't speak a word that made sense, or respond to a request he heard well enough. Egdalina, the boy's mother, had not been surprised. God had a purpose in everything, she said, even her son's affliction.

José María turned the clock over. Three minutes after four. He held it to his ear, blinking in rhythm to its ticking. Gabriel Lenín tilted his head to one side; the set of his eyes, the outer edges lower than the inner edges, made him look sad. At last, he put his hand out and José María gave the clock back.

A jet flew low over the house and José María looked up at the ceiling. When he looked down again, the boy had disappeared into the cubbyhole he shared with his mother. José María sighed. The boy's sadness tugged at him. There was something of a miracle in the very fact of his existence. At least the way Mario had explained it. An only child, the unexpected fruit of an act of charity Egdalina had bestowed on a blind beggar she'd taken in when he was sick and unable to care for himself. The beggar's health improved, he eventually went back home to Honduras, and in a few week's time, Egdalina discovered she was pregnant at the age of forty-seven. She, whose husband had left when she was twenty-three because of her barrenness; she, who had never in all the succeeding years attempted to prove him wrong with any other man, now produced a son to whom, in the absence of family, she gave the name Gabriel Lenín.

Another plane flew overhead, its jet engines howling against the resistance of flaps and landing gear. The late afternoon airport traffic had started. Coming from Panama or San José and heading for Mexico or Miami after a short pause in Managua. Or going in the opposite direction. He imagined Julia getting on a plane with her children, going up the ramp and disappearing into the plane's dark interior. From down here in the near captivity of a safe house, their life up there seemed so innocent. Untouched by the politics of naming a child Gabriel Lenín in a country where you could die for such an act.

There was a shout from the street, answered by another in the house next door. José María rose and looked out through the crack between the shutter and the window frame. One of Mario's shouters, the kid whose voice was changing, was alternately bellowing and squeaking at someone offstage, the younger brother who now appeared, waving a book and yelling back. The two were joined by a toddler bawling at the top of his lungs. For an instant the noise was deafening, but in the end the toddler won out, and the two older boys broke off their argument and bent to deal with him.

"Powerful lungs that kid," whispered Mario from behind him.

"Jesus! Don't come up on me like that!"

Mario grinned. "Get some sleep." He sat down at the table and tilted his chair against the wall. "You're jumpy as a cat."

"And you're not?" José María reached into his pocket and brought out a battered pack of cigarettes.

"Don't," said Mario.

"I know, I know." He tossed the pack in the air and batted it against the wall, then turned back to the shutter. "Egdalina come back yet?"

"No. See anything out there?"

"Nothing. But who knows, this place feels like a trap; anybody could be out there but we wouldn't know until he was right in front of us."

Egdalina's house was one of a series of attached, one-story houses on a wide, unpaved street, just off the back road to the airport. Each had a door and a window fronting the street. As a safe house, its only virtue was anonymity.

"There's always the back wall," said Mario.

It was like this: one minute Mario was wired tighter than a drum, and the next minute it was José María who twanged at the slightest touch. Each time, the other provided the slack or the steadiness.

"What's eating you?" asked Mario.

"Fuck all. That's what's eating me. Why isn't Egdalina back yet?"

"Hey, we did it. It worked. We're out, we got the money…"

"Some of it. And this…" José María looked around the dingy room. "…is not 'out.' We're as trapped here as we were in the bank. You realize we haven't spoken above a whisper in four days?"

"Yeah. And it could be weeks more. We knew that when we started. But we're alive. And that we didn't know when we started." Mario bent and picked up the packet of cigarettes. "There could be worse places." He leaned against the wall and bounced the pack in his hand. "I keep thinking of Pepe."

"Right." There were worse places. And Pepe could be in one right now. José María eyed the cigarettes. He hadn't had one since before the robbery. "He got away," he said.

"Yeah?" said Mario. "Well, where is he?"

"If they'd caught him, they'd have it all over the newspapers." The bouncing cigarette pack was beginning to annoy him.

"Maybe they don't want us to know they got him," said Mario.

José María snatched the cigarette pack out of the air and set it on the far side of the table. "You said it, I didn't. Everyone else got out."

Daniel and half the money were already in Matagalpa. But of Pepe, and the money he was carrying, there was no word.

"No way, man," whispered Mario suddenly. "No way he would turn on us."

"Who's to know? He sure was pissed we didn't get to the vault. He wanted all the money in that bank."

Mario sat still for a minute. "Well, at least he didn't know where the safe house would be. That was all in Augustín's head." He tapped the top of his forehead.

"Yeah." José María wondered why they weren't told where to go before the job in case they got split up. But he wasn't going to say it out loud. He walked through the house to the back patio, stepped behind the low modesty wall that shielded the toilet trench from the rest of the house and took a leak, then sprinkled lime from the can over it.

There were so many 'what ifs.' If they hadn't killed the bank guard. If he'd shot the Angel when he had the chance. If the Guard weren't doing maneuvers in the mountains, they'd all be gone from here by now. If Tacho weren't here, if his fucking father hadn't killed Sandino, if, if....he closed his eyes. The woman next door was singing again, stirring her sweets; the steady thump of wood against metal set the rhythm, a sad song, low and warbling. He remembered Katherine in those final weeks, humming between bouts of screaming, humming a low sound, like a slowing-down heartbeat.

When he opened his eyes, Mario was coming around the wall and unbuttoning his pants.

"Maybe," Mario lifted his chin toward the next door, "we could jump over in the middle of the night, and lick the pot." He grinned and, closing his eyes, sniffed appreciatively.

José María nodded; the innocence of Mario's gesture warmed him. It was good he was with Mario; it was good they were both alive. Still —

A noise at the front of the house startled them. Mario, still zipping his pants, ducked behind the modesty wall. José María stepped around the stone wash basin and crouched; the gun butt was warm in his hand. Carefully, with the gun between his legs to muffle the sound, he released the catch.

"Gabriel Lenín, wake up your lazy self and get out of that bed!" Egdalina stood in the doorway to the patio. She hooked her head back toward the front of the house and José María rose from his crouch. The boy came up behind his mother and put his arms around her and she pressed his hands into her belly. Again she motioned with her head to get them to come inside.

"Look," she said, when they were seated around the table. She laid a copy of *La Prensa* on the table and pointed to a photograph on the front page.

"Son-of-a-bitch!" Mario shook with silent laughter.

It was a picture of the scorched entrance of the Montoya bank branch with graffiti across the walls on either side of the door: "Tacho's Wallet" on the left, "*La billetera de Tacho*" on the right.

"*Mierda*," said José María. "Bi-fucking-lingual."

"And I hope they wrote it in shit, too," murmured Egdalina.

"Do you think it's Pepe?" asked Mario.

"Who knows?" said José María.

"There's more." Egdalina pushed the mop of gray hair from her forehead. "Augustín is gone. He won't be back for several weeks."

Unas semanas. That could be three or thirty. She spoke as if this had the same weight as the photograph, just something to think about.

"And us?"

"He said when the fucking Guard maneuvers are over and he comes back, you'll be moving out." She jerked her head back over her shoulder to indicate the mountains to the northwest. "You're safer here than out in the open."

José María looked at Mario, saw the same question in his face. How out in the open was Augustín, their only lifeline? Mario's fists clenched, unclenched. The balance was tipping, in a minute it would be José María's turn to supply the steadiness. Maybe not. They both looked to Egdalina.

"Food," she said. "I've brought you something special." She reached into her bag and brought out a small package wrapped in newspaper. Opening it, she held up four coconut candies. "There's one for each of us. Eat and enjoy. I'm taking the boy to vespers now."

Another early evening jet thundered by overhead.

438

Chapter 42

Julia stood for a moment in the shade of the hotel entrance, staring down at the city, a jumble of white walls and red tile roofs baking beneath the sun. There were vultures at war above Acahualinca and beyond the muddy lake.

To the west, dark clouds gathered, coming to swallow the sun. Julia gripped the small red knife in her pocket and tried to focus on the list of things she still had to do.

Their furniture was on its way, belatedly painted with gasoline against the termite eggs she had only discovered as the furniture was being crated. How had they survived the treatment in March? And how had she missed seeing them?

"May I call you a taxi, *señora*?" asked the doorman.

"No, thanks. I don't need one." She waved toward the battered Volkswagen. "Errands," she said.

She pulled the brim of her hat down and stepped out into the harsh sun. The children were happily installed in the hotel with Juanita, greedy for each other, greedy for this move and for the hotel pool and the magic of a journey with all they held to constitute security: a mother and a father together again. All she had to do now was tie up some loose ends. One more goodbye dinner party tonight and then tomorrow they were off. Without a backward glance? Did the contract count now that they were going to live in the States?

Julia stopped short and put her hand out to the nearest car to steady herself.

Is that what they had been doing all these years? Erasing all but a few memories from each place as they left it? As though everything they had experienced could be reduced to a collection of conversational tidbits to deploy at cocktail parties in the next place? She could even hear herself: oh yes, she'd eaten fried ants in Peru; she'd climbed all the way up to the shrine on Montserrat above Bogotá; in Nicaragua, she'd drunk chicha beneath a zinc roof, and had visited a maggot farm in a town called Acahualinca, and...

She lifted her head and looked out over the city. The vultures were still soaring over Acahualinca. Only the top of the mountain of garbage was visible. But hidden away at the foot of it were a thousand little houses that looked like trash until you walked inside and saw a faded photograph on a wooden shelf, and beside it a discarded brass lamp that had been polished until it gleamed. And below that, there was a neatly made cot that could no more fit two people than a sawhorse — but it had. More than once.

She pressed her arm into her stomach. A wail rose up within her and she forced it back. Is that what she had become? A drifter? Just passing through. Collecting pelt.

"May I help you, *señora*?" The doorman was standing beside her.

"No! Thank you."

"Would you like to sit down?"

Go away, she thought. Can't you see...She shook her head and made herself look at him squarely. His arm was out as though to steady her, his eyes were squinting in concern. He nodded back toward the lobby. "A drink of water, perhaps?"

"No."

His shoulders dropped and she was ashamed. He wasn't just a door-man. He belonged here in this world, he lived here, with a family and a history. He would be here when she was gone. He owned the air he breathed, the tiny piece of earth he stood on. He could take the sun and that unbearably blue sky for granted because he would be here tomorrow to see it, and the day after.

A small humming came from him, a gentle reminder that he was still here and his question was unanswered.

"Please. I don't want to go back. I need to..." As her voice soared, she grasped the knife in her pocket. "I need to walk," she said and looked into his face again. "I just want to think."

He stepped back. "Of course. It is good to walk. And to think, of course. They go well together. But be careful with the sidewalk, it's broken in places."

By the time she got to the Boer Market, she was sweating. Just inside the entrance, she snatched off her hat, took a swipe at the sweat sliding down into her eyes and began to thread her way between the fruit and vegetable stalls. The air, thick with the odors of earth and damp, enveloped her, the sourness of smashed fruit beginning to ferment, the gassiness of onions going bad. Oh God, how she would miss this. In the States there would be nothing so basic and natural; certainly not in a supermarket.

Even before she got to the meat stalls, she could smell the offal, the sharp scent of blood and the velvet gas of putrefaction. At the entrance to the food hall, she came to a halt. The place was alive with shouting, metal spoons clinking on tin plates, someone singing. Smoke from the cooking fires swirled up through those wonderful shafts of sunlight that pierced the corrugated zinc roof. And against the far wall, two stalls to the right of the long, central eating table, was the sausage stall and José María's aunt.

Round cheeks, knob of a nose, eyes, intelligent eyes, ironic eyes, not unkind. José María seldom spoke her name. *Mi tía*, my aunt, the person who had been the center of gravity for him for so many years. Julia took a deep breath and began to walk across, down a step and through those brilliant shafts of light and their gravity-defying dust motes. It was magic, like walking through a forest of light. She would miss that, and the tantalizing smells of the soups and stews, and of the freshly cooked tortillas which had a scent all their own. All this she wanted to keep with her forever.

So intent was she on everything around her, she didn't hear the hecklers at the long trestle table until she was past them. That too, she would miss. In some sense their heckling made her real. The heat from the metal roof on her scalp, the sweat trickling down between her breasts, this was real, so real that for an instant she wondered if she were actually dreaming this in some future time.

But the pain was now. In these minutes and the coming hours. She waited as a handcart loaded with potatoes lumbered past, then stopped at the first stall to buy a *córdoba's* worth of tortillas, wrapped in clean white paper. With no basket or bag, she pressed the warm packet between her arm and her ribs and walked to the sausage stall where the *tía* stood watching her.

Julia set the tortillas down a hand's breadth from the gleaming circle of light on the wooden table and inhaled the smell of sausages. The woman didn't move, and her gaze never left Julia's face.

"Is he well?" said Julia at last.

The *tía* shrugged, a slow heaving up of her shoulders.

Julia reached into her pocket for the knife. When she looked up, the woman was passing a packet of sausages to someone.

"And you, doña *Beisbolera?*" she said, turning to Julia. "May I help you?"

"*Beisbolera?*"

"*La Gringa Beisbolera,*" *la tía* corrected.

So José María and Miguel had talked to *la tía* about her. Had talked about the stone baseball game. No, it was Miguel who had called her that. He would have talked about her, but not directly to *la tía*; he would have said it to José María in front of her. It was a wild guess, but it felt right. At some point they had been together and he was still alive, thank God, and thinking of her.

"We are leaving Nicaragua."

There was no reaction, just those eyes boring into hers.

"Will you take something to him?"

The woman turned away to ladle sausages out of the pot and drop them onto a square of paper. She threw more sausages into the oil and turned back. If her face showed anything at all, it was sorrow, briefly held up in the eyebrows, the easing of the jaw, and then gone.

Julia pulled out the Swiss Army knife and laid it on top of the tortillas. Its red sheath glowed against the white paper.

The woman slowly nodded. "So," she said and wiped her wrist on her apron, then blew on it. "What is it you want?"

The question was so blunt it almost amounted to an insult. Julia pressed her fingertip against the knife to steady herself. She refused to quaver. "If there is any way to get this to him, I would be in your debt."

"In my debt?" *La tía* tilted her head to one side, and repeated the phrase. Then she leaned into the table, knuckles resting on the rough wood, arms straight. "You don't belong here, *doña*. This isn't your home." With a small shake of her head the woman went back to

443

her pot and her stirring and scooping. Hot sausages landed on paper. Sausage followed sausage. Stir, scoop and plop.

At last, she laid the scoop down. When she looked up, her face was different, longer and looser. "I thought he had come home for good. That maybe he had found what he wanted and there was no need to travel any more. But..." She paused and her voice dropped. "...it no longer matters. He has already gone too far away."

Has already? "Where? What does that mean?"

"He never came home. Because he doesn't have one."

Julia frowned. "He has your home."

La tía jerked her thumb back toward her chest. "This one. I'm talking about this one. This home."

"You've lost me."

"I don't believe that."

A man came up to the table and muttered something. *La tía* ignored him. "Tell me, *doña*," she said to Julia, "if there's no water in a glass, of what use is it?"

"Don't you mean, with no glass, there's no way to drink the water?"

The man had turned and was watching them, turning his head this way and that with each sentence.

"Don't fuck with me, you useless fart," said *la tía*, and the man slunk away.

"No..." She turned back to Julia, "...I mean if there's no water, the glass is empty. Dry."

Julia shook her head. "Then neither glass nor water would have any meaning without the other?"

A glint of a smile crossed the woman's face. "Well, that is one way to look at it." She went back to her pot and Julia waited. The bright spot of light on the table had moved fractionally toward the tortillas.

Or was it she herself who had moved and now saw it differently? She raised her head and stared at the dust motes floating within it until they were blurred by her tears.

"So who's the glass and who's the water?" She said when *la tía* returned.

"You are both," said *la tía* . "Unless you make your home here," she tapped her chest, "you are empty."

"The glass…"

"Yes. And any home you try to build will have no shape." She frowned and shook her head. "No. It's that your home will be empty." *La tía* took a breath and looked down at her hand, now clamped around the wooden handle of her scoop.

For a moment Julia couldn't breathe.

La tía flung her free arm wide. "You are a visitor here, a tourist." She pressed her index finger down onto the circle of sunlight as though to drill a hole in the wood to let it fall through. Again, she shook her head. "The home inside you is the only home you will always have." She lifted her hand and looked at her finger as though she were surprised the sunlight hadn't come off onto its tip. "You cannot be someone else's home, you can only share who you are with them. And they will learn."

She turned back to her pot, leaving Julia in a daze. Sausages changed hands. She hollered something to someone at the far end of the hall and flipped off the cheers of the people eating at the table.

Julia was about to turn away when *la tía* returned. "The truth is, *Doña*, I don't know where he is." There was a catch in her voice. "And I don't know if I will ever see him again."

"No," Julia whispered. She stared at the woman, his *tía*, the woman who had held him in her arms. Had held all of them, his sister and his cousins. She had raised them all by herself.

445

Julia slipped the Swiss Army knife into her pocket and put the tortillas under her arm again. Her head throbbed. Would she ever have that kind of strength? Could she be that for Becka and Caley? Could she ever be at home within herself? She looked up at the woman whose features were blurred by her tears. She wiped her own eyes with the back of her wrist, then reached down and placed that hand beneath the shaft of sunlight. She could almost feel its heat. Her fingers bent toward each other to hold it, but the light slipped through them and came to rest on her closing knuckles.

She brought the empty hand up to her chest and let the thought that had lain beneath all the comings and goings of the last two weeks, the tiny, hidden engine that had propelled her through all the ordering and the sifting and the packing, come to the surface...I'm coming back, I'll come back some day, after the children... But now, looking into those sorrowing eyes, she felt that tiny engine sputter and die away.

Chapter 43

Mattie's maid took away the dinner plates and brought the dessert plates. Julia ran her fingers up and down the flimsy stem of her wine glass. The dark red liquid, still nearly at the rim, shivered with her touch. It was almost over. An hour, maybe less and they could go. She longed to be alone, by herself, with this strange, sad day.

"So I've finally started learning Spanish," said Mattie, "and it's just as I suspected. I'm a dunce for languages."

"You'll learn," said Marshall.

"No, I won't." She smiled at Jaime. "But I'm going to die trying, this time."

Jaime chuckled. There was only the faintest of bruises on his left cheek from the beating at the Montoya Branch. His right eye was covered with a very elegant patch, but his cheek was swollen.

"Well," he said, "that's one way of dying I hadn't considered." Only his posture, a slight inclination toward Mattie, betrayed anything other than polite interest in his hostess. But all through the meal, there had been a kind of electricity between them that burned up all the energy at the table.

Julia looked across at Catalina. No jealousy, no anger to mar the peacefulness in her face. Only a small wrinkle between her eyebrows as she watched her husband.

"Julia, how long did it take you to learn your Spanish?" asked Mattie. "You must have studied it all your life."

"Not really. I started in college." Where was Mattie going with this? Julia smoothed her hand over the white tablecloth. "I took Latin in high school and that helped a lot. And I lived in Bogotá, and then in Peru before I met Marshall."

"And you dated Latin men?"

Ah, there it was — from here, Mattie would move to Nicaraguan men. And from there, to refrigerator repairmen. Julia gave a small shrug. "I dated some. I also ate fried ants."

Garv laughed. Marshall grimaced.

"We have those in Colombia too," said Catalina. "They come from the Vaupes. What did you think of them?"

"Not very good, mostly salt and legs that stuck in my teeth. And grease, a little rancid. But this dessert is very good Mattie; it's got orange peel in it?"

"Yes. It's a chocolate orange refrigerator cake."

"How will it feel to be living in the States after all these years?" asked Catalina.

"Strange, I suppose."

"I would think so," said Mattie. "Better you than me." She turned to Jaime. "Car pools make me shiver."

Garv pushed his plate back. "Did you hear about Beal Jackson?" Marshall lifted his head.

"God, that was terrible," said Mattie.

Julia sat forward. "What happened?"

"He's dead." Garv shook his head. "They found his body beaten to a pulp down on the coast this morning. I got it over the short wave."

The hair rose on Julia's neck; she pressed her hands against the table. "When? Who would — "

"Garv, you're not serious!" Marshall's voice cut across Julia's.

"Terrorists,"said Jaime. "Revolutionaries. He must have found something out and they killed him. Several days ago, from what I understand. You didn't know?"

"My God," said Marshall, "the poor bastard." He looked around. "Excuse me, it's just that the poor guy had so much happen to him. I mean, he loses everything and then he's murdered? Christ!"

"And his dog?" asked Julia. "He had a dog."

"Shot," said Jaime.

"He was a very sad man," said Catalina. "I don't think I've ever known a more gentle man." She glanced at Jaime. "And yet there was something very... strange about him." She turned to Marshall. "I remember when he had his accident, the airplane accident, Jaime offered to fly him to the States to get skin grafts, but he wouldn't accept. He preferred – " She broke off and stared at Julia.

All of them were staring at her; she could feel their eyes on her hand and the broken stem of the glass poking up out of her fist, the wine, a broad red pool soaking into the tablecloth. She looked up at Catalina first. Beaten to a pulp. Falling, falling, his child screaming.

A flash of recognition, of horror, came into Catalina's eyes, so stark that Julia turned away and looked toward Marshall. His mouth was working, he was saying something, he was standing, as was Mattie.

"I'm okay," Julia said quickly, "I'm okay. I'm sorry, Mattie."

"Have you cut yourself?" asked Jaime. She turned at last and looked at him. Behind his smooth face, the yellow-brown eyes, she saw a ball falling, unwinding, its legs kicking wildly, its hands tied behind its back, and she knew that this, too, she would hold within her. José María! Oh, my dearest love.

She glanced down at her hand. "No, I haven't cut myself."

"For God's sake, Julia, if you know something, tell me." Marshall flipped the right turn signal on and slowed for the turn onto the bypass. The car shuddered and he sawed at the clutch. His last night driving the fucking Bitchwagen.

"Not yet."

He made the turn. "What's that supposed to mean?" He'd never understand her. He thought of Mattie, how her lips looked in profile, how her hair floated down her back. Bitch and whore and still so beautiful. She was easier to understand than Julia. She wanted a fuck and if he wouldn't, someone else would do. It was as easy as that. Christ, he was glad he was going back to the States.

He threaded his way through a series of potholes. Thank God the moon was out.

"Did you ever go to bed with her?" asked Julia.

"Huh?"

"With Mattie. Did you ever go to bed with her?"

He gripped the wheel. "What the hell?"

"She's doing it with Jaime, you know."

He could feel his jaw working up and down. "I don't give a damn who she's doing it with. Why should I care?"

"Mattie told me."

"What?"

"No, she didn't tell me you'd made love; she told me she wanted to."

He caught his breath, glanced at her, but she was looking straight ahead, the bottom half of her profile backlit by the moon.

"Something like that," she said.

"Something like that? You have a lot of nerve!"

She turned toward him. "Have you ever done it with anyone else?"

"What?" The car lurched as he hit the brake, the accelerator and the brake in quick succession.

"Have you ever made love to another woman?"

"What the hell?" He swung the car wide and ran it up onto the side of the road. The engine died. "Who the fuck are you to ask me that? You're fucking some Yo-Yo man and......"

She was staring at him, her mouth slightly open.

"For Chrissakes," he yelled. "You sit there all evening, eating their food, talking with them, and this is what you're thinking? Who fucked who? In case you don't remember, we were talking about a man you know who has just been murdered and you're sitting there thinking about who's fucking who? Is that why you broke the glass? What kind of a person are you anyway? No, don't bother. I don't want to hear it!" He grabbed the key, turned it. The engine shook and died. He'd forgotten to engage the clutch. He turned the key again and the starter motor whined but the engine didn't turn over. Damn, he shouldn't have let them take the Olds so soon.

"It's the carburetor," she said.

"It's flooded." He tried again. And again, but nothing happened. Anger pounded inside his skull.

They waited in silence. It was she who broke it. "I want to get a job in the States. Teaching Spanish, maybe."

"Fine."

A shadow crossed the car as the moon rolled behind a cloud.

"I knew a storyteller once," she said softly. "He earned his living by traveling around the country telling stories. But he got into trouble because he kept making parables about Somoza..."

"Fine with me," he said roughly and jammed the key over into the starting position. The mechanism whined and he pumped his foot. The engine wouldn't turn over. And now he could smell the gas.

"It's the carburetor," she said again.

"You don't know what the hell you're talking about!"

She opened her door.

"Where are you going?" He flung his arm out to stop her but he was too late.

She closed the door and leaned back into the car window to lay her wrap on the seat. "Release the hood, will you?" She looked down into her hand and he saw that she was shifting her Swiss Army knife around as if looking for an appropriate blade.

"What do you think you're doing?"

She walked around the front of the car to his side and patted the hood.

"It's flooded," he said. "You're just going to screw it up."

"Release the hood," she said quietly. "I know what I'm doing."

"Shit!" he said, but he released the hood.

Chapter 44

Patiently, endlessly, Gabriel Lenín ground a stone across the rough, flat surface of a *metate*. No corn or any other grindable material, just the noise humming in José María's blood, jangling his nerves.

Neither Augustín nor Mario seemed to notice the noise. Back in the bedroom off the patio, Augustín slept like the dead, an M3 beside him, while Mario sat at the table writing a poem. Amazing! Waiting out the last hours before they were to leave, those two were cooler than ice.

José María stared through the crack in the shutter at the *siesta*-emptied street. Two messages in one day, each harder than the other.

The first had to have been from his *tía*. It had come through too many hands to be sure. Julia was leaving.

Of course she was leaving, she was free to go, this wasn't her country. Reason did nothing to ease the pain in his belly. Worse, it had brought her closer. He pressed the fleshy part of his thumb against his lips. Go then, go. But nothing helped. He could feel her beside him, a whisper, the faint stirring of her breath against his ear.

He had written her a letter. It had taken hours. What could he tell her except that he loved her. She would never receive it anyhow. She was going. And she'd probably never look back. No, not true. She had to leave because of her kids. In the next moment, he knew she would never be gone completely. A part of her would always be here. And that part he would take with him wherever he went. He would take her with him into the mountains. There she would see the sunlight slanting through the trees, the narrow, twisted, rising path, huge leaves dripping with rainwater. She would sleep in a hammock, eat beans and tortillas if they were lucky, and fight. Her beautiful warm skin would sprout pale patches of mountain leprosy and she would brush her teeth with a twig. And she would laugh, and walk, and cry.

He let his breath out slowly. Go, go with your children. But take me with you. Carry me into the hours and days of your new life. That soft hour at dawn that has no shape of its own yet. The ache of dusk. He remembered back in Missouri the scent of grass being cut at dusk in May, a sweet, longing smell.

Augustín had brought the other news before dawn this morning. Pepe had been sighted in Costa Rica, living off the money from the bank job. That meant they had to move on tonight. The fact of the money was significant: had Pepe been caught, the *guardia* would have taken the money; if he was a mole, he wouldn't have let himself be spotted. Still, they'd have to get out of Managua quickly. Pepe was just an end link in a tributary chain, but sooner or later he'd get drunk and say too much. Christ! If poverty withered men like Pepe, and wealth corrupted them, what was the answer?

The street was quiet. It was midday and the air traffic had stopped. He'd caught a glimpse of a Pan Am jet, making a tighter turn than usual, northeast, headed for the lake. Going to Miami before it headed for God knew where? Would Julia take a Pan Am flight? Probably not. But she might, she just might go to the airport via the road transecting this one. And if, he leaned to the right of the window and sighted with his left eye, he could see a section of that road, a few feet only, but a section nevertheless.

454

Gabriel Lenín's grinding took on a new rhythm, one, two, one, two, a little faster, a little sharper. José María tapped his forehead against the wall beside the shutter. If he took the stone away from the boy, what would that accomplish? Tears? Total silence? Either would be worse than the grinding. On one side of the house, the juvenile shouters all seemed to have left their house, or were in some early afternoon trance. On the other side, the candy maker's song had ceased, the smell of hot candy was fading.

A prop plane lumbered overhead, its bloated shadow flowed along the street. A Hercules transport. The Guard had two of them, plus a DC6. Could a Hercules be shot down with an M3?

He turned away from the window. Pepe was living it up in Costa Rica. The son- of-a-bitch had gotten out. And so had the Angel. Two fucking guns in his hands and he wasn't able to kill the bastard. Some revolutionary hero! Augustín had tried to comfort him with that bullshit about how he wasn't a killer, and the revolution needed loving. "In the end, this war's going to be won by loving," he'd said. And the guy really believed it.

Gabriel Lenín's grinding ceased. The boy was crossing to the trench; he carried the lime can, and the roll of toilet paper. He wouldn't come out for a while. Minutes of relief from the purgatory of that grinding. Minutes of silence. José María swung back to the window.

"A little restless?" asked Mario softly.

"A little."

"Then listen to this."

"Go ahead."

Mario held the poem up, then changed his mind. "You read it," he said, his face knotting with embarrassment. José María took it and carried it to the window.

If there were time,
I would walk with you to the river.
Together we'd dance in the water,
If there were time.
That river is pure, my love;
It flows from my heart in the mountains,
Unwinding into the ocean.
If there were time,
We could ride the cold mountains
To their source.
If there were time.

He could hardly breathe. It was as though he himself were talking. José María made himself read the poem again. And then he looked off into nothing. As far as he knew, Mario had never had a *novia*. He was too ugly, he would say. Scared women off with a face that was preternaturally old. The poem was pure pain. He hunted carefully for the right words to say. The grinding started again.

Mario smiled. "It's not finished, is it?" he said. His eyes slid past José María and the smile froze.

José María felt a pang of fear in his chest. He jumped back against the wall before his mind registered the roar of a diesel engine and the running feet. There was a loud rap of wood against wood. The door shook. He looked down and saw he had his gun in his hand, looked up, saw Mario dive for the submachine gun, fumble with the catch.

The door shuddered and one hinge broke. Mario brought the weapon up firing even as a bright patch of red sprang out of his shirt, but the firing went on, was taken up by the rapid bark of the M3 as Augustín stumbled in from the patio, his trousers half on, half off. José María turned back to the window, shot blindly, aware more of the recoil of the pistol than of the noise of the shot. Three, four, five.

Mario was on his knees, still firing. The bullet riddled door swung open, then slightly back as though closing. For a minute, the firing stopped, but the roar of the diesel engines went on, weapons carriers probably, more than two, a great many, and now there was shouting. "*HIJUEPUTA COMUNISTAS! QUE SE RINDAN!*"

"On your mother's grave I'll surrender!" shouted Mario. The entire front of his shirt was scarlet and blood ran down his left arm. With the barrel of his gun he slammed the door shut, then fell. José María crouched down and went to him under cover of Augustín's M3. He lifted Mario's head onto his arm.

Mario's mouth moved and José María bent down to hear. "What?"

"*Aymmm...chiquita.*" Mario's eyes were open and his face twisted into a rictus of a grin. Then all the fierce wrinkles smoothed out, and his eyelids trembled down over his eyes.

José María lowered Mario's head, bent over and called, "It's a beautiful poem, man, it's beautiful." He grabbed the submachine gun, straightened, fired off a few rounds through the window, knowing that from his kneeling position, the bullets only went skyward.

Chapter 45

"Shit!" The taxi-driver stopped the car and shifted into reverse.

"Damn!" said Marshall.

"What's happening?" Julia stuck her head out the window.

"Look, Daddy," yelled Caley. "It's a parade!"

At first Marshall thought she was right, a military convoy maybe, but then he saw the roadblock.

Looking over his shoulder, the driver swore.

But it was too late. Two, then three, then four cars piled into line behind them and then, to seal their fate, a bus braked to a stop, slewing to one side, effectively sealing the street off and causing a pandemonium of horns.

"I knew we shouldn't have come this way," said Marshall. He got out of the car and walked forward to the roadblock. He could hear the sound of automatic weapons up toward the airport. "What's going on here?" he asked the soldier who blocked his way.

The soldier swung his rifle forward without a word.

"Whoa!" Marshall stepped back. "Hold on. I was just asking."

Ahead he could see cars slowly feeding off into side streets, soldiers peering into them as they passed, and further on, another roadblock.

"Look," he said in Spanish. "We're on our way to the airport. We're leaving the country and have to catch a plane."

The soldier said nothing.

"Can't you see you've got us blocked in here?" He tried to keep his voice calm. "There are no side streets to help us get clear. Just let us through to the next side street."

The soldier jerked his head as if bothered by flies.

The taxi-driver had gotten as far as the bus driver and was yelling up at him. Julia had stepped halfway out of the car. "What is it?" she called.

The soldier looked over at her, interest sparking his face into momentary life.

"Look," said Marshall. "Just let us through to that next street."

The soldier's interest died away and the rifle rose.

"Damn," said Marshall. Not now! he thought. Not at the last minute. Just when he thought they'd made it out of here. Damn, goddamn!

Julia came toward him. "What is it?"

"Nothing. I don't know. They won't let us through."

"Did you tell him….?"

"I told him."

She looked at the soldier and Marshall was startled by the expression on her face. Holy shit! What was she going to do? He opened his mouth to speak and she glanced up at him, then turned and walked slowly to the end of the wooden barrier. The soldier brought his rifle up. The catch clicked off but she kept on going.

"Julia! Stop it. Get back in the car."

She got to the end of the barrier, turned slowly, put her hands underneath the top bar and looked at the soldier. The barrel of the gun was pointed right at her chest. Her eyes narrowed, she bent, picked up the barrier and began to pivot it around toward the side of the street. The guard stared at her bug-eyed, the rifle wavering.

459

"For God's sake, Marshall, help the woman."

Marshall whirled around and found himself staring at Jaime Salazar.

Chapter 46

Augustín was on his knees, still firing. Blood ran down his arm from a small wound in his cheek. He'd also been hit on the right shoulder and was working the M3 from the left.

José María ducked under the window and came up on the other side, closer to Augustín, should he fall. He was getting the hang of it now, using a spraying technique, down into the ground, aiming for legs, grunting each time he rose, and grunting again as he fell back. Mario, he kept saying to himself. This is for Mario.

How long had it been? Five minutes? The ammunition was low. There was more in back. Augustín was down now. José María went to him.

"Don't," said Augustín. "Get the rest of the ammo. I'll be alright." He pushed himself up on one arm, got his knees under him, then rose and lurched forward to one side of the window.

José María ran back through the patio, scooped up the ammunition from its place behind the washbasin. The M3 sounded again, Augustín was shouting.

He tore back into the front room; Augustín was down again. An explosion of mud and wood shot inward from the window frame. José María fired a few rounds from the submachine gun, fell to the ground and crawled to Augustín. He raised his head, placed his cheek next to Augustín's mouth. José María groaned. He could feel no breath.

He straightened and shot blindly in the direction of the window, then ducked, half jumped, half crawled over Augustín to the wall next to the window. As he turned to fire, he saw Gabriel Lenín standing in the doorway to the courtyard, watching him, his eyes wide and blank.

"Get back!" he yelled at the child. Something slammed into his arm, stung, and then his arm was numb. He looked down and saw a trickle of blood slide out from under his shirtsleeve. He ducked under the window and came up the other side again. He could see nothing, couldn't tell what he was aiming at, so he aimed hip-high where a man might be.

The child was coming toward him. A shower of wood chips drifted down from the beams overhead. "Go back!" screamed José María, but the kid kept coming.

"Fuck!" He dove forward and the child went limp as they hit the floor together and rolled up against Mario's body. A machine gun went off and chewed up a strip of the inside wall. José María rested his head on Mario's chest, looked up at the child's face so close to his and then over at Augustín. It was time to go.

Jaime held his hand up to the soldier, palm open. The soldier brought his gun down and went to help Julia.

"*Gracias,*" said Julia when they had finished. She took a step toward the taxi, another, she moved slowly, as if she were half asleep.

Jaime watched her, his eyes narrowed, his lips trembling with the beginnings of a smile.

Marshall found his voice. "What's going on here, Jaime?" Out of the corner of his eye, he could see Julia turn.

"Just a few Communists we caught down there." As Jaime spoke, a low boom shook the ground and then there was silence. He looked up at Marshall, the smile broadening. "Some get away, but most don't." His eyes flicked toward Julia, then widened as she came toward them. Marshall put his hand up to stop her, drew it back in astonishment at the expression on her face.

She stopped in front of Jaime and spoke softly, in English. "Did you see the expression on Catalina's face last night?"

"I beg your pardon?" Jaime looked at Marshall.

"I saw it, Jaime." There was a growl in her voice. "I don't think I'll ever forget it."

Marshall reached for her; her hand chopped down against his. The guard took a step toward them. There was another burst of machine gun fire up ahead.

"You don't know what you're talking about," said Jaime. "Marshall, help her to the car."

She nodded. "That's true. There's a lot I don't know. Too much."

"Go home, Mrs. Bennett. I have no fight with you."

She flushed, turned up her chin as if he'd struck her. "God help those who do."

Marshall froze. "For God's sake Julia! Not now. Not with Jaime."

But she was walking back to the car, moving easily now, with a grace that caught Marshall's breath. He turned back to Jaime. The cars behind him began to honk their horns.

"You were going to catch your plane, Marshall?" Jaime waved at the empty roadway ahead. "I wish you a safe journey." As though Marshall were the passenger and he the first mate.

Marshall thought of Horse, the red ledger clasped in his one hand, waiting for Jaime to decree his wife's use for the afternoon. 'Man proposes, God disposes,' Jaime had said, or something like that. Without a word, Marshall started back to the car.

Jaime's voice stopped him before he had gone ten feet, "I beg of you Marshall, keep an eye on her. She needs taking care of."

Behind the soft voice, the empty face, Marshall now heard the man's anger. He turned back.

"Julia's okay. She's fine. It's your — ," it was a strange word to use, but it was the right one, " — you take care of your soul." When it came out it sounded pretentious, laughable.

"Ah, how quick you are to judge, you of all people."

"Right." Marshall looked straight at him. Fear pressed up against his collarbone. "You're right." He took a small step forward. All the years he'd played by the rules, recorded in as precise a ledger as the one Horse had held in his hand, profits and losses, a careful accounting, for what? The gentle tug of that severed hand in the water? His fear turned, shifted up into his throat, became something else and, before Jaime could turn away, Marshall said. "And where is she now, Jaime? Where is Yelva Inez now?"

For a moment the smooth facade wavered. A moment only, then Jaime recovered, shook his head. "An accident," he said. "She had an accident."

"An accident?" Marshall shook his head. Like having her hand chopped off?

"Yes, poor woman." Again that small hesitation. So slight it was almost not there.

Marshall held his breath. He couldn't believe it. She'd gotten away. Poor, frightened woman, she'd gotten away and Jaime didn't know where she was.

"So it's over?" he said and saw the full-blown doubt spring into

Jaime's face, the unspoken question: do I know? Marshall nodded. "Well, as you say, a plane to catch. And a safe journey."

He got in next to the taxi driver, closed the door carefully, then punched the lock down as the taxi lurched forward. "It's okay," he said. "It's alright. We're on our way."

In the back seat, Julia held both children, one in each arm. She was crying silently, making no attempt to wipe the tears away as they slid down off her chin. He was shaking with anger, with relief, with panic, but he had no words left. He reached into his pocket for his handkerchief and passed it back over the seat without turning around to look through the rear window.

Chapter 47

José María started crawling, dragging Gabriel Lenín with him. The door to the courtyard was there. A burst of fire chewed the wall above him. There was a boom from outside. The ground shuddered. One of the narrow beams overhead cracked. A portion of the zinc roof fell in, scattering clouds of dust, blinding him for a minute. Where in God's name was the back door? He pushed forward, then saw it before him.

As he hoisted himself through, there was a terrifying scream behind him, shrill and full of rage. For an instant he thought it might be a plane in a dive. He looked back. Augustín had risen to his knees. The scream came again and with it Augustín brought himself up to his feet and lurched toward the window.

José María hung there, frozen. Beneath him the child stirred.

"Oh Christ!" he screamed, and then back over his shoulder, "I'm coming back!"

He swung Gabriel Lenín up with his left arm, staggered with the sudden pain, ran out across the courtyard. The boy was too heavy; he brought the barrel of the submachine gun underneath to support him. The thin arms clawed at his neck. He stumbled into the wall, dropped the gun, and scrambled up, pushing and shoving with his free hand until he had the boy up on top of the wall separating the houses. He swarmed up behind. A burst of fire along the wall sent him flying and he fell to the other side clutching at Gabriel Lenín. Pain shot through his knee and for a moment it wouldn't hold him. He rolled, his arms cradling the child, and finally got himself upright.

He was in a courtyard, a mirror to the one he had just left. There was another burst of fire along the wall above him. Bullets from above, an airplane. He lumbered with his burden to a stone wash-basin and dove beneath it. Gabriel Lenín coiled tightly into his belly.

The courtyard was empty. For a moment, the firing stopped. A Walkie-talkie crackled, someone spoke into a megaphone, the words no more than an incoherent yowling. There was another moment of silence. A shadow passed overhead and there was a tremendous roar. The ground shook and a portion of the wall blew away across the courtyard. Then there was no sound at all. A sweet, sweet silence. A breeze even. He rubbed his cheek against the child's hair, spoke and could not hear his own voice.

He coughed, sucked in dust, opened his eyes, stuck his head out from under the sink. Above him the wall was a foot lower but there was a huge mound of rubble blocking the way back to Augustin. To his right, there was a break in the wall. And beyond that, from one of the bedrooms, a figure emerged. A face, a woman, her mouth open, calling. She was coming to him, stepping over the rubble.

He met her halfway. She held her thick arms out and he walked into them, the smell of coconut enveloping him; then he stepped back and the child was hers. He stayed a moment looking into her eyes. His arms, his belly, his body, all empty. She turned and moved back across the rubble and disappeared into the room.

The broken rubble rolled away under his feet as he hit the wall again. He was up over it and down on the other side, running, running toward Augustín, the sun beating down, the dust in his mouth, his body moving as it had never moved before, in great surging

467

strides, a burst of joy in his chest, that shook him, lightly, almost tenderly. And there was sun, beating down on the jeep, and its silver Airstream trailer. A blinding ache in his eyes. The passenger door swung open and Maggie Peters leaned out, her gray hair flying, the whiskers still curling on her chin. "Hop in, Joseph," she shouted, grinning at him. "It's about time you got here."

The plane lifted off, banked to the south and the landing gear rumbled up into its belly. Through the window across the aisle, Julia saw a storm to the northeast. On the right, the crater of Santiago bobbed at the end of the wing as the plane held its sharp right turn. In minutes, they were heading north, crossing fields, flying over the houses to the south of the city. Their house, one of them. From where she sat, she couldn't see the lake yet. Nor Acahualinca, which would be off to the left of the plane.

They were over a blanket of roofs, some tile, some zinc, here and there a thatched roof, courtyards green with the rain, the gully of a stream, weeks ago so dry, now filled with vegetation.

Caley reached up and dabbed at Julia's chin with the handkerchief. Julia kissed the top of her head, the warm, soft hair.

"Will we ever see her again?" asked Caley.

She was talking about Juanita, who had stayed until the very last minute, waiting quietly for her hugs out in front of the hotel. One by one, even Marshall, though that hug gave her such a turn she could only put her hand to her mouth and look away.

"No, Honey, probably not." Ah the coolness of the words, the ease with which she said them!

"Will we ever come back?"

The question she'd been dreading. "Probably not." She could feel the bones crumbling inside her, all that had held her upright until this moment.

"Why not?"

She closed her eyes, she could hardly breathe. "Because we have a long, long journey to make and we can't think that far ahead." Then, as soon as she'd said it, she knew it was only one part of the truth, and that she would come back. But only when she had something to bring, something to give, to do. In an instant, this fragile new home of hers, this as yet unlived-in space of dreams, was lit with that knowledge, and she could breathe again. She could come back. She might come back. Anything was possible. "Maybe, after a long journey," she said. That seemed enough for Caley. A long, long journey. Journeys, she was used to. Surely it was enough for anyone.

"We forgot to bring the *lulo* plant with us," said Becka from across the aisle.

"I know," said Julia. "It probably wouldn't have traveled well."

"Look," said Caley, pointing out the window at a column of smoke rising just ahead of the wing. Black and rolling, it spiraled upward out of the mass of houses, dipped under the wing and disappeared for a moment. Out near the airport road. Probably what the roadblock was all about.

They turned and watched it reappear behind the wing. The wind blew it at an angle and for an instant the flames at its base were exposed. Then the dark column straightened and was gone beyond their sight.

Acknowledgment

I wish to thank those who have helped me along the way. My grateful thanks to Professor Art Edelstein and to the members of his classes for helping me learn to write and for giving me the confidence to take my work seriously; to Tima Smith, who honored me with her honesty and never glossed over my omissions. I want to thank my husband,Loren Schechter, for his loving support and encouragement, and for the endless hours of patient and meticulous editing he gave to it. Without his efforts *Home* would never have been completed.

And finally, I wish to thank the people of Nicaragua who taught me that in a world where inequality and repression reign, our only hope is to look into each other's eyes and see there our valued neighbor.

Afterword

In the early 1930's, Anastasio Somoza senior, father to the brutal dictator in this novel, squashed a popular movement toward democracy, and murdered its leader, Augusto Cesar Sandino. But the Movement lived on. The Somoza family, father and son, ruled Nicaragua from 1933 until 1979 when the Sandinista Front defeated Anastasio Somoza Debayle and his National Guard. Somoza fled to the United States with his entire family, their dogs, cats, cages of birds, his lover, two coffins, holding the remains of his father and brother, and ten million dollars packed into cardboard boxes. On September 17, 1980, in Asuncion, Paraguay, a guerilla command attacked his armored Mercedes with bazookas. Acetyline torches were necessary to extract his remains from the automobile.

Nicaragua celebrated for three days.

Made in the USA
Middletown, DE
03 October 2022

11767152R00291